Praise for *The City Beautiful*

★ "Polydoros seamlessly blends a murder mystery with Jewish folklore in this haunting historical fantasy." —*Publishers Weekly*, starred review

★ "A gorgeous, disturbing, visceral and mystical experience."
—*BookPage*, starred review

★ "A wild ride of a queer gothic fantasy that's a must-have for YA fantasy collections." —*School Library Journal*, starred review

★ "*The City Beautiful* is a triumph, showcasing queer love, illuminating historical events, and guiding readers to an enthralling ending that will leave them satiated yet desirous to return to the world in which they have become immersed." —*Booklist*, starred review

"Like a darkly compelling dream; I dare readers to try to put down this queer triumph of a book where myth, mystery, and death lurk around every corner of the Windy City."

—Sarah Glenn Marsh, author of the Reign of the Fallen series

"With a keen eye for historical details, Polydoros deftly weaves together a gruesome murder mystery, a beautiful romance, and a rich depiction of Jewish life in the 19th century." —Allison Saft, author of *Down Comes the Night*

"A gripping, fast-paced book that expertly marries thriller and murder mystery. Polydoros is not afraid to tear aside the façade of beauty and civility to confront the darkest aspects of human nature, no holds barred."

—Sophie Gonzales, author of *Only Mostly Devastated*

"Readers will become immersed in Alter's world, rooting for his survival, hoping for his reunion with his family, and wishing for him to find the love that he deserves." —*Kirkus Reviews*

"Details rich with specificity and research, and its joys tinged with sorrow... [make] it all the more moving." —*NPR.org*

Books by Aden Polydoros
available from Inkyard Press

Bone Weaver
The City Beautiful

ADEN POLYDOROS

BONE WEAVER

inkyard
PRESS

ISBN-13: 978-1-335-91582-5

Bone Weaver

Copyright © 2022 by Aden Polydoros

For questions and comments about the quality of this book, please contact us
at CustomerService@Harlequin.com.

Inkyard Press
22 Adelaide St. West, 41st Floor
Toronto, Ontario M5H 4E3, Canada
www.InkyardPress.com

Printed in U.S.A.

Dedicated to all those who've buried, silenced, and sacrificed parts of themselves in order to survive.

For more information about the terms and phrases used in this story, please see the glossary at the end of this book.

* * *

Additionally, this book contains content and themes that may be difficult for some readers. For a list of content warnings, please visit adenpolydoros.com.

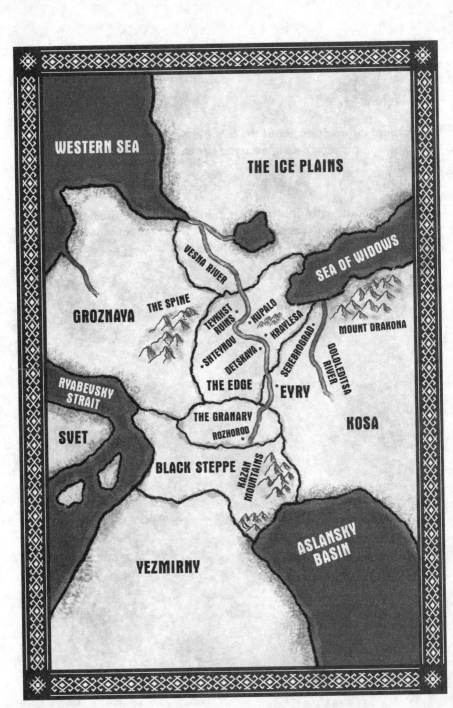

1

As the autumn wind pawed at the boarded windows like a wolf trying to break in, I arranged my medical supplies next to the teacup containing the severed finger. Needles and water, handspun thread, and clean rags.

"This is the second time this week, Galechka!" I exclaimed, picking up the finger. The first knuckle twitched when I touched it, then curled inward, prodding tentatively against my palm.

"I fell down again," Galina mumbled, extending her arm across the table. She was in better condition than the other upyri in my family and still had most of her hair and flesh.

"Be more careful. Keep losing fingers, and someday you won't have any left." I took her left hand, examining the damage. Her skin was discolored and withered, buffed with a sheen of lavender oil to keep from tearing. Mine was a reminder of what hers had once been—smooth and still warm, a sandy beige against her waxen complexion.

"Can you make a pretty one this time?" she asked. "Like one of your rushnyky?"

"Okay, but promise me you'll try not to lose anything else." I gently tapped a finger against her forehead. "You don't want me to reattach your head, do you?"

Galina giggled. "No."

She didn't wince when the needle pricked her. I used a geometrical stitch, embroidering her skin in a delicate red lattice of interlocking lines and diamonds. No blood welled up. The liquid had long since evaporated from her veins.

It made me proud being able to do this small deed for her. So much had fallen apart in my life, it was satisfying to know that I had the ability to sew things back together again. At least in this way, I could make a difference.

"This will protect you," I said, tying off the final knot. My birth mother had taught me that the embroidery was a talisman against ill luck and the Unclean Force, a corrupting energy that sickened the body and soul. Over the years, I had decorated the walls of our house with rushnyky I had made using found linen. Some good must have come from the tapestries and their lucky embroidery, because the wilderness had yet to claim me.

After snipping the tail of thread, I cleaned her hand then bandaged it. Later, I'd probably find the strips of velvet scattered across the floor, forgotten as she admired my embroidery.

When Galina flexed her reattached finger and laughed, I smiled. Just that raspy sound made all my effort worth it.

"Thank you, Toma." She curled her fingers to test them. "Will you come exploring?"

"I can't. It's too wet for me out there."

"We can search for treasures."

"Don't you have enough of those?" I teased, gesturing at the array of objects lining the shelves along the wall. Jars filled with ceramic pipe stems and tarnished coins sat alongside bottles dredged from the mud, the glass so old that it had acquired an iridescent gleam. She had found brass artillery shells, which I engraved and turned into vases, until each windowsill overflowed with cotton stems and wildflowers.

"Please." Galina scrounged through her dress pockets and came out with a handful of faceted barrel-shaped beads. "Look what I found in one of the houses."

"Is that how you lost your finger? You shouldn't be digging around in those kinds of places." I took the beads from her, rolling them around in my palm so they caught the firelight. "These are beautiful, Galechka. They're so blue, they look just like sapphires."

She smiled in excitement, revealing teeth like river pearls. "You think they're sapphires?"

"They could be," I said, although I doubted sapphires would be so heavily chipped.

"I didn't know they were blue."

I felt a twinge of sadness. Did Galina even remember what the color blue looked like? She admired things for their shape and feel, but she'd never know the ring of embroidery around her finger was as crimson as the berries of a guelder rose.

"I want to see if I can find the rest of the necklace, but I don't want to go alone." Galina pocketed the beads when I handed them back to her. "It's scary in there."

I sighed. I wasn't looking forward to caving my skull in

with a fallen beam, but how could I refuse her? "It's going to get dark soon. If it stops raining, we can go tomorrow, all right?"

"Oh, fine." Galina rose to her feet. A draft intruded through the door as she opened it, rustling the bundles of herbs and wild garlic nailed to the rafters. She looked so fragile standing there, framed by the bruised sky and dark tree line, as though the world might swallow her whole. There wasn't much of her left to give—year by year, more hair fell out in chunks, and just in the last summer, she had started carrying her lost milk-teeth in a sachet I'd sewn myself. It frightened me. Someone as small and delicate as her seemed prone to disappearing.

"Don't lose anything else!" I called after Galina as she closed the door. If she answered, a resounding thunder blast stole her words.

To fight off the chill, I busied myself by cleaning my supplies in the water basin. Once everything was put away, I added another log to the massive masonry stove that occupied nearly a third of the room. Every night, I cleared the ashes and made sure there was enough wood and tinder. I needed to be careful to keep the fire going. It wasn't as though I could conjure flames with magic.

Magic was a gift reserved for bogatyri and witches, not someone like me. Thinking back to my childhood among the living, I could recall only a handful of magically endowed individuals, all high-ranking soldiers or nobility. While the heroic bogatyri in Galina's storybooks were occasionally peasants, in reality the Three Sisters never bestowed their gift on commoners. It was always the duchesses, the earls, the captains, and the commanders who wore the deep-purple epaulets and sashes of the bogatyri. And in the tales, it was them who hunted creatures like my family for their kingdom's honor.

Witches, or kolduny, were a different story. Their powers came from the Unclean Force, and they infiltrated all levels of society. With a single glance, a koldun—or his female counterpart, the koldunia—could spoil a person, cursing them with disease and misfortune. Just a few words uttered from a koldun's mouth could be fatal, or so the stories told. I'd never met one myself, and unlike creatures like upyri or rusalki, I wasn't even sure if kolduny existed in the world. Perhaps they had died out years ago.

After closing the stove door, I sat down to work on my newest rushnyk. The tapestry was my most ambitious one yet—it was so long it billowed down to my feet, the folds of white linen covered in a wealth of geometrical embroidery. I'd dyed the thread myself, hand spinning it from flax and steeping it in madder. I couldn't wait to see how the rushnyk would look once I finished.

Just as I was done embroidering one corner, Galina burst through the door.

Smiling, I lowered my needle. "Too wet for you?"

"There's someone out there," she cried, her voice breaking on the last word.

"Someone?" I asked, baffled.

"Like you, Toma. Someone like you. I think he's still alive!"

I barely had enough time to grab my hunting satchel from the shelf and tug on my gloves and embroidered buckskin coat before Galina herded me into the downpour.

Windblown trees, craggy outcroppings, a couple of decaying houses, so much rain. So cold. The storm's chill worked its way into my bones.

Galina raced across the ground with coltish ease, a tiny figure held together by rags and leather belts. I hurried after her, swatting away the rain that stung my exposed cheeks.

Someone alive. Someone like me. How long had it been since I'd last seen a living person? More than a year, certainly. Two or three, at least. The moment the hunter had spotted me, he'd dropped his snared rabbits and rushed off, leaving me with a nice dinner but a sinking heart. I had spent the entire day afterward searching my dark eyes for any sign of blood or fading and pawing at my hair in terror that the black strands might break away in ash-tinged fistfuls, until I was reassured that I hadn't transformed into an upyr as well.

At the thought of encountering another living person, my breath seized in nervous excitement. One of my favorite pastimes was watching airships pass overhead and fantasizing about the distant lands they were traveling to. But it was a different thing altogether to look into another human's eyes.

Galina led me down to the river. As we approached the bridge, a pale figure flitted through the wind-torn shallows. I caught a glimpse of long hair and shining eyes before the rusalka retreated into deeper waters.

The river spirits ignored us as we crossed the bridge. I had never been attacked by rusalki, but I had once seen them swarm a caribou, all thrashing limbs and burgundy hair, until the water ran red with blood. It wasn't uncommon to find gnawed bones and scraps of hide littering the banks.

My feet touched down on solid ground. I lifted my gaze

to the horizon and gasped. A trail of smoke rose in the distance, black against the downpour.

"Come on, come on," Galina urged, tugging at my sleeve.

The wind changed directions, blowing the smoke toward us. Each breath I took was sullied by its acrid odor. Pressing my coat collar over my nose and mouth, I broke into a run, heading toward the fire's source.

Galina and I took a natural trail formed by decades of deer migration. When the underbrush thickened and obscured our path, we wove our way between red currant brambles and clumps of spurge laurel overladen with berries as black as ink drops. I curtained her with the flap of my buckskin coat when we strayed too close to a thornbush, wary of what its barbed branches might do to her skin and hair.

Before long, the forest thinned. Hornbeams and young oaks replaced the towering spruce and beech trees, admitting in sallow radiance. A pall of smoke caught the sunlight and trapped it in hazy columns.

Ahead, I spotted the deflated remains of an airship ensnared in the trees. Not one of those minnow-shaped vessels that occasionally passed overhead, but a smaller machine whose rowboat-like wicker compartment was open to the elements. Loose ropes and mounds of soot-blackened canvas hung from the branches. A man lay facedown beside the ruined basket, his blond hair streaked with mud.

Stepping carefully over the rubble, I made my way to his side. Here and there, broken machinery bristled from the soil. The barrel of a gun or cannon, and a scatter of brass shells each no longer than my finger. This vessel had been built for war.

I would know—to the south, the wilderness was scarred

with overgrown craters and trenches on the verge of collapse, and whenever I hunted in that area, I had to proceed warily. Unexploded ordnance studded the land there, and though the black powder had gone impotent with age or decay, barbed wire and broken glass lined the ground like teeth.

Galina hid behind me, her twig-like fingers grasping at my coat. Her eyes had long since wasted away, but I knew that in her own way, she could see. And while she was incapable of producing tears, I could tell when she cried because her sorrow twisted like a dagger deep inside me.

"Is he dead?" Galina whispered.

"I don't know." I sank to my knees beside the wheat-haired man. If he was dead or dying, I didn't want her to see it. Didn't want her to be reminded of her own last moments. "Go find Mama and Papa. Hurry."

Galina rushed into the forest. I waited until she was out of sight before turning back to the man.

"Hey, are you okay?" I lightly shook his shoulder. "Can you hear me?"

Groaning, he struggled into a sitting position and lifted his arms to ward me off. Weak veins of fire pulsed across his skin, sizzling in the rain.

I froze.

A bogatyr.

"You need...you need to help him." His voice was scarcely louder than a whisper as the flames throbbed, fizzled, and then receded. He sank against the basket, his eyes clouding over like silty puddles. "He needs a doctor."

"Who does?" I whispered.

Before he could answer, a pole clattered across the ground.

I turned, suspecting it had only been the wind, but then a scrap of canvas bulged as something stirred beneath it. Crawling over, I pulled back the flap.

There was another young man beneath the wreckage. He wore a gray wool coat and broadcloth trousers. His face was almost as pale as the ashes caught in his dark brown hair, his full lips chapped and blued from the cold. Even in unconsciousness, there was a cruel edge to his features, something hard about the cast of his mouth and his sunken cheeks.

"Is he alive?" the bogatyr mumbled, knitting his hands over his stomach as though to hold part of himself in. Blood darkened the crisp white linen of his uniform shirt. Though he was a bogatyr, there was no trace of indigo on him, not even a ribbon pinned to his collar or piping down his sleeves.

I took off my glove and pressed a palm against the dark-haired boy's cheek. The heat of his skin shocked me. When he drew in a shallow breath, I found myself holding my own breath in turn, feeling as though I was witnessing something precious.

My shoulders slumped in relief. "He's still breathing."

"Praise the Three," the bogatyr said with a sigh.

The dark-haired boy stirred and cracked open his eyes. They were the palest gray, as though they were simply reflections of the sky above. He flinched when he saw me, but he was too weak to shy away.

"My name's Toma." I returned my hand to my side, worried my touch might be hurting him. "Don't be afraid, I'm a friend."

"Mikhail." His voice was scarcely louder than a whisper.

"You're safe, Mikhail. Just hold on. My parents are on the way."

"They're coming."

A flash of alarm rippled through me. "Who's coming?"

"They'll kill me." His eyes fluttered shut, his breath slowing. "Run, or they'll kill you, too…"

I said his name once more and repeated my question. He muttered something unintelligible before slipping back into unconsciousness.

I turned to the bogatyr. "Who's he talking about? Who's coming?"

"The Fraktsiya," the bogatyr said grimly, his gaze planted on the horizon. "They're here."

I followed his line of sight. In the distance, a dark blotch surfaced behind the clouds like a bloodstain. Rising to my feet, I squinted against the rainfall. Slowly, the form took shape, materializing into a small dirigible much like the one scattered across the ground at my feet.

An explosive rattle shook the air, as loud as hail on an izba's roof. In an instant, holes appeared in the ground at my feet. A bush shuddered to my right, its boughs splintering as the projectiles struck it.

Heart hammering against my rib cage, I threw myself to the ground and scrambled toward the cover of the deflated balloon. The canvas would provide no protection from gunfire, but at least it would hide me.

As another volley of bullets pierced the glade around us, the bogatyr raised his bloodied hands toward the sky as though to beg the goddesses for intervention.

"Long live the Tsar." Blood bubbled from the bogatyr's

mouth and slid down his chin, diluted pink from the rainwater. Curls of smoke wafted off his palms and forearms. "Glory unto him. May the Three Sisters lead him to victory!"

Crackling flames raced up his arms and leapt from his spread palms in a blazing gout, setting his gaze afire with reflected light. Raindrops evaporated in an instant, forming a scalding cloud of steam as the blaze arched toward the balloon. The two pilots jumped out of the basket seconds before the craft exploded into flames. Bags of fabric spread out above their heads, slowing their fall to a smooth, slow descent.

Carried away by the wind, the pilots disappeared from sight. Smoke billowed from their balloon as it crashed in the depths of the forest.

"You got them!" I turned to the bogatyr.

My smile dropped from my lips as I saw that he had crumpled onto his side. His eyes confronted me, their pupils fixed on a distant point.

I couldn't stand his sightless gaze. Crawling over, I gently pressed my hand over his eyes and closed his lids. I waited for a moment after lowering my hand, hoping half-heartedly that the bogatyr would open them again. His eyes remained closed.

Only a small percentage of people came back, and even the magic-endowed bogatyri burned or dismembered their fallen to prevent resurrection. Still, after spending so much time among the dead, I had come to expect it.

Rising to my feet, I returned to Mikhail's side. He hadn't regained consciousness, but at least he was still breathing. I tried to wrestle him onto my back and nearly collapsed under his weight. Not good. I'd never make it back to the house this way.

I racked my brain for a solution. If I couldn't carry him, maybe I could drag him.

Drawing my hunting knife, I cut a square of canvas from the deflated balloon. I laid the sheet over Mikhail to shield him from the rain and retrieved rope and more rubberized cotton from among the wreckage.

Once I had gathered my supplies, I rolled the tarp over him, and bound it tightly. The layers of oilcloth enclosed his body, protecting him from the elements.

I looped the remaining rope through two of the holes riveted in the tarp, fashioning a rudimentary lead. Afraid that my sloppy invention would fall apart, I tugged carefully on the rope. The waterproofed canvas slid effortlessly across the mud.

Dragging Mikhail forward, I cast a worried glance behind me. The smoke from the boys' dirigible was as good as any beacon, and the downpour did little to conceal it. It would only be a matter of time before those two men—the Fraktsiya—made their way to the glade, and I intended for us to be long gone by then.

We headed deeper into the forest. As the minutes passed, the ache in my hands turned into a steady throbbing, and my legs wobbled from exhaustion. At last, I spotted a dark gash through the trees and sighed in relief. The river. Just a little farther.

Rusalki swam through the shallows, exposing a hand here, a webbed foot there. Their skin was even paler than Mikhail's ashen complexion, their limbs disproportionately long compared to their gill-split torsos. One lifted her head above the water as we neared, her burgundy hair curtaining her face. I couldn't see much more than her flared nostrils and the curve of her full lips—slick and crimson, like a gaping wound—but even that brief glimpse was enough to send a shiver down my spine.

I had never seen a rusalka lift her head above the water before. Maybe she could smell Mikhail. Smell his blood.

I swallowed the lump in my throat and stepped onto the rope-festooned bridge. The rusalki swam back and forth beneath us but didn't attempt to climb up. I avoided looking at them directly, instead focusing on the path ahead.

One step after another. The slick wood creaked, and the bridge swayed in the grasp of the storm. One step after another. Why couldn't I have been born a bogatyr? I would have killed to be able to levitate Mikhail right now.

No sooner had I reached the other side than two figures appeared ahead. Recognizing my parents' lurching gait, I sighed in relief. Galina followed behind them.

"We need to help him," I said as Mama pressed her hands against my face, my hair, my ears—all the parts of her that had withered.

"You're not hurt, are you?" Her voice crackled like frost underfoot; it grew softer each year, until I was afraid that one day it would fade away for good.

"I'm fine, but Mikhail isn't. I think he's dying, Mama." I swallowed hard. "And the other boy, the bogatyr, he's dead. They killed him."

"Toma, Galina, return home," Papa said, his words muffled by the wooden mask covering his face. His entire body was restrained in leather belts and scraps of hide and oilcloth, leaving no amount of withered flesh exposed. His garments were the only things keeping him together, with the rusty splints providing additional support for where his joints failed him.

"But, Papa, Mikhail—"

His mask turned to me, a careful construct of the face he had lost, carved by his own hands. No eye holes, just the bulbous shapes of eyes, uplifted like those on a saintly icon. "Return. We will take him back."

I wanted to argue, but I knew better. While my legs could fail me halfway up the next slope, Mama and Papa could go on until time tore them apart.

"All right." I took a step back. "Come, Galina. Let's go."

I hurried in the direction of home, only glancing back when Galina and I climbed a low hill. My adoptive parents held the makeshift sled's rope, soldiering on with grim determination. I hoped that the strain wouldn't lead to torn muscles or severed limbs, the unfortunate consequences of pushing their bodies past the breaking point.

Once Galina and I reached the homestead, I immediately filled a pot with well water and placed it on the stove in preparation to make herbal tea.

"Toma, what can I do?" Galina asked, tugging at my sleeve to catch my attention. She had followed me to the well and back like a ghost, always a step behind me. "Please, I want to help him."

Normally, the sleeping nook atop the masonry stove would've been the best place for an injured person to rest and recuperate. I knew from experience that the warmth radiating from the masonry could soothe even the worst fever chills. But considering how much trouble I'd had with just dragging him here, I doubted we'd be able to lift Mikhail onto the shelf.

"Can you get extra blankets from the chest?" I asked. "He's been out in the cold for so long, we need to make sure he's warm."

"Warm," Galina repeated softly, as though it were a spell or a blessing, and then she hurried upstairs. As I listened to the steps creaking beneath her feet, my heart swelled with nervous excitement.

I could count the number of living people I'd seen over the years on the fingers of one hand. Usually, after taking one glance at my family, they ran off screaming. If Mikhail survived, maybe we could become friends. And if he died, perhaps the same strange force that had resurrected my new family would also allow his sentience to remain after his body failed him.

Just as the pot of water started to boil, the door opened, and Mama and Papa dragged Mikhail inside.

I hurried over. "I've prepared my bedroom."

As I followed them into the room, Galina's fingers plucked anxiously at my skirt. I hadn't heard her approach, but she could be so silent sometimes, easing across the floorboards like a shadow.

Stopping next to my bed, I untied the ropes from around Mikhail's body and peeled back the oilcloth. My heart dropped. Against the fabric, he was white and deathly still. As I reached out to see if he was still breathing, he stirred briefly. His sharp face contorted in pain, shadows carving out the hollows in his cheeks as a low groan escaped his lips.

Mama and Papa hauled him onto the mattress. I leaned over

the bed and drew back the flaps of Mikhail's coat. Bloody gemstones spilled from the saturated fabric and scattered on the straw-stuffed mattress.

Stunned, I picked up a couple of the faceted jewels. They were cold and sticky against my palm. Rubies and diamonds, as if his blood itself had hardened into stone. I spotted the source sticking out of his coat's ripped lining—a pocket of fabric lighter than the rest, torn open and contents scattered.

Placing the gems on the nightstand, I unbuttoned his shirt. My stomach lurched at the devastation beneath—blood coursed from a hole in Mikhail's shoulder, slickening his entire left side.

Papa examined the wound.

"He's been shot." Papa's voice was low and gravelly through his wooden mask. As he spoke, he twisted the lead ring on his finger around and around, a memento forged from the bullet that had taken him.

My gaze drew to the flintlock musket above the fireplace. If the people in the other dirigible survived, and if they came searching for Mikhail, would I be able to protect us? How could an old musket compare to rapid gunfire, let alone the powers of bogatyri?

No. I hardened my heart to the fear that seized me. Mikhail was my responsibility now. The moment I had touched him, I had known in my heart that his life was something to safeguard and cherish.

Everything that was alive out here, I had to kill for my own survival, from the plants I farmed and foraged to the animals I hunted. But this was different. I *must* be the one to save him.

"How can I help?" I asked, my voice firming with resolution. "There must be something."

"We need to stop the bleeding," Mama said. "Galechka, fetch some samogon from the cellar. Toma, bring me your sewing kit, clean bandages, and a lit candle."

After finding the supplies, I returned to my bedroom and laid everything out on the bedside table. Already, Mama had started cleaning the skin surrounding Mikhail's wound with a samogon-soaked rag. As I leaned over him, the alcohol's pungent fumes stung my nostrils.

At Mama's instruction, I heated a sewing needle in the candle's flame. By the time the needle cooled enough for me to touch it with my bare hands, the rag that Mama held against Mikhail's shoulder was already dyed red. The blood had soaked through to her own hand-wrappings, staining the layers of deteriorated dowry lace and buckskin.

In the flickering candlelight, shadows settled under Mikhail's closed eyes. He was fading fast.

I threaded the needle and slid it beneath his skin. My fingers ached and blisters had risen on my palms from holding onto the rope lead, but I forced myself to steady my hands as I sutured his wound.

Blood welled from between the stitches the moment I knotted the thread and snipped its tail.

"It's not working..." The words came out choked and breathless, my voice tight with dismay. "I—the bleeding. I can't stop the bleeding."

Mama sighed deeply, resting her hand on my shoulder. "Toma, I'm afraid there's nothing else you can do for him. It's as I feared. He's lost too much—"

"Your rushnyk," Galina said suddenly. "Use your stitching like you did with me."

Drawing in a deep, shuddery breath, I turned to her. "Galina, that's not going to work."

"It works," she insisted, wiggling her reattached finger as though it was proof. "I promise. It really does. Please, just try it."

I hesitated, looking back at Mikhail. He had lost so much blood already that it was only a matter of time before he succumbed to his wounds.

My gaze drew to the rushnyk hanging above my bed. Unlike the other tapestries in my room, the embroidery was not of my own hand but my birth mother's. It was the only thing I had from the *before*, an inheritance I had carried from my village, past the border of the Kosa interior, and into the wilderness. I remembered now, my mother had wanted me to carry it, to wear it, because…

"If they come after you, this will protect you, Tomochka," my mother had said, and wound the rushnyk around my shoulders the way she had once draped it from the shelf in our altar corner. I remembered being cold and afraid, but I couldn't remember who she had been talking about. She'd squeezed my shoulders and stared at me, pale and drawn, with snow caught in her ebony hair. "Please, always keep it with you. No matter what happens."

Now, I looked to Mama, unrelated to me by blood but more substantial than the woman from my memories. She wore the mask Papa had carved for her—not her own face, but a visage modeled after the brass icon of the goddess Voyna that hung in the corner. Carved of curly birch and buffed to a sheen, the mask gleamed with a silken glow when the candlelight rippled over the wood's natural whorls. The sadness emanating from her was at odds with Voyna's proud, chiseled features and furrowed brow.

"He's going to die, Toma," Mama murmured.

"Not if I can save him," I said, and exchanged the black thread I had used to suture the bullet hole for thick floss dyed red with madder root. The moment I strung the needle, a calm settled over me. Once more, I looked at my birth mother's rushnyk, its embroidery so ornate that I had never been able to replicate the designs exactly. Something about this felt so right, so *familiar*.

I got to work. Interlaced chevrons, wheels, lines reminiscent of sown fields. With each stitch, I felt an intoxicating confidence swell inside of me. I could do this. I had to.

Between stitches, I blotted up the blood that swelled through the seam. Mikhail groaned, his muscles tensing. The design became just as elaborate as the rushnyk hanging over my bed, radiating out from his sutured wound like the sun's corona.

Once it was over, I snipped the remaining thread and washed away the blood. Mikhail's skin was almost as white as the linen he lay on, but his wounds had already clotted over. His chest rose and fell in deep, even breaths.

I sighed, my shoulders sagging as the last residual tension drained from my limbs. Somehow, I had managed to keep him on this side of our world, at least for tonight.

2

In the time it had taken me to stitch his wound, the candle's guttering flame had drowned in a puddle of wax. Blood stained the floorboards and blanket. I sat in the chair next to Mikhail's bed and mended the holes and tears in his clothes, keeping vigil.

Every few stitches, I glanced at Mikhail. It had been so long since I had lived among humans, I had almost forgotten what they looked like. He was beautiful in a severe sort of way, with a sharp jawline and cheekbones like honed blades. Even in sleep, he seemed ill at ease, shifting restlessly atop the mattress, his jaw tightening as though to ready himself for a blow.

I thought he must still be young. Not a child, but not a grown man either. I liked to imagine we were the same age.

As I waited for him to wake up, vague memories returned to me. A mining town bustling with people. My father returning from below ground, smelling of coal dust and wet earth. Countless hours spent by the fire as my mother taught me her embroidery. When we ran out of thread, she drew the stitches in the fireplace ashes, guiding my fingertips over the symbols until I memorized them completely.

Then there were darker memories of corpses lying on the cobblestones, gunfire and artillery blasts in the night, and streets filled with coal smoke and inky grease from the mining machines. The memory of the Groznaya War hung over me. My childhood had been plagued by executions—both of suspected spies for Groznaya, and those accused of being kolduny and heretics.

Each time, the condemned would be tethered to a steel post in the center square, before a bogatyr soldier released a lightning bolt down upon them. The stench had been so horrific that observers would press satchels of herbs over their noses. And once it was over, the scraps of the deceased's burnt clothes would be collected and sold—even relics of the bogatyri's wrath were considered holy.

But the worst memory of all from that time was the cave-in mere days before we left. It was one of my few memories that remained pristine. I would never forget my mother gripping my hand as we'd walked past the rows of bodies laid out in the dirt, some just piles of parts covered by sheets.

My father had been fortunate. His features had been recognizable still, unlike many of the others whose families had to resort to sifting through their clothing and pockets to identify them. It never mattered in the end though. Their tendons were severed by the same silver blade, and their bodies burnt on the same pyre.

I hissed as the needle slipped through the cloth and pricked my finger. A quivering drop of blood welled from the wound.

Staring at it, I found myself thinking back to the boy who had perished in the wreck.

I had asked my adoptive parents many times why some people came back and others simply died, and they had always been vague about their answers. Mama believed that there were springs of power in the world, areas where the barrier between the human realm and the goddesses' realm was a little thinner. Rivers, certain glades, caves, ponds, crossroads, sometimes potter's fields.

It was in those places the goddesses listened as we were dying and answered our deepest prayers—for another breath, for one more sunset, for the touch of a lover.

Papa told me once that he had been killed in a potter's field in the empire's far south, at the edge of the Black Steppe. He had been murdered by men who had hated him for no other reason than that he was a stranger. And once it was over, he had awoken with his mouth crammed with spindly yellow steppe-grass, and his skin already bloated, the bullet still inside him. He spent years living like an animal, hunting and scavenging, before Mama helped return him to his senses. Most upyri ate the dead and the living alike, but my family had found a way around it, by slowly starving themselves until they craved nothing at all.

A soft knock on the door stirred me from my contemplations. Galina peeped her head in.

"Is he still alive?" she asked timidly.

"Still alive," I confirmed, glancing over at Mikhail.

She edged into the room, shyly cradling her arms around herself. Her chestnut hair hung over her face. Someday Papa would carve her a mask of her own, but for now, there was still enough left of her that a ghost of her original features remained. "Are you sure?"

"I'm sure." I had to bite my inner cheek to keep myself from smiling, remembering how flustered Galina had been when she'd found me all those years ago. She had refused to leave my side for days, even waking me in the night to make sure I was still breathing.

Back then, I had quickly warmed to Galina. She became my best friend, and we spent countless hours exploring the forest together. Over the years, as I grew older and she remained the same, our roles had changed. Now, I felt a soft, sisterly affection toward her, and those days we were equal might as well have been a second lifetime ago.

"When will he wake up?" Galina asked as I folded his mended coat and put it on the dresser.

"I don't know," I said.

"Does he sleep as long as you do?"

I laughed. "I imagine."

She groaned. "But that's *hours.*"

"It's important that he gets his rest. He needs to recover."

"Can I help? I want to help him."

"We just have to wait, Galechka. There's nothing we can do."

She edged toward Mikhail's bed, her fingers plucking anxiously at her patched skirt. "Please?"

I sighed, picking his shirt off the floor. There were still some holes left to repair. I held it out to her. "Why don't you—"

Suddenly, Mikhail pushed back the blanket and lurched into a sitting position, the bed frame shuddering from his violent motion. His whole body trembled, chest rising and falling in urgent gasps.

"Aleksey?" His gaze darted around the room before landing on Galina, who stepped toward him with a little coo of excitement.

I rose to my feet, dropping the shirt. "Galina, wait—"

As she neared Mikhail's bedside, he shied away with a low cry. His feet tangled in the blankets and furs, and he fell over the side of the bed, landing on his hands and knees.

"Stay back!" Eyes blazing with terror, Mikhail lurched against the bed frame. He raised a hand to ward her off. "Get away from me!"

"It's okay," I said quickly, rushing to Mikhail's side to calm him. "You're safe. Stop moving. You're going to reopen your wound."

"What is that *thing*?" he demanded, looking past me.

My shock gave way to anger. "How dare you. That's my sister, Galina, and she's not a *thing*."

"Your sister?"

"She's an upyr and she won't hurt you."

"Upyri eat people!"

"Not my family." I took a deep breath, calming myself. After spending so many years in isolation, I had almost forgotten that living humans feared the undead. "Don't be afraid, you're safe here."

He looked from me to Galina then back again, his fearful grimace dissolving into an expression of blank confusion. "But…"

"Let me help you."

He flinched when I touched him, but after a brief hesitation, allowed me to guide him to his feet. His gaze darted toward Galina once more, and his hand tightened around mine.

I eased Mikhail onto the straw-stuffed mattress, supporting his back. Galina stepped away, her face contorted in such pain that I was afraid her fragile skin might tear. I wanted so badly to tell her that Mikhail was hurt and disoriented, that he didn't know what he was saying. But by the time I opened my mouth to speak, she had already fled from the room.

"I'll bring you something to eat and drink," I said hurriedly to Mikhail, backing away. "Just don't move any more."

"Who are you?" Pain and confusion fogged his silver eyes. "Where am I?"

"I'm Toma, and this is my home. Don't worry, nobody's going to harm you here, so please don't be afraid."

He didn't say anything, just stared at me with his teeth bared like a wolf readying to bite.

I left the room, shutting the door and locking it behind me. He was too hurt to be allowed to wander, and I couldn't risk him coming across Mama or Papa and attacking them in a panic.

"Galina," I called softly, going down the hall. "Are you still here?"

I found her in the kitchen, sorting pebbles into piles. The silk bag she carried in her pocket lay empty, her found treasures scattered over the floor. I stepped over a lead soldier, beads, old coins, spent bullets, and amulets.

"Are you okay?"

Galina shook her head, fumbling with her prizes. White stones, green stones, black.

"He shouldn't be here," she mumbled.

"Mikhail's hurt, Galechka," I said gently, sitting down beside her. I picked a tin horse with a missing leg from among her treasures, turning it around in my hands. "He needs our help. He didn't mean what he said."

"You don't understand," she said as I placed my hand over her own, stroking the rags and ribbons entwined around her palm. Whenever I came across fabric in the abandoned houses, whether it be dowry lace or an altar rushnyk embroidered with the signs of the Three Sisters, she was the first to claim it. Strannik goldwork was her favorite, black silk or cotton covered in an interlacing of metallic thread.

"He's just scared," I murmured gently. "Once he realizes how wonderful you are, he'll love you."

"He thinks I'm a monster." Her voice became choked.

"That's nonsense."

Galina lifted her head and regarded me with void eyes. Concealed by shrunken lids until they were just slits, the empty sockets unsettled me in a way they never had before. It was like staring into the night. "He's right."

She pushed to her feet and raced toward the door.

"Galechka, wait." As I stood, the door slammed shut behind her. "Don't go!"

I hurriedly put my boots on and stepped outside into the pouring rain. The sky had darkened to a sooty gray, and the downpour was so heavy, it was impossible to see where she had gone. She could be incredibly fast sometimes, and silent too.

"Galechka?" I called, shielding my eyes from the rain. "Please, come back."

There was no sign of her. Just ripples racing across puddles and the inkblot smudge of the forest. A lightning bolt bayoneted the sky, followed by an explosive crash of thunder so loud I flinched. I called her name twice more, but the howling wind was the only thing to answer.

Sighing, I went back inside. As I put a fresh pot of water atop the stove, I couldn't help but cast repeated glances through the gaps in the boarded window, waiting for Galina to reappear.

While the water warmed, I added a mixture of preserved vegetables and dried meats to the pot. It was mushroom season, and along with several sacks of dried mushrooms, I also had an entire basketful of fresh ones. I sautéed some of them with the precious amount of deer fat I could spare.

As the meal was cooking, I went down to the cellar, where jars of preserved vegetables and meat sat like dusty offerings on narrow shelves. Sacks contained herbs and spices. A small barrel of salt, gathered from natural deposits at a nearby stream, rested near the door.

As for drinks, there were plenty of barrels to choose from, not just of ale and stout, but also of nonalcoholic kvass. In the summer months, Mama would brew drinks from wild hops, rowanberries, grain, and beets. Using a makeshift still, she made samogon that was so potent, it scalded the throat like fire. I didn't know why she bothered, considering she rarely drank even well water. Maybe she did it for the same reason Papa carved wooden clock boxes and fiddled with broken clockworks scavenged from surrounding houses—as a reminder of the woman she had once been.

After filling a tankard with stout, I returned to the ground floor. Cool liquid sloshed across my hand as I tried to open the stubborn door to Mikhail's room. Locking him in had been pointless, considering the frame was so warped that I couldn't even wrench the door free.

Grunting, I pressed my shoulder against the panel and tried to force it inward. The door shuddered, then creaked open, and I stumbled into the room triumphant.

Blowing stray curls out of my face, I grinned at Mikhail, who sat on the bed. "I'm sorry I took…"

He held Papa's flintlock musket in his lap, the barrel angled toward me. His fingers frantically struggled to load the flash pan. In the process, his elbow struck the wooden box perched on the mattress beside him. Lead shot spilled across the blanket and tinkled to the floor.

"Get away from me," he snarled, his voice low and ragged. "Just stay back."

I took a step away, then hesitated. I had shot the gun enough times to know it was a fickle thing, quick to jam. Did it even have a flint still? I was sure I had removed it a few weeks ago after it had chipped, intending to chisel a replacement.

"I am Tsar Mikhail Vladimirovich of House Morev, and under the authority of the empire, I am ordering you to stay back!"

His royal authority had the opposite effect on me—instead of backing away, I froze where I stood. Just as I had never heard of a bogatyr of common blood, neither had I heard of a tsar who needed to fight someone off with a musket, not when he might have magic at his disposal. Was Mikhail too injured to use his powers? Did he even *have* powers?

Recovering from my shock, I lifted a hand to placate him. "I'm not going to hurt you. Please, just put that down."

"I know what you are."

"I'm Toma," I said gently. "Remember?"

"You're a koldunia."

I laughed abruptly, taken aback. If the legends were true, the witches of the wilderness lived in chicken-legged cottages surrounded by bone fences. They rode in giant mortars, wielded pestles, and ate children. Whereas I was pretty sure my house did not have scaly feet growing out of its foundation, and the last time I had seen a living child, I had been one myself.

"I'm not a witch," I assured him. "And that gun doesn't even work. It's just a decoration."

His eyes narrowed. "You're lying."

"I promise I'm telling the truth."

"The Edge is full of kolduny and heretics."

"Then it's a good thing I'm neither," I said, and was relieved to see a hint of doubt cloud Mikhail's features. "I wouldn't hurt you, not after I saved you."

Slowly, he set the musket on the mattress, keeping one hand over the wooden stock. Sweat glistened on his forehead. His pale, drawn features relaxed, but his silver eyes never left mine.

"I brought you stout," I said, taking a cautious step forward. Once I was sure he wouldn't try clobbering me with the musket, I covered the remaining distance to the bed and held out the tankard.

He stared down at the amber liquid and licked his lips, his eyes burning with thirst. Yet he didn't reach out. Realizing he was still afraid I was a koldunia, I took a sip.

"See? It's good." Maybe a bit on the vinegary side, but not nasty enough to poison him.

Mikhail accepted the tankard and took a hesitant taste. He rolled the liquid around in his mouth before swallowing. His thirst won him over after a few tentative sips, and he finished off the draught in one deep gulp.

While he was distracted, I picked up the musket. Even though its flash pan was empty, I didn't want to return it to the shelf, where it would remain a hazard.

Angling the gun's muzzle toward the ceiling, I said, "Some stew is warming in the kitchen. I'll bring you a bowl once it's ready."

"Thank you," he mumbled. "May I have some more stout?"

"Of course."

As I retreated to the door, he said my name, softly.

"Yes?" I asked, turning back.

Mikhail drew the blanket against his chest, his fingers worrying at the frayed hem. "Are there others here?"

"What do you mean?"

He hesitated, moistening his lips. "Like…your sister. Others like her."

"Oh, yes." I smiled. "I'll introduce you to them later once they return. Mama and Papa are searching for the people who hurt you, but they should be home soon."

I supposed the drink must have begun to disagree with him, because his face paled and his mouth pressed into a puckering line.

"You shouldn't have drunk it so fast." I studied him. "Are you going to be sick?"

"I'm dead," he said tonelessly.

"Not yet," I reassured him, and then left to find a safer place for the musket.

3

After hiding the musket in the cellar, I checked on the stew. The broth had darkened to a rich brown, with succulent chunks of rehydrated venison floating in it. I filled a bowl then fetched another mug of stout.

On my way back to Mikhail's room, a stone jabbed me in the foot. I winced and looked down, but it wasn't a pebble at all. It was one of Galina's blue beads. Balancing the tray in one hand, I picked up the bead and slipped it in my pocket.

Even if it snowed tomorrow, we'd go hunting for treasures. I'd spend all day crawling through the ruins, digging up broken keys and loose beads, if she wanted me to. We wouldn't come home until our pockets were crammed to the seams. I owed her that much.

When I returned to the room, Mikhail had gathered the spilled lead shot and put it in the box, along with the powder flask and other tools. He sat up as I shut the door behind me.

"Venison and mushrooms." I set the tray at the foot of his bed. "And more stout."

"Thank you, Toma," he said, taking the mug from my hand. He didn't waste time sampling the stew, much less using the spoon I had provided. After guzzling the stout, he cupped the bowl in both hands and drank from it deeply.

Was he really a tsar? He hardly seemed noble. Then again, the emperors in Galina's storybooks never ended up facedown in the wreckage of a ruined airship.

Once Mikhail was done, he returned the bowl to its tray and leaned back against the pillow, closing his eyes.

"How's your wound?"

He placed a hand over his bandaged shoulder. "It barely hurts at all."

"Good."

"What did you do to me?"

"I just sewed it up," I said, deciding that it would be best to not mention I had essentially embroidered him like a rushnyk. "I couldn't get the bullet out, but I think you'll survive."

"Are you sure you're not a witch?"

"Aren't you going to ask if I'm a bogatyr?" I retorted.

He looked around at the hewn-log walls, the cobwebs in the corners, the boarded-up windows. A blush colored his cheeks. "Uh… Are you?"

"No, but I'm not a koldunia either." I took the musket box and placed it on the fireplace mantel, then moved his meal tray over to the dresser. Settling into the chair by his bedside, I fiddled with the bead in my pocket, tracing its worn facets. "When we first met, you said that someone was coming. Do you mean the people in that other airship?"

"Yes. They're Koschei's men." Mikhail hesitated. "I need to know… There was a boy my age with me. My…friend. Aleksey. He pretended to be a Fraktsiya soldier and helped me escape. Is he… Did he…"

"I'm sorry." I looked down at my feet. "He died saving us. I don't think he's coming back."

A low, anguished moan tore from Mikhail's lips as though I had shot him myself. The hand he pressed over his mouth failed to suppress the miserable noise, nor did it hide the way his features contorted as he struggled to regain his composure. Pain darkened his gaze, and then he closed his eyes, squeezing them shut so tightly that wrinkles formed between his brows.

"I…I see." He spat out the words as if they were as heavy as bullets, like he wanted to force them out and be rid of them.

"He didn't suffer," I said softly.

When Mikhail didn't answer, I walked over to the window and peered through the cracks between the boards. It was pouring even harder now, and the droplets splattered against the glass as a grainy, half-frozen sleet.

I gauged Mikhail's emotional state before I spoke next. Although his eyes were glazed with unshed tears, the creases in his brow had smoothed out, and his hands were unfurled across the blanket. When his eyes met mine, a stir of surprise passed through me. His gaze blazed with fury.

"If you're the Tsar, why did they try to kill you?" I asked.

He answered my question with one of his own, his voice curt. "You sound like you're from the Kosa interior, so what are you doing in the Edge? Where's your family?"

I took a deep breath. If I tried hard to remember, I could

conjure my birth parents' faces in my mind. But each year my memories of them grew fainter, and that haunted me.

The Edge was the name for the Kosa Empire's westernmost territory, which centuries ago had been a separate kingdom. Centuries of imperialism had stolen the different territories' individual languages, but the accents were unique enough that Papa, who had grown up in a border town along the Black Steppe, sounded different than Mama, who had come from a town in the Edge's verdant south.

"You're right, I'm not from the Edge," I said. "My father died in a mining accident when I was just a child, and my mother and I… We were traveling. She said we were on our way to a faraway place, and then…"

Something terrible happened.

"…I lost her. I think I was ten or so. It was after the war."

"The war with Groznaya?"

I nodded. "About a year after."

"Seven years…" His voice was soft with awe. "You've been out here for seven years?"

The way he said it made my skin prickle uncomfortably. He made it sound like far too long.

"What about you?" I rested against the windowsill. "Shouldn't you be in your palace?"

"It's not my palace anymore." Mikhail gave a cold laugh. "It's been stolen by a bunch of barbarians who don't know the first thing about governing an empire."

I could tell that he was beginning to recover from the shock of his friend's death, or at least suppress it. Maybe he had a dark place inside him, too. A little hole where he buried all the things that were too painful to think about.

"What do you mean?" I asked.

"The Fraktsiya. They're a political group, or at least that's what they call themselves, but the fact is they're nothing more than anarchists controlled by a madman named Koschei. They say that power should be transferred from the nobility to the peasantry, in a rule of majority. It sounds good in theory, but when you get down to it, something like that would never work. Not in our country. My family has ruled this empire for centuries, and it has prospered under our guidance. Our dynasty was consecrated by the Three Sisters themselves."

Sometimes I liked to believe it was the Three's power that had brought my family back to life, but this raised painful questions. Such as, why hadn't the Three Sisters shown my birth parents the same mercy? Why did they bless noble families with powers, but never peasantry?

"What do you believe in, Toma?" Mikhail asked, when I didn't respond. His gaze landed on the dusty corner where an altar to the Three would have hung in a believer's home. "Are you Strannik?"

I shook my head. "No, I don't think so."

He lifted an eyebrow. "You don't think so?"

I hesitated. There were holes in my memory, dark spaces where time had gnawed away at my past. How could I even be sure of who I was, when I could no longer recall the name of my town or my birth parents' voices?

In the end, I supposed it didn't matter if my family had worshipped the Three Sisters like most of the Kosa Empire, or if they had been Strannik and worshipped the triple-faced goddess Voserka. Whichever entities my family had prayed to, they had forsaken us just the same.

"I don't remember enough to know for sure," I said. "But we had an altar to the Three in my home, and I remember the Stranniki who lived in my village. I remember the clothes they wore."

At one point, this area must have had a significant Strannik population, because even to this day, Galina still uncovered examples of their goldwork from the ruins surrounding us. She showcased the fragments of black silk on the wall by the stove, so that the firelight would glisten across the embroidery. Even the copper threads aged beautifully, and the rare gold and silver examples were remarkable, covered in lush, raised designs meant to resemble flowers and leaves.

I remembered there had been many Stranniki in my hometown too, because they specialized in metalwork and our mines were rich in silver and copper. Base ores were sacred and pure, with iron's red color representing the lifeblood of the Three and copper's green verdigris colored by the water of life itself. But it was considered cursed work to tear precious silver and gold ore from the earth's bosom, and just as heretical to smelt and shape it—work apt to spoil oneself with the Unclean Force—so by royal decree, the Stranniki had labored in both professions.

Only the temple priestesses and monks who crafted Troika icons had the holiness and knowledge to be capable of resisting the corruption of raw ore and would bless the metal en masse. In the past, gold and silver jewelry had been a luxury restricted to the nobility who could afford temple services. But when the Stranniki had come here, their conflicting beliefs about the uncleanness of ore had cheapened its value so that even peasants could afford a silver ring or dainty chain, if they were willing to buy it from a Strannik.

My father, though not Strannik, had been a miner, and to atone for his transgressions, he would burn wheat at our home altar and every three moons offer a rooster to the middle Sister, Seredina.

Fire purified all. Even the silver ore that had blackened my father's clothes. Even his body, after his sins had caught up to him far below the earth.

The Stranniki in my town had worn high leather boots and black tunics embroidered with silver mined from the mountains that surrounded us. I had been so enthralled by their hooded tent-cloaks, the grommeted hems decorated with silver hoops and polished malachite buttons, that I had approached a woman at the market and asked to touch hers.

The memory troubled me. It came from the dark like smoke and left an acrid taste in my mouth. Fear had shone in my mother's eyes when she'd stopped me. She yanked me back by the wrist, as though just touching the Strannik woman might sully me.

"Don't do that again!" my mother had cried once we were home. "If someone sees you…" The blood drained from her face. "If someone sees you, what will they think, Tomochka?"

That had been one of the last times I had seen a Strannik in our village. After a landslide claimed the lives of ten miners and talk of the Three Sisters' wrath permeated through the village, they had all left one day, their homes shuttered and ravaged, a long procession of wagons and horses trailing down the road. Banished.

Mikhail sank against the mattress and closed his eyes.

Somewhere in the house, a door opened and then creaked shut. Galina must have returned.

"You must be tired," I said. "I'll let you sleep. Just call my name if there's anything you need."

Silence. I supposed he must've drifted off already.

Taking care to be quiet, I left the room and eased the door shut behind me. Mama and Papa had returned from outside, tracking water across the floor before the hearth.

Sitting on the bench by the window, Papa rested a half-finished clock box on his leg and carved it, slivers of wood dropping to the floor. Once he finished the clock and assembled its mechanism from scavenged parts, it would join the rest of the quietly ticking timepieces located in every room of the house. Time meant nothing to him, but it meant so much to me. Each tick was a terrifying reminder that I grew older while my family remained the same, and any day now, that might change.

"Did you find the men?" I asked, going to his side. "The ones who hurt Mikhail?"

"We found the crash, but there was no trace of them," Mama said, lingering near the stove. She had taken off her mask to dry it. The fire cast its glow across her jutting features, gathering in her cheeks' hollows and the sunken pouches of her eyelids, frozen shut in perpetuity. Her skin was so thin that when she spoke, I could nearly see the ridges of her teeth beneath. "The rain must have washed away their tracks."

"We'll look again tomorrow morning," Papa added, his worry betrayed by the way he handled his knife, carving the wood in rough, swift strokes. "And we'll stand watch through the night. If they come through here, we'll know."

Thin beams of light intruded through the gaps in the boarded window, turning his body into an eerie shadow play of sunken contours and sharp edges. He looked so fragile sitting there, even with his wooden mask and layered clothes concealing the worst of the decay. Any moment, he might fall apart.

"Have you seen Galina?" I swallowed hard. "She went outside."

"No, but we only just returned," Mama said.

I took a deep breath, focusing on the whistling wind and the groan of timber, the rap of hail against the roof. For a reason I couldn't explain, the talk with Mikhail had unsettled me. Just thinking about the past was dangerous. That simple question—*Are you Strannik?*—had opened a door to allow darker memories to lurch in, if I allowed them.

I rubbed my arms, cold in spite of the oven's warmth. "Maybe she's exploring. I'll take a look."

I tugged on my boots and stepped outside, hoping to spot Galina climbing one of the boulders or building a fort from branches. An empty brown expanse confronted me, pebbles of ice melting in the rain puddles. I shielded my eyes with my hands, squinting as I studied the darkening horizon, where the forest cradled jagged mountains.

"Galina," I called.

No answer.

"Galina, come home now. It's getting late. Don't you want to string those pretty beads into a necklace?"

Silence.

Frowning, I went back inside. Undead or not, my sister would still be vulnerable to blustering winds and rocky out-croppings. If she fell into a crevice or was buried by a landslide, we might never find her. Goddesses forbid she lose a leg, a hand, or even her head.

I shuddered at the thought. I had never reattached a head before. The idea of confronting her windpipe, the bristling vertebrae, arteries and sinew and so many dried, delicate things made my skin crawl. Could she even survive decapitation?

"I can't find Galina anywhere," I said to my parents, crossing my arms as a sudden draft passed through the house. "She was upset earlier and ran off. I should have stopped her, but— but I didn't. I'm worried about her."

"We'll look outside," Mama said, her joints popping as she approached me.

"She couldn't have gone far in this weather," Papa said, rising to his feet. He set down his knife and unfinished clock box and brushed the splinters from his clothes. It was growing darker by the moment, the storm bearing down. Now, there was only enough light left to reveal the oiled gleam of his skin. His knuckles swelled like pickled walnuts through the layers of deteriorating fur and fabric.

"I'm scared for her," I whispered. Somehow, it came as an immense relief to give voice to my fears.

"Don't worry, we'll find her," Mama murmured, stroking my hair. She smelled faintly of juniper and dried flowers. I sighed and leaned against her, gently, resting my weight on the balls of my feet so I wouldn't burden her. Her papery skin, her fragrance, the ribbons garlanding her tufts of graying-blond hair. So comforting and familiar.

"Help by staying here," Papa said. The rusty hinges of his leg splints groaned as he crossed the room. "Watch over the boy and wait for Galina to return. Someone must be here, Toma."

I followed them to the entrance and stood in the doorway. The thought of being alone in this storm paralyzed me and left my mouth dry with fear. I recalled what it had been like as a child, shivering in the cold and calling for my mother, knowing nobody would respond.

Shoving the memory from my mind, I lingered at the threshold as Mama and Papa trudged through the hail. The downpour was so thick, it concealed them within five paces, first reducing them to snippets of lighter gray against the outer dark, then engulfing them entirely.

As night crawled on, the storm worsened, and my worry became dread. I stood by the window, waiting for a figure to emerge from the darkness. Squandering the precious amount of oil we still had left, I lit a lantern and set it in the upstairs window, whose pane was only cracked instead of shattered. I hoped Galina would be able to discern the wick's glow through the sleet storm.

When I came downstairs again, I found Mikhail in the hallway, slumped against the wall and panting. A fine dew of sweat shone on his brow, his gray eyes clouded with pain.

"I told you to rest," I said, reaching for his arm. He flinched away, but when I took another step closer, he allowed me to gently grasp his wrist.

"I need to go," he croaked.

"You're hurt."

"Koschei's men are going to come for me. As long as I'm here, they'll never stop searching."

"There's a storm and you won't be able to find your way home," I said, resting my arm across his lower back to support him. His skin burned hot against my palm. I couldn't decide if he had a fever or if this was a normal human temperature. Over the years, I'd grown familiar with the chill of the dead. "Please, you'll be safe here. Just let me take you back to bed."

By the time I guided Mikhail back to my room, I had already made up my mind—I would search for Galina as well. I refused to lose any more of the people precious to me, and there was no way a storm would get in my way.

I locked the door to Mikhail's room behind me. Prisoner or not, he couldn't be going anywhere in his condition. The last thing I needed was to hunt him down, too.

I brought the lantern down from the second floor and put on my coat and boots. As I tied my laces, I glanced at the cellar door. I had hidden the musket behind some barrels, wrapped in an oilcloth to protect it from the elements. It would make a good weapon, but the box of lead shot and the powder horn were still in Mikhail's room. If I went back in there, it would raise too many questions. Besides, I didn't plan to go far, and if rain damaged my musket, I'd never be able to repair it.

After slinging my satchel over my shoulder, I tamed my dark, disheveled hair into a bun that I tucked under my fur ushanka. I wrapped a scarf around my face to protect my skin from the biting wind and ventured out into the night.

Leaving the izba was like jumping into a frigid pond—a sudden immersive chill that took my breath away. Holding the lantern in front of me and ducking my chin down, I trudged forward.

"Galina?" I called as I headed toward the river, searching the ground for twitching fingers or torn rags. My teeth chattered uncontrollably, and cold water sank into my boots. "Are you out here?"

The wind responded by slapping another wave of sleet in my face. I doubted Galina would be able to hear me no matter how loudly I shouted, and her creaky voice was so soft, I'd never catch it over the howling storm.

The river was swollen to the edges of the banks, and sleet encrusted the bridge. Skidding across the wood, I gripped onto the railing to steady myself. Perhaps the rusalki ignored me, but there were other creatures in the river—I had seen their webbed footprints in the mud along the foreshore and the mauled animals left from their bloodlust.

Alder trees that only a few days ago had been covered in a wealth of gold leaves now stood threadbare. Sloshing through drifts of slimy leaves, I picked my way south along the riverside. After making it some distance, I spotted a light burning in the window of an abandoned home.

It couldn't be Galina. She wouldn't know how to set a fire, not that she even needed it except to keep the frightening darkness at bay. But she may have seen it and become curious.

Exposed rafters, rotten thatch and boards. Part of the decorative wooden trim that had once adorned the izba's roof now protruded from the mud like a dislocated jaw. Nearing the home, I extinguished my lantern, set it on the ground in the cover of the eaves, and crawled through a broken-out window. Sleet pounded against the roof, far louder than the taps of my boots as they touched down.

I had taken no more than three steps when someone coughed in a nearby room.

My breath solidified in my lungs as if frozen. I began to back against the window then hesitated. What if Galina had come here? It seemed unlikely, but I would never be able to forgive myself if I ran away now, even to warn my parents. By the time I returned, it might be too late.

"You think Koschei will accept it?" a man mused.

"He'll have to." The other cleared his throat before coughing once more. "Otherwise, it'll be your head or mine."

Steeling myself, I reached into my satchel, groping past the chunk of flint, the herbs, and heartwood, until my fingertips touched antler. I pulled my hunting knife from its sheath. The soft *snick* of the blade scraping against leather was the only sound that betrayed me.

I edged closer to the doorway where the light came from. Pressing my body against the wall, I peeked into the room.

A bearded man sat on the dirt floor, stoking a fire with a stick. Another one with blond hair leaned against the wall. They wore dark sage-green greatcoats emblazoned with black patches on the shoulders. No visible weapons. If they were the men who had shot at Mikhail and me, they could have lost their guns in the crash.

My gaze swept across the room. A burlap sack sat in the corner. It had once probably held onions or potatoes, but now it was filled with squirming cargo. A low moan escaped my lips before I could stop myself.

Galina.

"I don't see what's so special about upyri," the blond man said, nudging the sack lightly with the toe of his boot. "Back in my village, we used to spot them slinking through the graveyards. The feces pits, too. They're like swine. They'll eat anything."

"Are you sure that wasn't your mother?" The bearded man bellowed with laughter.

His partner shot him an ugly look. "Keep talking, Dima, and I'll tell Koschei that you were the one to let the Tsar escape. Then *you'll* end up in a feces pit."

"Easy there." A hint of nervousness wavered in Dima's voice. Restlessly, he tweaked at his beard. "Listen, once Koschei sees this thing, he'll give us another chance. He has to. Upyri are one thing, but child upyri? And a live one? They're rarer than gold."

Afraid they might spot me, I stepped back against the wall. My foot crunched down on a piece of broken pottery.

"What was that?" Dima rose to his feet, his bared teeth glistening in the dark thatch of his beard and mustache. "Did you hear that?"

"I didn't hear anything," the other man said. "You must be imagining things."

Holding my breath, I retreated deeper into the shadows.

"No, I definitely heard something."

"It's the wind, Dima. The storm."

"Shhh. Listen."

Holding my breath, I clenched the hunting knife in a vise-like grip. One minute passed. Then two. No voices.

As I loosened my hold, hands seized me from behind. With a wild cry, I swung my arm back, slashing blindly.

"It bit me!" Dima yelped, releasing me. "Damn it, it bit me!"

I swiveled around and retreated several paces, my knife brandished in front of me. Urgent gasps pushed from my lungs, trailing in fog from my lips.

"That isn't an upyr, you idiot," his companion growled, eying me warily. Strands of lank blond hair hung over his forehead, framing features nearly as emaciated as an upyr's. "It's a woman. A girl, at that."

"A koldunia," Dima spat, backing away from me. My knife had left a shallow cut across the back of his hand. "Only witches live out in the wilderness. And just look at her."

"Where is he?" The blond man's lips were so chapped, droplets of blood welled from their creases when he smiled—a thin, vicious sneer that left my throat dry. "You know, don't you?"

My blood pounded in my ears as I leveled my knife at the men. I felt struck mute, my voice reduced to raw, frantic panting. It wasn't just fear that had caught my tongue—staring into the soldiers' eyes, a strange, feral anticipation welled inside my veins.

"I asked, where is the boy?" the blond man snarled. "The dark-haired one. The one from the crash."

"Dead." My eyes darted from his head to his hands to his feet. If he lunged at me, what part of his body would move first? "Both of them are."

"She's lying," Dima hissed.

"You're not a koldunia at all." The blond man edged toward me, his gaze planted on my blade. "Just some farmer's daughter. Drop that knife now, before you hurt yourself."

Suddenly, he lunged. I thrust the knife forward, aiming for his throat. He ducked away and seized my wrist as the blade cut the empty space between us.

Growling, I tried to yank my hand free. In the corner of my eye, I spotted a haggard figure entering through the open door, backlit by a hazy burst of lightning.

"Mama!" I shouted. "Papa!"

The man's fist flew toward my face. I never felt it hit before succumbing to the darkness.

4

When I came to, the world was filled with a fiery golden light, my vision blurred behind a gossamer veil. Weight on my brow. The entire left half of my face felt swollen into one aching pustule. I groaned, closing my eyes. That helped the nausea somewhat, but it didn't reduce the pain that roared down my face at the slightest motion.

"Is there anything I can do to help her?" a low, hoarse voice said.

"Mikhail," I mumbled.

A hand squeezed mine. "I'm here."

"She needs to rest," Mama said.

"I'm fine. I'm fine." I opened my eyes and fought to sit up, grasping hold of the bed frame for support. The entire world turned slowly, twisting and twisting. I was afraid that if I moved too much, I'd fall off the bed and keep falling forever, through the dirt and permafrost into even stranger depths.

Two figures stood around my bedside. Mama. Papa? No. Mikhail.

"Galina," I whispered, searching the room. Where was Galina? I had saved her, hadn't I?

"I'm sorry, Toma," Mama said, her voice filled with sorrow. "We couldn't stop them. They took her."

"No, I need to find her!" As the world swung in dizzying circles around me, I struggled to climb from the mattress. I swung one foot over and lost my balance. Mikhail caught me before I could fall, grunting in pain when I grabbed his shoulder in reflex. He helped me back onto the mattress then took a step away, casting an apprehensive glance in Mama's direction as he pressed a hand over his healing shoulder.

"There's nothing left for you to do," Mama said. "She's gone."

Her words hit me like punches. There was such grief in her dry, rattling voice, as if there was no hope. As if she was already mourning Galina.

My vision blurred, my breath quickening into thick, urgent gasps. I pressed my hands against my face. When I touched the swollen area, tears welled to my eyes, half from pain and half from sorrow.

Galina couldn't be gone.

All I could think about was my mother striding away from me as the wind grew colder and the snowstorm rolled in—*Tomochka, whatever you hear, don't make a sound*—and then suddenly I was alone, and I tried to call her name, I screamed for her to find me, but it was so cold, so cold, and nobody answered.

I felt a sudden urge to scream and tear at my clothes. To run into this storm, so much like the blizzard that had led me to the upyri all those years ago. Instead, I curled on the bed and pressed my face into the pillow, wrapping my arms around my waist as I began to sob.

The rising sun crested the peaks, lighting up a hazy blue sky that seemed as insubstantial as a skin of ice. Looking up at the horizon, I traced the throbbing knot on my temple. Mama had applied a poultice to the swelling, and it had helped somewhat, but not enough. A shame I couldn't embroider my own scalp.

"Toma?"

I flinched, spinning around.

Mikhail stood in the doorway, blinking drowsily. While he had slept in my bedroom, I had tossed and turned on the small storage nook atop the stove. Even the gentle warmth radiating from the masonry had failed to lull me into peaceful sleep, instead singeing my nerves until I found solace outside.

"What are you doing out here?" His gaze lowered to my bare feet, and he frowned. "You must be cold. Let's go inside."

Mutely, I followed him into the main room, where I had left an oil lamp burning. He surveyed the supplies strewn across the table and bench: strips of dried venison; sacks of grain and salt; bandages and tins of herbal poultices; neatly-tied wire to build snares; my musket, already cleaned, oiled, and fitted with a new flint.

"You aren't planning on leaving, are you?" Mikhail asked. "Not after you were just injured."

"I need to find my sister," I said, clenching my hands into fists. "I can't just sit here, wondering what's happening to her.

You don't understand. If I don't find her, it'll…it'll be like I'm losing my family all over again."

"Toma, those men were soldiers." His voice was strained. "Koschei's men, I'm certain of it. If they see you again, they won't just knock you out. They'll kill you."

"I'll be ready for them this time," I insisted. "I'm good at hunting, Mikhail. Better than you think. I know how to follow tracks. I'll find them."

He looked back at the table. "You really intend to leave?"

I nodded. "Where do you think they would have taken my sister?"

"Probably to Koschei." Mikhail hesitated. "As a way of appeasing him for letting me escape. You need to know, Koschei is obsessed with supernatural creatures. Positively fixated on them. Especially the ones that people turn into after they're dead—mavki, rusalki, drekavcy, upyri. He believes that they're the key to deathlessness. He's even tried…"

I swallowed. "Tried what?"

"It's not important."

"Tell me!" I demanded, dismayed by the fearful waver in my voice. "What has he tried?"

"Grinding up the remains of dead monsters," he mumbled, scarcely louder than a whisper. "To see if he can make the Water of Life that the Three Sisters used to create the first men."

My stomach twisted and I gagged involuntarily, sickened by the images that passed through my head. What kind of torture would Koschei subject Galina to in his quest to find an elixir of eternal life? She was just a little girl, just a child. Wouldn't he be able to see that?

"But those upyri were already gone, just piles of body parts, too far past saving," Mikhail added hastily. "Upyri are rare to encounter in the wild, and children who come back, even more so. But an upyr who is resurrected *aware*, who can actually still talk and think? It's unheard of. If he finds one, he isn't going to waste it."

I struggled to speak. "My sister—she isn't an *it*."

Mikhail winced. "I know, I didn't mean that. What I'm trying to say is the soldiers who took her know her value, know how important it is for Koschei to possess a sentient upyr. They're going to do everything in their power to bring her to him unharmed, because that's the only way they'll survive. By showing him that they are still of value."

"I'll die before I let Koschei have her!" I took a deep breath, steadying myself. "Tell me where I can find him."

"I can't say for sure. Just before I escaped, he decided that it was too unsafe to stay in the capital, and he wanted to take me somewhere secluded. He was going to travel in the royal airship. I managed to escape when we arrived at the airfield. He never told me where he planned to go."

That settled it then. If I found the royal airship, I'd find Koschei.

"You can hide out here until you're fully recovered," I said. "There's a well outside and plenty of food in the cellar."

I reached into my skirt pocket for a ribbon to tie back my hair and touched something smooth and faceted. I took it out. Galina's blue bead.

You think they're sapphires?

My eyes burned. Instead of tying my hair with the ribbon, I strung it through the bead's worn hole and knotted it in a bracelet around my left wrist. Mikhail wouldn't understand how precious Galina was to me, and I feared that deep down even Mama and Papa viewed it as a mercy killing. A quicker route to the inevitable, something kinder than watching her fall apart piece by piece.

"I'm coming with you," Mikhail said as I piled supplies into my rucksack.

I looked up, bewildered. "What? But your wound."

He pressed his hand over his shoulder. "I saw how you stitched me up. Whatever you did, it saved me. My wound barely hurts at all."

"It's safer for you here, Mikhail."

"Nowhere is safe, Toma. I'll take you as far as the next town and we'll see if Koschei's men have gone there, but after that we're parting ways. The sooner I get out of the empire, the better."

His words dawned on me. "But this is your country. You're their tsar."

"You don't understand." He clenched his jaw, his features contorting in frustration. "I…I can't use magic."

I gasped. "What? But you're royalty."

Just as the peasants in Galina's storybooks were occasionally bogatyri, maybe it was also possible for a tsar to be born without magic. However, Mikhail's next words put my theory to rest.

"Koschei took my power." Mikhail stared down at his hands like he expected them to burst into flames at any moment. He curled his fingers into fists. "All of it. He's a koldun, a damn witch, and with just his hands, he took it. I can't… Every time I try to use my power, it's like I hit a wall. Don't you see? This isn't my empire anymore. I can't do anything here. I can't stay."

5

Just as I finished loading the first knapsack, Papa stepped in from outside. Backlit by the murky sunlight, he seemed shrunken, but as he prowled into the room, his gaunt form lengthened in the shadows, turned imposing and sinewy.

His chin dipped slightly as he regarded the supplies still littering the table. "What do you think you're doing?"

"Finding Galina," I declared, knotting the pack's suede straps. Mikhail discreetly removed himself from the kitchen, casting a lingering glance at Papa on the way out. "I'm not going to give up without even trying."

"Toma, you don't know what's out there." His flat timbre became strained with worry. "It's not safe."

"No," Mama said, entering from my bedroom. "It's time she leaves."

A part of me wanted Mama to forbid me from going, but when I saw the rushnyk she cradled in her arms, I knew at once that she never would.

The rushnyk's white linen had yellowed with age, yet its red embroidery was still as bright as blood. Somehow, seeing that heirloom piece made it all the more real for me. Mama knew how much the rushnyk meant to me, that it was the only thing I had left of my birth family. My most precious possession.

"You almost forgot this," she said, wrapping the rushnyk around my shoulders like a shawl.

"But I should just leave it here." I fingered the dusty hem of the tapestry with infinite care. "I don't want it to get damaged."

"No," Mama murmured, fastening the cloth with an amber brooch I had coveted for years. An heirloom of her own, the pin had survived her death and transformation. "Because if you cannot find her, you can't come back."

I flinched, stunned as if struck. A heavy stone formed in my throat, and I pressed my lips together to keep them from trembling uncontrollably.

"How can you say that?" I whispered.

Sighing, Mama took my hand in both of hers. Through the layers of silk and fur binding her hands, her fingers felt as fragile as sparrow bones. "Don't look at me like that. You know you're always welcome here, but this isn't your world, Toma. This isn't where you truly belong."

I sank against her. "But I love you."

"I love you, too. We all do."

"You're my family."

She gently brushed her hand through my hair. "No matter where you go, Toma, we always will be."

As the sun climbed higher into the sky, Mikhail and I set off through the woods. We carried buckskin rucksacks stocked full of supplies, with blankets tethered to the bags' wooden frames. My satchel slapped against my thigh with each step, and my musket rested heavily upon my shoulder.

I had traveled far enough south to know that there would be rivers and springs along our route where we could refresh our stocks and fish. Then there would also be gnawing cold, exhaustion, and hungry monsters. Some things we couldn't prepare for.

The sky was clear, but a nipping chill stropped the air so that each breath stung my nose and throat. I fashioned my rushnyk into a hood and tied the loose ends under my chin, my breath escaping in short, pallid puffs. The fabric smelled like home. I couldn't place a particular aroma, only revel in the familiarity of it.

As I walked, I absently rubbed the sore knot on my temple. Every time I touched it, the faces of the two men flashed through my mind. When they had taken Galina, it felt like a part of my body, an organ that was essential to live, had been ripped out and dragged off too. They hadn't even seen her as a person, just a monster to be captured.

If what Mikhail said was true, all hope would be lost if those men reached Koschei. My only chance at finding Galina would be out here in the wilderness.

I had hunted before, had tracked deer and wild boars. Even though the two men were soldiers, they were unarmed when I had found them and could still be unarmed. I didn't need to fight them. If I could find them and catch them off guard, it might be possible to rescue Galina without spilling blood.

We neared the river. The rusalki were nowhere in sight, but I searched the restless waters anyway for a glimpse of their pale limbs or algae-red hair—the intrusion of humans into my wilderness had forced me to confront the reality that I was human too, and that there were more differences between me and the resurrected dead than I wanted to acknowledge.

"I want to see him," Mikhail said as we crossed the bridge. He too eyed the water uneasily.

"Who?" I asked, glancing up.

"Aleksey."

I hesitated. "Mikhail, he isn't coming back."

He nodded, his jaw set firmly. "I know."

"Are you sure?"

"Yes, Toma. At the very least, I need to say farewell."

Reluctantly, I guided him along the overgrown path until the sunken cobblestones dissolved into grass and raw earth, and then from there took the deer trail that Galina and I had followed the day before. It was easy enough to find my way—when I had dragged Mikhail to safety, his tarp-wrapped body had cut a divot through the soil.

The forest was unnaturally quiet, with the birdsong absent and even the crunch of dead leaves strangely muted. When we entered the clearing, I felt the weight of the bogatyr's death pressing down on me, as though it were a massive object plummeting with great velocity. I drew in a deep breath of the early-morning air, crisp and scented of damp laurel. Dug my nails into my palms.

My dread only grew as we stepped over the rubble. The storm had filled in the bullet holes and lashed the shreds of balloon canvas from the trees, but had only managed to cast the bogatyr facedown on his stomach instead of washing him away entirely.

No. The dead bogatyr's coat lay on the ground several paces from his body, as if he'd hastily thrown it aside. And his arms were spread, his upturned palms bloodied as if…as if he'd been feeding.

A shiver racked my body.

"Aleksey," Mikhail murmured, taking a step forward before I seized his forearm. He turned to me, grief and confusion darkening his gaze.

"Wait." I edged closer, plucking a branch from among the rubble. I gently poked Aleksey's arm.

Even the corpses of deer stiffened within hours, the blood settling in their limbs. But when I nudged the bogatyr's body, his arm moved freely, scraping limply across the soil. His wrists and elbows had been cut at the joints, the tendons severed. It was not the blood of any victim that stained his wrists, but his own.

Revulsion and anger flared in Mikhail's gaze as he spun around to face me. "Did you do this?"

I shook my head. "It must have been the soldiers."

I realized now the men had probably found the burlap sack they used to hold Galina in this airship's wreckage. Maybe she had come back here hoping the boy would be resurrected, only to find that his killers had cut that chance away from him forever.

As I lowered the stick, Aleksey twitched, a single convulsive jerk that sent my heart jolting against my rib cage. I had seen dead animals move before and had even watched as snakes writhed upon the cutting board after being skinned and segmented. But in all cases, those last tremors of life had died down within minutes, and never had a creature slowly lifted its head, never had it fixed its eyes—already filmed over and sightless—on me and tried to speak.

"Lyosha!" Mikhail shouldered past me, a frantic smile passing over his lips. "Toma, we need to help him. He's still alive. He's—"

Crumpled purple flowers bulged from Aleksey's mouth and spilled down his chin; green shreds clung to his sharpening incisors. The soldiers had taken precautions, but not good enough. They had severed the tendons of his limbs and filled his mouth with moss and monkshood, and yet something had remained within him to cling to life and crawl laboriously, desperately back to this mortal coil.

6

Mute with shock, I stumbled back before I could stop myself. Beside me, Mikhail's face went dead white, and the hope that had welled in his eyes when Aleksey first stirred quickly dimmed into terror.

As Aleksey licked the grit of dirt and moss spores from his lips, his hazed eyes lifted. Dried blood beaded on his cheeks. His shirt was muddied with more of the same, and when he struggled to hoist himself from the ground, through his torn clothes I caught a terrible glimpse of his entrails' glistening coils.

My breath caught in my lungs. This was too much for me. I couldn't fix this.

"No, no." A low groan left Mikhail's lips as Aleksey lurched forward. The bogatyr couldn't stand anymore, could hardly even move. His limbs bent unnaturally at the wrists and heels, not just disfigured now, but *changing*.

"All hail the Tsar." The words left Aleksey's mouth in a

hoarse croak, his voice rattling deep in his lungs, as if there was dirt loose in his throat. "Glory. Glory..."

He spoke the words slowly, not at Mikhail, not at anyone— mumbling them to thin air the way an infant babbled. Sparks fizzled at his fingertips, weak pulses of flame that the damp soil snuffed in an instant. I could see it in his eyes; as he crawled closer to Mikhail, Aleksey was slowly circling those final moments that had taken him from this world.

I turned to Mikhail, placing my hand on his forearm as he shied away. "Don't be afraid. It's okay. He's not going to harm you."

"It's okay?" His voice rose with an undercurrent of anger. "No. Nothing about this is okay. Look at him, Toma. *Look* at him."

"Just say his name." Deep inside me, I felt a twinge of excitement. Couldn't Mikhail see? We were watching the creation of something wonderful. "Maybe we can bring him back, the way Mama did to Papa."

"I'm not going to—" He was about to say more when Aleksey lunged at him, the bogatyr shockingly fast in spite of his mutilated limbs. Before I even had time to react, he had driven Mikhail to the forest floor, splayed flat across the very soil the boys had bled into the day before.

Any cry Mikhail made was drowned out by the wrenching noises that pushed from Aleksey's bared teeth—strangled sobs punctuated by guttural gasps and growls that sounded barely human. He was trying to say something. What was he trying to *say*?

"Aleksey, stop!" I tried to wrench him off Mikhail, but he had the Tsar's collar in a bone-white grip, the drabcloth already smoldering. Beneath him, Mikhail twisted sideways, his teeth bared in the same pain and grief that contorted Aleksey's features, as though the same threads I had used to suture Mikhail's shoulder had irrevocably bound the pair together.

"Long may you reign." The words left Aleksey's mouth forcefully and all at once, like he'd had to spit them out with the same desperate strain he'd disgorged the moss and flowers. As Aleksey was about to say more, Mikhail brought his arm up, his fingers locked around a broken pipe snatched from the rubble.

Mouth dry, I reached out. "Mikhail, wait—"

A smatter of cold black blood gushed across my face as Mikhail slammed the rod against the side of Aleksey's head. Once, twice, until the bogatyr's grip loosened and he collapsed onto his stomach beside Mikhail.

Lurching to his knees, Mikhail spun the pipe around in his hands. He drove its jagged tip deep into Aleksey's back, in a motion so fluid it could have only been muscle memory. My stomach turned at the squelch of flesh giving way. As the pipe end tore through to the other side and buried in the soil, Aleksey's feeble twitching stilled, and the sparks that had smoldered at his fingertips winked out and crusted into white ashes.

Panting, Mikhail sank onto his haunches. Tears rose to his eyes, but even when they overflowed and streaked down his cheeks, he kept his hands unfurled in his lap. Blood gathered like drops of ink in his upturned palms.

"I had to, Toma," he said distantly, his gaze raised to the cloudy sky. "To leave him this way, spoiled by the Unclean

Force, would have severed him from the Three. It would have exiled him to the abyss forever."

I stared at him, shaken. I wasn't sure what was worse, the trained and ruthless ease with which Mikhail had handled the broken pipe—*he has killed before*—or the fact that the two had been close, so close that seconds before the strike, I had watched the pet name *Mishka* form on the bogatyr's lips.

We could have brought him back, I thought, biting my inner cheek to keep the words from flooding out.

"He deserves a funeral," Mikhail said, rising to his feet without looking at Aleksey. "If we were back in the capital, he would be burned with full rites and purified by the royal priestess. I would inter him in the royal sepulcher. He deserves that. A burial at least."

"I'm sorry." I swallowed hard. "The soil here is too hard, Mikhail. Even now in autumn, we'll be carving through ice before we can dig deep enough."

For a long moment, he didn't answer. His gaze drifted away from me to the line of blood inching across the soil, and his hand strayed to the blisters Aleksey's fingers had raised on his throat. "Would you go on ahead, Toma? I'd like a moment to pray for him. Alone."

"Of course," I said, retreating to the tree line.

Mikhail uncorked his canteen, knelt down, and washed the rancid blood from Aleksey's face with a trickle of water.

The rites themselves were unfamiliar to me, but I recalled the offering of grain and salt to the goddesses, the washing with water, the purification by fire. When my paternal great-grandmother had died, as a Troika priestess she had been cremated with full rites, in the red shrouds worn only

by the most pious. I remembered her funeral—a silent procession of miners and worshippers who had added wheat
sheafs and wooden spindles to her pyre, symbols of the Sisters
Kosa and Seredina. The eldest sister, Voyna, was not similarly
honored—she was the patron of bogatyri and bogatyri alone,
and blood and iron were her tithe.

As my birth mother had watched the smoke rising, she had
shaken her head in dismay.

"It shouldn't be this way," she murmured to my father, or
at least that was how I remembered it. "She shouldn't be divided. There should be someone to guard her."

And he had looked at her until she fell silent.

I drove the memories from my head as Mikhail returned to
my side. In the time it had taken him to wash Aleksey's face
and hands and sprinkle his body with dried oats and a pinch
of salt from our supplies, he had reinforced his barricades. His
features were smooth and without emotion.

"I'm sorry," I said.

"Please." He drew in a terse breath. "Don't even say it."

Now more than ever, I was aware of the differences between us. It felt like we had come from different worlds, and
the only thing we shared was the same language.

"About Aleksey..." I began, but Mikhail shook his head
firmly, once.

"What matters is that he died for his country. He died protecting me. For a bogatyr, that is the greatest honor—to de-
vote your blood and soul to your tsar." His silver eyes chilled
over. "Anyway, that thing was not him. It was scarcely even
his body."

To that I had no answer, except to wonder if Mikhail expected me to die for him as well, and if that too would be an honor.

As we moved beyond the glade, I was eager to put the memory of Aleksey's second death behind me. Something about watching Mikhail tend to the dead in this isolated place felt dangerously close to other memories, half-formed snippets from the *before* that I could only recall in disjointed fragments—bloody water sluicing down the rim of a washing basin, sheet-covered bodies lined along a rocky stretch, a man on fire and yet still walking.

And I was afraid. I was afraid that if I went down that road, I would be confronted by even darker recollections. Better to keep my distance and keep those things buried, where they couldn't touch me.

Yet not several hundred paces from the body, Mikhail spoke my name.

I looked over.

"Did Aleksey become like your family?" Even though his voice remained level, I caught a dark trace of grief lingering in his gaze. "An upyr, I mean."

"Not how they are now, but how they once were, maybe." I felt as if I was treading on thin ice. Anything might lurk beneath. "I think that once you die, you have to find your way back, and sometimes by the time you do, your body has already run off without you."

"So that wasn't actually him," Mikhail said after giving it some thought. "It was just the animal part of us. Like a mad dog."

I couldn't know for sure, but I nodded.

"And I put him out of his misery."

"Yes," I said, because I knew he needed it. But it relieved me once he turned away. It meant that I didn't have to speak up and really, physically, acknowledge the one absolute truth here—if Aleksey had transformed into an upyr, and Mikhail had managed to kill him, that meant there was a limit to the amount of damage one could take. Several hard blows to the head, or even just a stake to tether her to the earth, might be enough to take Galina from this world for good. And those men wouldn't treat her gently.

As Mikhail walked on ahead, I scuffed the ground with the toe of my boot, deep in thought. Maybe the reason I never came across other upyri was because they fell apart and had no one to sew them back together.

My earliest memories of Papa were of him as he was now—a soul smothered beneath layer after layer of cloth and leather, his wasted limbs tethered to rusty splints like vines to an arbor. And Mama wasn't much better; her wrists and ankles were garlanded with my embroidery, and the left side of her rib cage had collapsed inward.

I wondered what would have happened if I had never found my family. Probably, I would have died. And they would have, too. Everyone knew that the dead could not return twice, or if they did, it was as something even darker than their original resurrection. I was still haunted by the folktales my birth father told me of old gods, decrepit and corrupted, who had been born from the blood and bone of monsters. Long after my father's own face had been reduced to a shadow in my memory, his stories remained.

Beyond the forest, we reached a grassy span of land pocked with craters and trenches. The izbas here were just piles of rubble, so destroyed that Galina and I had seldom bothered to root through them.

No sooner had I stepped from the tree line than Mikhail seized my shoulder. "Wait."

I looked back, puzzled by the shock in his eyes. "What's wrong?"

"This is a blight ward. The entire Edge is strewn with them." He eyed a cannon peeping from the tall grass. The trunk of a young larch tree had grown around its barrel. "The ground here is likely still filled with unexploded ordnance."

"Relax, Galina and I pass through here all the time." To prove my point, I took a few steps backward until I tripped over a rolling object and fell onto my buttocks.

"Toma." Mikhail stepped forward then froze as I picked up the offending item. Composed entirely of brass, it was shaped like a bottle and small enough to fit in my hand, the metal corroded to such a degree that it had scaled. His face grew even paler. "By the Three."

"I hate these," I said, rising to my feet. "Galina digs them up all the time."

"D–don't drop that."

I cocked my head. "What's the matter?"

"That's a bomb!"

"I know, but don't worry. I've never had one explode before."

"Just hand it to me. Slowly."

I held it out to him, baffled by his reaction.

Drawing in a shaky breath, Mikhail took the brass shell from me and turned it around in his hands with infinite care. "Grozniy ordnance… It's from the war."

He scanned the field, his brow furrowed as he took in the sight of the overgrown trenches. A shadow crossed over his face.

"What is it?" I asked.

"Can you give me your knife?"

Curious, I relinquished it readily. He inserted the tip of the blade under the brass plate at the top of the device and carefully wiggled it free. For someone who had seemed so frightened by the explosive, he was certainly eager to tamper with it. When he upturned the metal bottle, bits of corroded metal and brown dust fell into his hand.

"The powder's spoiled," he murmured, rubbing the grit between his fingers. "And this pitting on the metal... You'd think that it's at least eighty years old, not just ten. It almost looks..."

"Like what?"

"Like something's eaten away at it." He allowed the explosive to fall to the ground and handed my knife back to me. Stepping deeper into the field, he scanned the overgrown trenches.

Through the tall grass, I caught a glimpse of a skull with purple wildflowers blooming through the socket, and knew that yet more skeletons waited farther in. Each spring and autumn, torrential rainfall would lure more bones to the surface, even as far back as my family's own izba.

Mikhail stopped at the cannon, running his hand along the barrel. It flaked to rust beneath his fingertips, and in one section, his index finger punched through up to the first knuckle. His face darkened as he regarded the reddish dust gathered in his palm.

"I think it must be the winters here," I said. "They're very damp and cold."

"No, that wouldn't have caused this. Not in just ten years." Mikhail turned away from me, but not before I caught the storm brewing in his gaze. He hitched up his rucksack and continued walking. "This was the work of a koldun."

As the hours passed, we found only traces of the two soldiers—footprints in the mud, the wreck of their dirigible, a spilled sack of grain. By the time Mikhail and I reached the mountain range that cradled the forest to the east, the sun had already met its zenith. My eyes ached from the glare, and each step I took sent glassy waves of pain darting up my calves. As I paused to take a sip of lukewarm water from my flask, my skull throbbed with the beginning of a nasty headache.

Fragile sheets of shale crumbled beneath our feet as we climbed the steep path, pebbles and dirt cascading down. During the monotony of the climb, my fingers strayed to my bead bracelet as though drawn by gravity. I held my wrist to the light so that the sunlight glossed across the bead's worn facets. I wanted to see the bead how Galina saw it—as a sapphire, as a treasure. But it was just a dirty chunk of glass to me. I was the sister with eyes, but Galina was the one who could *see*.

"Tell me more about what's out there, Mikhail," I said, pausing at the brink to allow him to catch up. "Aren't there still people who support you?"

He nodded, clearly relieved to break the silence. "The Otzvuk. They're formed from the deposed aristocracy and the remnants of the imperial army and military police, along with whatever peasantry they can recruit from the villages they've liberated from the enemy's command. Many of the nobles and military superiors are bogatyri, so it's only a matter of time before the Otzvuk regains control."

"What about the..." I had already forgotten the other side's name. "The soldiers who took Galina?"

"The Fraktsiya." Mikhail spoke the name with such venom, it might as well have been a curse. "Traitors who think they can lead a country on their own, who want to burn down everything my dynasty built, all in the name of so-called liberty. It's a joke. They don't give a damn about order or justice or the fate of our nation. They just want to take whatever they can get their hands on, even if it means destroying everything in their path. Some of the Fraktsiya served in the infantry, I suppose, but I highly doubt any of them are bogatyri. Most of us know where our place is and where our loyalties should lie."

Although I knew that by "us," he was referring to bogatyri collectively, his words made me vaguely uncomfortable. I had no powers; I was no bogatyri. Even though his world wasn't mine and I had no allegiances or loyalties, that hadn't stopped the war from coming to my doorstep.

"Are you going to try to find the Otzvuk?" I asked.

He mulled it over. "Not right away. Once the Otzvuk see that I can't use my powers anymore, they won't believe I am the Tsar."

"But won't they recognize your face?"

"I hate having my photograph taken, and I've never been one for official portraits. The last time I had artwork commissioned was for my coronation three years ago. They wanted to present the image of a noble tsar, a welcoming one." His fingertips traced along his chiseled jawline, the hard ridge of his cheekbone. Even at rest, there was something cold and unforgiving about his features. "It barely even looked like me, and a lot has changed since then. In any case, I can't risk it. I'll go to Svet and find allies there. As long as I'm in the empire, I'll be in danger."

I thought of asking Mikhail how he expected his would-be allies in Svet to recognize him, if he didn't trust his former soldiers to. But something in his voice held me back, and as he turned ahead, it dawned on me—he was *afraid*.

"Isn't Svet on the other side of the continent?" I asked instead, thinking back to the maps I had found in a moldering almanac. Painted green on the maps to represent its pastoral landscape, Svet was an archipelago resting southwest of the neighboring Groznaya Empire.

"Not quite, but it's far."

Everything seemed far from here. Svet. Galina. The two soldiers. They might as well have been a world away.

7

As night fell, Mikhail and I were rewarded with our first glimpse of civilization when we passed several farms, lights burning behind their half-shuttered windows. I paused, mesmerized by the glint of candlelight.

"What's wrong?" Mikhail asked.

"Nothing, it's just…it's beautiful." I had spent the last seven years searching through abandoned homes and decaying trenches. For all the books I had salvaged from the ruins, I had almost forgotten that the places described in their pages were real—that somewhere far beyond my izba, other people continued to live and prosper. Most days, I'd felt like the only person still alive.

"What do you mean?" Mikhail glanced up. "The stars?"

"No, the lights in the houses." I pointed at them.

He followed my gaze, and his expression softened. "Ah… They are, aren't they?"

As we left the lights behind, my wonder turned into deep

homesickness. If I didn't return, the fall vegetables in my garden would rot on the vine, and the wheat I'd just planted would remain unharvested come midsummer. If I didn't return, my parents' bodies might fall apart for good.

Mikhail and I continued on, the moon burning overhead as the cloud cover cleared. Nightingales and crickets chirped in peaceful harmony as we passed along a crumbling stone wall overtaken by ivy. Through breaches in the wall, I spotted crooked outcroppings of gravestones. Ahead, shingled domes swelled against the night sky—its triple domes identified it as a Troika chapel or monastery, devoted to the worship of the Three Sisters.

A low rasping sound distracted me. Several paces down the road, an animal slunk out from a breach in the fieldstone wall, emerging into the moonlight.

At first, I thought the creature was a crippled, emaciated hound, dragging itself along on stunted limbs. Its head was humanlike and grotesquely enlarged, dangling on a knobby neck like an apple rotting on the bough.

My heart jolted at the sight of its wrinkled ruddy skin, swollen brow, and crude features. It made me think of a horrible mistake I had made years ago, when I had shot and field-dressed a deer, only to find a fetal doe nestled among its steaming innards. Except this rudimentary creature was far more threatening.

A drekavac, a harbinger of doom.

As the monster neared, Mikhail seized my wrist and pulled me to the other side of the road.

"Don't let it step within your shadow, or you'll get sick," he warned.

If it touches you, it will bring death, Tomochka. You must never touch a drekavac.

I shivered at the memory. Not the fetal doe. This one came from beyond the veil, from the *before*, a hazy recollection of walking, and walking, and walking, cold and hungry, with my mother's hand in my own. We had stopped at an inn where she had introduced herself by another name and with a nervous laugh had told the innkeeper that we were on the way to visit relatives in the Edge. I remember how tightly she had gripped my hand as she'd said it.

That was the first night we had seen them—watching from the tree line, their swollen heads bobbing slowly. But it hadn't been the last.

The drekavac's shriek jolted me into the present. Its cry was as shrill as an infant's scream, filled with despair and need.

"What are you just standing there for?" Mikhail demanded, already several steps down the road. I hurried after him, glancing back at the drekavac as it lumbered after us.

When I looked ahead again, I spotted another crawling figure emerging from the darkness. Then two more, their bulbous heads dragging against the ground.

We were surrounded.

Mikhail thrust out his hands in front of him, his brow furrowing in concentration. After a moment, he slowly lowered his arms with a puzzled grimace. That sudden gesture—palms up and fingers spread, a motion that had seemed more offensive than defensive, as if his hands themselves were weapons— he had been trying to use his powers, hadn't he?

Raw, anguished shrieks filled the air as the monsters clambered closer. A drekavac lunged from the darkness, its malformed fingers reaching toward me.

"Get back!" I swung my musket toward it, hoping to drive it back by prodding it with the muzzle. Monster or not, I wasn't willing to shoot anything that even remotely resembled an infant. Then I realized that by trying to ward off the lone drekavac, I would be opening up my back for the others to cross within my shadow.

I stepped away, knocking into Mikhail in the process.

"Give me that," he said, and made a grab for my musket.

"No! It looks like a baby." I grimaced as another drekavac screamed at us, the noise driving into my ears as painfully as rusty nails.

His hand closed around the gun's barrel. "Well, it isn't one! If you're not going to—"

A massive black shape freed itself from the darkness, barking furiously. I leveled my musket and curled my finger around the trigger. The creature entered the gleam of our lantern, revealing the broad face and sagging jowls of a shepherd dog. I sighed, transferring my finger to the guard.

Frightened by the dog's barking, the creatures scattered. As they retreated into the cemetery, I slowly lowered my musket. The dog bounded toward me, wagging its tail as it nestled against my side.

"Good boy." Rubbing its fuzzy ears, I waited for my racing heartbeat to return to a normal rhythm.

The monastery's gate creaked open on rusty hinges, and an older woman stepped out. Her crimson robe hung loosely on her frame, its voluminous folds enveloping a lean face and deep-set blue eyes fanned with wrinkles. Silvery hair fell in straight, thick tufts to her shoulders.

"Come." She clucked at the dog, who returned to her side.

Glancing at our packed rucksacks, she furrowed her eyebrows. "Ah. Refugees?"

"Yes," Mikhail said, his shoulders sagging in visible relief.

"It's a bad night for travelers to be out wandering. The Unclean Force is heavy in these parts. The drekavcy are more active than usual, and if you keep going down this road, you'll pass through a potter's field. Come inside."

When the monastery was first built, it must have been beautiful. Now, the paint flaked from the walls, pieces of colored tile were missing from the mosaic floor, and cobwebs festooned the corners of every room we passed through. Paintings of the Three Sisters, minor deities, and saintly bogatyri decorated the walls and ceiling, chalked with dust so that they were nearly as ashen as their caretaker. The icons' eyes seemed to follow us from room to room.

The main hall contained a massive marble statue dedicated to the Three: Voyna, with her balance scales held aloft and her sovnya pointed skyward, the polearm so tall its curved blade nearly scraped the ceiling; Seredina, carrying her distaff and spindle; and the empire's namesake, Kosa, with her sheaf of wheat and reaping hook. Rarely were the goddesses referred to by their individual names. Mama and Papa had always called them by their formal title of the Troika or used some variant of the Three Sisters, speaking with quiet reverence.

Passing under their stone-cold faces, I found myself thinking back to Mikhail's question about who I worshipped. It had been important to Mikhail, a way for him to fit me into a tidy compartment—Strannik or Troika, koldunia or bogatyr.

Why was it so important who I was? The only thing that mattered in this world was the division between life and death.

"My name is Nikita Aleksandrovich," Mikhail said. "This is my sister, Tamara."

"Just Toma actually," I corrected, earning a hard look from him and a bemused smile from the priestess. I cleared my throat. "Thank you for offering us shelter, um…?"

"Irina Sergeyevna, and it is my pleasure." She led us into a large kitchen where a lone cauldron smoked atop the masonry stove. The oven's whitewashed stucco had fallen away in patches, revealing underlying bricks. "Sit. Rest."

"Thank you," I said, settling into one of the empty chairs. Mikhail chose a seat at the other end of the table, far enough from the hearth that his features were cloaked in darkness.

Irina leaned over the cauldron, stirring its contents. She ladled the stew into bowls and topped each one with a generous spoonful of what could only be sour cream. My mouth watered at the soup's savory fragrance.

Returning to us, she placed a bowl in front of me. Chunks of succulent meat and vegetables floated in the golden broth. "Eat. You look like you could use a warm meal and a good night's sleep."

As Irina gave Mikhail his bowl, a drekavac's shriek echoed past the fieldstone walls. The creatures sounded as though they waited just outside. I tensed, peering into the darkness on the other side of the grated window.

The screams didn't seem to bother Irina as she began eating. Taking that as a sign it was safe to begin my meal, I blew on a spoonful of soup to cool it and took a sip. Delicious. The broth was richened with herbs and silky duck fat.

"Where exactly are we in the Edge?" Mikhail asked as Irina fed bits of meat to the dog, who wagged its fluffy tail and accepted each morsel with a soft whine of pleasure. "I'm afraid we've strayed from our original route."

"You're in the northern interior," she said.

"How far from Groznaya?"

"Six days by wagon from their northwestern border or one by train. Unfortunately, our railroad lines have never quite recovered from the Groznaya War. The nearest international train depot is in Detskaya, and meanders south through the border's mountain pass. It'll be quicker to simply take a wagon."

Six days. Just six more days, and my mother and I would have crossed the border. I had never realized how close we had gotten to Groznaya. How would my life have gone if we'd made it?

"Whose control is this area under?" Mikhail asked as I scratched the dog behind its ears. "The loyalists or the Fraktsiya?"

"It changes all the time." Irina stirred her soup absently. "Each day, there are more and more refugees."

I decided to interject. "We're looking for two men with an up—"

"With a large, suspicious bundle," Mikhail interrupted. "One has a beard. The other has blond hair. Could they have passed through here?"

"I haven't seen anyone like that, but it's certainly possible. You'll want to check in the next town over. Everyone who goes down this road will pass through there."

Whether it was the next town over or the next country, I swore to myself that I wouldn't give up searching for Galina. I'd pursue her to the world's edge if I had to.

8

The next morning, Irina refreshed our rations of food and water and sent us on our way. She couldn't provide us a horse, but she told us that the town of Kupalo was less than a two-hour walk, a good five thousand strong, and that we'd be able to find someone there who would be willing to accept our money for transport.

In daylight, the cemetery and monastery weren't nearly as eerie as they had been at night. The drekavcy had left small handprints in the mud, like children had come out to play while we slept. When I saw the handprints, my heart ached for Galina. She must be so scared. Was she even still *alive*?

All night, I had lain awake, haunted by what Mikhail had told me about Koschei's obsession with immortality. If Koschei ground up dead upyri for rejuvenating elixirs, then what would he do to living ones? As I had watched the bedroom fill with the hazy glow of dawn, my mind came up with its own nightmarish scenarios. Each image of torture was more terrible than the last—bone saws, scalpels, dismemberment, fire.

"Mikhail, why do you think some people come back?" I asked, trailing my fingertips along the overgrown wall. Moss and wildflowers grew in the chinks between the stones.

He glanced at me warily, as if I were testing him. "I was taught that it's a result of the Unclean Force, that it's heretics, sinners, and kolduny who become monsters."

"Galina died alone in the forest," I said at last. "She was killed, Mikhail."

She hadn't been a sinner, just an innocent child. Her last moments in those dark, damp woods must have been terrifying, but in death she had grown to love the forest. She would look at the ghosts of things—the crumbling izba, the black river brimming with ice floes, tumbled glass and dove bones—and see their hidden beauty. I admired her for being able to move beyond her past when I still felt haunted by my own.

"I didn't mean to imply…" Mikhail cleared his throat. "It can also happen to murder victims like Aleksey, when someone cuts short their thread of life, or to people who die when it isn't their time, like with the drekavcy. A hole is unraveled in their soul, and the Unclean Force flows in."

"My parents aren't full of the Unclean Force," I said, bristly. "If anything's full of the Unclean Force, it's those men who took my sister."

"Maybe you're right," he said, but I could tell he disagreed.

"Besides, maybe it's not an *Unclean* Force," I added. "Maybe it's just a *different* one."

"Best be careful, Toma. If we were back in the capital,

they'd call that blasphemy and send the Holy Tribunal after you." He forced a chuckle. I stared at him until his laughter died down and he turned back ahead. "That was supposed to be a joke."

"It wasn't funny," I said flatly, then frowned. Something about that name, the Holy Tribunal, stuck like a nail in my throat. I sifted through my memories, trying to pair it with the fragments. "Mikhail, aren't those the people who hunt suspected kolduny?"

"I didn't mean it seriously, Toma."

"But aren't they?"

Sighing, he turned his attention back to the road. "Sometimes. Other times, it's the military police or auxiliary forces. But most kolduny are detained within town borders, so there's rarely a need to actually hunt them, if you're using that word literally. The Tribunal's role is in affording the accused the right to a fair trial and performing the executions. But the majority of their cases concern blasphemy, not witchcraft."

His mention of witchcraft made me think back to my home. Out of all my family, only Galina had come from this part of the Edge. In their search for peace and isolation, Mama and Papa had discovered her wandering among the trenches a mere two years before Galina herself had found me. She had still been mostly fleshed.

Galina's memories were disjointed and darkened as all upyri's were, but she remembered several key details of her death. She had been hiding in the forest from loud noises, and in the seconds before her death, she saw a man approaching. I had always assumed that her killer had targeted her in particular, but what if she had only been collateral damage? If the battlefield's decay had truly been caused by a koldun, could that same event have been what led to her death?

I mulled it over as Mikhail and I walked in silence. Within time, the monotony of the forest and patchwork blue sky was disrupted by twin pillars of smoke on the horizon. I felt a stir of excitement at the sight of them.

"Finally." Mikhail sighed in relief. "The town. Looks like there must be a factory."

"Will people be there?"

A wry smile touched his lips. "I imagine."

"Are you worried about soldiers recognizing you?"

"Of course. But as I said before, a lot has changed, even in just the last few months. I barely even recognize myself anymore." He plucked at his coat's singed hem. "Besides, do I look like a tsar to you?"

"Not really," I admitted, turning ahead as the trees thinned.

I expected to come across a ramshackle scatter of crumbling houses, much like the abandoned village I had grown up in. Instead, we emerged from the forest to find a street bustling with people. Living, breathing people.

I froze in awe. I couldn't recall the last time I had seen such a crowd, and their clothes were so beautiful. Printed and dyed fabric. Brass buttons as globular as the berries of a guelder rose. Long, ruffled skirts with no patches or tears, their collars and hems embroidered in red—a symbol of the Troika faithful, my birth mother had insisted on adorning my hems and collar with the color, as if it might protect me. The bogatyri among them proudly displayed their purple sashes and epaulets, while the most devout wore garments of pure white and crimson.

"Mikhail, isn't this amazing?" I turned to him, unable to stop myself from grinning. "Look at all these people. And look, some of them are bogatyri like you!"

"You should visit the capital," he said, clearly unimpressed. "We need to keep moving."

Wood smoke filled the air. A net of wires spread overhead, connected to tall poles. I remembered scenes like this from my childhood, but it was all so much brighter here. After enduring yesterday's horror, I felt like I had entered a beautiful new world.

"Wait," I said, grinding my heels into the cobblestones. "I want to look at this."

Mikhail shook his head. "We don't have time."

"You go on ahead." I pointed at a bridge that stretched across the river. "We'll meet there."

He looked conflicted. "Toma, I'm not leaving you here alone."

"I'll be fine," I assured him. "Besides, maybe those two soldiers stopped here. I want to ask around."

"Are you sure you'll be all right on your own?"

"I've hunted wolves and bears before, Mikhail. I'll be fine, trust me."

He sighed, relenting. "All right, but meet me at the bridge when the clock tower strikes the hour, and promise me you'll be careful. Don't go with any strange men—or any strangers in general—and don't stray far. I'm going to figure out whose command this town is under and try to find someone who will buy my jewels."

In my mind, trying to barter a pocketful of diamonds and rubies would be just as conspicuous as if he'd come in wearing a crown, but what did I know? Mikhail had gotten a royal education, after all.

He crossed the street and hesitated like he wanted me to follow. I smiled reassuringly then walked in the other direction, looking into shop windows and at people. They eyed me, wary of my clothes, or the musket slung skyward over my shoulder, or just an unfamiliar face.

Once I reached a crossroads, I circled back the way I came, walking along the river. There were more buildings on the other side of the waterway, and I crossed over the bridge connecting the two banks.

The river was calm and placid, as dark as a tarnished mirror. No rusalki swam in its depths, perhaps in part due to the spiked pilings lining its banks. Beneath the bridge, I caught glimpses of sunken copper caltrops, their barbs green with verdigris.

I had read about defenses like these. Before the introduction of the Yezmirskiy steam engine, cargo ships would be dragged upstream by troops of barge haulers, men and women yoked to vessels from the time the ice melted in the spring until the Vesna froze over once more. It was a deadly job for only the most desperate, and many fell victim to the rusalki and vodyanye if exhaustion didn't claim them first, or so the stories told. To protect the barge haulers, such barricades had been built along the major waterways, and even in the wilds, I still came across the mussel-encrusted remnants of pilings washed up along the strand.

For the first time, it occurred to me that out here, such precautions were still necessary. That the restless dead were something to be feared.

Clinging to the rocky shore like teeth along a decaying palate, the buildings on the other side of the river appeared in danger of crumbling away entirely. Some were built upon the ruins of even older structures, patches of new brick and stone clashing with the age-blackened wood and weathered plaster.

Turning down the street, I followed it along until I entered a market square. Stalls were set up along the courtyard's outer edge, while in the center, other vendors sold their wares out of pushcarts or simply piled them in baskets and atop rugs.

I stood to the side for a moment and studied the people walking past. Some dressed in the same fashion as their neighbors across the river, except there was not a hint of white or red upon them. The majority wore heavily embroidered black tunics, the stitching as elaborate as anything I'd created, although in the goldwork singular to Strannik craft.

I walked over to the nearest vendor. A handsome burgundy-haired boy sat on a stool beside the stall, a fountain of metallic thread spilling over his hand. His attention was devoted to the hooded hunting-style cloak in his lap, its grommeted hem already encircled with leaves sewn in silver and rose-gold. The embroidery prettied up the fact that the garment was hardly more than a rectangle of fabric tied off with cords and buttons, versatile enough that it could be used as a blanket, stretcher, or half tent—necessary for someone ready to move at a moment's notice, with little more than the clothes on their back.

As I approached, the boy's gaze landed on me. His eyes were the brightest green, like new grass after a spring thaw.

Slowly, he lowered his needle without pricking the fabric. His gaze flickered from my face to my feet to the rushnyk wrapped around my waist then back again, before settling on the musket I carried over my shoulder.

He set the cloak he was working on aside and said something in a rough, gargled language.

I blinked, bewildered. "I'm sorry, but I don't understand…"

"Can I help you?" His voice softened when he used the common tongue, but a hard accent still clipped the ends of his words. He sounded almost guarded.

"I'm looking for two men. One has bad teeth and blond hair, and the other has a beard."

"You've described twenty percent of the men in this town," he said dryly.

"I don't think they're from this town. They would just be passing through."

"Check the inn." He pointed across the square, in the direction of a pair of brick towers. "The Blue Raven Inn is that way, near the mill. It will be on the right, past the war memorial. You can't miss it. The only other one is in the New Quarter, across the river. The girl at the Blue Raven will be able to give you better directions. Tell her that Vanya sent you."

I glanced at the accessories hanging from hooks on the stall and overflowing across the counter. Not just hooded tent-cloaks, but sashes as well. It felt wrong to leave without saying something nice about them. "I like your wares."

"Thank you."

"The embroidery is beautiful."

"Not as nice as yours." He glanced down at my rushnyk, looking a touch wary. I remembered that in some regions, Stranniki were barred from dressing in red or bleached linen, to avoid being mistaken for the Troika faithful. I wondered if it was also taboo to even wear garments of those colors in their neighborhoods, or if the rushnyk itself was reason for offense.

"Did you make these all yourself?" I asked. "The clothing, I mean."

"No, only some of them, but I did most of the embroidery."

"Is the thread real gold?"

Vanya laughed, and for the first time, I caught a trace of genuine warmth in his features. "No, it's a brass alloy spun over silk, or gilt silver if you can afford it. Gold is only used in marriage and burial garments. Sorry to disappoint."

"You didn't," I assured him.

Slowly, his smile faded. His gaze focused on something over my shoulder, and his jaw tightened. Anger flashed in his eyes. "Get out."

"What?" I whispered.

Vanya reached into the stall's lower shelf and shifted aside a roll of black cotton. The sunlight gleamed across the barrel of a rifle.

9

"Go now!" Vanya snapped at me, his voice cutting. "What are you just standing there for? You don't belong here!"

I stepped back, knocking into someone. Turned around. Nothing significant appeared to have changed since my arrival, except there was a tension in the air that hadn't been there before.

For the first time, I noticed the young men loitering around the fountain and near stalls. Some had their hands in their pockets, and one boy gripped a section of iron pipe partially concealed inside his coat. Their faces were drawn rigid with agitation.

Vanya reached for his rifle but didn't take it from under the stall. His fingers curled around the edge of the shelf. Where he touched, hairline fissures formed. Buds and leaves threaded from the dead wood.

I froze. He was a bogatyr, but he was a commoner. Only in Galina's storybooks had I ever heard of a magic-user being born to the peasantry, and always at the blessing of the Three Sisters and to devout Troika families. Could he be a koldun?

At first, I thought the other boys were the source of his worry, then I followed his gaze to the eastern horizon. Black smoke billowed past the rooftops. Not benign wood smoke. Something was burning. Something big.

The whole market seemed to be holding its breath.

The boy smuggling the lead pole walked over and spoke to Vanya in a gruff, hushed voice. It took me a moment to realize they were talking in a different language.

Vanya pulled a square of felt over the buds of new growth stemming from the wood, concealing his magic from the other boy's view. He eased into his seat and drew the rifle from its hiding space, angling it across his knees.

They glanced my way, and the other boy raised his eyebrows. *"Iohna, hayst e Strannikit?"*

Vanya shook his head.

"E'nitz Strannikit," Vanya said with a nod to my rushnyk. *"Dreynikit."*

"I need to go," I said, taking another step away.

"That's a smart idea," he said quietly, switching back to Koskiy. "Best if you head across the bridge."

As I retreated to the edge of the market, searching for Mikhail amid the huddles of anxious townsfolk, a low chanting rose in the direction of the fire, growing steadily louder. Boot heels clattered against the cobblestones.

A woman turned to me and said something. Her words were drowned out as dozens of men stormed into the town square, shouting.

"Get out of our country, you damn kolduny!"

"Punish the filthy traitors! They helped the Fraktsiya kill the Tsar!"

"The Tsar's blood is on their hands!"

"They carry the Unclean Force!"

Some of the rioters carried guns, axes, and truncheons, while others held indigo flags and signs aloft, each banner emblazoned with a crossed sword and wheat sheaf. Uniformed men with sabers hanging from their belts flanked the mob; upon their shoulders, they wore the purple epaulets of the bogatyri.

"Leave us alone," the cheesemonger cried as the crowd filled the square. "We had nothing to do with what happened to the Tsar! We're not—"

A rock struck his face with the ghastly *crack* of broken bone, and he collapsed into a heap on the ground. A line of blood edged across the cobblestones.

"We're done letting you beat us with impunity!" Vanya rose to his feet, rifle in hand. "We have the right to defend ourselves!"

I ducked as a brick sailed over my head and slammed into the shopfront behind me. Glass tinkled to the ground, crunching beneath my shoes as I stumbled away.

Gunshots rang out—then one of the uniformed men stepped forward and lifted his hands. A surge of fire roared through the square, incinerating a produce-laden cart in an instant. A torrent of water followed quickly after, snaking over the cobblestones, washing fleeing vendors to their knees. The shouts of protest became screams of pain and terror.

I skidded on the water that spread from the wave, grasping onto a wall to keep myself from falling. A stray fireball split the air above my head, close enough that a wave of heat rolled over me. The flames should have singed my hair and caught my rushnyk aflame, but instead, the heat became a subtle warmth through the embroidered fabric. Sparks fell on the rushnyk and sizzled out in an instant, leaving not a trace of soot.

As I reached the cover of an alley, I looked over my shoulder.

Brawling rioters swamped the square. A wagon levitated in the air, spinning lazily, before slamming into a nearby shopfront. Splinters nipped into my back, and a falling piece of wood slammed into my shoulder. Broiled bits of vegetables and broken rinds squelched underfoot as I raced down the alley, fleeing from the screams and gunfire erupting behind me.

At the end of the alley, I turned the corner—and slammed into someone. Hands reached out and steadied me. I raised my arms to push away my attacker, then froze as I confronted a pair of iron-gray eyes.

"What's going on?" Mikhail demanded, looking back the way I had come. "I've been searching everywhere for you, and then I saw smoke."

"I was talking to one of the vendors, and suddenly, a mob came, and everyone started fighting," I said breathlessly. "They're using magic."

Suddenly, Mikhail pushed me behind him and shielded me with his body. A man ran down the alley. No. Not a man.

Panting, Vanya skidded to a stop in front of us. A line of blood trickled down his cheek from a shallow cut.

"If you don't want to get killed, follow me. It's worse than we thought it would be. They're not alone." He rushed past.

I seized Mikhail's hand so we wouldn't get separated and ran after Vanya. When we reached the end of the alley, Vanya dashed through the street and into another alleyway that flanked an abandoned building on the verge of collapse.

He climbed onto a crate, slung his rifle over his shoulder, and slipped through an opening in a boarded window. Apprehensively, I clambered in after him, and Mikhail followed.

I landed on a packed dirt floor, blinking as I waited for my eyes to adjust to the gloom. Raw brick walls. Rubble.

"I hope that antique's not just for show," Vanya said, reloading his rifle. Unlike my musket, the weapon didn't rely on lead balls and loose powder. It took him only seconds to trade out the small metal box attached to the weapon's underside.

"I'm sorry, but I can't fight with you," I said, and he frowned, clearly disappointed. "I need to find my little sister. I think she's somewhere in this town."

"The New Quarter or the Old?" He sighed at my confused expression. "Is she across the river or on our side of town?"

"I don't know," I admitted.

A loud *bang* echoed from outside. The building shuddered, and a chunk of plaster crashed to the floor in a cloud of dust.

Vanya winced. "Those Otzvuk bastards are going to destroy the whole damn quarter."

"Otzvuk?" I said blankly.

Hadn't Mikhail said that the Otzvuk was composed of deposed nobility, the former military police, and the imperial army? Why would tsarists target the empire's citizens?

"The Otzvuk is doing this?" Mikhail asked, his brow furrowed in confusion.

Vanya scoffed. "Who else?"

"The Fraktsiya?"

"I doubt the Fraktsiya have many bogatyri in their ranks," Vanya said. "Or that our neighbors across the bridge would join in to help."

A stricken look passed over Mikhail's face. "What? Why?"

"You sound like a city type. Is this your first time in the Edge?" His chuckle was as flat as a hatchet blade. "Right, that's what I thought. I don't have time to explain this to you now. I need to get to the temple."

"What's in the temple?" I asked.

"It's where the children and elderly will have taken refuge, but it's also the first place the militia will go after they loot the market. If we go there, I think I know a way to stop this. But first, we need to cause a distraction. Make some noise. Just enough so that some of the soldiers split off from the main group, or we'll never make it that far."

"I can do that," Mikhail said firmly.

"Good. Your best bet will be to hit the rich part of town. The bogatyr part. It's on the other side of the river." He retrieved a leather pouch from his cloak's inner pocket. An iron striker hung from its string. "You know how to start a fire, city boy?"

Mikhail's jaw tightened. "What are you—"

"I'm not suggesting that you level the New Quarter. Don't target homes, just pick a shop or two. If it's empty, then it means their owners have probably joined in on the festivities. The fire brigade will be on it before anyone can get hurt."

"You want to destroy the town to save it?" I asked, taken aback.

"Buildings can be rebuilt. Lives can't."

"All right, I'll do it," Mikhail said gravely, and accepted the pouch Vanya offered him.

"Go to the temple once you're done. It's the large wooden building in the center of the Old Quarter. Single dome, traditional style. You can't miss it." Vanya's vivid green eyes flickered toward me. "You should come with me. I don't think this place is going to last, and before long, the temple will be the safest place in town."

There was no time to consider. As a larger piece of plaster came crashing down, I nodded and slid my musket sling from over my shoulder, my finger straying to the trigger.

10

As Mikhail ran across the bridge dividing the older part of town from the New Quarter, Vanya and I headed in the opposite direction. We took the alleyways and the narrow side streets, occasionally crossing through private courtyards or over stone walls. Although we managed to avoid encountering any Otzvuk soldiers or rioters, the noise of fighting roared like thunder in my ears. Screams. Gunfire. The crackling of burning wood.

Frantic thoughts pounded through my head as I gripped onto my musket, which I had prepped and loaded in the abandoned building. Fear knotted my stomach. Why was I even doing this? I never should have agreed to go with Vanya when Galina was still out there, and Mikhail was all alone in the New Quarter with his injured shoulder.

Even as doubt pressed down on me like an anchor, I kept running. As much as I wanted to find Galina, I suddenly felt obligated to help Vanya reach the temple. Because he had been kind to me. Because I couldn't stop thinking about the Strannik villagers from my childhood, the ones who had disappeared never to return. I had stood still by the window and watched them leave, a black trail of horses and carts winding down the mountainside. I had let Galina run stumbling into the sleet and darkness. I would not stand aside and watch Kupalo's residents die now.

"Why are they doing this?" I coughed on the smoke billowing in from a burning home we passed. After entering a patch of clean air, I slowed to a stop to catch my breath. "I don't understand."

Vanya stopped running, too. His body shook with panting gasps. "Have you been living in a cave this whole time?"

"No, I'm just...I'm not from around here."

"I can tell." He scoffed. "Where do you come from?"

I pointed toward the mountains Mikhail and I had scaled the day before.

"That's cursed land." A wary edge honed Vanya's voice. "Nobody's lived out there since the war, unless you count kolduny and monsters."

"I'm not a witch." I paused. "At least I don't think I am."

"That's not very reassuring," he said dryly, then turned ahead again. "They're doing this because the aristocrats need someone to blame for their own shortcomings, so they turn everyone else against us. Usually, the other villagers will just beat us. Maybe set a few fires. Loot some stores. But this time, they have the Otzvuk to help them, and I think they intend to kill us."

Try as I might, I couldn't make sense of it. After years in the wilderness, killing had become a matter of necessity, done solely for the sake of survival. Something died so that I could live. It had been easy to forget that people killed each other all the time, sometimes for no reason at all.

In the street ahead, the air turned sallow like deer fat, beams of sunlight captured in the gelatinous atmosphere. Vanya grabbed my shoulder and yanked me behind a wagon. He squatted to hide himself, pulling me down with him.

Through the gaps between the wheel spokes, I watched as rocks flew in slow motion, as if the flow of time had thinned to a trickle. A boy staggered forward, his run reduced to a sluggish, jerky dance. A man in uniform lunged into view, as fast as a wolf in comparison, and drove the fleeing boy to the ground.

"Shit," Vanya whispered as the man reached for his saber. Resting one knee against the ground, he drew his rifle into a shooting position, its stock snug against his shoulder. As the saber blade emerged from its sheath, Vanya's finger curled around the rifle's trigger.

The rifle blast reverberated against the alley's walls. In the street ahead, the air's jaundiced tint dissipated, and the uniformed man collapsed onto his side.

Even before the soldier's sword clattered against the ground, Vanya was rising to his feet. The scent of gunpowder hung in the air like a gasp. I stumbled to follow, my fingers clammy against my musket's oak understock. By the moment, the gun felt as if it were changing in my hands, its shape becoming bulky and unfamiliar. Even as I found the familiar curve of the trigger, the sense of disorientation remained.

"These bastards will prey on anyone they can," he growled, twisting back his rifle's bolt to clear the spent shell from its chamber. The brass casing tinkled to the cobblestones. "That's Yuriy. He just turned thirteen. That damn idiot. He shouldn't even be out here."

As we ran from the alleyway, I caught a brief glimpse of the dead soldier's disfigured and gore-stained face—and then we passed him. Vanya yanked up the sniveling boy by the arm.

"Come on, there's no time to cry," Vanya urged, his voice as sharp as a saber blade.

"B-b-blood," the boy blubbered, gripping onto Vanya's sleeve with both hands. Red flecks were streaked across his cheeks. "Blood. There's blood on me."

"Be glad it's not your own. We're going to the temple. You have to keep up."

"You're okay," I said gently, trying to comfort the younger boy. Something about the way he clung to Vanya's sleeve made me think of Galina. "Just breathe in and out. You're safe now."

Yuriy sniffled and nodded, wiping his teary eyes with his shirtsleeve.

Vanya released Yuriy's arm and ran forward, slowing to a manageable speed to allow the weeping boy to maintain pace. When Yuriy fell behind, I took his wrist and led him.

Even after leaving the dead soldier behind us, I couldn't escape from the memory of his face. I had seen carcasses before. I had tended to them for years, suturing torn skin and reattaching missing fingers.

This was different. With the damage the bullet had done to his head, the man wouldn't be coming back, and I was glad for that.

A towering hewn-log building rose before us, crowned with a large aspen-shingled dome. Yuriy ran past us and hurried inside, Vanya and I following at his heels. As I stepped inside, the doors closed behind us with a deep, solemn *thud*, blocking out the distant shouts.

Overhead, a circular amber-glass window allowed light to come in. At the rear of the temple, a wooden statue of the Goddess was adorned with fresh flowers and goldwork tapestries even more ornate than the rushnyk I wore around my waist. An offering basket of guelder rose branches rested at the idol's feet, the boughs drooping under the weight of red berries and green leaves tinged an autumnal crimson.

Women, children, and elders crowded the vast hall, withdrawn and silent. The majority were dressed in loose, black garments like Vanya's, embroidered with metallic threads along the sleeves and hems.

I gnawed my lower lip, my thoughts straying to Mikhail. He shouldn't have offered to cause a distraction, not with his injured shoulder.

Yuriy sank against a pew, sobbing violently. I felt so bad for him. I wanted to do something. As Vanya caught his breath, I walked over to Yuriy and placed my hands on his shoulders. Although he was only thirteen, he was almost as tall as I was.

"Are you all right?" I asked, forcing a smile to let Yuriy know he was safe now.

He nodded wordlessly. Teardrops cut lines through the streaks of blood fanned across his cheeks. His eyes were a dark, velvety brown; wide and terrified, they reminded me of a doe's eyes just before I pulled my musket's trigger.

I searched my pockets for a handkerchief to wipe the blood from his face. When I couldn't find one, I settled for using the corner of my rushnyk instead. I gently blotted up the blood;

the rushnyk took it all in, leaving not a single trace of red on his pale cheeks.

"All gone," I murmured.

Yuriy gulped hard, staring at me. "Thank you."

Vanya came up to us. He glanced down at my soiled rushnyk. "You aren't going to use that blood for a spell, are you?"

"I told you, I'm not a koldunia!" I said, exasperated.

"Don't believe her, kid," Vanya whispered loudly to Yuriy. "She's definitely a koldunia."

A weak smile trembled on Vanya's lips as he looked over to see my reaction. If he was trying to be funny, his joke fell short. His body shook with rapid, heavy breaths, and his pupils were swollen with fear.

"Keep calling me that, and I'll put a curse on you," I said, glancing up in concern as a volley of gunfire rang out. "This building is all wood. If the Otzvuk come here..."

"Fire isn't what we have to worry about," Vanya said. "After Kupalo's old temple was burned down two hundred years ago, we rebuilt it with wood that's been specially treated so that it's practically fireproof. I doubt even a bogatyr's flames would have much effect on it."

A nearby explosion shook the building. Dust fell from the ceiling, and the floorboards rattled beneath our feet.

Vanya grimaced, holding on to a pew. As the temple's shuddering ceased, something broke inside of him. His lips disappeared into a puckered line, a gruff choking sound coming from deep inside his throat. He lifted his hand to his mouth and turned his face away from me, gripping the back of the pew even tighter than before.

"It's never been this bad before," he said, features gaunt

with anxiety. "I never...I never had to shoot someone. I've hunted before, but what I did back there, it...was different. Just pulling the trigger. It was easy. I don't understand it. Taking another person's life, how can it be so *easy*? Shit. Shit! How could they have come prepared to do this? Damn it! How could anyone be prepared to do this?"

Slowly, he sank down on the pew, his gaze focusing on the glow filtering through the dome's oculus. In shadow, his wavy, unkempt hair was almost black, but in sunlight it was the color of dried blood. "Just give me a moment, please. I just... My chest hurts. I need to breathe."

"Of course." I sat down next to him, resting my musket muzzle-up against the seat.

Listening to Vanya's rough breaths and watching his strength fissure, I felt a piercing urge to comfort him. I reached out and placed my hand over his, rubbing gentle circles over the area between his thumb and index finger. The gesture had always soothed Galina, and I hoped it would have the same effect on Vanya.

Exhaling slowly, he closed his eyes. We were strangers, but that didn't stop him from leaning against me, shoulder to shoulder. Subdued tremors racked his body, as though he was still feeling the explosion's aftermath.

"My name is Ivan Zoravich," he mumbled.

It struck me as slightly ridiculous that he would introduce himself so formally, as though we were both adults, but then I realized that he needed to do it this way. Because someone his age shouldn't have been forced to shoot a grown man in the face. Because this outer world did not favor youth or innocence.

"It's Tamar, right?" He squeezed my hand softly. "Or Ta-mara?"

"No, just Toma."

"Short for what?"

"Nothing."

"Nothing," he repeated, and laughed as if I had made a joke without realizing it. "What's your matronym?"

"I'm not Strannik."

"Your patronym then."

"I don't have one either," I said, because I didn't want to think about my biological father or my birth family at all.

Papa—once Anatoly, when he had still breathed—had always been just Papa to me. Even though he was more important to me than my real father had ever been, I couldn't bring myself to take the patronym of Anatolyevna.

Culture. Customs. Expectations. Those things had ceased to exist in the wilderness. Death had stripped away even the most rigid societal restraints, leaving my family desperately grasping for the things they'd cared about in their former lives. It was why Papa never scolded me, but why he still carved clock boxes and assembled mechanisms from salvaged parts. Why Mama still brewed drinks she likely couldn't even taste. Why I was always Toma now, and never Tamar Dmitrievna Volkova. That girl had perished in the forest.

Civilization had driven my birth family into the wilderness and had been the death of them. What I had witnessed so far only confirmed my deep-rooted certainty that the outside world's beauty was only exceeded by its venom and cruelty.

"No matronym *or* patronym?" Vanya raised his eyebrows.

"You don't have a mother or a father? Are you sure you're not a witch?"

"Just call me Toma," I said sharply.

"Okay, okay, don't spoil me. Since we're past formalities, I suppose you can call me Vanya like everyone else. Better to die as friends than as strangers, right?"

"Speak for yourself." I stood up. "I don't intend to die anytime soon."

"I like your optimism, Toma-short-for-nothing," he said, and rose to his feet. "Let's hope it lasts."

I followed Vanya to the center of the room. As he climbed onto the idol's pedestal, faces turned toward him. A man shouted something at him in Strannitsky, and Vanya responded in a tone just as sharp.

Whatever Vanya said, his words charged the crowd. Whispers rippled through the room, and in a far corner, a child began wailing.

"What did you say?" I whispered.

"That if they stay here, they're all going to die. And that I'm the only one who can save them." Vanya exhaled slowly. "But I think I'll have to be a little more convincing. You might want to step back for this, just in case they decide to stone me."

He selected a branch from the offering basket at the idol's feet and raised it like a torch. Every eye in the room was on him now, staring transfixed as the bough spilled forth in a flood of new leaves and twigs. White flower heads bloomed amid the autumnal berries, as though the seasons had been reversed.

The child's sobs were joined by cries of alarm and anger.

"Koldun!" bellowed the man who had shouted at Vanya before. Now, *that* I understood.

Others echoed the accusation, emboldening the man to advance forward. Before he could reach us, a regal black-haired woman stepped from the crowd.

Her spun-silver wreath was as ornate as the silverwork covering her black robe. I didn't need Vanya to tell me she was a priestess. He made that clear when he stepped down from the pedestal and sank to one knee before her, laying the bough at her feet like an offering.

She listened in silence as he spoke. When he gestured toward the door, she nodded. He rose to his feet, his relief evident in the faint smile he gave me.

"They're going to the textile mill down the road," he said as the people filed from the room. "You should go with them. It has a gate at least, and maybe the mob will prioritize this town's economy over their glee at killing a few Stranniki."

If I had looked for Galina sooner, I might have been able to save her. But I refused to stand by while more people got hurt, even if it meant delaying my search for the men who had taken her.

"I'm staying here with you," I said sternly, ready to argue if Vanya put up a fight.

Instead, his shoulders sagged in relief, and he nodded. "I was hoping you would say that."

We watched the others file from the temple. I wanted to ask him what the plan was, but I was afraid to know the answer.

"Too bad you're not a witch," Vanya said at last. His voice sounded very small, alone in the domed hall. "We could really use one right now."

"Let's hope your magic is enough."

He smiled thinly. "Surprised you're not trying to stone me like all the rest."

Before I could respond, the temple's doors flew open, and Mikhail rushed inside. He skidded to a stop before us.

"They're coming," he croaked between panting breaths. "They're heading right this way."

A change passed over Vanya's features. His gaze hardened, and as he turned to me, his lips curled up in a mirthless smile.

"You know, Toma, in the past, we weren't called Strannik but *Strazhnik*. Guards. Protectors. Our skill in battle was renowned." He shifted his rifle's sling from over his shoulder. "I suppose it's time to remind these bastards of that fact."

11

The second-floor balcony offered a view of abandoned pews, forgotten belongings, and crushed offerings of grain and berries. I crouched just shy of the railing, my musket aimed at the level below, eyes on the door. Waiting.

I dreaded the thought of having to pull my musket's trigger. Vanya had called it shockingly easy to shoot a human being, but I didn't believe him. I thought that must have just been something he told himself so that he'd be prepared to do it again.

Mikhail took up post at the other end of the balcony, a haunted look on his face. He held Vanya's rifle in a tight, white-knuckled grip. I didn't know what he had seen out there. I didn't want to know.

My gaze shifted to the idol of the goddess Voserka. Vanya crouched behind the wooden statue. From where I stood, I could only catch a glimpse of his black tunic and burgundy hair. He yanked up his hood, and then he was hardly more than a shadow filigreed in gold.

The explosions and gunfire had died into an eerie calm. It didn't last. Down below, the door crashed inward with a sickening thud and the rioters poured into the room.

"Where are they?" a man roared in anger. I flinched as a pew slammed into the opposite wall, hurled by a mere wave of his hand. Ducking low against the floor, I held my breath. If he looked up here, would he see us?

"I saw that bastard run in here," someone else said.

"They're hiding. Burrowing somewhere like rats. We'll have to smoke them out."

"No, not yet. They keep their gold and treasures hidden in here. You know that."

"Hey, assholes!" Vanya shouted, darting out from behind the idol. As the men turned, he dropped to his knees and pressed his palms against the floor.

Before the rioters could attack, the entire room quivered as beams groaned and began to bend. The basket of guelder rose at the icon's feet burst into garish bloom, white flowers unfurling amid the red berries. As for the idol itself, it began to fissure. It had been carved with three faces, and the one that faced us cracked into a maw of splinters. Although the idol was not jointed, as it fell from its pedestal, its limbs began to bend as though they were flesh. Sap prickled from the wood like lifeblood.

It was magnificent. It was terrifying.

Even for the bogatyri, it was hard to keep their calm with the wood of an entire forest bearing down on them. Fire blasts splashed harmlessly across the rafters. A bogatyr sent a burst of lightning blazing toward the idol, only to have a log strike him in the chest and slam him into the wall as though he weighed nothing at all. My stomach twisted at the snap of breaking bones.

At the other end of the balcony, Mikhail looked up in shock and wonder. "I've never… This isn't…"

More branches sprouted from the walls, the new boughs forming deadly points. Some of the civilian men tried shooting the branches or hacking at them with swords and axes, but even that wasn't enough. Some were skewered. Some were crushed. Many fell victim to their companions' gunfire and magic.

Mikhail exhausted the rest of his ammunition, but I couldn't bring myself to open fire. My finger trembled on the trigger, refusing to move. I just…I couldn't do it.

The remaining marauders poured from the temple as eagerly as they had rushed in, trampling the fallen. The idol stilled, now festooned in leaves and flowers, and rooted itself to the floor. Once I was sure that the men wouldn't return, I moved out from behind cover and rushed downstairs.

Vanya lay motionless by the idol.

"Vanya?" I dropped to his side, shaking him. For a terrifying moment, I was certain he'd stopped breathing. Then he groaned, stirred. I released my held breath, my shoulders sagging in relief.

"Toma!" Mikhail ran over to us, carrying Vanya's rifle slung over his shoulder. "Get away from him!"

Vanya opened his eyes and slowly, laboriously sat up. I rested a hand on his back to support him.

"It's fine," I called to Mikhail. "He's okay."

"That wasn't magic." Mikhail stopped in front of us. When he looked down at Vanya, his face hardened, gray eyes chilling with guarded suspicion. "It was the Unclean Force. He's a koldun."

"Ah, so that's how it is? When it's a noble, it's divine, a gift from the Three. But when it's a peasant—or, even better, a peasant who's Strannik—it's witchcraft." Vanya laughed hoarsely. He tried to stand, couldn't. "I hate to break it to you, city boy, but I'm no koldun. I'm a bogatyr."

12

Vanya lived in an apartment located above a clothing store not far from the town square. At his firm insistence, we helped him back there, hobbling through deserted streets and clambering over rubble. After the first several blocks, he regained enough strength to walk on his own, but I kept one hand on his forearm just in case.

He made it sound like he just wanted to recuperate at home, but I could tell he was afraid to stay.

"What I did in there was a sacrilege," he said, once we were on the street again. "I spilled blood in a holy place. Not to mention wrecked the grandest temple from here to Detskaya. Voserka will probably curse me now, if my neighbors don't tear me apart first."

He added the last part with a hint of humor, like he was trying to maintain face. But the moment he turned back ahead, his smile slipped from his lips, and he dug his nails into his palms.

The lock on the storefront door had been bashed into pieces. When Vanya held the door open for us, one of the hinges snapped off. Mikhail steadied the panel with both hands.

"It doesn't look too bad," Vanya said, glancing around at the ramshackle shelves and broken glass. "Good thing nobody wants to steal clothes."

"Where are your parents?" I asked.

He picked up a few rumpled shirts and returned them to their shelf. "I never met my mother, and my father died ten years ago."

"In the trenches?" Mikhail asked.

"That's right. Not far from here, in what used to be the village of Teykhst." His gaze shifted to me. "You might actually know the place, Toma. In the early days of the war, the Grozniy troops came as far north as your mountains."

A shiver swept through my body as I recalled the overgrown trenches, the bones that surfaced with rainfall. I had known the destruction was a product of war, but I hadn't actually ever considered how the victims might have had friends and family. They were just relics at that point, no more substantial than the portraits and letters I found in abandoned houses.

"Anyway, for about a year now, I've been renting the room on the second floor," Vanya continued, sparing me from having to answer as he turned back ahead. "It gets lonely sometimes, but it's better than having to clean up people's vomit at the inn or listening to another lecture from my godmother."

There was another door at the other end of the room. Vanya climbed onto a stool and retrieved a key from atop the lintel. He opened the door, held it for me, and then promptly let go of the knob when Mikhail tried to walk through.

"Why did you do that?" Mikhail asked sourly, rubbing his arm, where the door had struck him.

Vanya shrugged. "The knob slipped from my hand. Who knows, city boy? Maybe it was witchcraft."

"Stop calling me that."

"You never told me your name."

"Mik—" His mouth snapped shut. The sudden look of mortification that crossed over his face might have confused Vanya, if Vanya wasn't in the process of walking upstairs and blissfully oblivious to it.

"Nikolai?" Vanya asked, glancing back.

"Yes. Nikolai Ruslanovich."

A hint of a smile touched Vanya's lips. "Ah, so you have a father."

I blushed, realizing that Vanya was referring to our conversation in the temple.

"Why wouldn't I?" Mikhail asked, mystified.

"Because she has neither a patronym nor a matronym." Vanya looked at me. "How is it that a city boy—"

Mikhail flushed. "I told you not to call me that."

"—and a witch from the wilds ended up traveling together?"

"First of all, I'm not a witch," I huffed. "Secondly, it's a long story."

"Good. You can tell me all about it over tea."

As Vanya climbed the stairs, Mikhail leaned close to me.

"Let me do the talking, Toma," he whispered. "We need to keep our story consistent."

I gave it some thought. Wasn't the best way to keep a story consistent simply to say it exactly how it happened?

In the small sitting room upstairs, Vanya took off his shoes and hung his coat on the rack. After we removed our shoes, he gave us felt slippers that were well-worn, but so soft and cozy that I curled my toes in satisfaction. A tabby cat ran into the room the moment Vanya shut the door. The feline sauntered up to him, meowing.

"Ah, Liliya," Vanya cooed, scooping up the cat. He kissed her head. "All this time, you were hiding up here? Why didn't you defend our home, you little coward?"

Cradled in his arms, Liliya studied me with dull yellow eyes. When I reached out to touch the cat, she hissed.

"Don't be unfriendly now." Vanya set the cat down. "Sometimes, I think she is a koldunia in disguise."

After Mikhail and I had taken off our coats, Vanya led us into a cramped kitchen. A bathtub was shoved up next to the cast-iron water heater and sink. An oven occupied the other corner. There was only enough room left for a small table and an ironing board.

"I'm sorry, it's not very clean." Vanya eased his rifle's sling from over his shoulder and leaned the weapon against the wall. He washed his hands at the basin, working the iron pump until clean water flushed from the spigot. "The domovoi ignores me, even when I leave him offerings. You'd think he'd at least do a little dusting for all I give him, but he's never shown himself."

"They rarely do," I said, smiling a bit. If my family's izba had once hosted a household spirit, he had abandoned the home long before I came there. Occasionally, when entering an abandoned cottage, I would hear a domovoi whisper or croon plaintively, as if mourning his masters, only I had never seen one's true form. They were supposed to be little bearded men with dusty fingers and the nubs of horns, but I liked to imagine they were as majestic and imposing as the rusalki.

As Vanya busied himself with preparing a kettle of tea, I allowed my gaze to wander around the room. A pheasant hung by its twine-bound legs from a hook above the icebox, a recent kill left to air-dry and tenderize. On the floor by the cast-iron stove, he had left a small dish filled with porridge. I grimaced. No wonder the domovoi never lent a hand to household chores—judging by the surface crust, it had been a good month since Vanya had remembered to refresh the gruel.

"Is it really safe to just be standing around here?" Mikhail asked, crossing his arms. When he wasn't eying Vanya, he kept glancing out the window.

"Probably not." Using a bit of burning paper, Vanya lit the potbelly stove. "But I'd say my little trick in the temple gave us another day or two of calm, and nowhere is safe unless you want to hide in the forest. Which raises the question... Why did you come here?"

"We're just passing through," Mikhail said. "Do you know of a wagon we can hire to take us to the Grozniy border?"

"Sure, but that's a good way to get yourself killed. If you're looking to get into Groznaya, it would be safer for you two to take a train or ferry and avoid the border entirely."

"I'm not going to Groznaya," I interrupted.

Vanya furrowed his brows. "But I thought you two were traveling together."

"Toma," Mikhail said like it was a warning.

"I'm looking for my sister," I reminded Vanya. "The

Fraktsiya took her. She's an upyr, and I think they're going to kill her!"

"An upyr?" Vanya asked in disbelief. "Is that a joke? You can't be serious."

My cheeks flushed in indignation. "Stop laughing, Vanya! There's nothing funny about it. I'm telling the truth."

Vanya's amused smile faded. "Shit. You mean it. How is… do you mean an actual upyr? Decaying, hunger for human blood and flesh, upyr?"

"Upyri don't eat humans. They don't eat anything. They raised me and protected me."

"I see…" He studied me. "Since you were an infant?"

"No, a child."

"I really don't think now's a good time for this discussion," Mikhail cut in.

Vanya ignored him, his full attention on me. "What happened to your parents?"

"I…I don't remember much of my parents. There are just fragments, but they were alive. I know that. We lived in a small village. I can't remember its name. My father…" I closed my eyes, trying to remember his face, but it was just a blur. Instead, I imagined Papa, whose decrepit face I had only seen in bits and pieces over the years. "My father worked in a mine. He died in a cave-in. I know that."

The smell of rust and coal smoke always brought back memories of my childhood. Sitting on my father's lap by the fire. My mother's lithe hands ensnared in thread as she worked on her embroidery. Beautiful shards of the life I once knew.

"After my father died, my mother and I left," I said. "I

don't know why. Something...something happened. I think we were going to cross through the Edge, into Groznaya."

"Were you driven out?" Vanya asked. "If it was around that time, it could have been during an expulsion."

"No. I'm not Strannik."

"We aren't the only people who've been banished," he said. "People of Grozniy descent were, too."

I gave it some thought. Our move had occurred during the night. My mother hadn't even had time to sell our house or pack more than a bag each. Because... "It was something else. I think my mother was running from something. Something personal."

"Go on," Vanya said.

There was a wall in my memory that divided my childhood in the village from my life in the wilderness. On one side of the wall, there were darkness and cobblestones, my father reduced to ashes atop the pyre, and an eternity of exhausted walking. On the other side, there was the snow, the cold, and Galina clothed in rags, excitedly asking if I was alive.

My most distinct memory of the time between was an image that had haunted me since childhood—a man crossing between the snow-burdened pines, cloaked in flames that liquefied the ice beneath his feet and caused the bark on nearby trees to blister and blacken. Even knowing the power of bogatyri, the vision seemed so surreal that I wasn't sure whether it was a dream or a genuine memory.

"I...I don't remember much. I just know my sister, Galina, found me and brought me to Mama and Papa. I've been with them ever since."

A heavy lump formed in my throat. Galina had saved me

from certain death. Why was I just standing here? Every second I wasted meant another step her captors were putting between us.

It made me uncomfortable to linger on my past, so I skipped through it, jumping past the hunting, the gathering, the small garden and wheat crop I tended to, until I reached our current situation.

Mikhail kept looking at me like he wanted to say something. The way I saw it, if he had something to add, he might as well speak up. But he didn't.

Once I had finished, Vanya gave it some thought. "This sister of yours, the one who was taken—"

"Galina."

"She was taken by the Fraktsiya, right?"

"I've already told you this," I said, growing frustrated. "Why is it so—"

Vanya lifted his hands. "I'm just trying to get my facts straight. You aren't the most eloquent of storytellers, and I need to hear a story twice to really understand it."

I huffed, crossing my arms. "I'm not a bad storyteller! I tell stories to Galina all the time!"

"Most people want to run away from upyri, not keep them as pets," Vanya said. "Why would they take her?"

"Toma, I don't think we should inconvenience Ivan with our—" Mikhail began.

"Because Mikhail is the Tsar and they needed to appease Koschei for failing to find him!" I blurted out before I could stop myself. The moment the words left my mouth, I felt a sudden horror, and wanted desperately to take them back.

Mikhail rose quickly from his seat, and Vanya's jaw came unhinged.

"What did you say?" Vanya whispered.

I swallowed hard, trying to dislodge the boulder in my throat. "I..."

Vanya turned to Mikhail. His gaze swept from his tattered clothing to his face. I could see him trying to piece together Mikhail's contradictions, the same way I had—the refined lilt of Mikhail's voice, his cold and distant bearing, the unscarred softness of his palms.

"You," Vanya said. "You're the Tsar?"

Mikhail took a step back, seeming at a loss about what to say. Even if he had lied, the truth shone clearly in his expression. In his silence. In the way his gaze flickered toward the rifle propped against the wall near the door.

"You're the Tsar?" Vanya repeated quietly.

"We're just passing through, Ivan," Mikhail said, his voice low and wary. "We won't impose on you any longer. Toma, let's go."

Vanya's gaze chilled in an instant. He stepped in our way, blocking the route to the door. "No."

"Vanya, we don't want to fight you," I said, suddenly conscious of the weight of the musket slung against my back. It would take Vanya only a second to load the rifle. By the time I slid my ramrod down my musket's barrel to secure the lead shot, he would have already fired—and that was if he didn't use his powers. This was wrong. All of this was terribly wrong.

"This isn't about you, Toma." His cat-green eyes remained on Mikhail. "This is between me and the Tsar."

Mikhail took a velvet sack from his coat pocket and shook its contents into his hands. Two rubies and a diamond. The rest of the gems were hidden in his shoes and in both of our coat linings.

"In return for your kindness and your discretion," Mikhail said, holding out his hand.

Vanya looked down at the jewels, his features darkening. "Is that it?"

"What?" Mikhail asked, befuddled. "You want more?"

"No, I want none of it. I can't believe you're going to try to *bribe* me and run away from everything you witnessed today like it has nothing to do with you!" Vanya's eyes flashed with anger. "You think it was just a coincidence the Otzvuk targeted the Strannik side of town, or that this is the first time it's happened?"

As Vanya spoke, the floorboards beneath his feet began to fissure, beads of ruby sap bursting like blood to the surface. Knobby branches emerged from the wood.

"Vanya, just calm down," I stammered, shifting restlessly from foot to foot. My fingers strayed to the hunting knife secured to my belt. The musket would be too slow, but the blade would involve getting close. I prayed it wouldn't come down to that.

"Even under your father, the imperial army and bogatyr militias terrorized us!" Vanya snarled as though he didn't even hear me. "You know what it's like to be marched out of your house at gunpoint, Tsar Mikhail, and be made to dig trenches in the dead of winter? To be harassed and beaten, and to know our attackers would never be court-martialed, Tsar Mikhail? To watch our neighbors be hanged because the imperial army thought they might be conspiring with the Groznaya Empire? No! You can take those jewels and shove them up your ass, Your Highness, because I'd sooner drag you back to the Fraktsiya myself than let you leave our country to tear itself in two!"

Mikhail flinched like he had been struck in the chest, but even now, he was sparing with his words. His jaw worked silently as he considered what to say, before at last responding. "You have it wrong. I have no intention of abandoning our empire. I simply need to leave so that I can find allies."

I hesitated. Although I didn't understand this conflict, one thing remained abundantly clear to me. "Mikhail, these people need you."

"Svet's royal family supported my reign, Toma," he said, looking from Vanya to me. "They can lend me their forces and put this insurrection to an end. To face the Fraktsiya alone would be the definition of suicide."

"So, you're fine with piling all your shit onto other people?" Vanya scoffed. "Running away with your tail between your legs like a beaten dog?"

"You don't understand," Mikhail snapped, curling his hands into fists. "Koschei is able to take bogatyri's powers, and he stole mine!"

A flicker of shock raced across Vanya's features. "What?"

"He's a koldun." Mikhail's voice lost some of its force and became hesitant, almost haunted. "All he did was lay his hands on me, and it was like—it's like decaying from the inside out."

If Mikhail's confession inspired any sympathy, it was fleeting. Vanya's expression hardened once more, and he took a step forward.

"Is that so?" he growled.

"I can't do anything, not the way I am now," Mikhail said hollowly. "I'm powerless."

"Vanya, the floor," I whispered as another board split. Leaves sprouted on the branches growing from the hewn planks. I felt frozen. Nothing I could say would stop this. After all, until today I hadn't been a part of their world.

"Ninety-nine percent of people are born without powers, but they still fight and die for the good of their country," Vanya shouted. "Thousands of normal, ordinary people died fighting against the Groznaya Empire, while you were hiding in your castle, detached from it all. My *father* died, and there wasn't even enough of him left to ship back in a *hat box*! What excuse do you have?"

The tension drained from Mikhail's body, his shoulders sagging in defeat. He muttered something under his breath, too soft for me to hear.

"What did you say?" Vanya asked sharply.

"If I go back there, Koschei will kill me."

"Don't you think it is the greatest honor for a soldier to lay his life down for his country?"

"I'm not a soldier," Mikhail said through clenched teeth.

"Personally, I believe that leaders should be held to the same standards they expect of the people they send into battle." Vanya brushed a hand through his hair, his gaze flicking to the bronze and silver medals in a shadowbox on the wall. "Besides, if Koschei is a koldun like you say, then it's a curse what he did to you. You won't get your powers back by running away."

Mikhail's eyes narrowed. "You think I can get my powers back?"

"We have our own legends about witches," Vanya said. "About how the only way to break a koldun's curse is to repay it threefold. He took your throne, your magic, your birthright—so take them back the only way you can."

"You mean kill him."

Vanya smiled dully. "Blood for blood."

13

As the sun set, Vanya took me through the Old Quarter. Unlike Mikhail, Vanya had a lot to say about everything. He couldn't take more than twenty steps without pointing out another landmark, bringing up the Old Quarter's historical past, or telling me about his friends and neighbors. I began to wonder if he loved the sound of his own voice or if he viewed this as a rare opportunity to practice the common tongue instead of Strannitsky.

I liked the sound of his voice, too, but I didn't want to sightsee when Galina was still out there. Vanya had generously allowed us to spend the night, but every moment I wasn't actively searching for Galina, I felt trapped in inertia. For Mikhail, I suspected it was much the same—when Vanya and I had left, he had been pacing the room restlessly.

"Didn't you say that you had something to show me?" I asked, rubbing my arms. "Something about my sister?"

"Don't you want to see the town?" Vanya frowned, looking a tad offended. He kept his hood raised, and every time we passed another Strannik, he turned his face away, as if a little afraid they might attack him.

"I just want to find Galina."

"Relax, Toma. You only have control over what you have control over. Look around. Look at the town you helped save." He gestured toward a tan three-story building with marble cornerstones and a pitched roof of black slate. Climbing ivy ensnared the high walls, red leaves quivering in the breeze. "That's where Yuriy, the boy we rescued earlier, lives. It was a scary thing, but I think he'll be okay."

We turned down an alley and climbed a flight of narrow limestone stairs to the street on the hill above. Vanya stopped on the top step and glowered at the scenery. Steeples and towers cut through the haze of smoke that lingered in the air. On the other side of the river, a ruined limestone castle stooped over Kupalo like a widow in mourning. The mountains that Mikhail and I had crossed the day before were mere shadows past the rise of forested hills.

"The way we're living now, it's disgraceful," Vanya growled. "After we fled the Black Steppe, the nobles *welcomed* us here. Now we're living like cattle."

Papa had grown up in a border town at the Steppe's edge and had described it to me in detail—an expanse of rolling grasslands ridged with bald mountains. Entire stretches of the Steppe were littered in black glass and molten sand, and of the once-great cities, only centuries-old ruins remained.

When Papa had been alive, nomadic tribes had still occasionally passed through the Steppe, although due to the scarcity of resources, most travelers preferred instead to go by sea or on the winding, southern tributary of the Vesna River. Unlike the empire and its surrounding lands, the primary danger of the Black Steppe wasn't monsters, but starvation and dehydration. Yet Papa told me that some still believed the burning hadn't destroyed the undead, but simply trapped them beneath the surface, and that one day they were bound to re-emerge.

"If you were welcomed once, what changed?" I asked Vanya, gesturing at the smoke-filled streets. "Why did this happen?"

"Like I said back at the temple, we used to serve as guards. We protected noble estates when there were still different kingdoms. It's never talked about now, but over the years, all the nonmagical noble houses were destroyed. Wiped out entirely by the bogatyri, or integrated by marriage if they were lucky. Strannik guards were considered obsolete, traitors, a threat to the new order. And that's followed us. For hundreds of years, it's followed." Underneath his voice's harsh staccato, there rolled an undercurrent of profound sorrow. "We're not people to the bogatyri, just heretics and the enemy. They kill us…and it means nothing. We mean nothing."

Vanya strode into the street, his boots' hobnails clacking on the cobblestones. As I trailed behind him, his words lingered in my head. I remembered that after all the Stranniki had left my village, people had blamed their problems on suspected kolduny. It was never the wealthy landowners who were accused of being witches, but the elderly peasants, or workers crippled in mining accidents, or young women. There had been many executions in that year alone.

Vanya and I stopped in front of a two-story building with a red terra-cotta roof. A sign hung above the door, depicting a raven in flaking shades of blue and indigo.

"Those two men you talked about, whether they're on their way to the capital or any other major city, they would have passed through here," Vanya said. "If they spent the night, they'd want somewhere discreet, and the only other inn is in the New Quarter. It's crawling with bogatyri."

He opened the inn's door, releasing the savory aroma of roasted meat. People sat at tables, in deep, solemn conversations over pipes and drinks. I recognized a few from the temple, but the rest were strangers. Their talking stilled when we entered. They looked at us coldly as we passed, and more than a few touched the amulets around their throats or slipped their hands beneath their hooded tent-cloaks, reaching for concealed weapons no doubt.

"Lovely as usual, Annushka," Vanya said, offering the chestnut-haired girl behind the counter a charming smile.

She rolled her eyes. "Admirable effort, but flattery won't make me come back to you, Vanya."

"You mustn't hate me too much," he said, resting his elbows on the counter. "You're still wearing that hat I made for you, and indoors, no less! Too cold in here for you?"

"Thank you for reminding me to throw this old, fraying thing away." Annushka flushed, tugging off the low velvet cap embroidered around its crown with a bold geometrical border in burnished copper. Her hair was so thick and glossy that I found my fingers straying to my own lank, dark locks.

Vanya groaned as she shoved the cap beneath the counter, pressing a hand over his heart. "You injure me. There's nothing lower than insulting a man's hard work."

"Luckily for you, I think I've got something to soften the blow." Smiling, Annushka retrieved a bottle of pale gold liquid from the shelf and filled three small cups. She transferred some slices of meat and pickled vegetables to a plate and placed them on the counter, along with a fork for each of us. "For saving the Old Quarter."

Judging by her earlier comments, she must have been very close to him. Watching them interact so carelessly, so openly, I felt a stir of envy for something I didn't have. Something I had only read about. I desperately wanted to be able to talk to Vanya or Mikhail that way. To have the boys talk that way to me. But what could I say? *Hello, my name is Toma, and I was raised by upyri?* Right. As if that would impress either of them.

"Ah, steppe grass." Vanya picked up a cup and handed me another. "You have good taste, Annushka."

She lifted her cup. "To our health."

"To wrecking the grandest temple from here to Detskaya," Vanya said, earning a few resentful glances as he downed his cup in one swallow.

Feeling out of my element, I mumbled, "To health," and took a sip from the cup.

My eyes watered instantly. Samogon, maybe, but even more potent than the spirits Mama distilled. It had a pleasant nutty flavor at least, likely thanks to the steppe grass it'd been steeped in. When I lowered my cup, I noticed Vanya and Annushka staring at me.

"What?" I asked, mystified by their bemused expressions. "Is there something on my face?"

"Nothing." Vanya lowered the slice of sausage that he had raised halfway to his mouth without taking a bite. "It's just, it would go down smoother if you drank it all at once. It's not something you sip unless you want to torch your tastebuds."

Annushka nodded. "The steppe grass is very—" She turned to Vanya. *"Shtrestkiy?"*

"Harsh," Vanya explained. "The first sips are good, but any more and it'll pickle your tongue."

"Oh." I blushed, embarrassed. I had never much cared for strong spirits or the jolt of taking a single serving in one gulp. Even the stouts Mama brewed were less refreshing than cold, bubbly kvass or hot chaga tea. I hadn't thought that my inexperience would shine through in the way I took my drinks.

Annushka turned to Vanya. *"Mühre, Iohna?"*

"Of course," he said, and she splashed a little more samogon into her cup and his. I shook my head when she offered me the bottle, busying myself with the food she had brought out. The salty sausages and vinegary pickles and tomatoes cut the drink's lingering sharpness.

When Annushka set down the bottle, her fingertips brushed against Vanya's forearm. He shifted his hand to place it over hers. The gesture was intimate but unconscious, like the way I sometimes brushed my hand through Galina's wispy hair without thinking about it. Except there was heat here. This was a different kind of love.

I felt vaguely uncomfortable, like I was observing the mating ritual of a different species. Mama and Papa never touched each other this way, and instead seemed to intentionally avoid it, keeping a wide berth from one another as though they were the opposite poles of a magnet.

"So, now everyone knows," Annushka said, on a more somber note. "About what you can do."

Vanya waved a hand dismissively. "Let's not get started on that. We have more important things to discuss."

"You're lucky you have your own roof over your head now, because even my dad thinks you're a koldun."

"Good to know. I'll remember that next time I come over for dinner." As Annushka rolled her eyes, he turned to me. "Toma, tell her about the two men you're looking for."

I choked on the piece of sausage I'd been chewing and swallowed it hastily. "Yes. A man with a black beard, and another with blond hair and bad teeth. Fraktsiya soldiers."

"Fraktsiya?" Annushka narrowed her eyes. "Why are you looking for Fraktsiya soldiers?"

"That's none of your concern," Vanya said.

Restlessly, she rubbed a smudge on the counter. "This isn't your war, Vanya."

"It's all our war," he said. "Just tell us, did two men like that pass by here yesterday?"

"Who knows?" She confronted him coolly. "It's none of my concern, as you said."

"Annushka." His smile remained, but his voice lost some of its warmth. He glanced back toward the tables at the opposite end of the room, where the other patrons were still eying us with suspicious and resentful expressions. "Are you really going to make me wait here all evening? I'd say we're a good ten minutes from a bar fight, and then I think your father will like me even less."

She sighed. "All right. Two strangers like that spent the night yesterday. Kosa nationals, by the sound of their accents."

"Did they have any luggage?" Vanya asked. "Or strange cargo?"

"A trunk. It looked like the one Gershka's been trying to sell." She nodded across the bar, to a haggard man slumped asleep at a table in the corner, surrounded by more than a few tankards. "They must've given him a good price. He slept right through the *tsurästvo*."

"The riot," Vanya explained, before setting down his glass. "I'd better talk to him. Maybe he knows more."

"Did they tell you where they were going?" I asked Annushka as Vanya crossed the room.

She shook her head.

Sighing, I glanced back at Gershka, who had jolted awake at Vanya's touch. The man raised his tankard with a crooked smile, nearly splashing Vanya in the process. When I looked back, Annushka was watching me.

"Those men you're looking for, did they do that to your face?" she asked, and there was a hard edge in her voice that hadn't been there before.

Absently, I raised my fingers to the tender bruise on my temple. "One of them punched me."

"When you find them, may you pay it back threefold." Then, as if sensing the deepening tension, she offered me a small smile. "I like your rushnyk."

"Thank you. I like your hair. It reminds me of a fox's pelt." I blushed, realizing that she might not find it as much a compliment as I hoped. "I'm sorry, I didn't mean—"

She laughed. "That's a new one, but thank you. Yours is nice, too. It's so dark and sleek. Mine is a nightmare to brush in the damp seasons. It puffs up like a fox's *schväst* then, too."

Vanya returned to us and put a few coins on the counter. "Gershka wants another round, Annushka. Anyway, he says those men were looking for a way to Eyry."

"Eyry?" I asked.

"A city just past the border with the Kosa interior," Annushka said.

Vanya nodded. "They asked if he had a wagon. Obviously, he doesn't, but they were carrying enough money that I imagine they didn't have any trouble finding a ride."

Where would they have gotten money? I frowned, recalling the dirigible wreck and the bogatyr's corpse, his coat disturbed and tendons severed. After the two soldiers had mutilated him in an attempt to prevent resurrection, they must have searched him for valuables.

"Detskaya is the closest depot that services the Kosa mainland," Vanya added, mulling it over. "There's a train to Eyry that passes through there."

My legs weakened. "So, it's already too late then?"

"Not necessarily. See, the thing is that before those Otzvuk soldiers showed up here, they were probably in Detskaya. Two weeks ago, the Fraktsiya regained control of the city. From what I've heard, the battle damaged the railway tracks, so all trains out of Detskaya have been delayed until they're repaired." A thin smile touched his lips. "And you know how bad the roads are here, especially during the rainy season? Add in an old dray-mare and a farmer's wagon, and it'll take a good four days to get to Detskaya."

"We don't even have a wagon!"

"No, but for that lovely little bribe your friend offered me, you'd easily be able to get your hands on a pair of horses. If you take the old logging routes through the eastern mountains, with a bit of luck and some determination, you might even be able to reach Detskaya before them."

14

Night crept over Kupalo's gabled rooftops and domed temples. After the three of us had reinforced the windows and broken door downstairs, Vanya had banished Mikhail and me to the sitting room while he cooked and cleaned, refusing to let us in until everything was complete. Entering the kitchen, I was immediately overwhelmed by the delicious fragrances of roasted meat and vegetables.

Mikhail and I sat at the table while Vanya carved the small pheasant. Ever since I had told Mikhail about the train to Eyry, he had seemed in a daze. I could tell that he didn't want to return to the Kosa mainland, even if he wouldn't say it aloud.

"Are you all right?" I asked as Mikhail traced the whorls in the oak table with the pad of his thumb.

"I'm just hungry and tired."

"What about your wound? How did it look when you washed up?"

"It's fine," he said, shifting his gaze across the kitchen. He kept looking at Vanya when the other boy wasn't paying attention. I couldn't decide if he was suspicious of Vanya's hospitality or merely intrigued.

As for Vanya, it was just as impossible to decipher what was going through his head. He kept glancing out the window or at the rifle propped in the rack against the wall, and even as he prepared our meal, he handled the knife with rough, hard strokes.

Vanya transferred crispy golden slices of roasted pheasant onto a porcelain platter and carried it to the table. He served us tea from an old brass samovar and brought out china so delicate that it must have been an heirloom set. There were only two chairs, but he dragged up a wooden crate that he upturned and sat on.

The pheasant was juicy and succulent, while the braised cabbage was sweet and tangy with a pleasant bite. Hardly like the bitter, stunted cabbages I grew at home.

"This is delicious, Ivan," Mikhail said, after the first few bites. "You'd put the royal cook out of work."

"I know it's probably not what you're used to, Tsar," Vanya said, blushing as he looked down at his hardly touched plate. He had been watching us eat so keenly, he had only taken a few bites. Now, he sliced off a massive chunk of meat and shoveled it into his mouth as if he wanted to avoid saying more.

"It's ten times better than what I can find out in the wilderness," I said.

"I'll bet," Vanya said, once he had managed to swallow

his mouthful of food. He wiped his mouth with his napkin. "Shocking you didn't starve to death over the years."

"I wasn't the only one scavenging. My family would help me, and I had a small garden and wheat field."

I took a sip of tea, savoring its sweet, grassy flavor. Mint leaves and tree bark were nothing in comparison. Nor could anything made of acorn flour rival the thick golden slabs of spiced honey cake that Vanya brought out for dessert.

I broke off chunks of the dense cake with my fingertips and savored it a bite at a time, the rich flavors of honey and cinnamon melting on my tongue. A dark, sugary crust had formed on the surface during baking, but the inside was moist and crumbled lusciously.

As I licked the crumbs off my fingertips, someone knocked downstairs. Heavy, jarring blows—once, twice, three times. The strain that had been buried beneath Vanya's smile all throughout dinner suddenly rose to the surface. He climbed to his feet, his gaze wary.

"Wait here. Maybe my boss is back early." He nodded to the rifle propped against the wall. "If you hear anything suspicious, it's loaded."

Mikhail and I sat stiffly as Vanya opened the door and stepped onto the landing. The air thickened with tension as we waited for him to return, and the cake's sweetness soured on my tongue.

"If I just had my powers…" Mikhail trailed off, staring at the rifle.

The mention of powers reminded me of what had happened at the temple. "Mikhail, those men were Otzvuk soldiers, weren't they?"

He gave a weary sigh. "They were carrying their flags and wearing their uniforms, but I don't think they were actually Otzvuk. Not the way you think."

"But they were bogatyri."

"It's not uncommon for soldiers to desert. That's what must have happened. Or…"

"Or what?"

He glanced toward the door that led downstairs, before continuing in a lower voice. "There have been reports of Stranniki stockpiling weapons in preparation to stage rebellions. Ivan shouldn't even have that rifle—his people aren't allowed to craft guns or bladed weapons, much less own them."

"Why?" I asked, taken aback.

Mikhail frowned. "Why what?"

"Why aren't Stranniki allowed to own weapons?"

"That's how it's always been, for hundreds of years." He looked vaguely uncomfortable. "It's as Ivan mentioned back at his temple. In the past, Stranniki served as guards."

"And they were called Strazhniki," I recalled.

"Yes, but it's more complicated than that. After fleeing the Great Burning of the southern steppe, they became mercenaries for the old gentry. When the bogatyr ruling families came into power, they took up arms against us. They used the Unclean Force to fight back, and many died before we were able to quell their insurrection."

"But that was hundreds of years ago."

"Even now, there are many Stranniki fighting for the Fraktsiya."

"Weapons could have stopped what happened today," I pointed out.

"What I'm trying to tell you is that it could have been what caused the violence today. I'm not saying that it was justified, but you need to understand, these things don't just happen without reason."

I wanted to argue, but I held my tongue. Mikhail hadn't witnessed what happened in the marketplace. He hadn't seen the looks of hatred on those men's faces.

Quiet voices. Creaking stairs.

"Refugees," Vanya said, opening the kitchen door again. "The girl I was with earlier, and a boy who was caught in the attack."

Dressed in a rain-drenched cloak fastened by rows of niello buckles and embroidered with ornate silverwork, the temple priestess stepped into the room.

Favoring Mikhail and me with a solemn nod, she set her small linen sack on the floorboards. She hung up her cloak. As she leaned over to remove her boots, Vanya said, "There's no need. I imagine you won't be here long."

"No, I'm afraid not." Her jet eyes flicked toward us. "Perhaps it would be better to continue this conversation in our own tongue."

Vanya's gaze darkened. "What is it? Why did you come here?"

"Something this personal should be kept between us."

"Just say it," he snapped.

"Tomorrow morning, I will go to the New Quarter to formally announce your execution."

Vanya's face drained of color. "Wh-what?"

"What did you say?" I stammered, certain I had misheard her. Mikhail glanced at the rifle, his face hardening.

"As long as you stay here, our safety will be jeopardized. You killed six people, do you know that?"

Vanya didn't answer, but from the stricken look on his face, I could tell he hadn't realized it in the moment. Using his power must have been even more impersonal than pulling his rifle's trigger—simply giving over to the uncontrollable force that raged within and allowing it to enact change on the world in his stead.

"Three of those men were prominent residents of the New Quarter. You will never be able to wash their blood from your hands." She regarded him levelly. "As high priestess, it is my duty to protect the citizens of the Old Quarter. Even if it means doing something I find morally reprehensible."

"That's not fair!" I cried, shooting to my feet. "You can't do this. Vanya saved this town. He saved your people."

"At seven o'clock tomorrow morning, the koldun Ivan Zoravich Azarov will be taken out to the swamp, administered purification rites, and quietly executed. His body will be dismembered, a stake driven through his back, and his mouth filled with moss."

"This is illegal," Mikhail said, rising from his chair. "Under imperial law, even kolduny are deserving of a trial. Anyone accused of being a witch must face the Holy Tribunal—"

"Shut up, city boy," Vanya said quietly. The color hadn't yet returned to his face, but he no longer looked shocked. Just wary.

"As a representative of the bogatyr elite, Duke Kirill will serve as witness to the execution."

Vanya's eyes narrowed. "Duke Kirill. He's—"

"Yes, the nobleman who warned the council that tensions

had started to rise." Her lips rose in a bitter smile. "It pained him to hear what happened this morning. He sends you his deepest sympathies."

Vanya nodded slowly, lifting his hand to his face to discreetly wipe his eyes.

"I brought you new clothes," the high priestess said, nodding to the bag. "I'll take the ones you wore today, along with your identification papers and work permit. There's a small amount of money in there. Enough to get you to Kraylesa at least. I spoke with Inga Elenovna over the telephone to explain the situation, and she told me that if you end up in Detskaya, you should pay a visit to her factory."

Vanya laughed, but it was a wrenching sound, deep with misery. "You've killed me."

"Not yet." She took her cloak from the rack and slid it on. She picked up her hat and held it in her hands. "You still have tonight. Just make sure you leave before daybreak."

"What about my cat?" Vanya asked.

"I'll find someone to take care of it for you," she said.

"Her."

"Her. Now." She held out the bag. "Your clothes, please."

Snatching the bag from her hand, Vanya strode into the other room. When he returned several minutes later, he had exchanged his dark shirt for one of bleached linen, adorned around the cuffs and collar with red. The pants were similar enough to his own, but sewn of brown gabardine with looser legs, meant to be rolled and tucked into one's boots.

He rummaged through the kitchen cupboards until he found a stack of envelopes and thin leather-bound booklets. He threw the whole lot into a burlap sack, carried it back to the high priestess, and shoved it into her hands. "Just go and take them. Take my name, my life, my only other set of clothes, why don't you just take everything from me?"

"Farewell, Ivan Zoravich." She held out her right hand. "You will not be forgotten here. I can assure you of that. Don't think to come back, or you will truly die a heretic."

Referring to Vanya by his first name and matronym was a sign of respect, a way to show that the priestess and the boy stood on equal footing. Yet Vanya stared suspiciously at the woman's offered hand like he expected her to strike him. At last, he extended his own hand and gave a firm, brief shake.

As the door closed behind her, Vanya trudged back to the table and stared down at the cake and tea. His expression was unreadable.

Hesitantly, I approached him. "Vanya, I'm so sorry."

I laid my hand on his shoulder, and he shuddered like he hadn't noticed me standing there. He brushed my hand away without saying anything, walked over to the counter, and retrieved a bottle of clear liquid from the bottom cabinet.

Turning back to us with the bottle cradled against his chest, he smiled brightly. "Didn't you two hear? They're going to execute me tomorrow. I think this calls for a celebration."

The night brought uneasy dreams of Galina trapped in a sack, writhing and screaming until she disintegrated into a pile of bones and ashes. I woke alone in Vanya's bed in a heavy sweat, gasping for breath and shivering. My mouth tasted sour, and my head ached.

Still exhausted, I sank against the pillow and stared at the yellow bars of light that the streetlamp outside painted across the ceiling. I couldn't stop thinking about Vanya's banishment or what Mikhail had told me about Koschei's obsession with the resurrected dead.

"Just don't think about it," I whispered, my fingers drawn to the bead strung around my wrist. I traced its weathered facets to soothe myself.

You think they're sapphires?

Tears prickled my eyes, threatening to spill free. How long would it be before I forgot the sound of Galina's voice? Before her features faded from my memory like so much smoke? Soon, she might become no more substantial than my birth parents, just another phantom to join the procession.

"You're going to save her," I told myself sternly. "She's going to be fine."

The floorboards were cold beneath my bare feet as I padded around the partition wall separating the bedroom from the parlor. Mikhail lay asleep on the sofa. A rumpled pile of blankets and furs on the floor marked where Vanya had slept.

The lamps in the kitchen were extinguished, but I paused to marvel at them. Electrical lamps, Mikhail had called them. I gently touched one of the glass orbs that had once contained pure gold light. It was cool to the touch.

Galina would have loved it so much. She would think it was magic.

"Impressed?" a voice behind me said softly.

I swiveled around.

Vanya smiled at me from the stairway. Along with the clothes the priestess had brought him, he wore a mink fur ushanka and had a dark brown outercoat folded over his arm.

"It's amazing," I said as he walked over. "There's noth–

ing like this back home. It's like fire, but it's in a glass and it doesn't flicker."

"Some people are afraid of technology, but I think it's a beautiful thing," he said, tracing his fingertips over the lamp's glass orb. "The nobles have their magic, so the proletariat should have machines."

I blushed, becoming aware of how close we stood to each other. I could reach out and touch him if I wanted to, trace the fine curve of his cheekbones, or run my fingers through his thick burgundy hair. And his skin would be warm.

"It's different in other countries," Vanya said. "In Yezmirny, I've heard that nobody outside of the priestly class uses magic. Anyone who shows an affinity for it is cloistered, even nobility. They're the ones who invented these lights in the first place."

He went on to explain how despite being a powerful and wealthy kingdom, Yezmirny had so far remained a neutral observer in the civil war. Their wealth of natural resources and diverse climate, ranging from the acrid northern steppes to fertile coastland in the west and vast deserts in the south, had contributed to their prosperity.

Although Yezmirny lacked the same magical might as Kosa, they were renowned for their technological advances, and many of the war machines used by both Otzvuk and Fraktsiya forces were derived directly from Yezmirskiy design. Due to the buffer zone created by the Steppe, past conflicts between Kosa and Yezmirny had been mainly limited to skirmishes along the major trade routes.

"You seem to really admire Yezmirny," I said, once he had finished telling me about how the latest advances in Yezmirskiy naval steam-engines and their invention of the rigid-framed airship had renewed interest in attempting to cross the Western Sea.

"They have the right idea," he said. "Technology can be an equalizing force."

"Is that why you didn't use your power at the market? Because you thought your gun would be an equalizing force?"

"No. I've never used my powers to fight before, and I was afraid that I might hurt innocent people." He crossed his arms, frowning at the floor. "We've been anticipating something like this for a while now, but not with bogatyri. Usually, when tensions flare up, it's with the other villagers, the ones who aren't Strannik. Farmers, workers, not trained soldiers or bogatyri. We thought arranging a self-defense squad would be enough. I don't think anyone expected it to...to be what it was yesterday."

It took me a moment to fully process his words, and the vague pleasure I'd felt at our closeness vanished into shock. "Are you saying that some of those people were your *neighbors*?"

"You need to understand, until now, it's never been the politicians or bogatyri who get their hands dirty. They're just the ones to point the finger." Vanya sighed. "What I did yesterday, I just provided a respite. The people in the New Quarter are going to be a lot warier from now on, knowing we'll fight back, but it's only a matter of time before they attack again. And I'm not going to let that happen."

"But Vanya, if you stay here, they'll kill you," I stammered. The truly frightening part was that it might not even be the villagers in the New Quarter. Remembering the priestess's grim warning—*His body will be dismembered, a stake driven through his back, and his mouth filled with moss*—I realized there must be people in the Old Quarter who feared Vanya as well. Who saw him as a monster.

"I know they will." His lips rose in a ghost of a smile. "That's why I'm going to help you find Koschei."

15

It was still dark when we set out on foot, and a dense fog choked the streets. Instead of going toward Kupalo's gates, we headed deeper into the Old Quarter, crossing through alleyways and behind houses.

"This morning, I went down to the inn and made a few calls," Vanya explained. "I know a shortcut through the mountains. It won't be a comfortable journey, but it'll be quick."

Up ahead, an imposing brick building emerged from the darkness. Thin arched windows with segmented panes overlooked the riverfront.

"What's that?" I asked, eying the structure's metal chimneys and bud-domed cupolas.

"It looks like a mill," Mikhail said.

Vanya nodded. "Flax. It's how most people on this side of the river make our living."

A guard loitered in front of the gate. As we approached, he stepped forward.

"Come to destroy this one, too, koldun?" the man asked, and just when I thought he was serious, a hint of a smile touched his lips.

"It's hardly worth the effort," Vanya said, stopping in front of him, smiling now as well. "Inga Elenovna should have called ahead to let you know we were coming."

The guard nodded. "She did. The stable is in the back, next to the loading bay. They're in the pen."

"Inga Elenovna is my godmother and the woman our priestess was talking about last night," Vanya explained as we walked to the stables. "She lives in Detskaya and owns the mill here. Even so, she won't be making large deliveries from Kupalo anytime soon, not with the main roads being shelled, so she's going to let me take three of her draft horses. Her main factory's a short distance from Detskaya. We'll drop them off there."

Three horses waited in a pen outside the stable. They were brown, with long white fur on the lower halves of their legs as though they were wearing stockings.

"Wouldn't it be easier to simply take a ferry down the Vesna?" Mikhail asked as Vanya tacked up a horse.

"It would be a good way to get killed. The Vesna is too rough in these parts, and the last place you want to be right now is on a main travel route." Vanya glanced over his shoulder. "Not everyone has airships at their disposal."

"I've never ridden a horse before," I admitted, staring uneasily at the animals.

"It's not hard," Mikhail said. "All you need is good balance."

"You'll be a natural, Toma," Vanya added, buckling the first saddle. "I can tell just by looking at you."

I was taken off guard by his charming words. "You think so?"

"I know it." He extended his palm. "Give me your hand."

Hesitantly, I placed my palm in his. His touch was like lightning, sending a pleasant shiver running down my spine as I allowed him to guide my hand toward the horse's muzzle.

The animal's nostrils flared, and its hot, moist breath brushed against the back of my hand. Gently, Vanya placed my fingers atop its snout. It nuzzled my palm, its thick tongue flicking out to deposit a gritty green skim of saliva upon my skin.

I laughed, surprised. I had half expected the horse to bite me. As I stroked its nose and forehead, it leaned its head forward, encouraging me to continue petting it.

In the corner of my eye, I spotted Mikhail watching us with a strange expression. Not angry or anything, just distant, his gray eyes clouding over as if he were lost in a dream. The moment he noticed me staring, he turned away and began tacking up his horse.

"Ready to get on him?" Vanya asked.

"I don't think I can," I confessed, my stomach fluttering with apprehension. The saddle was so high off the ground. "I'm going to fall off and break my neck."

"Maybe just a leg."

I looked at him quickly, surprised to see his smile grow, his green eyes bright with amusement.

"I'm just teasing you. You'll do fine." He guided the horse to a hay bale. "Step up."

Hesitantly, I stepped onto the hay bale. At Vanya's guidance, I put my foot in the stirrup and hoisted myself up, holding on to the saddle horn to balance myself as I swung my other leg over. I smoothed out my skirt to keep it from bunching.

"Good. I told you you'd be good at this. Now, let's try walking." Clucking twice under his breath, Vanya led the horse forward.

I clung to the saddle horn, adjusting to the animal's slow, jostling gait. After circling the stable twice, I felt comfortable enough to take the reins. I rode back and forth across the yard as Vanya tacked up the remaining horse.

"You did a pretty good job," he said to Mikhail, who had already strapped on his horse's bridle and saddle. "I thought you'd just have servants to do that for you."

"Right, because I've never put on a belt before and am incapable of buckling straps on my own," Mikhail said sarcastically.

I flushed, embarrassed to admit that I hadn't even known which way the saddle was supposed to go. It was strange how all my skills were, in some ways, useless out here. Instead of relying on candles handcrafted from deer tallow and beeswax, people had lights they could turn on with the flick of a switch. And although I had practiced firing the musket until it took me less than thirty seconds to prime and reload it, how could that ever compare to artillery capable of firing hundreds of rounds a minute?

It didn't matter how many books I had salvaged from the homes and trenches, poring over the water-stained pages until the bindings disintegrated in my hands. Nothing could have prepared me for this.

We returned to Vanya's apartment and lingered only long enough to retrieve the supplies we had prepared the night before. I tied my bedroll and knapsack to the back of the saddle, slid my musket into a leather scabbard Vanya attached to the tack, and set off beside him and Mikhail.

As we rode through Kupalo, I trailed behind, observing the wreckage. Although many broken windows already had boards nailed over them, there was still so much rubble piled in the street. Splintered timber, loose bricks, and fallen shingles. It was hard to imagine how so much destruction could have been wrought in a single day.

The fog intensified once we entered the forests surrounding Kupalo, as if in some way the town's stone walls and iron fences had been the dam that kept the mist at bay. As we passed through a birch thicket, I thought I saw a beautiful nude woman stalking us from tree to tree, and asked Mikhail if he had seen her, too.

"That's a mavka," he said, staring straight ahead. "Don't look at her directly, and she won't harm you."

"You're lucky, Toma," Vanya said. "The forest spirits only tickle men."

"Did you say tickle?" I asked, certain I had misheard him.

He glanced back, grinning. "That's how they kill you. A pleasant death, if you ask me. Wouldn't you agree, Mikhail?"

"Not really," Mikhail said dryly.

"Ah, too feminine for your tastes?"

Cheeks reddening, Mikhail sputtered for a response. "What—what exactly are you trying to imply, Ivan?"

"Nothing at all, Tsarushka," Vanya purred, before turning back ahead.

Against my better judgment, I looked into the forest once more, unable to resist taking another glance at the strange and fascinating creature. I only caught a glimpse of the mavka this time, staring at me with eyes as green as Vanya's. Twigs, cocoons, and clumps of moss were trapped in her untamed black curls.

Her very presence radiated a fierce and uncontrollable power, so palpable that I couldn't help but feel a twinge of awe as I met her gaze. She smiled, displaying rotting brown teeth, and then turned from me. As she retreated into the dappled shadows, she revealed a flayed back like a broken vase. Her spine and ribs were exposed, as pale as the birch branches surrounding us. There was nothing left inside of her.

16

Hours elapsed on the road.

As we headed deeper into the mountains, we passed through several dilapidated hamlets where livestock outnumbered the people. Glimpses of hewn-log izbas and stone cottages appeared every now and then past the trees, while the occasional temple or monastery added its domes and steeples to the skyline. Some sanctuaries had impressive tented roofs that curved into sharp points like the helmets worn by the bogatyri of lore, and yet others rose in a single dome that marked them as Strannik.

Vanya told us interesting facts about each of the hamlets, pointing out war monuments and landmarks. He regularly visited the surrounding villages to purchase materials for his boss and wasn't shy about sharing the funny or interesting things that had happened to him over the years.

Vanya spoke so openly about his past. I felt a twinge of envy, a craving to learn more about my own history. Just because my family had been running from something didn't mean that I needed to keep running. It didn't mean that my past was poisoned. Maybe it was time to reclaim myself.

"Mikhail, where do you think I came from?" I asked, riding up alongside him. "Back when we first met, you said I sounded like I was from Kosa."

"Somewhere along the northern coast, for sure," he said. "Maybe one of the port cities. You have a certain way of pronouncing 'tse' and 'zhe' sounds. My physician came from the north, and he sounded just like you."

No, I hadn't lived along the ocean, but I remembered being taken there once. A vision of it swam through my head—an endless expanse of dark, frothing water, flowing and ebbing, crashing hard against the limestone cliffs and the black pebble shore.

The ocean had both frightened and mesmerized me. Its destructive strength and brute force had made it seem even more powerful than the bogatyri, who were the closest thing to divinity in our lives.

Just as the empire's southern edge was bordered by the Black Steppe, so was the north crested with a steppe of its own—a vast and hostile tundra of ice and raw stone fragmented by glacial seas and rivers, stretching as far west as the Edge and Groznaya. Though wealthy in natural resources and precious metals, the Ice Plains were rumored to be cursed land. My own birth father had told me tales of how the tsarina of witches ruled that hostile expanse.

"Not on the coast, but near it," I said. "A day's wagon ride from there. Somewhere in the mountains, where there were silver mines. A small village. Do you know where that might be?"

Mikhail shook his head. "I'm sorry, I don't. There are dozens of villages in the north, many of them centered around silver or coal mines."

"What about you, Vanya?" I asked.

"I've never been outside the Edge, Toma," Vanya said, then cocked his head. "But, you know, a lot of Stranniki used to live in the north because of our skill in metalwork. There are some beautiful shrines and temples there. Was there any that you can remember? Maybe if you describe it, I can help."

I shivered. Yes, there had been a Strannik temple, hadn't there? A towering building of age-silvered wood. But several years before we had left, the temple had burned to the ground. I still remembered the skeletal ruins, the onion dome caved in. The massive wooden idol of the goddess Voserka had been reduced to a charred husk.

I hadn't known it at the time, but looking back, I realized that the fire had probably been deliberate. A way to tell the Stranniki they weren't welcome in the village. A way to prevent them from coming back.

"I can't remember," I lied, looking at the fog-ensnared hills rising before us. "I just know it was in the mountains."

We rode on. Although in his descriptions Vanya had made the hamlets sound charming, the villagers we came across were cold and reserved, eying us warily as we drew well water for the horses. A chill dampened the air, turning our breaths into vapor as white and dense as the fog surrounding us. Farmers tending to autumn harvests of apples and wheat glared our way, keeping their hoes and sickles close at hand.

Within the hour, we passed through one village called Dimatsk, and another smaller one named Osoka, where Vanya insisted on taking a detour.

"In the square, there's a statue of Dinara Tagaeva, the hero of the Siege of Morevgorod," he said as we rode past the simple wooden houses roofed in tin sheets overgrown with moss. "If you kiss her hand, she blesses you with good luck. Trust me. The last time I did it, I won a hundred grevka at cards two days later."

"That sounds like a good way to catch a disease," Mikhail said dryly. "Just go and put your mouth on something that's touched the mouths of a thousand other people over the years."

"Don't tell me you're scared," Vanya teased.

He looked unamused. "I don't believe in luck, especially the kind that comes from praying to idols."

"What about you, Toma?" Vanya asked, turning to me.

I gave it some thought. Mikhail made it sound bad, but what if the statue truly was lucky? "Well, I guess. I could use some luck after all."

We arrived at the statue—a woman standing on a marble plinth, sword in hand and chin raised as though to confront an encroaching opponent. Her hand lay outstretched, the knuckles burnished to a soft gold while the rest of her brass form was enveloped in a dark patina.

Vanya jumped from his horse. "Allow me to demonstrate."

Guiding the horse by its reins, he made a show of kissing the statue's hand and then turned to us, grinning victoriously. "That's another two years of good luck for me."

"More like another two years of brainlessness," Mikhail said, rolling his eyes.

"Oh, don't want to lose your first kiss to a statue?" Vanya replied, before turning to me expectantly. "Want to give it a try, Toma?"

"Is it that bad?" I asked, climbing down from my horse. "To lose your first kiss to a statue?"

Vanya's smile slipped from his lips in an instant. "Oh, no. No. I was just joking. I didn't mean to suggest that if you've never kissed someone before..."

"I'll have you know, I've kissed people before, Ivan," Mikhail snapped.

"Who?" I asked, and his mouth puckered as though I'd left him with a bad taste.

"You shouldn't ask people questions like that, Toma," he muttered.

I winced. "Sorry."

"Oh, come now, Misha," Vanya encouraged. "Entertain us with all the court intrigue."

"Fine, it was a few years ago," Mikhail said after a long pause. "Aleksandra. She was the daughter of a visiting duchess. It, uh, it couldn't have worked."

I approached the statue and pressed my lips against its knuckles. The metal was cool and silken against my skin, and it came as a strange thrill to know that just mere moments before, Vanya's lips had touched the same place.

Vanya clapped. "Another two years of luck."

I laughed. This time, Mikhail didn't comment, although he still looked mildly annoyed.

"What about you?" I asked Vanya, once I had wrangled myself back into my horse's stirrups. "Was it Annushka?"

"No, actually, this was before she and I got together." He

chuckled. "She's a nice kisser, but Ios'ka, he was a terrible one."

Beside me, Mikhail tensed, his jaw tightening. He turned his horse forward and continued past me, muttering under his breath, "He truly has no shame."

"Oh, pardon me, Misha," Vanya called after him, climbing onto his own horse. "Did I offend your good sensibilities?"

As we continued through the village, I followed after, feeling mildly befuddled. So, it wasn't a bad thing to lose your first kiss to a statue, but it was shameful to kiss more than one person? There was so much I didn't know about the world. I felt like I'd never manage to catch up.

The day dragged on, and we headed deeper into the mountains. We didn't come across any more villages, but occasionally I spotted lone log houses through the trees. They reminded me of my own izba and made me yearn for home.

As the sun began its slow descent, we stopped in a meadow off the road and ate an early dinner around the fire we built. Kasha, dense rye bread, pickled beef tongue garnished with horseradish. I rubbed my hips and back to ease my saddle-sore muscles, eager to unroll my bedroll and take a nap.

Vanya pointed to the river snaking through the valley below. "I once caught a trout there as big as my arm. People say rusalki live there, but I've never seen one. I hear they leave the water in search of husbands. They're supposed to be beautiful."

"Why don't you jump in the river and find out?" Mikhail suggested.

"I'm not *that* desperate," Vanya said.

I laughed. "I should hope not."

Meeting my gaze, Vanya smiled. I had spent so much time among the dead that just looking into his eyes felt like a challenge, as intimate as a touch. I was the first to look away.

"What about you, Toma?" Vanya asked, after a couple more bites. "Have you ever seen a rusalka?"

I nodded, still averting my gaze. "Yes, but I've never gotten a good look at one. It's only just a leg, or a hand, or some red hair, and then they're gone. Although, I did see them swarming a caribou once, but there was so much blood..."

All this talk about monsters gave me an idea.

"Let's tell stories," I said. "I want to hear something wonderful, scary, or exciting."

"Like what?" Mikhail asked, setting down his bowl.

"I don't know. Anything. I'll go first. A few years ago, Galina lost her arm in the snow. It just fell off. Just like this." I tucked my arm against my chest and waved my elbow in the air. "We looked for hours trying to find it. I thought we never would. Then, a week later, I heard a *tick, tick, tick*. Something was tapping at the door. I thought it might be snow at first, but it was a clear night. I opened the door, and it was lying there." I laughed, warmed by the memory. "Her arm. It was waiting for us. Mama says all that you love returns to you, no matter what. I want to believe that. That she'll come back."

"I'd like to believe that, too," Vanya said thoughtfully, lifting a spoonful of kasha to his lips. Midbite, his gaze shifted to Mikhail, who until now had been staring fixedly at Vanya. Eyes widening in horror, Vanya choked on his food. "Have you no shame, Tsar?"

"What?" Mikhail asked, blushing.

"Your *bread*."

Throughout our meal, Mikhail had spent more time rearranging the tender slices of pickled beef tongue than actually eating them. Since setting his bowl aside, he had turned his attention to the slice of black bread and was in the process of tearing it into tiny chunks.

"You're supposed to eat it," Vanya said.

"It's bitter."

"That doesn't mean it deserves to be mutilated."

Mikhail thrust a sizable piece into his mouth, chewed, and swallowed. "There. Satisfied?"

"Yes. Thank you." Vanya turned back to me. "I suppose I'll go next… This isn't my story, but it's my father's. When he was around my age, he would always fish along the Vesna. Along the bend, where the trout were most plentiful. One day, he saw a beautiful red-haired woman bathing in the river. She beckoned to him, and he realized that she was a rusalka. Naturally, he didn't go to her, but he visited that area of the river every day, hoping that he would see her again. He would leave her presents. Sometimes just the fish he caught, but also fresh fruit and wooden figures he had carved for her."

"What happened next?" I asked, mesmerized. It sounded like something out of Galina's beloved stories.

"One day, he went fishing and she was waiting for him with her feet dipped in the river. He said her hair was like garnets in the sun." Vanya ran a hand through his own loose curls, which were indeed the same color as the gemstone. "And her eyes, they were like the sun itself."

"So, we're supposed to believe that you're half rusalka?" Mikhail asked sarcastically.

"I'm not telling you to believe anything." Vanya shrugged.

"It's just a story. If I had to make a guess, I'd say that my mother was probably a girl who lived in a neighboring village. Still, I've always felt drawn to the Vesna—" he looked at me, one corner of his mouth lifting in a vague smile "—and it's nice to think that the things you've lost will come back to you."

"I've seen dead rusalki before," Mikhail said. "They're not beautiful. They're grotesque."

"Well, maybe that's because they were dead, Tsarushka," Vanya said bluntly.

Mikhail frowned. "Didn't I tell you to stop calling me that?"

Vanya cocked his head. "Did you?"

"What about you?" I asked, turning to Mikhail. "Do you have a story to tell?"

He rolled his eyes. "I don't think I'll be able to top that one."

"Try," I said with a smile.

He gave it some thought. "Well, you know the legends about how bogatyri came to be, don't you?"

"Of course," I said, recalling the heroic stories I had grown up on, and that for years now, I had retold to Galina. "Many centuries ago, nobody could use powers, and people worshipped different goddesses and gods. When the monsters first appeared, humans weren't able to defend themselves. They had to build fortresses and walled cities, but even that wasn't enough. Many people died before the first bogatyri were born into ruling families."

"There's more to it than that," Mikhail said. "After my father died, I inherited the throne, and the imperial archives along with it. I read everything I could get my hands on, including the holy writings of the Oracle of Serebrograd. In her prophecies, she explains that it is our destiny as bogatyri to cleanse this land of the Unclean Force. In the future, a great evil will spread across the land, setting into motion a final war between bogatyri and monsters. During that time, a bogatyr will rise to usher in a new golden age and liberate all of humanity."

I felt a twinge of disappointment. I had hoped for a story about heroic ventures or castle life, not a tale about the bogatyri's divine destiny less than a day after seeing their violence and cruelty.

As for the Unclean Force, I was beginning to wonder what exactly Mikhail meant by that. I had heard that phrase used more in the last several days than in the last seven years, and it was beginning to seem vastly more complicated than I had previously thought.

From the scholarly books and religious texts I had salvaged over the years, I knew the Unclean Force was supposed to be the malevolent energy that gave kolduny their powers. Except Mikhail had told me that it was also the power that resurrected the dead, while the militants in Kupalo had accused the Strannik villagers of being carriers of it. Men and women who had been going about their daily lives, shopkeepers, children playing in the shadows of the market stalls. Innocents.

Did the Unclean Force even exist, or was it just a way to justify violence?

"Splendid sermon, Tsarushka." Vanya clapped slowly. "I'd love to know what role overtaxing the poor and terrorizing peasants plays in our divine destiny, but all in good time, I suppose?"

"You know what, Ivan?" Mikhail rose to his feet, throwing what remained of his bread onto the grass. "Just listening to you makes me lose my appetite!"

"Strangely, that's how I feel looking at your face," Vanya said pleasantly.

"You're lucky I don't have my powers, otherwise you wouldn't have one," Mikhail shot back, before storming over to the other end of the clearing.

"Vanya, there isn't really an Unclean Force, is there?" I asked as he broke the discarded crust into crumbs for the birds.

"I think there's the Unclean Force, and then I think there's something that people call the Unclean Force." He pressed his palm against a bare patch of dirt, and within seconds, blades of new grass sprouted between his fingers. "What I can do, people would call witchcraft. But my grandmother was able to make things grow, too. And I could trace our power back even further. A hundred years ago, two of my ancestors were burned for the same gift."

His words slowly dawned on me. "It follows bloodlines."

He nodded. "Just like with the aristocracy. You wonder why all the noble families have powers? It's because it's bred into them. You'll find the same thing in small, isolated villages. Being a bogatyr isn't a marker of divinity at all. Neither is it a sign of the Unclean Force. It's in the blood, it's that simple."

I mulled it over. For something that held so much significance in our world, could it really be that simple? And if bogatyri were no different than kolduny at their core, then what did that mean?

"Of course, don't tell Mikhail this or his head will explode." Vanya rolled his eyes.

I looked over to see if Mikhail was listening, but he no longer stood at the tree line. "Speaking of Mikhail, where is he?"

"He probably wandered away to blow off some steam. Sulk a bit. Maybe have a good cry." Vanya turned his attention back to the remnants of his meal.

All of a sudden, I realized the birds had gone silent. At their tethers, the horses shifted uneasily, steam wafting from their flared nostrils as they pawed the ground. The air grew heavy, burdened by an unseen presence.

I knew this feeling, knew the dread that crawled down my spine and raised the hairs on the nape of my neck. It was the feeling of standing at the river's edge and watching as the rusalki mauled an elk, thrashing up the rapids into a crimson froth.

"Something is wrong," I said, but by then Vanya was already rising to his feet. As he went to my side, the grass grew long and tangled in his wake. A shiver passed through me. This was the full force of his ability when allowed to flourish unbidden—powerful and uncontrollable, sprouting brambles and profusions of stunted white flowers.

"Hey, Tsarushka!" he called.

Silence except for the low gurgle of the river below and the rustling of creatures moving unseen through the underbrush.

Vanya swore, hurrying to my side to slip the rifle free from the leather scabbard mounted across his saddle. By the time he undid the scabbard's buckle, I had already taken my own musket and powder horn in hand.

As we headed deeper into the forest, the ground turned

marshy, water puddling beneath our feet. Here and there, I spotted humanlike footprints in the loose black soil—not the tiptoed tread of a mavka, but heavy feet webbed at the toes.

I swallowed hard, my mouth suddenly dry.

"Seen anything like this?" Vanya asked, nodding toward the footprints.

"Back in the wilds. But I've never seen the creature they belonged to." I left the rest unsaid—that aside from its footprints, the only omens of the creature's existence had been the relics of its insatiable hunger. Disemboweled deer and rabbits torn apart, and once the mangled half of a fisherman floating in marshy shallows, the bruises of fingers around his throat and forearms.

"You think it could be a rusalka?" Vanya asked.

I shook my head. "They always stay by rivers, never swamps or ponds. And I've never seen one walk on dry land before."

Still, I supposed there were always exceptions. In the wealth of taxonomy journals I had recovered from the trenches, I had read of rare instances of men returning as rusalki and women as vodyanye; sailor boys dragging themselves ashore to the shock of observers, with their hair running red down their backs and the new buds of breasts rising on their chests. A mavka with the face of a son, or a vodyanoy with the face of a daughter, and some returning as neither one sex nor the other. Perhaps this was no different.

"Mikhail!" Vanya called again, but the only answer was the rustling of the branches and then, faintly, the splash of unsettled water.

I had used my musket so many times through the years, it took me but twenty seconds to load and prime it. Vanya followed suit, jacking a round into his rifle's chamber. Edging deeper into the underbrush, now up to our ankles in the marsh, we scoured the algae-streaked water for any sign of disturbance.

"Just like a noble to wander from the path," Vanya muttered. "As if monsters have any respect for royalty."

Despite his scathing words, I caught an edge of fear in his voice. His jaw worked silently as he turned away.

"I hope this swamp doesn't get much deeper," he said under his breath.

"Afraid you'll drown?" The joke came out weaker than I intended, and he shot me a look.

"Yeah, actually, I am." Vanya turned his gaze back ahead, restlessly fingering the rifle's barrel. "I can't swim."

"You can't swim," I repeated, befuddled.

"Every time I go in the water, I sink like a rock." He laughed dryly. "So much for being half rusalka, huh?"

We followed the sound of water until we reached a shallow pond at the marsh's edge. As we neared, I caught a glimpse of two figures writhing beneath the surface—the pale gleam of flesh, and then the billowing fold of Mikhail's coat.

Swearing, Vanya aimed his rifle at the water, but hesitated at the last moment. This close, our weapons were useless. I set mine down, my body moving on its own, and lurched into the water, up to my thighs, up to my shoulders, and under.

Sediment clouded the water, reducing Mikhail and his assailant to mere shadows—thrashing limbs, the sinewy swell of a greenish-white amphibious tail—and then I wrenched Mikhail free. The moment my fingers closed around the creature's wrist, it jerked away in surprise, and I hauled Mikhail against myself as the monster retreated into deeper waters.

I broke the surface just as a gunshot erupted in my ears, and several meters away, a pool of blood bloomed across the pond's surface, darkly iridescent like machine oil.

Mikhail hung limp in my arms as I towed him toward the shallows. Jumping into the water, Vanya waded up to his thighs and helped me maneuver Mikhail onto solid ground. Together, we dragged him several paces from the edge.

"What do we do?" I asked frantically, shaking Mikhail's shoulder. His head lolled to the side, water welling from his parted lips.

Vanya shouldered me aside and leaned down, his hand upon Mikhail's chest. He tipped Mikhail's chin up and pressed his lips against his mouth, breathing in until Mikhail's chest swelled with borrowed air.

"Keep an eye on the water," Vanya croaked, pulling away to take a breath. "That thing is still in there."

I settled onto my haunches and snatched Vanya's rifle from the ground. Blinking silty water from my eyes, I scanned the pond's still surface. The trail of blood had diminished into an inky haze. We had wounded the creature, but not enough.

At the far end of the pond, a young man rose slowly from the surface. Streams of water raced down his skin, which was a sallow shade of white, dappled gray and green in places, like the belly of a fish that had started to spoil. Droplets caught in the tendrils of greenish-gold hair coiled over his shoulders. His eyes were as brilliantly gold as a frog's, with the same charcoal flecks, the pupils slantwise.

My breath caught in my throat. A vodyanoy. I had only seen

pictures of them before, printed in moldering almanacs and physiology manuals I'd retrieved from the rubble—creatures split open and segmented, their bisected organs rendered in water-stained ink.

The water spirit's strange beauty couldn't hide the devastation of his rebirth. Scaly black lesions covered his chest, trailing downward. Some were puckered and circular, others sunken inward. They reminded me of the white gouges of the gunshot wounds that had taken Papa from this world and into the Edge, or the livid scar necklacing Mama's throat.

Whatever had happened to this vodyanoy during his first death, it had been grotesque. He still wore a warrior's pauldron upon one shoulder, although the iron was scabbed with rust and the leather strap had begun to rot. In places, flaps of chain mail grew from his blackened scar tissue, the links encrusted in verdigris.

The water spirit's searing gold eyes confronted me, and his fish-pale lips twisted in a smile—a bared rictus devoid of mirth or amusement, simply muscle memory or the warning grin of a stalking wildcat. His first row of teeth was dull and knobby, designed for crushing bone, but behind it I discerned another row much sharper, the kind of fangs meant for bloodletting.

My finger trembled over the trigger. Somehow shooting the vodyanoy seemed even more vicious than turning my weapon against human opponents. When Mama had drawn Papa back from the brink, she had brought him old books and rusted chunks of machinery until his wasted fingers relearned the cogs and gearwork. Perhaps there was a way to help the water spirit recall who he had once been.

"I don't want to shoot you," I called as he waded toward us. "Please, don't make me do this. Just go away, and we won't hurt you."

"Toma, you can't talk this one down," Vanya shouted as Mikhail lurched into a sitting position, coughing and spitting up muddy water. "It's not human."

"You *were* a person once," I insisted, talking faster now, propelled by the same desperate urge that had once led me to search for my mother in every ruined building and hollow, as though, if I looked hard enough, she would return to me alive and well. "I know you can understand me. I know you're listening. Please, I don't want to fight you."

The water spirit hesitated. His webbed fingers strayed to the scale-encrusted scars twisting down his belly, the memory of disembowelment.

His lips puckered around a sound, a word even, but all that came out was a low, plaintive groan. In his gaze, I caught a trace of anger flanked by the deepest sorrow. Turning away from us, he retreated beneath the surface, swimming upstream and leaving in his wake a trail of ripples.

"By Voserka," Vanya whispered, staring at me. "How did you do that?"

I shook my head, my fingers straying to the rushnyk around my waist. "It wasn't me."

Once more, my mother's keepsake had protected me. I could feel it in my heart.

"You okay, Mikhail?" I asked, turning to him as he wiped the mud from his face with the back of his hand.

"I thought it was a man," Mikhail croaked, his features

stricken. "I don't know what I was thinking. I just…I was just trying to help him."

His body trembled uncontrollably. When I reached out to place a hand on his forearm, he slapped it away hard enough to sting my fingers. I recoiled in surprise.

"I'll admit, Tsarushka, that wasn't exactly how I envisioned our first kiss," Vanya said with a strained laugh, and Mikhail shot him a look sharp enough to draw blood.

"Go jump in the pond, Ivan," Mikhail snarled, staggering to his feet. "I'm sure the vodyanoy will give you plenty."

"Wait, you shouldn't get up—" I began.

"Thank you for your concern, Toma, but I'm fine." Without even waiting for us to rise to our feet, Mikhail strode from the clearing, leaving a drizzle of mud and water in his wake.

Vanya and I exchanged a look before picking up our guns and hurrying after him.

"You shouldn't have said that," I said, shaking out my damp hair. My body trembled from the cold, and with each step I took, water squelched between my toes. "You just made things worse."

"I can't help it, Toma," Vanya insisted. "When I get scared, my mouth develops a mind of its own."

By the time we returned to the roadside, Mikhail had wrapped a blanket around himself and was glowering at the ashen remnants of the campfire.

"We'd better get the fire going before I freeze my—" Vanya chuckled awkwardly. "My feet off. Toss me the matchbox from my pack, will you, Tsar?"

"Get it yourself, Ivan," Mikhail said without looking up.

"Or better yet, don't. If we're lucky, maybe you'll freeze your tongue off, too."

"I've got it," I said. After gathering a few handfuls of dry golden grass to feed the dying embers, I rasped the sharp edge of my flint along my fire-steel's curved length. Sparks flew onto the tinder, and with a few soft breaths, I coaxed a flame to life.

It made me feel good to be able to do this for them. Vanya and Mikhail weren't my family like the upyri were, but I felt like I had the potential to hold us together just the same. Or at least keep Vanya and Mikhail from going for each other's throats.

Vanya returned to the campfire with two more blankets.

"You need to take off your clothes," I told Mikhail, who was shivering miserably beneath his own blanket.

"Excuse me?" he said in disbelief.

"You'll never get warm with your wet clothes on," I explained.

"She has a point," Vanya said, handing one of the blankets to me.

For a long moment, Mikhail just stared at us. Then he huffed and rose to his feet, retreating behind a nearby tree to change in private. When he returned, he had the blanket wrapped around himself. He cast his drenched clothes over a log by the fire and settled down once more.

My buckskin coat, skirt, and blouse were soaked through entirely. Not to mention my shoes. While Vanya stripped out of his pants and boots beneath his blanket, I found privacy in the bushes and did the same. It was strange, knowing that if I had been among upyri, I wouldn't have felt the need to hide my body. But there were different rules out here, even this far from civilization.

Across the fire, Mikhail drew the blanket tighter around himself. His hand strayed to his throat, fingers slowly closing and opening, closing and opening.

"Mikhail, did you once have a necklace?" I asked, eating a heel of bread left over from our dinner. The blanket's voluminous folds of wool enveloped me.

He blinked and looked up. "What?"

I mimicked the motion.

"Good eye." He gave a small chuckle, running a hand through his dripping hair. "It was a triptych icon of the Three Sisters in gold and niello."

"Did you lose it during the crash?"

He shook his head. "No, it was taken from me before that. When I was first captured. I guess Koschei likes his trinkets."

"You know what?" Vanya perked up suddenly. "You're right, Tsar."

"About what?" Mikhail studied him warily. "You mean jumping in the pond?"

"No. That bread was like chewing on sawdust. Let's see what I have here. I know it's around here somewhere."

Leaning forward, he scrounged through his pack. At last, he drew a colorful dented tin from the bottom of the sack and hoisted it victoriously. "Chocolates all the way from Svet! Annushka got two from a traveling merchant and gave me one as a gift."

"I can't believe you brought that on the trip with us instead of something useful," Mikhail said.

"What? And leave it back home for the rats to eat?" He

pried off the lid with the tip of his knife and groaned. "No. They're all melted. Wait—" he popped one in his mouth "—they still taste good."

A stifled chuckle came from the other side of the camp-fire. Mikhail caught himself before it could turn into a full-blown laugh, and he shook his head with a thin smile. "You're such an idiot."

"Luckily, it takes one to know one." Vanya offered a choc-olate to me, but I held my towel shut with one hand and had the other filled with bread. As I searched for a place to put my food, he laughed and raised the candy to my lips. "Here, just try it."

I couldn't remember the last time I'd eaten chocolate. In my childhood among the living, it had been a precious deli-cacy only doled out on saint days. There had been nothing as sweet in the wilds, except for honey gained through smoke-charred lungs and throbbing bee stings, and the rare wild beet.

I held the chocolate in my mouth until it melted away, sa-voring its richness. Galina wouldn't have been able to enjoy it, but she would have loved the tin's ornate embossing. Maybe once we saved her, I would ask Vanya if she could have it.

"What do you think?" Vanya asked.

"Delicious."

He took a piece of chocolate for himself and passed the tin to Mikhail.

"I'm not hungry—" Mikhail began, and Vanya chuckled.

"Don't tell me you want me to feed you too?"

With a disgruntled look, Mikhail accepted the tin. "You know, I'm beginning to realize why you were going to be executed as a koldun."

"If it hadn't been witchcraft, it would have probably been my wonderful sense of humor. Some people just can't appreciate it."

We all laughed, but soon it died down into a calm, comfortable silence that even the memory of the vodyanoy couldn't shake. I leaned against Vanya, not even thinking about it, watching the fire's glow snake across his hands. And for the first time since leaving my home, I felt safe and warm.

17

Once our clothes had dried off enough to change back into them, we rode for another hour through darkness until the river was just a memory. We set up camp at the top of a low hill, but not before walking a perimeter around the area, alert for vodyanye and other wandering spirits.

Back home, I would've been comfortable setting up camp in the forest, but here it was different—this land felt hostile to me, and not just because of the encounter with the vodyanoy. I was an outsider. This was not my home, not my conflict, not my country.

It was decided that we would sleep in three-hour shifts, one awake at all times to stoke the fire and pace the outskirts. We drew twigs to see who would go first, and when Mikhail got the short one, I snapped mine in my hand. Out of all of us, he needed the most rest, and I could tell by the way he glanced warily into the woods and traced the bruises the vodyanoy had raised on his wrists that he wouldn't escape from the memory of the water spirit anytime soon.

"I can stay up with you," Vanya offered, but I shook my head.

"You need your rest, too," I said.

"Oh." He turned away, sounding almost disappointed. As he settled onto his bedroll, I felt a pang of regret.

During my watch, the only thing I encountered was an owl who alit upon a branch and regarded me for a long moment with its lantern-bright eyes before scarfing down the rat snared in its beak. The bald coil of a tail snaked down its throat; droplets of blood plopped to the forest floor. Even after the owl had vanished into the night, I thought I could hear its wings cutting through the air overhead, slowly circling through the outer darkness.

When it came my turn to rest, I tossed and turned atop my bedroll, grimacing each time stones prodded me through the oilcloth. I drifted off then jolted awake again, drifted off once more. After a disorienting tumble through a dream of snow-burdened trees and a flaming beast that pursued me relentlessly, sometimes on two feet and sometimes on all fours, I awoke to find the other bedrolls empty.

Groggily, I hoisted myself onto one elbow, blinking until my wobbly vision steadied. Across the clearing, Vanya squatted by the fire, poking at the embers with a stick while Mikhail paced the tree line.

"It's nothing to be ashamed of, what you felt for Aleksey," Vanya said, feeding the stick to the flames. "Nor is it disgraceful, like you say."

"You just think that because of how you were raised."

Mikhail's voice was tight with frustration and—what was that? Was that anger?

"How I was raised?" Vanya laughed. "Let's see. I was raised to speak my mind."

"Regurgitate all your thoughts, more like it."

"I was raised to be proud of my identity, even if it means being hated for it. I was raised to love all aspects of myself, irrevocably. Can you say the same, Tsarushka?"

Slowly, I sank back against my bedroll. I wanted to join in their conversation, even though I knew that I'd have nothing to say. I'd just sit back in silence, wishing desperately to have a part to add. To be a part of their world. Even now, I could only vaguely grasp at what Vanya was implying.

Still, there was some comfort in just being here with them, close enough to hear their voices and the shifting of their bodies. And to know I was not alone in being scared to confront parts of myself I'd kept buried all along.

"Quit 'Tsarushka'-ing me," Mikhail said in exasperation.

"Your Highness, then," Vanya said pleasantly. "If I may be so bold, here is how I see it: if you can't accept who you are and who you love, you will live and die alone. Resenting yourself."

Despite our precautions, the next morning I found footprints in the soil around our camp. Slim, high-arched feet with delicate toes, as if a woman had circled around us while we slept. Near where the boys had rested, the footprints were the most numerous, and there was more than one pair. I got the shivers just looking at them.

"Damn mavki," Mikhail muttered, blotting out the foot-prints beneath his boot heel.

Scanning the foggy forest, I thought I saw staring faces. Upon closer inspection, they proved to be only the trunks of moss-speckled aspens.

I rubbed my arms, unsettled. I hadn't noticed it the night before, but we had set up camp near an alder grove. Bad luck.

"I don't like this," I said. "There's something wrong here."

"I never would have guessed," Vanya said dryly, retrieving his mink fur hat from the forest floor. After one day on the road, his thick burgundy hair was matted in the shape of his ushanka. He ran his hands through his unkempt curls, grimacing. "Ugh. It always gets like this before it rains."

"I know how that feels." I rubbed my own hair, which was well on its way to becoming a tangled disaster.

We hurriedly ate breakfast and continued on our way. Even as we left the alder grove behind us, the food settled in my stomach like mortar.

We spent the first hour in silence punctuated only by bird-song, the rustling of leaves, and the gurgle of a nearby stream. A carpet of golden larch needles crunched beneath our horses' hooves, adding to the forest's symphony. Slowly, my unease faded.

I enjoyed watching the two boys ride. Vanya rode with an innate, relaxed grace, and never had to give more than a gentle tug on the reins or a single tap of his heel. On the other hand, Mikhail's pose was far more refined, his back as straight as a rifle barrel, his gaze always ahead. He handled the reins firmly, shifting his weight and testing his stallion's flank to maneuver the animal completely. I envied him for his ease and control—each time my horse stumbled or broke into a trot, I felt like I was going to be thrown off.

Vanya fell into place beside me. We rode so close, he could have reached over and touched me if he'd wanted to, tracing his hand over my thigh or arm. I wished he would. I wondered if Mikhail felt the same way about Vanya, but the prospect didn't bother me any more than the confession I had overheard the night before. It just seemed like a part of the natural order, no different than the laws of gravity that kept us tethered to the soil.

Around midday, the forest began to thin, showing signs of logging. Squinting through the fog, I spotted the broken remnants of an ancient defensive wall, and beyond it, the rooftops of houses.

"Are we getting close to Detskaya?" I asked. "Is that it?"

Vanya rode up beside me. "No, that's a town called—well, you imperials call it Kraylesa. There used to be a little railway station here, but it was shelled during the war with Groznaya and never rebuilt. It's been a year or two since I've gone this way. Last time I was here, there was a cook at the bathhouse who made some delicious cheese blinis. I hope she's still working there. I'm starving, and I hate to break it to you two, but we all smell like horseshit."

As we passed through the crumbling archway of the town gates, the horses shifted restlessly. Doors slammed shut as we neared, and the townsfolk who remained turned to watch us pass.

"Are people always this unfriendly here?" I gave a nervous laugh, hoping to coax out Vanya's reassuring humor.

Instead, a trace of worry darkened his eyes to malachite,

and he remained silent as he rode past. His only response was to shift his reins to one hand so that he could unbuckle his rifle's leather scabbard.

Talismans carved from protective birch and aspen hung on many of the doors, and bundles of berry-laden rowan branches and wild garlic bunches were tied to eaves and shutters with red string.

Something had happened here. Something terrible. There were no signs of outward destruction, but I could feel it in the air, a cloying presence that weighed down on me from all sides. What did the people here feel such a need to protect themselves from?

As we passed a tavern, my gaze strayed to a pair of men sitting outside, drawn to the garishness of their double-breasted greatcoats, with two sets of brass buttons running down the front and fabric dyed so heavily with madder that its color resembled raw liver. An uncontrollable shiver passed through me as I caught sight of the badges on their caps—a breaking wheel in gilt and red enamel.

"Lovely, the Tribunal is here," Vanya muttered, turning his face away. "I suppose even the Fraktsiya needs their protection."

One of the men turned to watch us pass. Underneath his cap's leather brim, his eyes were a frosty and unforgiving blue, at contrast with his baby-smooth complexion and mild, chinless features. Even after we had left the two far behind us, it was as though I could feel that gaze tracing over the back of my neck, searching.

The Tribunal had been deeply feared and revered in my town, but compared to the warring factions, their power was strictly provincial. To the Fraktsiya, I imagined they were viewed as a necessary service for the empire to function, no different than fire brigades or the city watch.

"The bathhouse is just this way," Vanya said as we passed through the courtyard of a crumbling keep.

"I don't think we should stop for a bath, Ivan." Mikhail tugged at his coat collar, eying the dark windows warily. "Or even a bite to eat."

I rode up alongside the two. "I have to agree with Mikhail. Washing up can wait until Detskaya. Besides, we still have enough grain left for porridge, and if it comes down to it, I know how to make a delicious roasted squirrel. Let's just keep riding."

It wasn't just the town's silence that put me on edge. The Holy Tribunal disturbed me, too. There had been a sect in my village. During prayer, they took the seats of honor at the same Troika temple where my great-grandmother had served as priestess—rows of stern-faced men in crimson frocks embroidered upon the shoulders and back with a breaking wheel, the symbol of their devotion to wiping out all evils. I remembered looking up at them during the services from their straight-back chairs on the second-floor balcony, and how they would peer down, cold and distant.

"We're going to the bathhouse," Vanya said, his voice oddly flat and off-key. His grip had tightened around the reins, and when he shifted in his saddle to scan the crossroads, I caught it in his eyes—a shadow of dread rising from their emerald depths.

Kraylesa was on the road from Detskaya. Now that we were out of the mountains, it was likely the same route the Otzvuk troops had taken upon fleeing the city, before marching to sow blood in Vanya's hometown of Kupalo.

A sick nausea grew in my stomach. And if the Holy Tribunal was here…

We crossed a bridge built over a dry canal and found ourselves in a part of Kraylesa still enclosed within a segment of its defensive wall—the narrow two-story structures built precariously into the soot-blackened limestone. The signs propped in windows and hanging over doors were inscribed with Strannitsky's flowing script, the letters all circles or interlocking lines with flame-shaped terminals.

"Are you really that desperate for pancakes?" I asked in an attempt to make Vanya smile and was about to say more when we entered a market square. At this time of day, the area should have been bustling with life, but the only loiterers aside from the masses of crows were a Strannik couple sitting under the shadow of an ancient oak growing in the square's center. One slept with an axe resting across his thighs. The other rose as we approached, her short field cloak shifting to reveal a pair of hunting knives strapped to her belt.

Long, dark silhouettes hung from the oak tree's lower branches. At first, I thought discarded clothes had been strung up to scare away the crows. As we neared, the shapes' true nature became apparent to me. Soiled black tunics whose goldwork lay tarnished beneath a liver-toned patina of filth and dried blood, naked ankles bound together.

Horrified, I squeezed my eyes shut. The reins nipped into my palms as I clenched down hard, trying to escape from the agonized faces and bulging eyes that assaulted my mind.

Two of the bodies hanging from the trees were men, but

the other three were women. One girl appeared even younger than we were, her face bloated and purple with gangrene.

Coming to a stop beside me, Mikhail stared up at the corpses, his jaw slack with shock and his eyes dazed.

"Who are they?" he asked, looking from Vanya to me, although neither of us could have given him an answer.

"Kolduny," the woman said blandly, her accent so thick it took me a moment to recognize the word.

"By whose decree?" Vanya spoke in the common tongue, likely for our benefit.

"Sudrekht."

"The Holy Tribunal, she says." Vanya's lips rose in a mirthless, bitter smile. "Of course. Even in the middle of a civil war, the imperial courts never fail. Very effective system, no?"

Mikhail's jaw tightened as Vanya looked at him for validation. "I had no part in this," he hissed. "The Tribunal is under the Ministry of Heritage's jurisdiction, not the crown's."

"Yes, and the upyr rots from the head down."

It was just a saying, one even my birth mother had used, but it left a sinking weight in my stomach anyway. Under the shadow of the hanging tree, I felt a growing sense of disquiet, as if Vanya had predicted the future soon to come.

"Let's go," Mikhail muttered, steering his horse away.

"They are kolduny," the woman said as the boys turned to leave, her voice rising in defiance, "and our neighbors, and our sisters."

Her eyes flared as I met them. She knew we were strangers, that we didn't belong here, but she needed to say this. To leave her mark and remind us of the dead's.

Vanya rode across the market square and didn't look back,

but I found myself still immobile, gaze lifted to the hanging tree. *Sudrekht.* The Holy Tribunal. A memory circled around the edge of my consciousness with the slow, malevolent prowl of a lynx—*my mother bending over the porcelain washing basin, scrubbing at her hands until a pink cloud spread through the water. She turned around and stared at me, her nostrils flared and urgent breaths pushing from her lungs.*

"What are you waiting for?" She seized me by the shoulders. "Don't just stand there, Tomochka. Get your coat on."

"Are you hurt?"

"No, love. No. Not me." Tears welled in her eyes, and her grip tightened. Bloodied water dripped down my arms. "Someday, you will understand all that we sacrifice for the ones we love."

I flinched, stirred back into the present by Mikhail's voice.

"Aren't you coming?" he asked, looking back from the other end of the courtyard.

"Y-yeah." I lightly tapped my foot against my horse's flank, catching up to Mikhail and Vanya.

As we turned down a winding alleyway, I avoided glancing back, unable to shake the conviction that if I looked over my shoulder, one of the women's swaying bodies would turn slowly, slowly, until those distorted features revealed themselves to be my own.

18

Steam snaked across the bath's surface like a nest of silver serpents, coiling sinuously and ever moving, before rising to the vaulted ceiling in a humid haze. Kicking back, I soaked up to my neck in the water, resting my back against the pool's stone border to ease my aching muscles.

For years now, I had drawn my bathwater from the well and heated it on the stove, filling the old copper tub bucket-by-bucket until there was just enough for me to sit in. When I had the fever chills, I'd lay atop the masonry stove or shuffle out to the dilapidated banya raised against our house's southern wall—a wooden sweat-shack with walls blackened from smoke, so neglected that over the years, its residential bannik had withered into a scraggily-haired husk glowering from beneath the benches, all splintered claws and eroded teeth.

The bathhouse Vanya brought us to was beyond comparison. Housed in a centuries-old building across the street from the Strannik temple, its pipes were fed by the hot water springs that merged downstream with the Vesna. With its steam baths and tearoom, the experience was a luxury fit for royalty next to my typical rituals, and all for just forty grevka a person.

Rolling my shoulders to work out the knots, I leaned my head back and breathed in the steam until it felt as though my lungs themselves were sweating out their impurities. The scents of myrtle grass, birch tar, and amber resin hung in the air, joined by the aroma of crushed pine needles. In the corner, an offering of fresh fir trimmings had been left for the bannik I'd heard muttering from the pall of steam when I'd first entered, his well-oiled claws scratching across the tiles.

I felt a vague guilt knowing that Galina was still out there alone, and I was sitting here soaking blissfully. But Vanya was right—we all needed a bath. When the attendant had plucked my clothes up by her fingertips, dust and dead leaves had sifted to the ground from the garments' folds. No doubt, we'd be denied entry at Detskaya's gates for violating the laws of common decency.

As I soaked, I allowed my thoughts to wander, but all I could think about was what we had just witnessed. The hanging tree roused something in my memory, a vague and troubling sense that I had seen the same exact moment before, sometime far in the past. The corpses dangling from the branches, the guards in black waiting to cut them down if they returned, and of course, the Tribunal in their crimson frocks and greatcoats.

Stifled laughter came from nearby. On the verge of drifting off, I cracked open my eyes reluctantly. The only other patrons at this odd hour were two girls my age or slightly older, resting languidly at the bath's edge with their dark hair spilling across the water like twin oil spills. Both watched me with suppressed smiles.

"*Tza slovanakh,*" the hazel-eyed one muttered, and my cheeks prickled. Something told me she wasn't exactly lauding me with compliments.

The other nodded and pinched her nose. "*Prahvekht.*"

"Do you have something you want to say?" I snarled.

Their smiles slipped from their lips in an instant. Retreating to the other end of the pool, they regarded me with furrowed brows and tight mouths, their expressions cold and brooding. Somehow, their wary glowers stung even harsher than their mockery. They knew I didn't belong here now.

With my cheeks scalding in mortification and anger, I rose to my feet and tugged the linen wrap around myself. As I padded across the marble floor, one made a sound like the nickering of a mare. *That* meaning was abundantly clear.

The men's bath was separated from the women's by a high stone barrier with keyhole-shaped embrasures where the wall met the ceiling, so that I could hear the boys' indistinct voices, but I couldn't see them. Easing open the door leading from the women's bath, I followed the corridor along until I came to another identical door and strode inside without hesitation.

At this hour, the men's section was mostly unoccupied. Aside from Vanya and Mikhail, the only other bather was a burly man who froze at the sight of me and fled as though afraid I'd spoil him, clutching his towel around himself as he pushed through the door.

Mikhail and Vanya sat on submerged ledges at separate ends of the bath, no doubt enjoying the hot water just as much as I had. They turned as I approached.

"Toma, what are you doing in here?" Mikhail sputtered, grabbing his own towel from the floor and yanking it into the water.

Vanya's reaction was just as absurd. He sloshed deeper into the pool and turned his back to me, hands shielding himself as he yelled at me not to look.

"I can't even see anything!" The water was so murky with minerals that everything below the surface was reduced to a pale blur. But his torso was exposed, and I found my gaze lingering on the smooth, lithe muscularity of his back, following the trough of his spine up to where his damp hair coursed over his nape, slick and the deepest maroon, like a partial decapitation.

A long, narrow scratch arched from his left shoulder blade downward, so fresh that ruby droplets welled to the surface. I wondered if the same dour attendant who had tortured me with a scourge of birch leaves, her kneading knuckles, and handfuls of anise-scented sea salt had also thrashed him hard enough to draw blood.

"Vanya, how'd you get that scratch?" I asked.

"The idiot tried having the bannik read his fortune," Mikhail said dryly, but I caught a hint of worry in his voice. Being clawed by a bathhouse spirit was never a good omen.

"Forget about the bannik. Toma, you're going to get us kicked out." Vanya hastily waved a hand in the direction of the door. "Go back to your own. This isn't a mixed bath."

"I won't bathe then." I sat at the pool's edge, dipping my legs in the water but keeping my towel wrapped around myself. "I'll just sit."

"What's wrong with the women's bath?" Mikhail asked,

still pressing his drenched towel over his lap. He had left his bandages on, and the lowest fold of gauze drooped in the water. I could just barely make out my crimson embroidery against his chest's mottled bruising.

"There's nothing wrong with the bath." I flushed, embarrassed to even say it. "All right, the girls there laughed at me. And one said, *'Tza slovanakh.'* What does that even mean?"

Slowly, Vanya turned back around, staring down at the water. "Um, that you smell a little...ripe."

My mouth twitched as I recalled the other girl's neigh. So, it meant that not only did I stink, but that I stank like a horse. Lovely.

"But don't worry," Vanya added quickly, glancing up just for a moment. "We all do after two days on the road. I mean, even Tsarushka here isn't exactly pissing perfume."

Mikhail shot him a disgruntled look.

I sighed. "You're not helping. You're supposed to say something nice, like tell me I don't smell like horses."

"All right, how about this?" Although a blush lingered on his cheeks, Vanya smiled easily as he lifted his gaze from the water. "You have beautiful hair. It's dark in the shadows, but when the sunlight catches it just right, it glows like embers. And you can tell from your eyes that you're kind. And your skin..."

As Vanya's gaze lowered from my face, his smile faltered.

Across the pool, Mikhail stared at me, looking stricken. "Toma, what..."

I stared down at the parts of me the flax cloth failed to hide, and all in a brutal instant, I saw myself through their eyes—the old burn scar encircling my upper arm like a grasping hand; the pale, raised scars scoured across my limbs from years of hunting prey through thickets and thornbushes; fresh scabs, and a patina of bruises atop older bruises, and the livid suckling of ticks and leeches.

Vanya cleared his throat. "Your skin—"

"It's not bad, truly it's not bad," Mikhail added, but I was already turning away.

I didn't want to hear the lies they were going to say. I didn't want Vanya to tell me that my skin was beautiful, when he had not a blemish to mark his own ivory complexion, as if all the harm the world poured out on him did not linger.

As I rose from the ledge, warm fingers locked around my wrist. I looked back.

"Your skin shows just how strong you are, Toma," Vanya finished, smiling at me sadly. "It shows that you survived."

19

Long after we had left Kraylesa behind us, I lingered over Vanya's words. He and Mikhail might not see it the same way, but if scars were proof of one's survival, then so was monstrosity. And there was beauty and power to be found in that—becoming something different, something not just capable of surviving the agony that took you from this world but paying it back threefold.

As our shadows lengthened across the cobblestone road, the first glint of Detskaya appeared in the valley below—a soot-stained sprawl of rising stone towers and temples crested with slate-shingled onion domes, with the Vesna River coiled along its length like a black eel.

Vanya pointed out Szternova Company to us. Located at the city's outskirts, the textile factory loomed along the riverbank, its brick pipes and iron scaffolding tearing open the skyline.

"Inga served with my father in the imperial army," Vanya

said as we trailed down the road. "I suppose some of her loyalty must remain there."

"What do you mean?" I asked.

"A few months ago, when the tensions were starting to rise in my village, the Old Quarter's council asked her to lobby the Otzvuk commanders in Detskaya to issue a statement affirming their support for all of the empire's citizens, including Stranniki. It could have prevented what happened a few days ago. Instead, she refused. Two weeks later, the first poster appeared in my village, accusing us of witchcraft and blasphemy." Vanya's hands tightened around his horse's reins as the words left his mouth in a growl. "All this time, she's been using our labor to provide uniforms for their army, and she won't even lift a finger to help her own people."

"Do you think she might be able to make contact with the Otzvuk leadership still?" Mikhail asked.

"Why?" Vanya said flatly. "Looking to hang more kolduny?"

I drew in a sharp breath, and Mikhail came to a halt alongside the road. There was a genuine edge of anger in Vanya's voice, resentment even, and I realized then that all this time it had been brewing beneath the surface, festering from the moment we passed under the shadow of the hanging tree.

Vanya kept on riding. He looked back after several steps. "What are you two waiting for?"

"What did you just say?" Mikhail said tightly, through gritted teeth.

"You heard me."

"Hey, let's just keep going." I tried to keep my voice light, but by the moment, I could sense the tension rising. Not good. Desperately, I racked my brain for something to add.

"As I told you earlier, the Tribunal is under the authority of the Ministry of Heritage, as per the Blasphemy Act. It's been that way for a hundred years. Every person accused of witchcraft is entitled to a fair trial."

I gave a nervous laugh. "I don't know about you two, but I can't wait to sleep in a real bed toni—"

"Except, that isn't quite how it works, is it, Mikhail?" Vanya said, wheeling his horse around to face us. "I'm curious, what percentage of accused kolduny are Strannik?"

Mikhail's features darkened. "What exactly are you implying, Ivan?"

"What percentage?"

"I imagine," Mikhail said levelly, "that it is the same percentage as the total population. In the Edge, just over seven percent."

"You imagine? So, you don't know."

Mikhail didn't answer, his face stricken.

"How about the percentage of blasphemy cases?" With each second, Vanya's voice rose. "Or the percentage of condemned? Well?"

"Vanya, stop!" I said, and he flinched, looking at me as though he'd forgotten I was even there. "You can't just blame—"

"He's right, Toma," Mikhail said quietly, coming up alongside me. "The truth is, I don't know, and until now, I didn't care. I never asked to be tsar. Never wanted to be. After my father died, I thought that if I just listened to my advisors, everything would be okay, but it isn't, and I'm sorry."

"Apologizing won't resurrect the dead," Vanya said.

"I can't change the past, but I can promise you both this,"

Mikhail said, looking from Vanya to me. His face hardened in resolve. "Once we kill Koschei, once we end this war, I'll revoke all discriminatory laws against minorities and disband the Tribunal. I'll take power away from the nobility and give it to the common people, and you, Ivan, I'll pardon you. You'll be able to go home."

The anger drained from Vanya's face. Exhaling slowly, he turned away. "Kupalo will never be my home again, Mikhail. I'm beginning to think it never was in the first place... But thank you."

With its exposed brick walls and windows as narrow as castle arrow-slits, the lobby of Stzernova Company had all the aesthetic of a prison cell. Vanya had stretched out in one of the chairs the moment we entered, but a nervous energy kept me pacing and glancing repeatedly at the double doors.

If Inga had once provided uniforms for the Otzvuk, her clientele appeared to have shifted in the months since Kupalo's Strannik counsel had requested her aid. Two Fraktsiya guards had been posted outside her factory's doors, and yet more milled around the factory's loading bay, stacking crates onto a waiting wagon. We had been forced to leave Mikhail at the forest's edge with our weapons and supplies and continue ahead with his horse roped to my own.

Maybe it was the grinding purr of steam-powered engines, or the questions Vanya's accusations had put into my head, or the fact that each moment, Galina's captors were straying farther and farther away from us, but I couldn't sit still. Standing didn't help, only made the wait slightly more tolerable.

"You look suspicious when you pace like that, Toma," Vanya said as I began my third circuit around the room.

"You should be, too, considering who's waiting just outside," I hissed.

"Relax. I suspect the Fraktsiya didn't give her much choice in who she makes uniforms for."

I flinched as the door at the other end of the lobby swung open, expecting Fraktsiya soldiers to flood the room.

A brown-haired woman stepped out, regarding us levelly. "Inga Elenovna will see you now."

Vanya rose to his feet. "You might as well come, too, Toma."

The woman led us down the hallway and into a spacious office backlit by two arched windows. Luxurious rosewood furniture occupied the space, and the walls were hung with gilt frames containing swathes of Strannik goldwork.

Behind the malachite-topped desk sat a tall, imposing woman wearing an elegantly tailored dress suit. As we entered, she regarded us with piercing blue eyes as pale as her hair. The bold goldwork adorning the shoulders and hemline of her black silk jacket was the only display of her heritage.

"Ivan Zoravich, I suppose you're here to return my horses?" Her low voice was clipped by the faintest trace of a Strannitsky accent, subtler than the smoky edge that colored Vanya's own words, but clearly of the same origin.

"Yes, ma'am. They're safe in your stable as we speak." Vanya gestured toward me. "This is my friend, Toma."

"Is that so?" Inga's gaze shifted to me. A faint scar snaked down the right side of her face, hooking beneath her angu-

lar jawline. I offered her a small smile, and though she didn't
return it, she dipped her chin in acknowledgment.

"How was your journey?" she asked, turning her attention back to Vanya.

"Oh. I'll tell you all about it, beginning with what we just
saw in Kraylesa." Vanya glanced at me. "But first, may we
continue this conversation in Strannitsky, ma'am?"

She nodded.

Vanya sat down in the chair in front of Inga's desk, folded
his hands in his lap, and began speaking in a subdued murmur. At first, his demeanor was calm and polite. But his
voice quickly lost its natural inflection, growing in volume
and harshness until his words shot out as rapidly as gunfire.

I had thought that he'd exhausted his anger on the road
from Kraylesa, but now I realized that it went much deeper.
There was so much I didn't know about him, so much he
kept buried even as he remained honest to a fault.

Slowly, Inga's expression changed. A muscle ticked in one
corner of her mouth, and she stopped fiddling with the ink-
well to fold her hands on the desk. Her knuckles tightened,
blanching white. Once, her pale gaze shifted to me, but in
all other instances it remained fixed on a distant point above
Vanya's head.

Even though I couldn't understand his language, I knew
what he was talking about. Second by second, he took a blind
step back down that muddy road, retreating into the hanging tree's shadow.

"You just stood back and did nothing," Vanya snarled, re-
verting back to the common tongue as fluidly as he had transi-
tioned to Strannitsky. His fingers grasped onto the chair arms,
twigs sprouting from the carved wood, buds bursting into white

bloom. "You say you had no choice, but you could have refused to work with the Otzvuk. You could have done *something*. Instead, you waited, and because of that, the Old Quarter burned. And do you want to know what happened in Kraylesa?"

"Stop," Inga said quietly as roots grew wormlike from the chair legs, twining down and burying into the exquisite woven rug. "Ivan. Ivan Zoravich. Vanya. Stop."

"No, you need to hear this. As a Strannik, it is your duty to hear this. You can't pretend it's not happening—"

Inga slammed her fist into the desktop, causing the brass lamp to topple over upon the typewriter with the loud *ding* of a bell. "I said stop!"

Vanya flinched and looked down at his trembling arms, embraced by slim, willowy branches. With a low moan of surprise, he ripped a hand free and tore at the twigs and leaves, exposing splotches of blood where half a dozen sprigs had nipped his skin.

"That chair is nearly two hundred years old," Inga said flatly, righting her lamp. "It's hand-carved cherrywood."

Rising to his feet, Vanya cleared his throat and rubbed absently at the scratches, as if thorns remained embedded beneath his skin. "I don't know what came over me."

"I suppose it adds a rather…rustic charm to it." Inga sighed, drumming her fingers on the desk. Her gaze remained distant, focused on the wall behind us. "A rather rustic charm indeed. You should know before making such baseless accusations that I did reach out to the general of the Western Provence Volunteer Army, the Otzvuk faction that was stationed here. Whether at the top or by his subordinates in Kupalo and Kraylesa, it appears my request was ignored. I made a choice. I chose to continue to keep my family's legacy afloat and prevent my workers from starving on the streets."

"I'm sorry, ma'am," Vanya muttered, looking at the floor.

"Apology accepted." A thin smile touched her lips. "I suppose I can expect no less from you. You are foolish and headstrong, just like your father."

I found myself still fixated on the chair. Its wooden arms weren't the only thing that Vanya's magic had affected; sooty cow's fur had grown in patches atop the leather upholstery, as if, for only a moment, he had bridged the boundary between life and death.

I took a tentative step toward the chair. Sweat beaded on the leather. The tufted upholstery swelled shallowly in inhalation, once, twice, before stilling.

Vanya hadn't lied to me when he said he could make plants grow, but I suspected that was only half of the truth. This wasn't just accelerating the growth of something. It was bringing life back. If I cut the cushion open, would there be pulsing guts nestled among the stuffing?

Inga steepled her hands on the desk. "Now, on the topic of travel passes and false papers... I won't ask why you need them or where you're going—I am aware of the blood you spilled in Kupalo—but I do know someone who can provide them. Give me the information you need on the forms."

Vanya stepped up to the desk, took Inga's fountain pen, and wrote on a notebook page. He glanced over at me. "How tall do you suppose Mikhail is? And how much does he weigh?"

"I don't know."

"Right." Vanya sighed and jotted down a few more symbols. "And you?"

"I don't know," I repeated sheepishly.

"I'll make an estimate."

"You," Inga said suddenly, and I turned to her.

"Me?" I asked, only to realize she couldn't have meant anyone else.

"Yes. Where did you get that rushnyk?"

"It was my mother's," I said, surprised. "Why?"

She extended her hand. "Come closer. May I see it?"

As I walked up to the desk, Vanya paused to watch me. I undid the amber brooch's clasp and unwound the rushnyk from around my waist.

Inga took the cloth from my hands, tracing her fingers over its red embroidery. "These designs…"

"I don't know what they mean," I admitted.

"They're Strannik."

"What?" Vanya and I said in unison. I was certain I had misheard her, until she repeated herself.

"Strannik," she said, studying the rushnyk closely.

"That can't be," Vanya said, recovering his voice. "The thread is red and it's on linen. Besides, I've never seen a Strannik rushnyk before. It has to be Troika."

"I'm not talking about the materials or the rushnyk itself, Ivan," she said blandly. "You're correct in that both would suggest a Troika origin, but these symbols woven into the pattern are something else entirely."

"But I don't recognize them."

"That's because these are ancient wards, dating back to the time we guarded noble estates. Runes of protection that would've been engraved on our armor and embroidered into our clothes. You'll see the same carved into the beams and lintels of old temples."

If they come after you, this will protect you, Tomochka, my birth mother had said as she wrapped the rushnyk around my shoulders, snow raging in a flurry around her. *Please, always keep it with you. No matter what happens.*

"Protection against what?" My voice came out in an unsteady warble.

"It depends on the runes as much as the intent of the scribe." Inga traced her fingertips over the snare of crimson embroidery along the rushnyk's hem, twisting geometrical designs that I had always thought were simply a way to fill in the empty spaces. "Some against the Unclean Force, others to protect against natural disasters, disease, ill will, or magic."

"Magic?" I asked, startled. "You mean bogatyri?"

She nodded. "In all my years of collecting, I've only found fragments of them. Most were destroyed centuries ago in purges. But this linen is not old. Did your mother buy it from a Strannik?"

"No, she made it," I whispered.

"Toma, are you Strannik?" Vanya asked, his voice soft with wonder.

"I...I don't know." I racked my brain for a single memory that could confirm it. "We...we kept an altar to the Three Sisters, and—"

On the day the Stranniki were banished from our village, she was terrified. Do you remember? She wouldn't leave her room, not even when Father tried to comfort her.

Back then, her fear had confused and troubled me, but I had been too young to understand where it was coming from. I had never even considered that my mother might be

Strannik, and I knew for a fact that my father was not one, for his grandmother had been the priestess of our village's Troika temple. By the time I was old enough to realize that not everything was so black and white, I had just wanted to leave the past behind me. Cut my ties with the girl I had once been. I should have known that the past would always follow.

"What about healing?" I asked as Inga studied the rush-nyk. Her fingers remained poised over the embroidery, tracing it almost fondly.

She glanced up. "Pardon?"

"Are those symbols capable of healing people?"

"When I speak of protective abilities, it is merely in speculation. I have never actually attempted to test my collection." She nodded toward the shadowboxes on the wall. "And no, Ivan, this is not an invitation to try. Those specimens are even more priceless than the chair you just destroyed."

"I would do no such thing," Vanya said, clearly offended. "It's not as if I spoil everything I touch."

"The telegram from your village suggests otherwise."

"So, in the legends, the runes were never used to bring someone back to full health?" I persisted, and her steely blue eyes returned to me.

"No. During the time these runes were used, the Strazhniki would have considered healing to either be a gift bestowed by the Goddess or an act of witchcraft, depending on the circumstance. These are the exact opposite."

"What do you mean?"

"These symbols are meant to be wards against magic and human violence alike. They date to the uprising."

I frowned. If my mother's rushnyk hadn't been responsible for healing Mikhail, then what had? Could it have been something Galina had done?

"Here," Inga said, handing my rushnyk back to me. "If you happen to remember anything else, consider paying me another visit. Ancient textiles are a passion of mine."

"I will." I cradled the rushnyk in my arms, troubled by the empty spaces in my memory. They didn't just feel like holes anymore; they felt like wounds, like someone had torn pieces of my past from me.

Inga uncapped her fountain pen. On the margin of a pamphlet, she wrote a sentence in neat, efficient script. She flicked the paper across the desktop. "This is the address of a warehouse in the waterfront district. Drop by there after dark. The documents should be ready by then."

Vanya picked up the pamphlet, folded it, and slipped it into his coat pocket. "Thank you."

"Be careful," Inga said.

"We will."

"One day when this is over, we'll discuss how you'll repay me for the chair. I expect you to come back here, do you understand? I don't want to stand guard for you, Vanya."

"As tempting as it is, I'll try not to die on you, ma'am." As Vanya walked to the door, he brushed the remnants of leaves and bark from his clothes. "Come on, Toma."

"One more thing," Inga said.

Vanya turned around. "Yes, ma'am?"

Inga's blue eyes turned hard and icy. "You say that my business is part of the problem. That I've abandoned our people for greed and ambition. But what does that make you, when you possess the same weapon as the enemy?"

Vanya smiled. "The revolution."

20

The moon trembled on the water. Sour fog rolled down from the factories upstream. The Vesna River carried other evidence of the industrial processes at work behind those citadel-like brick walls—animal bones, chunks of vulcanized rubber, scraps of cloth and paper. It was nothing like the pristine waterways back home.

It was decided that Vanya would go to the dockside warehouse alone, since the wharfs abutted a Strannik neighbourhood and if he was stopped, he could simply claim to be on his way home. Besides, according to Mikhail, a group of three stood out more than a pair.

While we waited for Vanya to return, Mikhail and I milled around a small market set up by the riverfront. Fishermen sold their catches straight from their boats—writhing black river-shrimp, smelt and baby glass eels ready to be fried, entire jarfuls of pearlescent eggs harvested from the Vesna funnelfish.

Though the city had fallen under Fraktsiya control in recent weeks, that hadn't prevented Vanya from finding someone to buy Mikhail's gems after leaving Inga's factory. We had traded his rifle and my musket for three revolvers and a box of ammunition. I resented having to give up Papa's musket, but with Fraktsiya patrols roaming the streets, anyone carrying an unconcealed weapon was apt to be detained and interrogated.

After what had happened at Kupalo, it made me nervous to linger at the market. As Mikhail and I wandered past the booths, the lively chatter of the people around us abraded my nerves until I felt on the verge of jumping into the river.

"Maybe I should get a haircut," Mikhail said, when we passed a man with a sign advertising trims for three grevka.

"At that price, you'll probably end up losing a good bit of scalp, too," I pointed out.

"New clothes then." His gaze scanned over the stalls before landing on a peddler whose cart overflowed with more clothing than I'd collected in seven years of scavenging. "You could probably use some too, Toma."

I sputtered for a response, my cheeks blazing. "What's wrong with mine?"

"I'm not entirely sure they'll last the journey," he said, glancing at my threadbare skirt hem.

"You go look," I said sourly. "I'm going to see what else there is."

"Don't go far. I'd rather not have a repeat of Kupalo. And don't spend more than twenty grevka."

I fingered the coins in my pocket. Twenty grevka felt like a tsar's ransom—it was enough to buy an entire quarter of lamb, more potatoes than I could carry, or a sack of flour the size of Galina.

As Mikhail strayed to the secondhand clothing peddler, I paused to admire the foreign fruits and jars teeming with strange delicacies at a nearby food stall. I bought a rolled pastry all for myself and ate it as I scanned over the assortment of goods piled at the next stall.

Used wares, dented pots, a few trinkets here and there. Fingering Galina's bead around my wrist, I thought how much she would enjoy scrounging through the clutter of antique bottles and tarnished spoons. I turned a lead toy horse around in my hand, before a gleam of brass caught my eye at the bottom of the pile.

Cramming the rest of the poppyseed pastry in my mouth, I picked up the trifold pendant and studied the crude form cast in its paneled surface. The engravings were blackened with niello, but over the years, the dark pigment had worn away to shadows and the subjects' features had eroded. Yet despite being faceless, the forms imprinted on its three folding panels were unmistakable—the goddess Kosa with her raised reaping hook and a bundle of wheat overflowing from her left hand, Seredina with her distaff and spindle, and Voyna in all her ruthless glory, holding her sovnya at her side and her balance scales raised aloft.

"This is it," I whispered, a smile spilling across my lips. It certainly wasn't crafted by the Imperial Temple's finest goldsmith, but it was still an icon of the Three Sisters. At the very least, it would make a suitable substitute until Mikhail could reclaim his original heirloom.

After trading the man five grevka for the travel icon, I

slipped it in my pocket and made my way back to Mikhail, who was carrying a cotton worker's cap. He sniffed the fabric as I approached and made a face but slipped it on his head. Shadowed by the hat's brim, his features were strikingly sharp, unkind even. When he lowered his face from the hissing streetlamps, his silver eyes tarnished to the color of smog.

"How do I look?" he asked.

"Good." I cocked my head, studying him closely. "You know, I'm pretty sure that Papa used to have a hat like that."

His eyes narrowed. "Lovely. So, I remind you of a walking corpse now?"

"Not at all." I chuckled, although a touch offended by the term *walking corpse*. "Just the hat does."

"Well, it certainly smells like one." He tugged down on the cap's brim. "Find anything interesting?"

"Maybe." Fighting to contain my glee, I slipped the pendant from my pocket and held it out to him. For a long moment, he merely stared, looking so confused that I was afraid the icon wasn't Troika at all. Then he took it from me and opened it, tracing his finger over the engravings.

"The Three Sisters," he murmured, lifting his gaze. The chill had thawed from his eyes—he'd let his guard down, just for a moment—and all I could think was how exhausted and lonely he looked, like he'd been walking for hours alone through the dark. "Toma, did you...did you get this for me?"

I nodded. "To replace the one that was taken from you."

"Why?"

My smile slipped from my face in an instant. Heat rose in my cheeks, and my throat tightened in mortification. He didn't like it. Of course, he didn't like it. It was just a cheap icon that cost less than the blinis we had eaten at the bath-house's tearoom.

"Sorry." My voice came out very small. I reached for the icon, but he kept his fingers curled around it.

"No, no, I want it." He laughed, sounding a touch shaky. "Thank you."

"So, you don't hate it?"

"Toma, this is probably one of the most thoughtful gifts I've ever received." He paused to set his rucksack down and freed one of the thin suede strings securing his bedroll. Stringing the cord through the icon's hoop, he tied it around his neck. "Thank you. It feels just like my old one."

Minutes passed and the market began to empty. The warm feeling Mikhail's reaction had left in my stomach slowly chilled into unease. I shifted from foot to foot as the vendors locked in place the metal shades and wooden boxes securing their wares. Where was Vanya?

"What's taking him so long?" Mikhail muttered under his breath.

As I opened my mouth to answer, a hand landed on my shoulder. I swiveled around, reaching to my waist for the hunting belt hidden in my rushnyk's folds.

"Hey, don't disembowel me." Vanya pulled his hand back, offering me a smile as I loosened my hold around the knife handle. "Sorry, I didn't mean to scare you."

"Where were you?" I yanked up my rushnyk to conceal the sheath once more.

"I was waiting there forever. I never thought they'd show, and once they did, you'll never believe it! It was my friend Ilyushka from Kupalo."

"Did you get the documents?" Mikhail asked.

Vanya reached into his coat and pulled out several booklets bound in red pebbled leather. "It's all here, including travel passes to the Kosa interior. Here you go, Kazimir Nikolaevich and Tamara Nikolaevna."

As Vanya passed me one of the booklets, his fingers brushed against the side of my wrist, just for a moment, but long enough to cause a pleasant shiver to trail down my spine. I would have liked to take his hand and hold it, savor the warmth radiating from beneath his skin—proof that he was alive and human.

As Vanya slipped his own passbook into his dark brown greatcoat's breast pocket, his gaze lowered to my rushnyk. Ever since we had left the factory, he kept looking at my rushnyk, and I sensed he wanted to talk about it more. I wasn't sure what I wanted, only that the idea of talking about my past frightened me.

"These look real," Mikhail said, studying his identification papers as we made our way along the foreshore path.

"That's because they are," Vanya said. "They're made using official seals."

"How did Inga get these?" I asked.

"Uh, I don't know, but I had an idea she might know someone who could provide them. My old papers identified me as Strannik, and sometimes that's enough to get a person killed. Even wealthy Stranniki like Inga Elenovna, and especially now." His vivid green eyes flickered toward me. "If hostilities against us spiral out of control, it's good to have a way out."

Was that what my mother had wanted—a way out? A way to be someone else? She had loved my father deeply. I knew that. I could still remember it. I wondered if that was the reason for it—a love so deep, she had been willing to reshape herself.

On a brick wall ahead, a large poster fluttered in the breeze amid the torn remnants of older fliers. The poster depicted a man in a green greatcoat, breaking the chain of a shackle between his raised hands.

HELP BREAK THE CHAIN OF OPPRESSION! the poster declared in bold letters. NO BOGATYRI, NO TSARS!

I paused. "What's this about?"

Mikhail's face darkened. "It's a Fraktsiya recruitment poster."

"Who's the man?"

His jaw tightened, and he hissed out the name as though it were a curse: "Koschei."

My gaze returned to the poster. The artist had depicted Koschei with his chin raised and his gaze boring down on us, his cropped blond hair brushed back. His face was handsome but in an imposing sort of way, his cheekbones flared and his leonine eyes shadowed beneath the hard shelf of his browbone.

My jaw tightened. So, this was the enemy.

With a scoff of disgust, Mikhail grabbed the edge of the poster and ripped it through the middle. As half of Koschei's face peeled away from the brick, a water-stained corner of paper was exposed beneath it—the moldering fragments of the same face executed in black and red, his lips peeled back like a dog about to bite. Koschei had been drawn with a cruel touch, his teeth as sharp as any vodyanoy's, his ears enlarged and pointed, his bulging yellow eyes roving ravenously, and his hair blanched white. Instead of holding a chain, he squatted over a shattered outline of the Kosa Empire, tearing out bleeding chunks of the country, with one gore-drenched hand raised to his mouth as though preparing to feed.

Emblazoned across the poster were the words SAVE YOUR COUNTRY! KILL THE KOLDUN, RECLAIM THE THRONE!

"This one's Otzvuk," Vanya said. "The city was under their occupation up until two weeks ago."

As the boys continued along the foreshore path, another flyer plastered to the wall caught my eye. It was painted almost as garishly as the Otzvuk propaganda poster—a full-color ad emblazoned with a drawing of an upyr, its teeth bared and eye sockets barren. Across the bottom, the poster read:

THE HALL OF WONDERS

TRAINED RUSALKA—ANCIENT ARTIFACTS—LIVE UPYR AND MUCH MORE!

"Hey, look at this," I said to the others.

Mikhail returned to my side and studied the advertisement. "Toma, I doubt you'd find a live upyr in this city. At most, it's probably a stuffed one."

"What if it isn't?" I said, and he hesitated. "Think about it. If this person knows how to catch upyri, he probably knows how to transport them, too. He might even have sold some to Koschei."

"Let's check it out," Vanya said. "It's not as though we have anything else to do."

"Now's not exactly the time to sightsee," Mikhail said dully. "In case you haven't noticed, this entire city is crawling with Fraktsiya soldiers."

"Even more reason." Vanya nudged me in the side with a grin. "By the time we leave, they'll all be so drunk, they won't be able to tell their heads from their asses. Right, Toma?"

"Can people actually get that drunk?" I asked Mikhail as Vanya sauntered on ahead.

"I'm sure Ivan has." Mikhail rolled his eyes. "Just look at what it's done to his brain."

We turned down a cobblestone street caged in by ivy-encumbered houses and dark storefronts. The Hall of Wonders was located by the riverside, in a three-story building that had probably once been painted blue, but over the years had faded to a mottled gray. Chunks of plaster had broken free of the walls, revealing the red brick beneath like bloodied scabs. Bars curled over the ground floor's windows, and past them, a silhouette drifted across the gauzy white curtains.

As we entered, the shadow resolved itself into a lean dark-haired man in an ankle-length crimson robe fastened with a sash adorned with brass scales. Setting aside the book he'd been leafing through, he offered us a warm smile.

"Ah, visitors." His words were colored by a subtle accent that reminded me of Papa's, somewhere as far south as the Black Steppe or beyond it. "Come to see the beast tamer Emre's marvelous monsters?"

I cleared my throat. "We were actually wondering—"

"Don't believe what you've heard about Adélard's Emporium of Oddities. His so-called 'stuffed rusalka' is nothing more than half a bear cub sewn onto a Vesna funnelfish tail. Now, *my* collection of beasties, on the other hand, is a true sight to be marveled at. It is unrivaled in the empire, exceeded only by the great menagerie of Svet." He emphasized his point with a flourish of his hand. "I spent my youth traveling to distant lands, collecting oddities and rare treasures.

For just thirty grevka a person, I'll give you an experience you won't soon forget."

"Deal!" Vanya said, before holding out his hand to Mikhail.

Sighing, Mikhail took three silver coins from the stash in his coat pocket.

As soon as the coins plopped into Emre's palm, they disappeared into the leather pouch fastened to his sash belt.

"Wonderful." His accent remained, but his voice lost some of its theatrical flair. "Are you three from around here or just passing through?"

"We're traveling to the mainland," I said.

"Good thing you stopped by. Few get an opportunity to see the fabled Hall of Wonders. Now, follow me." Emre ushered us across the room and through a narrow doorway screened by a black velvet curtain.

Shelves lined the next room from floor to ceiling, and precarious display cases made a cramped maze out of the space. Leisurely, he guided us down the rows, pointing out objects of interest.

Strewn amid books and relics, specimen jars contained cloudy fluid and piecemeal remnants—a vodyanoy's webbed hand, severed at the wrist; some black, knotted husk the beast tamer claimed was the heart of an upyr; the misshapen forms of more mundane animals.

"Did you see that baby pig?" Vanya said, looking as enthralled as Galina on her treasure hunts. "It had two heads."

I shook my head. I'd felt too sickened by the upyr's heart to even notice.

"It was probably sewn on," Mikhail muttered.

Vanya turned to him, clearly aghast. "Have you no sense of wonder, Misha? Are you not entertained?"

"My idea of entertainment isn't as provincial as sideshow acts," he said dully.

"Excuse me, but when are we going to see the upyr?" I asked Emre as he paused to admire a rug he claimed was woven from rusalka hair.

"All in good time." He winked. "There's still much to see."

"It's alive, right?"

"Indeed it is."

"Did you kill the vodyanoy yourself?" Mikhail asked, tracing his fingertips over the specimen jar.

"No, I acquired it from a Grozniy sailor," he said. "The sailors believe that the teeth protect against drowning, so they hunt them at their leisure and wear the teeth on chains across their waist."

I shivered, recalling the flicker of anguished awareness that had swept over the vodyanoy's face moments before he had retreated underwater. In his previous life, he might have been a killer; he might have been a young serf plucked from the field, shoved into chain mail, and given a sword in hands more accustomed to handling a hoe. No matter who he was in his past, it seemed so cruel that such a creature could endure one bitter fate, just to fall victim to another.

"Why do you think some people come back?" I asked Emre.

"We all want to leave our mark on the world," he said as though that answered it all, before turning back ahead and continuing with our tour. Along with the remains, the Hall of Wonders had a wealth of other artifacts. An early steam engine prototype from Yezmirny. Ancient icons in enamelled bronze.

"Ah, Strannik, this will be interesting to you," Emre said, picking up a slim black blade. "Made of glass salvaged from the southern steppes. Your homeland, no?"

"Kosa is my homeland," Vanya said dryly, and Emre chuckled.

"Aren't we all strangers here?"

As the man continued on, I turned to Vanya. "What was that about?"

"I suppose my accent is a little more obvious than I thought."

As we followed Emre down the winding aisles, Vanya explained to me that the Stranniki had arrived here many centuries ago from that region, fleeing an event known only as the Great Burning. Before the disaster, they had lived in small tribes strewn along the steppes. Though those communities had long since vanished beneath plains of molten ebony sand and scorched rubble, the refugees of that crisis had brought with them their own language and interpretation of the divine, along with the tools and skill for blacksmithing. With the restrictions imposed by Tsarina Yelena on the crafting of armor and weapons, Stranniki had applied their training to tinkering and jewelry making.

"What caused it?" I asked.

"Some say it was a dragon," Emre said, smiling our way. "In Yezmirny, we believe it to be the work of what you imperials call a koldun. We won't even cross through the Steppe. To get to Kosa, we braved the rusalki and traveled upriver."

Fire to the south, ruin to the north. If the Great Burning

had been the work of a koldun, I wondered if the same witch had cursed the wilds.

"But enough about that. The rusalka is waiting." Emre led us into the next room. It was smaller than the first, only large enough to contain a towering tank of glass and brass, riveted along its sides with bolts as large as my knuckles.

The rusalka treaded water beneath the surface, her long burgundy hair streaming behind her. All of the rusalki I had seen had come bare as the day they'd been born, although they weren't uninclined to steal the clothes I hung up to dry by the riverside. I had always viewed it as a mischievous sort of game instead of any genuine desire, but this creature seemed to favor her flowing blue gown, which was adorned with seed pearls and silk ribbons. She fingered it as she drifted in the water, smoothing it down in startling modesty.

Her clothing wasn't the only unusual thing about her. Even under the lamp's sallow glow, her skin was the rich brown of burlwood, unlike the bloodless tones of the rusalki back home. I supposed that Emre had brought her with him from beyond the Black Steppe, somewhere warmer and sunnier than here.

She couldn't have been much older than us when she died. A year at most, perhaps less.

Mikhail nudged Vanya in the shoulder. "I think that's your mom."

"She's too young," Vanya muttered, but his gaze lingered on the tank. "And we look nothing alike."

"A moment of silence, please." Emre cleared his throat before continuing in a loftier tone: "Renowned for their beauty as much as their viciousness, the rusalki are rumored to seduce men to their watery graves. However, our friend here is different. She was a fair maiden before her husband grew jealous of the attention doted upon her and drowned her in the river as she was collecting flowers. Ever since then, she has been searching for the love she was denied in life."

As Emre spoke, the rusalka drifted down to the tank bottom, her limbs moving slowly. The container wasn't large enough for her to swim in, only drift from the surface to the bottom and then back again.

My stomach tightened. Somehow, this was even worse than the previous room's grisly treasures. It sickened me to think of Galina being put on display like this, not even in a cage large enough to move around in. How could people know that monsters were birthed from pain and cruelty and then subject them to more of the same?

As we stepped up to the tank, the rusalka drifted silently in the water, her plum-dark eyes studying us through tendrils of burgundy hair. Vanya reached out to lay a hand on the glass, and she mirrored the gesture on the other side. He stared at her, his lips parted in wonder.

For how often Vanya had joked about having a rusalka for a mother, it dawned on me suddenly that he believed it. Or he wanted to, because the alternative—that he would never meet the woman who had given birth to him, that she was gone from this world before he'd even had a chance to actually know her, was even more devastating than the possibility of her being alive but changed.

I understood the desire. How many times had I scanned the dark waters, praying for a glimpse of the rusalki beneath—just a look long enough to catch a familiar face peering up at me?

"Did you buy this rusalka from someone?" I asked, tearing my eyes away from the tank.

Emre blinked, looking mildly befuddled. "Uh, no. Didn't you just hear my story? She was once a fair—"

"Yes, I know, a fair maiden. But do people ever come around trying to buy or sell monsters to you? Did Koschei—"

"What our friend is trying to say here," Mikhail interrupted, fixing me with a warning look, "is that she would like to see the upyr."

The man studied me for a long moment before smiling. "Of course. Follow me."

Vanya lingered at the tank, his palm still against the glass. "You two go on ahead. I just want to stay here for a few minutes longer."

As we turned to follow Emre out, Mikhail stifled a chuckle. "What?" I asked.

"Oh, nothing." A half-suppressed smile twitched on his lips. "Let Ivan have his reunion."

Emre guided us into the next room, a dim and unwelcoming chamber lit by the glow of a single oil lamp. As we entered, a chain scraped across the floor. My eyes slowly adjusted to the room's dimness, and I caught a glimpse of a shrunken form huddled in the corner.

The upyr's body was engulfed in a tattered dress. She shrunk away as we neared, ducking her head low against her chest. She was older than Galina, but not by far. My breath caught in my throat at the sight of her.

"Behold, the fearsome upyr." Though Emre kept his bombastic tone, he sounded slightly less enthusiastic than before.

"A terrifying creature, known to feed upon human flesh and blood. Don't get too close now. She bites."

As he rapped his heel on the floor, the upyr edged against the wall, her eyes glistening deep within her sunken sockets. Her scalp was bare, but remnants of ebony hair cradled the back of her head.

"Toma," Mikhail said reaching out for me. "It's not—"

"Who are you?" I asked, sinking to my knees to show her that I was not a threat. "What's your name?"

"What are you doing?" Emre yelped. "I told you not to get close!"

The upyr scrambled forward with a howl so forceful that it should have dislocated her jaw. As the chain rattled across the floor, she tripped over its coiled links and fell into me, her arms flailing. She was heavier than I expected—still fully fleshed, no doubt—and her hot breath fanned across my face. Gasping, I reached up to push her away, and my fingers snagged onto the edge of her face and tore it clean off.

I flinched back in horror, expecting to be confronted by raw bone and the still gnashing stubs of her incisors.

A small olive-toned face peered up at me. A girl. A living, breathing girl. She pushed wisps of dark hair out of her face, grimacing as she settled cross-legged on the floor.

"Why did you get so close?" she demanded. "You are supposed to run away or start screaming."

Across the room, Emre groaned, putting a palm to his face in dismay.

"You're still alive," I stammered.

"Of course." She rolled her eyes, picking up the upyr mask

with a groan of disgust. "This thing is so gross. Why can't Pelin be the upyr for once?"

Emre extended a hand toward us. "I can explain."

"The rusalka is fake, too," Mikhail said. "I saw a similar act a few years ago. There'll be enough room at the top for her to breathe or a hidden tube attached to an air canister, like the sort used with dirigibles."

"All right, so they're both fake," Emre said quickly. "But the rest of the artifacts in the Hall of Wonders are real. Let me explain. We did have a real upyr once, but it was taken a few weeks ago by the Fraktsiya. My youngest daughter Aergul volunteered to take over until we acquired a new one."

"Taken?" I demanded, stepping forward. "Taken where?"

"Wh-what?" he stuttered.

"Where did the Fraktsiya take the upyr? Did they take her to Koschei? Answer me!"

"Toma," Mikhail said, placing his hand on my wrist. I shook his arm away and turned my attention back to Emre, who had stepped in front of Aergul and was eying me uneasily, as though I were halfway to becoming an upyr myself.

Emre lifted his palms placatingly. "All right, look—"

"You're disgusting for keeping an upyr prisoner, you know that? And for this!" I snatched up the mask and hurled it at him. "Skinning one? You do realize that they're people, don't you? That they have feelings?"

"Now listen, I don't know what's with you and upyri, but this is just calfskin," Emre said, catching the mask only to wave it in my face. "It's been bleached and painted, see? And okay, fine, I lied. We never had an upyr. Do you really think

I'd try to keep one captive in the same house as an eight-year-old?"

"I don't believe you!"

"I'm telling you the truth. In our faith, we believe that all revenants still contain a spark of holiness. Of humanity." His words held genuine sincerity. "Enslaving another human being, dead or otherwise, goes against one of our highest tenets. The greatest kindness we can give the restless dead is by returning them to their graves."

Placing his hand on my shoulder, Mikhail steered me toward the door. "Come on, let's get Ivan and go."

I huffed. "Fine."

In the other room, Vanya stood before the tank, staring mesmerized at the rusalka's slow, graceful motions. By now, she was looking rather annoyed and confused.

"Isn't she amazing?" Vanya said. "I think she can actually understand me. I've been trying to talk to her."

Taking a deep breath, I readied myself to break him the unfortunate news. "Vanya, she isn't real."

He blinked, turning to me. "What do you mean?"

"Pelin, the act is up," Aergul called. "They know."

The rusalka stopped treading water and kicked up to the top of her tank, pushing against the lid. It lifted with ease, and as Mikhail burst into laughter, Vanya turned around with an appalled look.

"You knew," he said. "I can't believe it. You knew."

"That's right," Mikhail said. "Shockingly, I can tell the difference between stage performers and genuine monsters."

"Don't tell me—" Vanya turned to Emre "—even the two-headed piglet is fake?"

He sighed. "No, that one's real."

Pelin climbed out of the tank and leapt to the floor. As she approached, a stray breeze wafted across the room, stirring the drenched coils of her hair and her dress's sodden folds. Emre gave her a sharp warning look before turning to us hastily.

"It's all sleight of hand," he said quickly, running a hand through his hair. "There's enough air on top for her to breathe between moves."

Mikhail and I exchanged a look. True, there might be no monsters here, but the same uncontrollable power I had sensed in Vanya and the other bogatyri radiated from Pelin, faint but perceptible.

"The darkness helps as well," Pelin said, her lips rising in a sardonic smirk. As she stepped under the caged electrical light, its glow revealed inky roots beneath her burgundy hair. "Although, I'll admit, for a moment there, I thought you could see through my disguise."

Vanya groaned, his blush only deepening.

"You need to understand, we didn't come to Kosa with this in mind," Emre said with a sigh. "Back in Yezmirny, I was a surgeon in the medical corps. But here, even rural doctors require a permit from the governorate, and in a city as large as Detskaya, I would need a certificate from an imperial university as well."

"Then why didn't you get one?" I asked, still a bit skeptical.

"Because he can't," Vanya said bluntly.

Startled, I looked over at him. "Why not?"

"There's a university quota in place to prevent Kosa's citizens from being displaced by foreigners," Mikhail explained, and then turned as Vanya scoffed. "Something you want to add, Ivan?"

"No, no." Vanya raised his hands. "Keep talking, Misha. Enlighten us with your grand and infinite wisdom."

"Are they always like this?" Pelin asked, glancing my way.

I rolled my eyes. "You have no idea."

"As I was about to say before Ivan interrupted me, imperial citizens fund the universities with their taxes," Mikhail said evenly, turning back to me. "It would be a drain on resources to admit foreigners."

"Call it what you will, young man. In any case, disregarding the university quota, the cap on medical permits issued to Yezmirskiy expats and Stranniki is one-tenth of a percent of each governorate's respective populations." Emre's accent still softened the hard edges of his words, but his voice took on a different tone, becoming cool and clinical. I realized he was like Vanya—stepping between the roles he was expected to play, showing only parts of himself. "So, you do the math. One doctor per every thousand Yezmirskiy expats and Kosaborn residents of Yezmirskiy descent, and these include not just surgeons, but apothecarists, dentists, and physicians."

"At first, we just showed off my father's specimens and the medical devices we brought with us," Pelin added. "But then Adélard's Emporium of Oddities opened in the waterfront district."

"After that, it became an arms race." Emre smiled dryly. "If Adélard and his so-called 'stuffed rusalka' taught me anything, it's that the reality doesn't matter as much as the idea, the *feeling*. We needed a new angle, to reinvent ourselves."

"It was my idea to bring in the rusalka act," Pelin said, with a touch of satisfaction.

"And mine to be the upyr!" Aergul piped in.

Pelin rolled her eyes and lightly nudged her sister's head. "No, it wasn't."

"I don't care whose idea it was," Vanya cut in. "I want my money back."

Emre sighed.

"All right, all right." He retrieved our coins from his leather pouch then hesitated. "You know what, forget the money. I think I can do you folks something even better. You say you're traveling? Well, do you have a place to stay yet?"

"Not yet," Mikhail said.

Emre jerked his chin upward. "We've got a spare room in the attic. It's nice, airy, and we'll throw in a free dinner too. Just as long as this act stays between us."

21

The attic proved to be a large, drafty space crammed with such an assortment of oddities that, as we headed deeper in, I was a little nervous the floor might collapse beneath our feet. There was only one cot, shoved between a precarious stack of steamer trunks and a taxidermied creature that looked eerily human.

Vanya poked the creature's snout, sending a scatter of sawdust seeping from a tear in its side. "There goes my sleep tonight. Forever, I should say."

"What is it?" I asked, studying it closer. Half the creature's face had been eaten away by mites, revealing the pale shelf of bone beneath its short brown fur.

He shrugged. "Your guess is as good as mine. A bear, maybe?"

"It's a monkey," Mikhail said, laying his knapsack on the floor.

"Is that a type of monster?" I asked.

"No, an animal. I've seen them before at the imperial menagerie."

"Can you eat them?"

Vanya shot me a horrified look. "Don't tell me this makes you hungry, Toma?"

I huffed. "I'm sorry, but back home, I didn't exactly come across freshly baked bread or Svetskiy chocolates in the wild. If I see a 'monkey' in the forest and there's nothing else to eat, it's ending up on my dinner table."

Mikhail glanced over from where he was busy dusting off the worn sofa in the corner. "They aren't native to our lands, only warmer climates beyond the Black Steppe."

"Oh." I settled onto the bed, testing it beneath my fingertips. Ah, an actual mattress instead of a bedroll. And it wasn't even straw-stuffed.

"You can take the bed, Toma." Vanya grinned. "In case you get hungry during the night."

My brow twitched. "I'm beginning to see why Mikhail doesn't like your sense of humor, Vanya."

He chuckled. "Forgive me, I couldn't resist."

Along with the cot and broken sofa, there was a leather-padded examination table that Vanya claimed as his own. He stole a pillow from the bed and rolled out his bedroll atop the lot.

"Are you sure you don't want the bed?" I asked Vanya as he settled down with a contented sigh. "You let me use yours at your apartment."

"Who needs a bed when you have this? I mean, it even has a footrest." Stretching out, he propped his feet up in the elevated stirrup-like holders at the foot of the table.

"I don't think that's a footrest," Mikhail said, looking up from untying his boots.

"Well, whatever it is then." Vanya sat up and swung his legs over the side of the table. "Anyway, the bed's all yours, Toma. If I get any closer to Mikhail, I won't be able to fall asleep."

"How so?" Mikhail asked dryly.

"I hate to break it to you, Tsarushka, but you snore in your sleep."

Mikhail scoffed. "I don't snore."

"You're noisier than a horse," Vanya said.

I laughed, because it was true.

Aghast, Mikhail turned to me. "Wait. Do I?"

"I'm afraid so," I said, once I had gotten my helpless giggling under control. "But you're not noisier than a horse. You're noisier than a train!"

Vanya burst into laughter. "Isn't he?"

"You're a terrible influence on her," Mikhail said to Vanya.

"Don't look at me." Vanya lifted his hands. "This is all Toma."

I smiled, secretly pleased that I had made them laugh. It felt like I had broken through a barrier somehow, becoming a part of their world. I wished Galina was here. She would love them too.

"You know, for the Tsar, you really ought to have some manners," Vanya teased, and was about to say more when we heard the shatter of glass.

I turned to find Aergul standing in the doorway, a tray at her feet. Broken teacups littered the floor, their contents already soaking through her wool slippers.

"S-sorry," she stammered, leaning down to gather the porcelain shards. Mikhail was on his feet in an instant, and Vanya's face had drained of color until even his lips were blanched.

"Let me help you," I said, rising to my feet. By the time I managed to make my way through the labyrinth of crates and oddities, she had already piled the teacup fragments on the tray.

"This happens all the time," she said with a nervous laugh. "Pelin says I was born with two left feet, and I think she's right. I'll be right back and get you more."

Once she had disappeared down the stairs, I turned back to the others, not realizing I'd been holding my breath until I felt it hiss between my teeth.

"Do you think she heard?" Mikhail asked gravely, his knapsack already in hand. His fingers were tucked into the pocket containing his freshly bought revolver.

"Tsar could mean anything," I said. "It could be your nickname."

"Toma's right," Vanya said, but sounded a touch uncertain. "I mean, just look at you. You hardly look like royalty."

"Do you have to turn everything into an insult?" Mikhail snapped.

Vanya raised his palms defensively. "Hey, it's not an insult this time."

"Shouldn't we stop her?" I interrupted. "You know, instead of arguing?"

Mikhail swore, pushing to his feet. "Come on, let's go."

We hurried down the stairs, leaving our belongings behind. As we entered the kitchen, Aergul hastily pulled away from where she stood by the kettle, talking to Emre.

Pelin leaned against the counter, having exchanged her

soaked costume for a fashionable fawn-brown dress like the ones I'd seen in Detskaya's boutique windows, with two sets of brass buttons running down the front and a fox-fur collar. Her eyes shifted to us, unreadable.

Emre brightened at the sight of us. "Ah, just in time. Dinner is ready. You'll have to forgive my daughter. She's always been this clumsy. That's why we gave her the upyr role."

I exchanged a look with the others, waiting for one of them to make the first move. Leaving now might be even more dangerous than staying, erasing all shadow of doubt in Emre's mind of who we were. If he notified the city guard, they'd tear up the streets in search of us.

Vanya must have thought the same, because he laughed and stepped forward. "Great, I'm starving. I'm pretty sure Toma here is, too. Even that stuffed monkey was starting to look appetizing."

I groaned inwardly. He was never going to forget that, was he?

"Fortunately for you three, I have something a bit more appetizing than that moth-bitten thing," Emre said with a laugh. He stepped aside and extended a hand to the table. "Sit down. I've made you quite the feast."

I eased into an empty seat with a nervous glance toward the barred windows. They were likely just a security precaution to protect his supposedly priceless collection, but with each moment, I felt with increasing certainty that we had walked into a cage.

True to his word, Emre had prepared enough food to feed a small army. Within moments, he, Aergul, and Pelin had set before us plates heaped with stuffed cabbage leaves, flatbreads fried to golden-brown, and slivers of meat still steaming from the stovetop. In small porcelain bowls, he served a rich red soup that was so spicy my eyes watered from the first sip.

Eager to change the subject and lift any suspicion, I turned to Pelin as she settled into the chair beside me. "I like your dress."

"Thank you. I made it myself, patterned after the latest Svetskiy fashion. This style is very popular among Kosa's nobility these days." She looked at Mikhail as she said it. "Don't you think?"

Mikhail choked on his tea. "I wouldn't know."

"I made my clothes, too," I said, pleased we had something in common.

Pelin glanced down at my embroidered buckskin coat, madder-dyed cotton blouse, and skirt, which admittedly were in even worse condition than when I started on this journey. "I can tell."

"Pelin is a great admirer of everything Svetskiy," Emre said with a chuckle. "If I didn't know any better, I'd be afraid she'd run off to join Adélard's Emporium of Oddities for that reason alone."

As Emre began to spoon some of the meat onto Mikhail's plate, Vanya blocked him with a raised palm.

"If that's meat, he won't eat it," Vanya said, offering the man an easy smile. "Only the best fish and roe for our tsar."

I nearly spat out my stew. Across the table, Mikhail's jaw came unhinged.

"That's what we call him at least," Vanya continued. "Meat is too common for him, so if you put it on his plate, it'll go bad before he touches it."

"He's right," I added hastily, wiping the spilled soup from my chin. "And don't even try giving the Tsar stout."

Vanya nodded. "By royal decree, only the grandest Svetskiy wines shall pass Tsarushka's lips."

Mikhail gave Vanya an icy look before turning to Emre. "Despite what my friends say, the truth is that meat gives me horrible indigestion. I wish I was the Tsar. Maybe then I'd be able to travel with some better company."

I winced. Hopefully, that didn't include me.

Aergul narrowed her eyes, her own bowl of soup untouched. Pelin had started eating, but between bites, she studied Mikhail with keen interest.

Emre chuckled. "Well, if you have a sensitive stomach, you may want to avoid the stew as well, my friend. But the bread and cabbage rolls are safe."

"Thank you," Mikhail said, and helped himself to both.

"I'd be careful with nicknames like those," Pelin said, her jet eyes meeting mine. "I don't imagine Fraktsiya soldiers will find it nearly as amusing as you three do."

"Undoubtfully so," Mikhail said.

"We're not exactly known for making good choices," I said, my shoulders slowly loosening. I offered Pelin a smile, but she had already turned her attention back to her plate, tearing her flatbread into small pieces which she dipped into her soup.

Dinner continued uneventfully. Emre asked us a few questions about where we were going—down south to the Fraktsiya-controlled border towns at the edge of the Steppe—and why a Strannik happened to be traveling with two Kosa mainlanders—purely by chance and great misfortune, Mikhail explained—but aside from that, Emre allowed the conversation to fizzle out between bites. Once the plates were cleared and the last drop of spiced black tea plopped from the kettle, Emre glanced at his pocket watch.

"It's time," he said, rising to his feet. He went to the other side of the kitchen, where he fiddled with a large wooden box atop the counter. I thought that it must be some sort of cooking device, but as he twisted the brass knobs mounted on its face, a trickle of garbled voices rose from the machine.

"What is that?" I asked.

"It's called a radio," he said. "I brought it with us from Yezmirny, but there are also imitations built in Kosa."

"I think I remember my family having something similar to that." I gave it more thought. "You'd put a copper disc inside, and when you wound it, it would play the most beautiful music."

"This doesn't just play music," Pelin interjected, meeting my gaze over her teacup. "These are actual voices. They're not recorded."

"Every night at seven, the Fraktsiya broadcasts messages to the public," Emre explained, adjusting the knobs. "Mostly propaganda, but sometimes there's useful information like the shelling of the railway tracks."

After fiddling a little more with the radio, the voices resolved into a man's smooth baritone: *"—and above all, loyalty."*

Beside me, Mikhail tensed, his fingers clenching tight.

"Koschei," he whispered, and I felt a tremor pass through my own body.

"For centuries, the nobility has led us to believe that their very existence is ordained by the divine, and that it is by such will that we serve them. I too once believed in their grandiose claims. I de-

voted my life to serving the nobility, and I was good at my job. A trained dog. I would fight for them, kill for them, burn and defile for them. And during the Groznaya War, I was repaid for that devotion in blood and pain. The truth, the absolute truth is that there is very little difference between the ruling bogatyri and ordinary human beings. Their power is not given by the goddesses, and in fact can be taken with ease—as I have done to your tsar, and will continue to do until the bogatyri submit."

"So, it's true then," Vanya murmured.

"I'll confess, I don't have much fondness for nobility, but this is something else entirely," Emre said, a furrow forming between his brows. "This isn't how you gain justice."

Across the table, Pelin glowered at her tea until small ripples danced across the drink's surface and her hair wisped around her face as though teased by an unseen breeze. When she caught me staring, her lips pinched into a flat line and the stirred burgundy-black strands fell flat in an instant.

Koschei's voice echoed from the device, a low and compelling intonation that rose and fell like a chant. I could understand how it might have compelled the masses. It was the kind of voice you had no choice but to listen to, and the longer I listened to it, the more mesmerizing it became. Without reason, it made me think of my own father, not Papa, but the stranger I could only remember in bits and pieces like a phantom.

It was the kind of voice that held you.

"No bogatyri, no tsars," Koschei declared, and even across the room, his words pierced me to the core. "Soon, this will cease to merely be a slogan. It will become our future."

22

Midnight found me on the terra-cotta rooftop, on the widow's walk accessible through the attic's skylight. I dangled my legs through the gaps in the wrought-iron railing, peering out across Detskaya.

Past the spiderweb of cables, streetlamps glinted in the night and danced like flames across the river. I sighed, pressing my forehead to the railing as I fingered the bead strung around my wrist. Galina could be anywhere in this city. Could she see this same view now, or was she locked away somewhere, trapped in the darkness?

Soon, my thoughts strayed to my past among the living. No matter how hard I tried to remember, I could only dredge up snippets. The black stains on my father's pants from the silver mine, and the bristly roughness of his unshaven cheeks. My mother's laughter. My mother...

My earliest memories were of my mother, strands of thread streaming over her fingers as she taught me to embroider. She had made it seem so important, as if somewhere inside her meticulous stitching, there was the secret for how to hold together everything.

I rested my face in my palms, trying to follow that snowy road step-by-step, seven years back, southeast from the Edge, over the border, into the mainland and the mountains. My mother and I had taken a wagon from our village—the farmer's wife had smiled and given me an apple—and I had jostled awake in a city, yes, the city of Serebrograd.

Look, Tomochka, our town made those, my mother had said, pointing at the noble white-stone buildings lining the city streets. She meant that the silver from our mines had made those, that these were the people who flourished while people like my father mined deep below the earth and died for their good fortune. They didn't have to stain their hands black from the silver ore, or red with a sacrificial cock's blood to atone for the sin of digging. By the time our ingots of silver reached them, the ore had been purified by Troika priestesses or smelted down by someone else who would take the Unclean Force unto them.

I felt so close to a revelation. I just needed to go back a little further, back to the village, back to my mother.

While my father labored on his hands and knees in the silver mines, she had taken odd jobs around the village. I remembered going with her for hours from house to house. Her skill as a seamstress had been what led her to the homes of the wealthy, even taking her as far as the Troika temple's sanctuary, where she'd spend hours repairing antique altar cloths and holy rushnyky. She had been a faithful attendee, too, hadn't she? Never missing a service, her knees bowed in prayer.

I know in my heart, they are one and the same, she had said as she stepped past the snowbound trees. *And that they are listening. Whatever you do to me, may they pay it back threefold.*

The memory took me aback. What was that? That hadn't been in the village. It had happened when we were still traveling on the road from Serebrograd, this time on foot through the forests and mountains.

Because someone had been following us that entire time. They had been hunting us.

My thoughts scattered as a train roared down the track below. The roof shuddered in the resounding whistle and clang of bells. I didn't hear the creak of the ladder's rungs or the sound of the skylight opening, so when Vanya eased onto the platform beside me, it was as though he had materialized from the night itself.

"Something on your mind?" he asked, stretching out his legs.

I swallowed hard. What did he see in my face?

"Too much," I said with a weak laugh.

"Me too." He sighed, running a hand through his hair. "I can't stop thinking about Kraylesa."

"I'm sorry."

"It's grotesque."

I had no response to that. We fell into silence, watching the trains pass below.

"Do you want to talk about it?" Even as he spoke, his gaze remained on the scenery beyond, the glow of streetlamps reflecting in his eyes. "About what Inga Elenovna said?"

I sighed, running a hand through my hair. "I just…I know something terrible happened."

"To your mother?" Vanya ventured quietly.

"Yes, and I don't want to remember," I said, surprised by the harshness in my voice. "I don't want to think about that time ever again."

"I'd want to remember if something happened to me."

"It's different for you." I glanced over at him. "You already know everything."

A thin smile played on his lips. "That's not quite true. I never knew my mother."

"But you know your past. You know who you are."

"Sometimes I wonder about that." Still smiling, he regarded the city lights. "When I was a child, I was so scared, do you know that? I didn't have a mother, and none of the other kids let me forget that. And even the adults never accepted me as one of their own, not really. Not even after my father died. We have words for someone like me, and by five or six, I had been called them all. So, I learned to laugh it off when they hurt or insulted me, and after a while, I learned how to use that humor like a weapon. But the truth is, I feel like I haven't changed at all. That deep down, there's still that scared, angry boy."

His words struck me harder than I cared to admit. I could understand that feeling very well, of both being too old for my body while at the same time stumbling through life as the very same child who had fled through those winter woods, preserved in that instant as if under permafrost. Sometimes, I thought about Tamar—how innocent that girl had been, and how she might've turned out if her life had gone just a little bit differently—but then I realized that the person I was now was who I needed to be. I was this way because this was the Toma who had survived, scars and all.

Perhaps for the undead, it was the same. Maybe it was not punishment but empowerment—to seize hold of the life that had been taken from you and reclaim it the only way you could. Even if it meant sacrificing parts of yourself along the way. Maybe that was how it was for everyone in this world.

"What do you think happened to her?" I asked Vanya. "To your mother?"

"I wish I knew, but I suppose it was something terrible, too. Sometimes, I dream about drowning." His gaze sank to the dark river snaking below. "Before my father left for the trenches, he said that once he came back, he had something to show me, something about my mother. But then he died, and I never did find out what he was talking about. I ended up visiting all the surrounding villages, searching for someone with my hair, or my nose, or my mouth. I never found her, but what I did find were inconsistencies, like how Annushka's mother thought I was at least two months old when my father asked her to nurse me. So, what do you suppose that means? If my mother didn't die in childbirth, then did she raise me? Did she die later on, or did she just grow tired of me?"

"Vanya, whatever happened to her, you're not to blame." I searched desperately for something else to add, just another kind word that would clear the bitter sorrow from his gaze. "I don't think anyone could grow tired of you."

"Give me another two days, and you might think differently. I even get on Annushka's nerves sometimes, and we've been friends since childhood." He chuckled, rubbing the back of his head. "We've gone off topic. I guess what I'm trying to say is that I think there's at least some importance in knowing where you came from, even if the truth is painful. If there's anything you think I can do to help you remember, or if you have any questions about being Strannik, let me know."

"Thank you."

Vanya glanced over at me. "I guess this means I can't call you a koldunia anymore?"

Laughing, I shoved him lightly on the shoulder. "Not unless you want to be cursed."

"Honestly, I don't think I'd mind it."

We sat there for another few moments, laughing and smiling at each other. Then, I edged closer to him, and he scooted closer to me, until our shoulders brushed. I reached down and found his hand.

Just to sit with our fingers entwined, close enough that our breath mingled, was enjoyable. A gentle warmth radiated through my chest, melting away all the stress and trauma of the last few days, if only for a moment.

"Do you think they're ugly?" I asked as his fingers found the jagged scar that trailed down my wrist, courtesy of a lynx I'd caught in a snare one summer. "The scars, I mean. There are more you didn't see on my stomach and back. I guess I never thought about them until today, because my family, well, everybody in my family is just scar tissue at this point. That's all they're held together by—things that happened in the past, that left a mark, that they carry with them. And all I can do is try keeping them sewn together."

"When I saw your scars, I wasn't even thinking about whether they were ugly or not, Toma. I was just thinking how sad it was that you suffered through all this alone. But I suppose you weren't really alone." His fingers were so warm against my arm, as if the same sparks that tingled in my stomach had also found their way into his bloodstream. "I'm not going to lie to you and say I think they're pretty. I think they're what makes you human. They show that you've lived so much more than—" he gestured at the skyline "—than this. And I think that's beautiful in its own right, and far more intriguing."

Something slowly loosened inside me, like a clenched muscle I hadn't known existed until this moment. If he'd told me he found the scars beautiful, I never would have believed him. These words were real. They came from the heart, and the relief they gave me went so much deeper than any strained compliment.

"Tell me about this one," he murmured, tracing his thumb over the scar that curved along the base of my wrist bone.

Feeling my cheeks heat up, I found my voice. "The first time I caught a lynx in a trap, I tried to release it."

"Ah, that couldn't have gone well."

I chuckled. "It didn't."

"Something tells me that lynx got off with a whole lot worse than just a tiny scar."

"Oh, of course." I rolled my eyes. "It ended up as a hat."

"What about these?" Easing up my sleeve, he followed the warpath of pale pocks left over from thorns or splinters. His touch was slow and teasing, lingering on each gouge and pinprick.

I blushed, my breath catching in my throat as his palm cradled my forearm. I couldn't feel his skin's heat anymore—it was the same temperature now as my own, as if by the second, the barrier between our bodies was slowly dissolving.

"I got caught in a thistle patch, I think," I said, although the truth was that I couldn't remember how it had happened, only that it had been so long ago, that it could have come from the *before* time.

"And this?" His fingers poised over the burn scar encircling my upper arm.

"I don't remember."

"The way it curls around, it almost looks like a handprint, doesn't it?"

I chuckled, feeling a twinge of disquiet. "Maybe I strayed too close to the oven in a steam bath, and a bannik grabbed me."

The bathhouse spirits were known to scratch, and more than once, I'd felt the bannik in our house's run-down banya rake a claw down my back. But this scar too had come from the past, and it disturbed me even more than the marks left by thorns. All I could think about was the nightmare I'd had since childhood—a man set afire, striding between the white birches even as his clothes smouldered.

Tomochka, whatever you hear, don't make a sound.

As if sensing my unease, Vanya lowered his hand from my arm. His gaze searched mine. In the moonlight, his eyes were the deepest malachite. Slowly, he lifted his hand to my face, cradling my cheek in his palm. I held my hand over his, cupping the warmth of him. My disquiet slowly faded. I wanted this.

"And this?" His thumb traced the side of my mouth.

"There's no scar there," I whispered.

"I know."

Vanya leaned in closer, or I leaned in, and somehow the

rest of the distance between us dissolved until his lips brushed against my own. The kiss lasted only as long as a spark in a storm, but it left me with a warmth that lingered.

"Toma, we all have scars," he murmured, searching my eyes. "Some people just carry them more visibly than others. Nobody leaves this world untouched."

He was right. Something was happening to me. Just being next to Vanya, breathing the same air as him, staring into his striking green eyes—he was *changing* me.

As another train scoured the darkness below, I leaned against him and rested my head on his shoulder, watching as the light skidded across the riverside before slowly, silently sinking into the night.

23

It was drizzling when I awoke, and a small puddle had gathered on the floorboards by my bed. I settled back for a moment, watching the rain streak down the skylight. I felt mildly disoriented, as if I hadn't just woken up in a strange place, but a different era as well.

Faint voices came from down below—the metallic clatter of silverware and pans, Aergul's silvery laughter, Pelin's own bored drawl, the hazard whistle of a passing train. I closed my eyes, trying to summon the dream that had slipped through my head moments before waking and that had left me in a cold terror sweat.

No good. Just darkness and a sensation like running, as though I'd been dragged forward with sickening velocity.

Through the skylight, the sky was a putrid shade of yellowish gray, already fogged with the smoke trails of the riverside factories. It made me think of the mining machines back in my hometown, grinding behemoths of steel that swallowed entire wheelbarrows filled with coal and spat out black grease and gouts of smoke until the mud ran black. Strange how the more I thought about my past, the more distinct the memories became, like the excavation of a grave.

The evening before, we had studied the train charts with Emre and Pelin. No matter whether the soldiers had arrived in the city by riverboat the very morning Vanya had set out with us on the road, or if they had come later on horseback or wagon, they wouldn't have been able to reach Eyry by train. Only yesterday evening had the lines to the mainland resumed service, and until this morning, all outgoing trains had been diverted down south through the Granary.

As I contemplated getting out of bed, a door slammed below and then Emre cried out in protest, "Wait, you can't just walk in here like this!"

Wide-awake in an instant, I lurched out from under the covers, scrambled over the chaotic jumble of boxes and old furniture, and shook Mikhail's shoulder.

His eyes flashed open. As he began to rise, I raised a finger to my lips.

"What is it?" he whispered.

"Something is going on downstairs. There's someone here."

"Are you sure you weren't just dreaming?"

"Listen."

The sound of cooking had died into silence. Terse voices filtered from the rooms below. Glass shattered, and Aergul cried out for Emre in a warbling sob. My stomach tightened, nerves on fire.

Silently, we got dressed. As Mikhail tied his boots, I went to Vanya's side and shook him awake.

"Just another few minutes, Toma," he groaned.

"We need to go now," I said.

"Five minutes, I swear."

"Don't make me drag you off that table," Mikhail growled, and Vanya sighed.

"All right, you don't have to get violent."

We hadn't even unpacked, and it took only a minute to gather up our things. I wrapped my mother's rushnyk around my waist, my fingers straying to its familiar mends and embroidery. If the symbols she'd sewn in crimson truly were runes of protection, then I hoped they'd work their magic if we had to resort to violence.

"We know you have more than this," a man snarled, sounding even closer than before.

"It's just a bunch of old rubbish up there," Emre stammered. "I swear, we don't have any monsters, no matter what the fliers say."

The stairs groaned outside our door. There was no time to even ascend to the skylight above, and the attic was so high up that we would no doubt break our legs if we tried to jump.

"Mikhail, hide behind the monkey," Vanya whispered, but the other boy had already dropped to the ground. No sooner had Mikhail rolled under the bed than the door swung open, and a tall mustached man strode in, his burly frame squeezed into a sage-green greatcoat. A rifle hung from a sling over his shoulder.

From under the glossy leather band of his hat, he regarded us through narrowed lids. "Just a bunch of rubbish, you say."

Emre stepped into the room, one hand cupped over his

face. His left cheek was an angry maroon, and his lower lip had already started to swell.

"These are..." He trailed off at the sight of Vanya and me. By the way he looked around the room, I could tell he was doing the math in his head. I offered him a strained smile, begging him with my eyes not to say anything.

"Ivan Nikolaevich, sir," Vanya said with a polite nod, his voice off-key and his accent strangled. "This is my sister, Tamara."

Emre cleared his throat, smoothing back the strands of coal-black hair that had slipped over his eyes. "Just two of my daughter's friends. They'll be staying here a short while. But as I said before, we have no monsters, despite what the sign says. You people already came and took them."

The soldier stepped deeper into the attic, his flinty eyes scanning the room. He paused for a moment on the moth-eaten stuffed monkey, curled his upper lip in disgust, and then turned to Vanya and me.

"Papers." The man held out his hand expectantly.

"Of course," I stammered, searching through my coat pockets until I found the leather booklet.

He took the passbook from me and wordlessly flipped through it, before returning to the first page. "You're from the north, eh?"

"Yes."

"I have family there. A small town named Zoltsk." He handed the book back to me before turning to Vanya, who relinquished his own papers readily enough. This time, the soldier gave them only a cursory glance.

Slowly, I released a breath. Across the room, Emre and Pelin stood motionless, their faces blanched to wan tones. As I met Emre's eyes, a jolt passed through me. He was trembling ever so slightly, his hands curled into fists.

He *knew*.

"Ah, I almost forgot." The soldier nonchalantly dropped Vanya's passbook on the cot. "By order of the Fraktsiya, all residents of each household must be registered at city hall, including visitors. I'll let you two off easy this time and instead of giving you a citation, you'll just have to pay a small fine. A hundred and fifty grevka each should cover it."

I searched my pockets, but all I uncovered were the two grimy ten-pieces that the icon seller had given me in change.

"Here," Vanya said, holding out a wad of crumpled banknotes he had taken from his bag. "This should be enough."

Licking the pad of his thumb, the man counted out the bills, then did it a second time after reaching the end of the stack. With a grunt of satisfaction, he slid the wad into his breast pocket. One note slipped from the pile and landed on the floor by the cot.

I swallowed hard.

"I got it," Vanya said, but the man was already bending down.

Movement shifted in the corner of my eye. Silently, Pelin extended one hand, curling her fingers around thin air, and tugged back as though grasping at an invisible rope. A mild breeze passed through the room, stirring my hair over my eyes and sending the dropped banknote wafting across the floorboards.

"It gets drafty up here," Pelin said, leaning down to retrieve the crumpled paper.

The soldier turned to watch her, his eyes glassy and his mouth cocked oddly. At first, I thought he realized what she was and began to reach for my hunting knife. Then it dawned on me that the look in his eyes wasn't suspicion or hatred, but something else, something hungry. As she rose, she offered him a warm smile and held out the twenty-grevka note.

"Beast tamer, it appears as though your monsters aren't the only thing you've trained well," the man said, cramming the bill into his pocket. As soon as his back was turned, Pelin's face distorted in disgust, and she wiped her hand on the back of her lacy Svetskiy-style dressing gown.

"Your upyr will have to do, Dima," the man said, stepping into the hall. Just before the door slipped shut behind him, I caught a glimpse of a broad face engulfed by an untamed black beard and the same pale eyes that, in my memory, had been filled with firelight.

Him. My vision pulsed to crimson around the edges. It was *him*.

I took a step toward the door, my hand already going to the hunting knife I'd slipped under my rushnyk. Before I could pull it from the sheath, Vanya grabbed my wrist and shook his head.

"Let's go, Stanislav," Dima's voice called from the stairway, growing fainter with each word. "Gather up those jars and stop dawdling with your thumb up your ass. In case you forgot, we've got a train to catch."

24

Every nerve within my body screamed at me to go, until it felt as if at any moment, I'd tear from my own skin. I tried to make a beeline for the door, but Vanya kept a steady grip on my wrist.

"Let go of me," I snarled, turning around.

His green eyes flashed. "No."

Growling, I tore free of him and reached for my hunting knife once more, my body moving on its own. I'd threaten him if I had to. Anything to get to Galina.

"Those men are armed with rifles," Vanya hissed, and my fingers stilled. "And in the streets beyond, there will be more soldiers with rifles, and once they hear the gunfire, they'll come here. If you act now, you'll have all six of us killed."

"I can't just let them take her!"

"They won't," Mikhail said, pushing himself out from under the bed. With a grimace, he brushed the dust and mice droppings from his front. "We know where they're going, Toma. All we have to do is follow and bide our time."

Slowly, I lowered my hand. My cheeks felt scalded, and a sickening shame settled like a stone in my gut. How could I have even considered threatening Vanya, especially after I'd given him my first kiss? I needed to remember that this wasn't the wilderness. Those soldiers were people, not animals to be hunted, and there were rules here that must be followed.

"Just trust me," Vanya said, squeezing my shoulder gently. "We'll save her."

"I apologize for not being immediately forthcoming, Tsar Mikhail," Emre said with a respectful tip of his chin. "When my daughter told me what she overheard, I thought it would be better to allow you to safely continue on your way without my family's interference, if indeed you were the Tsar."

"Thank you, Emre," Mikhail said, and even as he spoke, there was a subtle change in his demeanor. His shoulders squared off and his chin lifted. His face remained fixed in an expression of careful neutrality. "I'll remember your hospitality."

Vanya chuckled. "Lucky for that draft, huh? He almost caught you, Tsarushka."

Before I could break the news to him, Pelin gave a jerk of her hand, smacking Vanya with a burst of condensed air so forceful, he stumbled back a step.

Vanya's jaw fell in disbelief. "You're a bogatyr?"

"How else do you think I could stay in that tank so long?" Her lips quirked in a smirk. "With enough concentration, I can draw air from the water."

She looked at Mikhail like she expected him to say something. He was still staring at the stairway, his shoulders tensed and hands fisted at his sides. Slowly, her smile faded, and she blew the hair out of her eyes with an annoyed huff.

"Best be careful around Mikhail then," Vanya said, earning a disgruntled look from him.

Pelin's brow furrowed. "Why?"

"He'll call you a koldunia."

I followed the others downstairs, my fingers aching to curl around my knife's antler handle. My nerves sparked with tension. Each step I took, those men were getting a step farther and I was just letting them.

But the others were right. The moment I tried to stop Dima and Stanislav, I would be endangering everyone around me, including Vanya and Mikhail. At the very least, I owed them some self-control.

Downstairs, the museum was in shambles. Shattered specimen jars encrusted the floor, the boards slickened with formaldehyde and worse. One bookshelf lay upturned, while another had been stripped of its artifacts.

"They even took the two-headed pig," Vanya said in disbelief. "What did they think it was? A drekavac?"

"No, the rat-faced blond one wanted it as a souvenir," Emre said dryly, rubbing his swollen cheek. He opened the door to the foyer. "Pelin will show you three to the train station. It sounds as though you too have a train to catch."

The main railway station was located in the city's old town, resting in the shadow of an ancient stone wall. I stopped to gawk. Though the train station was several stories tall, only its twin cupolas managed to reach beyond the wall's notched battlements. Over the centuries, the wall had crumbled, so that only a few short, coiling passages remained, limestone

structures that rose between buildings and roads like the severed spinal column of some vast serpent.

"What's that?" I asked Pelin, who had changed hastily into
a dress and overcoat.

She blinked. "The wall."

"Yes, but why is it so *big*?"

"In the time before the bogatyri, it was all Detskaya had
to protect its citizens from monsters," Pelin said, turning her
attention back to the road ahead. "The bogatyri were the
ones who broke it down, as a reminder that we'd never have
to live in fear again."

As she spoke, there was a hint of reverence in her voice, and it
became only more apparent as she shifted her gaze to Mikhail.
She looked at him the same way I had once watched rusalki
maul an elk, with breathless awe at their force and power. It
dawned on me that though she too was a bogatyr, he was so
much more than that to her. And he didn't even see it at all.

As we passed through the station's doors, Mikhail tucked
down the brim of his cap and lowered his gaze to the floor.
Inside, the circular entry hall terminated in a domed ceiling
adorned on all sides with the painted heraldic crests of what
Vanya informed me were the nearby towns' noble families.

High on the northern wall, a metal bulletin sign had been
hung over a gangway. A man was in the process of chalk-
ing in the times and numbers of the arriving trains, and the
routes associated with them.

I squinted at the writing. "Do you see Eyry?"

"Looks like platform ten," Pelin said. "You can buy a ticket
there."

As Vanya strode toward the platform entrance, I turned

to Mikhail, who had kept his back hunched and head down ever since we had entered the station. "Are you all right?"

"Not really, seeing as this place is crawling with soldiers," he said, his voice strained as tightly as a noose.

"You'll be fine," I said. "No one will expect you to be here."

Mikhail didn't answer, but he bit down on his lower lip and turned away, and in his gaze gleamed a shallow edge of dread. He fingered the brass icon I had given him, tracing the Three Sisters' eroded faces.

We made our way to platform ten. There was already a train parked along the tracks, over fifteen cars long and painted red with a white roof.

"That's a hospital train," Pelin said.

"You don't think they could be traveling in that?" Vanya muttered.

The narrow strip of brick was too crowded to even stand still on, with people sitting on the ground or grouped in huddles. Unpleasant odors cloyed the air—dirt, human waste, infection, smoke. As we headed down the platform, I recognized the malodor's source.

Set in a line along the length of the platform, men and women lay motionless on stretchers. Some wore the Fraktsiya green, while others were stripped to their undershirts and woolen drawers, with gore-stained bandages covering the rest.

Horrified, I pressed my rushnyk against my mouth, inhaling its gentle, dusty fragrance. If I closed my eyes, I could almost pretend I was home. Except for the moans. Except for the rumble of trains coming down the tracks and Mikhail's hand on my shoulder.

"Are you okay, Toma?" he whispered, easing his palm down to my forearm.

"This is a nightmare." I didn't want to open my eyes again, afraid of what I might see.

"This is war," Vanya said blandly.

I opened my eyes and stared at him in shock. "How can you just…"

Vanya's gaze darkened. "Just what?"

"Just say that like it's nothing?"

"Because it's the truth, and pretending otherwise won't prevent soldiers from dying in battle or protect children from being blown to bits when their towns are shelled." Vanya scanned the platform. "It won't save us."

I found myself at a loss for words. What I had mistaken for cold disregard was really resignation. This was the way things were out here, as much a rule of life as watching a wolf fell a rabbit. This world was not kind.

Turning my gaze ahead, I watched as several of the train-car doors slid open. Out marched even rows of men and women, some in the coats and caped gray dresses of medics, others in the sage-green greatcoats of the Fraktsiya, and among them, even a few garbed in the crimson sashes and robes of Troika priestesses.

"Excuse me," Vanya said, going to a nearby conductor. "When is the next train to Eyry?"

"Only military transport trains are being routed through that area," he said, nodding toward the hospital train. "If you want to get to Eyry, you'll have to take the long way around and travel south, then up through the Granary, and loop around."

"Are you sure about that?" I interrupted. "Are you absolutely sure?"

"Look, I don't know what you want me to tell you," the

man said, grumbling in annoyance. "If you're really that desperate, join the Fraktsiya and get your legs blown off by a bogatyr. Then they'll take you there free of charge."

As the conductor strolled away, I turned to the others. "If that's a Fraktsiya train, then the men who took Galina must be on there, too. We'll have to sneak on."

"In case you didn't realize, that train is filled with soldiers," Mikhail said tightly. "It's the equivalent of walking into a bear's den. And chances are, it's not just wounded soldiers on that train. It is armed battalions as well."

"Why would a medic train be transporting troops?"

"Because I know that train. It's a Yezmirskiy Ö-59, and one of the few in the Kosa Empire. We would use the same kind of train to transport emissaries and ambassadors from their residences to the palace or airfields. Trust me, the Fraktsiya have painted it up like a hospital train, but it will be built like a vault in there. It might…"

"Might what?" Vanya asked.

"Even contain high-ranking Fraktsiya officials," he said quietly.

"You think Koschei could be in there?" I asked as Mikhail tugged down the brim of his cap, averting his eyes from a passing soldier.

Mikhail didn't answer, but the flash of anger in his gaze said all I needed to know. He gritted his teeth and drew up his collar. "We need to get inside somehow."

"How are we going to do that?" I asked.

A dark silence fell over us, and then Vanya's gaze shifted to something over my shoulder, and he smiled. "I have a plan, but first, Toma, give Mikhail your rushnyk."

25

"'A plan,' he says," Mikhail said spitefully as Vanya strolled down the platform. "The last time Vanya had a plan, it ended up with me nearly being drowned by a vodyanoy. And the time before that, I had to run through a burning village while being shot at. I wonder what delights he will subject us to this time."

"I'm sure we'll be fine," I said, then paused as a realization occurred to me. Lightly nudging Mikhail in the shoulder, I grinned. "What did you just call him?"

"Iva—" His cheeks reddened. With a sheepish scowl, he shifted his gaze away from me and folded my rushnyk over his arm.

"You like him, don't you?"

"Wh-what?" Mikhail blushed. "Of course not. He's—he's a bullheaded idiot, he won't shut up, and half the time he's either goading me on or insulting me."

I chuckled. "Don't deny it."

"I'm not—" His mouth snapped shut as Pelin returned carrying a paper sack and two milk bottles.

"I hope you like bread." She looked around. "Where's your friend?"

While Mikhail told her about the plan, I stepped around the kiosk to see where Vanya had gone. Across the train yard, he walked up the row of wounded soldiers lying on stretchers. With his relaxed stride and dark brown greatcoat, he hardly looked out of place amid the railway workers and loiterers.

When I pointed out the number of civilians carrying rifles, Mikhail told me there was a shortage of uniforms among the Fraktsiya. Many of the plainclothes men and women were soldiers, identified by the green patches hand sewn onto the shoulders of their coats or the gilt badges on their caps and shirt collars.

But if there were officials onboard, they would be wearing the issued uniforms, and so would the soldiers close to them. We'd have no luck blending in without disguises of our own.

At several of the cars, bodies were being unloaded rather than brought on. Already, the Troika priestesses were tending to the dead—one by severing the tendons in the arms and legs using a silver blade, and the other by tying the jaw shut with red ribbon until it could be filled with cleansing herbs. Near the end of the row, a lone man in Strannik garb knelt beside a corpse, slipped the boots free, and chained the naked feet together.

While explaining his plan, Vanya had told us that the Strannik dead were attended to by guards rather than priestesses, strong and healthy men and women who would stand watch over the corpses for three days—that was how long the goddess Voserka had labored to shape the first humans at the hearth of creation, and the same window of time it took the dead to return to life. Typically, this final watch would occur at the site of the person's death, as in Kraylesa. When that wasn't possible, it would happen in an isolated field or glade, far from settlements where the living might be polluted by the Unclean forces that gathered near the dead.

Those who came back were considered cursed. They would be put down without mercy and incinerated until nothing but ashes remained.

Vanya stopped beside the other Strannik and spoke to him. I wasn't close enough to hear what they were saying or even which language they used, but after a minute, Vanya turned and looked around the platform. Spotting me, he waved his hand and gestured for me to approach.

I took a deep breath. *This is who you could have been*, I thought as I walked over. *It's still a part of you.*

As I stopped before them, I offered the man a weak smile. He growled something in Strannitsky, and I nodded, then nodded again. Vanya took me a step aside and hugged me, turning me away from the man so that he could whisper in my ear.

"He's going to escort you to the car. Once you get there, you're going to tell him that you want a moment alone with our brother and you can find your way back. Listen carefully. These exact words." As he whispered them to me, his warm breath brushed against the nape of my neck, lifting the fine hairs there.

It felt so good to be touched by another human, to be held by one. I didn't want to let Vanya go, and when he finally did pull away, I had to fist my hands at my sides to keep from reaching out for him again.

With the same nonchalant professionalism with which he had chained the feet of the dead, the man offered me his hand as he climbed into the train car. I took it, knowing that as the grieving sister, this was my part to play.

Though electrical lights were strung along the walls, it was dim within the cars. Weak sunlight intruded through the narrow portholes of windows, faint and grayish beams as thin as bayonet blades.

At one point, this train must have been meant for nobility. The car bore signs of its former splendor in the polished floorboards and floral wallpaper. The ceiling was adorned with raised plasterwork, gilded and resembling a briar of roses.

The original booths had at some point been ripped out to make room for rows of cots, except for those at the far end and those in front, which still had their original carved burl details and tufted leather seats. Of the rest, only brackets and scarred wood remained.

And the smell. The smell was horrific—a nauseating brew of gangrene, piss, and vomit. I breathed through my mouth as we headed deeper in, now more than ever longing for the familiar, dusty aroma of my mother's rushnyk, or the scent of the forest after a storm.

Fingering my bead bracelet, I followed the Strannik down the aisle. On most of the cots, a red ribbon had been tied to the footrail. He paused beside every cot marked by a black ribbon, turning to me expectantly.

I peered into the soldiers' faces as they slept or slowly drifted away to death. Some were so young that in another life, a life where my parents had lived, they could have been a brother of mine. Each time the Strannik man looked my way, I shook my head.

As we entered the second car, my skin prickled, and without reason, goose bumps rose on the back of my neck. Yet more soldiers lay wounded on the cots, only these men and women were more bandages than people, some with their faces oddly sunken beneath their shrouds, others with bloodied pads of gauze where limbs had been.

The windows had been boarded shut. It was so dim that all I could see of the dying soldiers on either side of me was the gleam of their slitted eyes and the saliva coating their parched, searching tongues. As they stirred, chains rattled—each had a wrist or ankle shackled to bolts in the floor, as much a sign of their encroaching fates as the shadow of death that roosted on their ashen features.

A blond soldier sat beside one of the beds, a bowl of water resting in his lap. As we neared, I watched as he gently sponged down the dying patient's unbandaged arm. In areas, the skin had blackened, and several of the fingers were missing.

Frostbite, I thought.

Slowly, the soldier looked up. He was a strikingly handsome man, although his features were whetted by a cruel edge. His dark-gold hair was brushed back and trimmed at the sides, but a few long strands had spilled over his brow, framing leonine eyes that pierced me to the core.

"Sir, forgive me," the Strannik said, lowering his gaze respectfully. "This girl came to me on the platform. She was looking to see if her brother is among the dying. He's a soldier from Kupalo."

"Is that so?" His voice was low and languid. He turned his attention back to the wounded soldier, his fingers trained over the bloody water's surface, sponge forgotten.

"I'll have her leave."

"No, she may continue her search," the blond soldier said aloofly.

Whoever this was, he must have been a high-ranking official to command such respect. The leader of a troop perhaps. I edged closer, peering into the faces of the wounded. All strangers to me, of course, but in another life, they might have been friends or family.

"Would you like to know something?" the blond man said as I passed his bedside.

I looked over. "Pardon me?"

He dipped the sponge back into the bowl, watching the blood muddy the water. "When something dies, it creates an echo. In exceptional cases, a rather loud one. Sometimes, that is loud enough for something to hear it. For something to answer."

"What do you mean?" I whispered.

"I think you know." He turned slightly in his chair, raising his chin. A vague smile passed over his mouth, his lips so full that they were almost pretty. "I think you have heard it."

An inexplicable shiver passed through me as I met his gaze. His eyes were as bright as a lynx's, a rare amber flecked with green striations.

"Do you see him?" the man asked, turning his attention back to the wounded.

I moistened my lips. "Who?"

"Your brother." He began to unroll the gauze from the boy's shoulder, revealing even more devastation.

"Not yet."

He gave a dismissive flick of his hand. "Then you may keep searching."

"Thank you, sir," I mumbled.

With the Strannik guard trailing behind me, I entered the next car and the one after that. I froze in the third car beside the cot of a boy with half his face encased in bandages. Dark hair peeked out from under the layers of linen, and in the side of his face that was still exposed, I caught a glimpse of what I would've liked to pretend was a part of myself—the bold, furrowed brows, maybe, or the restless line of his mouth.

I traced my hand over his arm, his skin waxen beneath my fingertips. Once I was sure he hadn't awoken, I turned to the man and repeated what Vanya had whispered in my ear. The language was strange on my tongue, filled with undulating vowels and hard stops that vibrated in the back of my throat.

With a nod, the man responded in a low, consolatory tone, words I couldn't understand but that I wished I could, that I wished had been meant for me and me alone. When I didn't answer, he turned around and made his way back down the rows of beds, which in the encroaching shadows might as well have been funeral biers.

As soon as he was gone, I turned to continue on my way, but scarcely had I taken a step before a hand seized me by the wrist. I yanked it away and looked back.

The wounded boy gazed up at me, his parched lips moving silently, struggling to speak. At last, he forced out the word in a single gasp: *"Vasyem."*

"I don't…"

He pointed at the pitcher of water on one of the bolted shelves.

I retrieved it and returned to his side. Pouring a glass from the carafe, I held the brim to his lips as he drank greedily.

I wished I could ask him why he had joined the Fraktsiya. What had he been hoping for? But he just drank, and once he was done, he slumped against the mattress, ragged breaths pushing from his lungs. As I turned to leave, his fingers grasped at my sleeve.

"Wait," he croaked, and I leaned forward. His voice crackled in my ear, crisp, like dead leaves crushed underfoot. "Save me."

I wrenched my hand away without thinking, taking a step back. His mouth trembled. He repeated those two words, but I shook my head, moisture prickling my eyes. How could I save him when I couldn't even save Galina? When I couldn't even save myself?

I hurried to the next car over, a windowless compartment whose shelves were stacked with folded linen, rolls of gauze, and metal tins. Sinking to my knees, I unlatched the sliding door in the middle of the compartment.

The door shifted sideways on ball bearings, heavy enough that I had to lean against it until it locked in place. Across the platform, Mikhail met my gaze and lifted his hand. I mimicked the gesture before easing the door shut once more, until only a crack remained. Peering through the opening, I watched as Pelin retreated into an alcove along the side of the train station, her burgundy-black hair already whipping around her face by an unseen breeze.

At first, nothing happened. Then the wind shifted directions.

Within seconds, the breeze became a gale, casting trash and pebbles against the train's hull, and sending hats and scarves flying. Dust rolled in off the tracks and filled the air with a brown haze as thick as smoke.

The wind intensified until the entire train shuddered in its onslaught. People ran for cover, shielding their faces from the scouring wind and abrasive dust.

"Ready yourselves," a man shouted as he unshouldered his rifle. His gaze roved the platform. "This is the work of bogatyri."

But even as he spoke, the dust immersed him. In the haze, individual forms were reduced to silhouettes, flickering and insubstantial, like shadows cast by candlelight.

Holding my breath, I pushed the door open wider, grasping onto the handlebar to keep the wind from tearing the door closed again. Through the billowing dust cloud, I caught a glimpse of Vanya and Mikhail running toward me, shielding themselves with my mother's rushnyk. The wind stilled around them, and they carried with them a bubble of calm, the only breeze that which was created by their own harried movements.

As they neared, the undercarriage shuddered beneath me. The air filled with the hard clack of gears moving and levers being disengaged. Rolling down the tracks, the train released a shrieking whistle so loud it dwarfed even the howling wind that consumed us.

"Hurry," I shouted, but the train was already beginning to pick up speed. I held out my hand to Mikhail, felt his fingertips scrape against mine, and then the train surged forward, and the pair of them disappeared from sight.

Slowly, I sank onto my knees, my fingers curled around thin air. A crushing weight pressed down on my chest. Gone. They were gone in an instant, as if they'd never existed at all, and I was alone again.

I swallowed down the hard lump in my throat.

This was what it always came down to for me, wasn't it? Being alone, in a strange place, searching.

It should have been easy to let them go. Maybe it was better this way. All I had to worry about now was finding Galina. This wasn't my war after all, and this had never been my world, not really.

Beyond the open door of the train car swept the smoke-tinged walls of a winding passage the builders had hewn into the hillside. Numbly, I stared at the bricks until they were reduced to a maroon smear. As we passed through a tunnel, the car was engulfed in darkness. The dimness soothed my aching eyes. I wished it would stay that way.

Much too soon, we emerged into the light, through a stand of birch saplings growing haphazardly along several moss-choked tracks, routes that led nowhere now. As I began to rise from my knees, a shadow fell over me.

"Koldunia," a voice growled in raw hatred, and I lifted my eyes to confront Dima's seething gaze.

26

As I began to rise, Dima's foot shot out. The hard toe of his boot caught me in my stomach, driving me down again. Curling over myself, I pressed my palm over my side and gasped desperately to regain my lost breath. It felt as though my rib cage had been transformed into a bear trap, seizing my lungs in its merciless grip.

Before I could recover, Dima snared his fingers through my hair, throwing me off balance and casting me onto my stomach. I writhed beneath him, snarling and kicking as he seized my arm and twisted it behind my back. His weight anchored me to the floorboards, crushing what little breath I had managed to draw in.

"I could sense it in you from the moment I saw you," he hissed, his rancid breath clogging my nostrils. His fingers were moist and clammy, but mercilessly tight, the untrimmed edges of his nails digging into my skin. "You carry the Unclean Force inside you. You are filth."

Terror seized me in its iron grip, spurring my heartbeat into a wild panic. I felt something rise within me, a scream I thought, but the only sounds to escape my clenched teeth were strained groans and growls, the sound of an upyr gone feral.

"Let go of me," I snarled as he dragged me forward by the hair and wrist, hauling me over the edge of the door so that my head and shoulders hung over empty space.

Below, the tracks were just a blur of steel and gravel. I felt the air being sucked beneath the wheels, forming a vacuum that I knew would drag me in if I fell, casting me under the crushing weight of the carriages.

"Where is the Tsar?" Dima demanded.

"I said, let go!"

"You really want that?"

Keeping a merciless grip on my arm and scalp, he pushed me even farther through the open door until my chest hung over the edge. If not for the counterweight of his own body, I would certainly fall. My free hand reached back blindly, scraping against his drabcloth trousers. Searching for something, anything, bare skin to gouge or a fallen instrument.

"Tell me where he is!"

"Right here," a voice said, and I heard the wet squelch of flesh giving way and the crisp snap of bone. Dima's hand loosened around me in an instant, and he collapsed on the floorboards beside me, blood trickling down his scalp.

I began to tip forward, my fingers scrambling for purchase. Below, the ground whizzed by in a dizzying blur. As I started to fall, a pair of hands seized me and wrenched me onto solid ground.

I rolled onto my back the moment the hands released me,

scooting away in a blind panic until my back struck the metal frame of a shelf. Vanya knelt beside me, while Mikhail stood several paces away, gripping an unused bedpan whose porcelain edge dripped with blood.

"Are you okay?" Vanya asked. "Can you walk?"

"I'm fine," I croaked, pushing my hair out of my face. "Just give me…give me a moment to breathe."

My scalp burned as if Dima had wrenched out a fistful of hair. As I massaged my side, the pain in my ribs quickly subsided into a low, throbbing ache. But even as I watched a wide ribbon of blood inch down Dima's face, my heart wouldn't stop pounding, my mouth so dry it hurt to swallow.

"How did you two get here?" I asked.

"We were able to jump onto a car farther back," Vanya said, helping me to my feet. The floorboards had already started to splinter at his feet, scales of bark forming on the surface amid the buds of new leaves.

Movement shifted in the corner of my eye. I turned just as Dima lumbered onto his hands and knees.

Teeth bared in a bloodied snarl, he drew the pistol from the holster at his waist. As he cocked back the hammer, Vanya stomped his foot down. The tender sprigs of new branches erupted from the floorboards, twisting into a bough that slammed into Dima's chest, casting him through the train car's open door and into the void beyond. If he made a sound, it was lost beneath the crunch of his body striking earth.

I stared out the open door, watching the trees pass by. I thought I should feel something. Relief, happiness even. But all I could think was how I wished I'd been the one to kill him, and as I turned back to the others, an acidic anger scalded the back of my throat. My body trembled with rage that swelled from within like a dark tide, rage so violent it shocked me. I wanted to push Dima out myself. I wanted to rip at my own hair. I should have heard him coming. I should have done *something*.

"You know, I think I'm beginning to get the hang of this bogatyr thing," Vanya said, retrieving the pistol Dima had dropped. But even though he kept his voice lighthearted, his hand was trembling, and the words stumbled over his lips. He turned away from us, but not before I watched him grasp his right hand and dig his nails into his own wrist, clenching down until the skin blanched even paler still, and the trembling subsided.

"Great job, except now they'll know a bogatyr is here," Mikhail said dryly, eying the exposed branches.

"Oh, so I'm not a koldun anymore?" From the outer pocket of his rucksack, Vanya retrieved the serrated blade he'd used to build our campfire spit. With a few hard jerks, he sawed the new bough through at its base and hurled it through the open door. "There."

"Thank you," I said, taking a shallow breath. I buried the anger deep down, digging my nails into my palms to center myself. "Both of you. I don't know what would've happened if you hadn't shown up."

"What are friends for, eh?" Vanya nudged Mikhail in the shoulder.

"Here," Mikhail said, handing me my mother's rushnyk.

I folded it over my arm, fingering one fraying edge. Just the tapestry's familiar weight and feel calmed me.

"We better get moving," Mikhail said as Vanya closed the

train door and latched it shut. "Help me look. There have to be some uniforms on one of these shelves."

Next to the folded bedsheets, we unearthed a steel washboard and a wicker basket containing a mishmash of uniform parts, the clothes still damp from the laundry. The boys found suitable matches within moments, but after trying on several shirts that fit like tents, I decided on a medic's uniform.

Along with the utilitarian gray dress that reached just past the knees, the uniform also came with a short sage-green cape and a belt containing multiple rings for tools and bags. We changed with our backs to each other, and though I despised getting rid of my familiar clothes, which I'd mended and embroidered myself, the nurse's uniform felt good against my skin, the cloth still crisp. It smelled better, too.

"Toma, are you ready?" Mikhail asked. I looked over. He had already exchanged his worn worker's clothes for the industrial, sage-green uniform of the Fraktsiya. White shirt tucked into his brown gabardine pants, leather belt cinched and adorned with a brass buckle featuring the Fraktsiya's broken chain motif. Underneath the leather brim of his cap, his cool gray eyes confronted me.

Beside him, Vanya offered me a small smile. Even more than Mikhail, he seemed at ease in his uniform, and I thought about how easily he could step from one part of his identity to another—always adapting, always moving. I envied that, his ease of transformation.

"Let's go," I said after fashioning my mother's rushnyk into a makeshift headscarf. It wasn't quite like the white veils worn by medics, but it would have to do.

We entered the same car I had passed through just minutes before. I avoided looking at the dark-haired boy who'd begged for water, though I could feel his gaze burning into me as we passed. The blond soldier was gone from the next car, leaving only the dying to observe our passage. Midway down the row of cots, the door at the other end of the compartment swung open and a young medic stepped out.

"You!" she exclaimed the moment her gaze landed on me.

"Me?" I stammered.

Her capelet was stained by a smatter of fresh blood, and her cheeks as well. Her black hair fell to her chin in a severe bob, framing dark eyes bordered by round gunmetal glasses.

"You have to come with me," the girl said, her voice strict and no-nonsense.

"What? Why?"

"There is a medical emergency in car eight."

"But—"

"This nurse is in the middle of assisting another patient," Mikhail interrupted.

"With what?" the girl asked, arching a bold eyebrow.

"One of them asked for water," I said weakly.

"How about you serve your fellow soldier and get him water yourself?" she snapped at Mikhail, before pivoting on her heel. "Please, come with me now."

With a helpless look in the boys' direction, I followed after the medic, adjusting the rushnyk that drew my hair back. I hoped that whatever the issue was, the blond soldier I had passed on my way into the train wouldn't be there. Then again, he had barely looked at me. He probably wouldn't even recognize my face.

Stanislav would be a different story.

27

The medical emergency in car eight was followed by another in car nine, and more after that. For three hours, I found myself dragged from station to station. I was no medic, but the waxed thread they used for suturing was no different than the thread I spun from flax. So, I closed gaping wounds and stuffed others with cotton, clamped perforated entrails, and salved burns. When we arrived at a patient whose foot had bloated within its boot to such a degree that we were forced to cut away the leather folds, I was the one who held him down as the other girl retrieved a bone saw.

Twice between errands, I tried to slip away, but each time she would catch me and chastise me. "There is still much work to be done, and the day is young."

She curtly introduced herself as Zemfirka Akhatova. But despite her strictness, when I told her to call me Toma, she huffed and said, "I suppose Zemfirka will do. Just don't call me Zemfirochka."

I wondered where Vanya and Mikhail were. I doubted they had gone far—Mikhail had been right in suspecting that the train was as much a mobile hospital as a means of transporting troops. Several cars I passed through were crammed with soldiers.

Past noon, Zemfirka and I stopped in the canteen for a brief lunch. Weak tea and another hot bitter drink made of roasted cornflower root, and slices of pickled herring served atop black bread. From behind some sacks of flour, Zemfirka retrieved a fresh red apple and cut it into segments. She offered me half.

I didn't realize how ravenous I was until we sat down and my legs started quivering. I crammed half a slice of bread into my mouth, nearly groaning at the herring's tangy bite and silken texture.

"Hey, slow down." She laughed. "Keep eating like that and people are going to start thinking you're an upyr."

"Sorry." I licked the salty brine off my fingertips and took a few smaller bites to show her I still had manners.

"When was the last time you ate?"

"Not since last night." Aside from a few gulps of copper-tasting water from the bottom of my canteen during our rush to the train station, I hadn't drunk anything either. "Speaking about an upyr, I heard there was one onboard."

"Mmm." Zemfirka cocked her head, resting her cheek in her palm. "Did Dima tell you that, too?"

A herring spine snapped between my molars. I winced involuntarily, recalling in an instant the sound Dima's body had made when he struck the ground. Slowly, I lowered the remnants of my bread.

"You know him?" I said, taking my tea in both hands to still my trembling fingers. The glass rattled in its metal holder. I told myself it was only from the jostling of the train, that my face revealed nothing.

"We were stationed in the same unit until a few months ago." She sipped her tea nonchalantly. "Serebrograd brigade, along the front lines. When I saw him this morning, he was bragging about catching an upyr on some top-secret mission he took with that blond soldier, the skinny one, er..."

"Stanislav," I said quietly.

She cocked a finger. "That one. Dima said he'd show me later, but honestly, he scares me more than an upyr!"

"Did he say where she—er, it was?" I asked.

"The morgue, I believe."

"And where is that?"

Zemfirka looked at me as though I were daft. "By the pharmacy car. You know, the windowless ones in the middle of the train. Maybe once we arrive in Eyry, we'll be able to see them unload it."

"Why don't we just sneak into the compartment?" I said, trying to keep my voice lighthearted. "It can't be too hard, right?"

"Considering they're monitoring the side entrance, so the only other way in would be through the door in the center of the car, I'd say it would be pretty hard," she said dryly, thrusting an apple slice in my direction for emphasis. "Besides, there's still much to do. If we aren't careful, we might end up with more than one upyr on our hands."

We turned our attention back to our meals. A few minutes later, as I finished my second slice of bread, I couldn't resist asking another question.

"How old are you?"

Zemfirka lowered her apple slice. "Eighteen. What about you?"

"Seventeen," I said, which I thought was a good guess. "Why do this?"

"What do you mean?"

"Fight."

"I don't fight, simply mend. Or try to." Zemfirka paused, slipping off her glasses. Gently, she nibbled on the end of one earpiece, her gaze turning pensive. "Have you ever seen what fire does to a person?"

My mouth was dry. I moistened my lips, feeling a memory stalk around the periphery of my consciousness—a man striding through the trees, engulfed in flames and as bright as a beacon. Even as the snow melted beneath his feet and wisps of steam trailed in his wake, he did not relent. He kept walking. Searching. Hunting.

Whatever you do to me, may they pay it back threefold, my mother had said as she'd stepped past the trees, and I'd remained under the bush where I lay, both hands over my mouth to choke my frantic panting.

Then she'd started screaming.

"The destruction, I mean," Zemfirka said, confronting me with her owlish black eyes. "How the skin burns. How the hair does. The smell."

I didn't answer, shaken to the core.

Tomochka, do not make a sound.

Moisture rose in my eyes. I wiped it away hastily, reaching under the table to pinch at my bare knee, dig my nails in. Show nothing. It didn't happen that way. It wasn't real. None of it was real.

She screamed, and you ran.

"Where you come from, who performs the executions?" Zemfirka asked, not even looking in my direction anymore. She cleaned her glasses lens with the corner of her linen napkin.

"The Tribunal," I whispered.

"I mean civil executions, like for theft or murder."

"Bogatyri as well." I could still recall the metal poles driven into the cobblestones in front of the courthouse, sometimes used as whipping posts, but more often for executions. In the darkness behind my eyes danced the crackling blue blaze that had engulfed the condemned. "By electrocution."

A thin smile rose on her lips. "For our town, it was fire. The same noble family who performed the executions also owned the farmland my family tilled and most of the businesses in Rozhorod. Before Tsarina Inessa abolished the practice, my ancestors served under them as serfs. This family had their fingers in everything, including the Tribunal, and when they came to collect, you gave them what they wanted. You gave them anything. Do you understand me?"

I didn't want to hear more. With each word Zemfirka spoke, she took me back to my past. With each word, she muddied the waters of what I wanted to believe was a simple battle between good and evil, the noble ruler and the ruthless usurper. I knew Mikhail wasn't a bad person, but what did that mean of the system he'd inherited?

"You gave them what they wanted," she repeated once more, before slipping her glasses back on. "That is why I joined. Now, how about some more fish?"

As Zemfirka rose to retrieve the rest from the tin, the train shuddered so violently that my tea glass tipped over, metal holder and all. Lukewarm tea flew across the table, and a bit of her herring flopped onto my hand. I rose to my feet, gripping onto the table for stability.

Beneath my feet, I felt the sudden jolt of levers shifting into place and wheels grinding to a screeching halt. Glasses tinkled against each other in the cabinets, and cans rolled across the floor as the train braked.

The train rolled for another fifteen seconds before coming to a shuddering halt. Slowly, I eased from my crouch.

"Why are we stopping?" I asked.

"I don't know. We can't be far from Eyry." Zemfirka went to the window and peered out, and I followed behind her. Past the window, the pine trees appeared as sharp as rusalka teeth, drowned in a haze of fog.

"What do you see?" I asked.

"Nothing. Maybe there's something on the tracks."

As she pulled away, an idea occurred to me.

"I'll check on the patients in cars nine and ten," I said. "You take seven and eight."

She nodded. "Okay."

I slipped past her, hurrying from one car to the next. The wounded soldiers groaned in their cots, and I helped up one who had fallen before continuing on my way. In car ten, I found Vanya retrieving a spilled hand of cards from the floor.

"Just my luck," he said to his companions—a soldier with bandages crossing over his nose and left eye and a girl wearing a black ribbon tied around his bandaged arm. "I swear, I was going to win this round."

"What are you doing?" I asked sharply, and he glanced up.

"Oh, nurse, just in time. Care to join us for another round?"

"Where's…" I trailed off, catching a glimpse of the wounded soldier's gray eye. Mikhail offered me a strained smile, rising to his feet. The uniform had already been an adequate disguise, but the bandages were even more so.

"I need some help in car eleven," I said, thinking quickly. "Can you two be of assistance?"

"Of course," Vanya said, before nodding to the girl and tossing her the pack of cards. "Why don't you hold on to these? They'll keep you entertained."

We entered the storage car, finding a private niche behind the laundry baskets.

"Do you think they found out that we're onboard?" I whispered.

"I doubt it," Mikhail said. "It's not unusual for a train to stop en route. It's possible we're stuck behind some kind of convoy or that there's an issue with the tracks. We passed the border crossing about an hour ago, so we can't be more than twenty minutes outside the city. We're deep in Fraktsiya territory."

"Listen, I know where Galina is," I said, struggling to keep my voice level and contain my excitement. "They're holding her in the morgue car. This might be our only opportunity to get to her."

With the train locked at a dead stop, I could climb out the train and hurry to the middle cars. Her captors wouldn't even know she was gone until the train arrived in Eyry, and by then, we would already have smuggled her out.

Mikhail shook his head vehemently. "It's too dangerous. The train can start up again at any moment, and if we get off now, we'll never be able to find Koschei."

His blunt words struck me like a blow to the stomach. It slowly dawned on me. "You don't care about her at all, do you?"

He looked at me, pained. "Toma, it's not like that."

"Mikhail, even if you find Koschei, are you going to sacrifice everything just so you can kill him?"

"This is more than just revenge, Toma. You've seen what he's done—he's sacrificed these people all in a desperate attempt to maintain control. The only way this bloody insurrection will end is if I take him down."

"Toma, Mikhail is right," Vanya added, and I turned to him in disbelief.

"I can't believe it. You too? I thought you were on my side." We'd even kissed. Did that mean nothing?

Vanya grimaced. "I'm not taking *anyone's* side here, Toma."

"Really? Because it certainly sounds like you're taking his."

"I'm just trying to keep all three of us from getting killed."

"You know what? Fine." I swiveled around. "You two have fun with your game."

"Where are you going?" Mikhail called as I strode across the car.

"Back to the medic's station. At least there, people actually appreciate me." I slammed the door shut behind me, glowering at my feet as I crossed down the row of cots. So many things could happen between here and Eyry. So many things could go wrong.

"All clear?" Zemfirka asked as I entered car eight.

"All clear," I snapped, passing her without stopping.

She blinked. "Where are you going?"

"Lavatory." I walked to the end of the next car, searching for the water closet I had used on a break between suturing. I found it at the other end of car seven, in a compartment so small

I could scarcely turn around in it. Shutting the door, I thumbed the lock and forced the window open. Nets of billowing mist ensnared the train and surrounding pine trees, and the sour tang of wood smoke sullied the air. No sign of patrolling guards.

I stepped onto the wooden toilet seat and crawled through the window feetfirst, grasping onto the upper frame to maintain my balance. The moment my feet touched the ground, I broke into a run.

When we had passed through villages, the train's resounding whistle echoed against the walls of buildings, distorted into a bestial screech. Now, it curled like a corpse upon the tracks, deathly silent, the fog seeping down its windows.

Ahead, a pillar of dark smoke cut through the fog bank. I couldn't make out the source of the obstruction, but several of the trees in the distance were engulfed with flames, and as I watched, one collapsed onto the tracks in a wave of sparks.

This wasn't the work of a lightning strike or forest fire, not when the fog enveloped me like a wet blanket and overhead sifted only more mist. It had to be bogatyri.

I unwrapped my rushnyk from around my hair and tented it over myself, protecting my head and vitals as I rushed toward the front of the train. Wary of being spotted, I kept close to the tracks, ducking my head low.

I counted the cars under my breath, envisioning my place on the maps that had been pinned up by each door. Car five! This had to be it. Slamming to a stop beside the windowless car, I climbed onto the metal step and eased open the sliding door.

Warily, I wrapped the rushnyk into a hood and stepped inside. Wisps of vapor trailed from grates at either end of the car, filling the compartment with a damp, frigid fog. Bodies were stacked in open shelves, their ankles chained together.

Some had already developed a film of hoarfrost upon their boots and pant legs.

Against the farther wall sat a wooden crate, the sort used to transport animals. Holes had been drilled into its side, and its hasp was fitted with a padlock. Fingers peeped from one of those holes—small, fragile fingers that were more bone than flesh, swaddled in layer after layer of decayed lace and silk. Around the pinky finger, I caught a glimpse of the same delicate embroidery I had sewn just days before.

I stepped forward. "Galina—"

I froze. Resting in the shadows across the room, Stanislav leaned against the wall, his eyes fidgeting restlessly beneath his closed lids. He cradled a rifle as though it were a child, with the bayonet angled upward and his cheek resting against the barrel.

He mumbled in his sleep, the words slurred into incoherence. His tongue darted out to lick at his lips, as though to catch a trace of something sweet.

"Toma?" Galina rasped, her faint voice nearly bringing tears to my eyes. Her fingers grasped through the holes, searching for me. It took all I had not to rush to her side.

I edged closer, sinking into a crouch and keeping to the shadows. Kneeling before the crate, I pressed my lips against a hole and whispered, "It's me. Don't make a sound. I'm going to get you out of here."

"I'm so scared." Her voice trembled. "I was afraid I'd never see you again."

"I know. Don't worry, I'm here now. Just hold on and be quiet. We're not alone."

"Is it the scary men?"

"Yes, but don't be afraid. I won't let them hurt you. Never

again." I tested the padlock. It held, and the jiggling of the bolt made me wince.

Across the room, Stanislav shifted and groaned, still in the confines of sleep.

I eased my knife from my dress's utilitarian pocket, creeping closer and closer. A bottle of hazy fluid rested at his side. Samogon.

The ring of keys dangled on his belt. It would've been easy, so incredibly easy, to bury my blade up to the hilt in his neck. It could be over in an instant, and he wouldn't even wake up. He likely wouldn't even feel a thing. How was that any different than stalking a deer through the underbrush or snaring a rabbit as it scavenged for spring grass? If anything, it would be a mercy.

Closer. Closer. Six paces away now, my fingers tightened around my knife's handle.

Underneath the scruff bristling under his chin, I caught sight of the rapid palpitation of his pulse. His heart was beating rabbit-quick. A dream, maybe, or a nightmare.

As I got within four paces of him, my foot struck something smooth and hard. The object gave way in an instant, tipping over and shattering.

I looked down. Milky formaldehyde sluiced over shards of broken glass. The two-headed piglet flopped across the floor, pale and shrunken, like a squashed maggot.

When I looked up again, Stanislav's eyes were open.

28

For a moment, I froze in absolute stillness, my legs immobile beneath me. It must've only been a fragment of a second, but in that time, the world came to a standstill, and all I could do was think about the harsh snap of Dima's spine giving way, the slap of flesh striking gravel.

Then, as if possessed by something much greater than myself, my body moved on its own. I lunged forward, closing the distance between us even before Stanislav managed to shift the rifle out from its resting position.

He met me head-on. The bayonet blade swooped over my head, carving a path a mere finger's width from my scalp, close enough that I felt the air part around it.

I dropped down to a crouch, twirling my knife in my hand so that its tip pointed forward, and lunged at him, aiming for the fatty pouch of flesh beneath his jaw. As I brought the blade up, he shifted the barrel and blocked my knife's ascent. The blade scraped against the iron barrel, sending off a rain of sparks that fizzled out in an instant, but not before briefly illuminating his crazed blue eyes.

"You again," he growled, fumbling for the rifle's bolt. The rank odor of samogon muddled his breath. His fingers were slow and clumsy from sleep, or drink, or both. "How did you get here?"

"I killed Dima," I spat, hoping to throw him off balance. It worked. For a moment he froze, giving me the opportunity to circle around him, searching for an opening. In these close quarters, with the walls insulated behind thick panels of metal that would be prone to ricochet, I doubted he would fire the gun. But if he did, I wanted to be prepared.

Then, just as quickly, the shock in his eyes flared into rage. Baring his teeth at me, he lunged forward. "You bitch!"

Stanislav swept the bayonet at me in rapid, aggressive stabs and slashes. The bayonet had three times the range of my simple hunting knife, and unlike the knife, it parried my blows with ease. Each impact resounded through my arm until my fingers numbed.

I stumbled back, dancing away from the sweeping edge of the bayonet. Its tip tore through my frock, drawing a seething trail from my shoulder to my collarbone. The pain was harsh enough to tear a gasp from my lips. Just a flesh wound, I prayed.

I ducked as Stanislav drove the bayonet forward. We were nearly to the brink now. Against my back, I felt the breeze enter through the open door.

The bayonet skittered across the wall and snapped free of its holder, landing at our feet. I made to kick it away, and as I did so, Stanislav switched the rifle to a two-handed grip.

He drove the heavy wooden stock against my chest, slamming the air from my lungs and casting me backward into thin air. For a moment I was airborne, the world reduced to a blur of fog and greenery, and then I landed hard and tumbled across gravel.

Slowly, I came to a rolling halt. A filmy grayness spread its petals across the edges of my vision as I struggled to rise to my feet. The harsh taste of blood filled my mouth, and more of the same trickled down my cheek in a hot ripple. My body felt loosely strung, like a marionette jointed by barbed wire.

"Koldunia or not, this time you will stay dead," Stanislav snarled, jumping down from the train car. As he aimed the rifle at my head, a searing bolt of light shimmered off the barrel and his entire being dissolved into a bluish glow. The stench struck me moments later—burnt hair, burnt skin. He collapsed to the earth in a charred pile, fingers of lightning crackling off his body and receding into the earth.

I blinked slowly, one eye gummed shut with blood. Could I have done this?

The source revealed itself moments later, emerging from the trees to my right. A young man dressed in white, with the indigo sash and epaulets of the bogatyri adorning his uniform jacket. Veins of electricity skittered up his cheeks, framing his golden hair and refined features in a saint's glowing nimbus. He gazed down at me, his brow furled in puzzlement, and I realized then that he hadn't been trying to save me—he had intended to execute us both indiscriminately.

"What are you?" Lightning crackled up his arms, smoldering at his fingertips.

"W-wait, I'm on your side."

"I doubt that." As the bogatyr raised his hand, there was a sound like the snap of a frozen branch. He stumbled against the tree behind him, a crimson circle of blood blooming across his uniform jacket as he sank to the ground.

Weakly, I turned my head.

Mikhail stood no more than fifteen paces away, smoke trailing from the revolver he held in both hands. He slowly lowered the weapon, his features ashen. Vanya raced after him and came to my side.

"You two came," I croaked.

"Of course, we came," Vanya said, resting his hand on my back as I struggled to sit up. "Easy. Don't get up just yet."

"We need to get Galina." Blood poured down the side of my face, leaking onto my lips. Wiping my eyes with the back of my hand, I waited for my blurred vision to clear. I tried to stand, but Vanya kept a steady grip on my shoulder, his gaze straying to the front of the train.

"Tsar, get down," he said quietly.

Other Otzvuk soldiers emerged from the trees forty or fifty paces to our right, a good two dozen of them decked in full regalia. Yet more stood at the front of the train.

"What's going on?" Vanya asked Mikhail, who sank to a crouch beside us. "This is a hospital train."

"Even a wounded soldier is a soldier," Mikhail said gravely, resting a palm on a tree trunk. "Most of these men have been trained with that in mind. It's imperial protocol—when you're in enemy territory, you take no prisoners. Toma, don't move just yet."

"My sister—"

"You won't be able to help your sister if you're set on fire," he said as a train door opened near the front of the line.

"Can't you do something?"

"Not dressed like the Fraktsiya."

A lone man stepped out, his hands raised above his head. It was the blond soldier who had been tending to the wounded.

An Otzvuk soldier emerged from the ranks to greet him. Gold epaulets and medals adorned his white greatcoat. The gilt elements glistened in the glow of the flames roosted at his fingertips.

My stomach twisted, and the pulsing gray fog edging around the corners of my vision threatened to overtake me. It wasn't the same man from my memory, but just like that time, I felt frozen. Helpless. My legs trembled beneath me, and I pressed my palms over my mouth to stifle my breathing.

"Are you the captain of this train?" the bogatyr shouted, his voice filtering through the fog. As he stepped forward, he left a trail of scorched earth in his wake. "Tell your men that if they surrender the train now, no innocent lives will be lost."

"I too believe in sparing the innocent," the blond soldier called back, his voice reverberating through the clearing with all the presence of an earthquake. From where I knelt, I only caught a glimpse of his smile. "Unfortunately for you bogatyri, you've spent centuries bathing your hands in blood."

29

"That poor fool is going to get himself killed," Vanya muttered, shaking his head in dismay.

Beside me, Mikhail's hand trembled upon my shoulder. The blood drained from his face as he stared at the blond soldier.

"Koschei," he whispered.

Koschei was young. Far younger than I had imagined, younger than my birth mother had been when she died. If he'd fought in the Groznaya War ten years ago, he couldn't have been any older than us at the time.

At first, nothing happened. Then it was as though the breeze had changed directions, and I felt something pass over me, pass through me.

Beneath my knees, the grass browned. I struggled to my feet despite the boys' protests and took a trembling step toward the train car. Vanya tried to grab my shoulder and snagged my rushnyk instead, unintentionally pulling it off as I wrenched free of him. Scabs of red rot spread across the toes of my boots in an instant. Before the leather could fall apart entirely, Vanya and Mikhail yanked me back to the shelter of the trees.

Koschei's head shifted ever so slightly in our direction, his golden-green eyes boring into the underbrush. My breath caught in my throat. Had he seen me?

The bogatyri closer to Koschei didn't immediately realize what was happening. Not until the Otzvuk commander tried setting him alight, and halfway across the field, the fireball disintegrated into smoke and ashes. The commander himself collapsed to his knees, writhing and screaming. Even from a distance, I could see the way his body distorted—his hair draining of color and his limbs withering into emaciated husks.

Shock and horror swept over me. This was the Unclean Force. This was what it meant to be spoiled, to be cursed—a decay strong enough to tear your power out from within, or cause the body to collapse into bones and sinew, or neutralize the gunpowder in munitions.

"Wait, what about Galina?" I cried as Vanya and Mikhail dragged me deeper into the underbrush. I struggled against them, but by the second, my vision narrowed into a pinhole.

"Galina is already dead, Toma!" Mikhail said sternly. "You're not."

Fueled by a sudden burst of strength, I broke free of their grasps and made a dash for the tree line. My legs gave out beneath me after three steps, and the world dissolved into darkness. I never felt myself hit the ground.

Drifting in and out of consciousness, I found myself torn between two places at once—a forest ensnared in fog, and then a town high in the mountains, built in the shadow of silver mines. Like the petals of a dying rose, memories peeled free and floated down to me.

I remembered my mother embroidering the rushnyky for the Troika altars, at peace in her sewing. She had always seemed comfortable sitting in the thronelike chairs lining the walls of the sanctuary, surrounded on all sides by frescoes of saintly bogatyri and minor deities.

But every so often on our way home, she would turn down a side street and guide me by the hand down a narrow stairway cut into the mountainside. We'd enter the neighborhood below ours—dark, winding alleys hewn into a precarious cliff overlooking the valley below, either side of us blocked in by tightly-packed shops and houses. She spoke to no one we passed, but she took the streets as though they were familiar to her. And when we arrived at the aspen-shingled Strannik temple perched at the edge of the precipice, she'd peer through the door if it were open—it rarely was—or pause to slip a few coins through the collection slot. She had never explained these rituals to me, except to say that in days like these, everybody needed kindness and charity. At the time, it had seemed no different than why she insisted on teaching me embroidery—not the patterns on Troika rushnyky or northern regional dress, but the symbols singular to the heirloom she had bequeathed me.

It had never been about embroidery at all for her, had it? It had been a way to pass on the protection of the runes, something her family must have carried with them from mother to daughter over the centuries, back to the days the Stranniki had carved the symbols into their swords and armor.

But that memory was not important. It was just accessory.

By the time I was six, the Strannik temple had been reduced to smoldering ruins, and that dim, labyrinthine neighborhood cradling the cliffside lay deserted and plundered. It would be another year until the Groznaya War ended, and another four until the snowy night my mother strode boldly to her death in order to save me.

What came next was the magistrate's wife.

When my mother had brought me to the magistrate's house for the first time, I remember shying away in fear, recognizing the young woman from the second-floor balcony of the Troika temple, where she sat alongside her husband and gazed disinterestedly at her feet. With her flaxen hair, waxen complexion, and rheumy blue eyes, when she sat in the shadows, she appeared on the verge of fading away entirely. I didn't realize how young she was then. Everyone was an adult to me.

Even in her own estate, the magistrate's wife seemed lethargic, sprawled on the window seat like a wilted hothouse flower while my mother tailored the armfuls of lace and silk clothing the magistrate had mail-ordered from Svet. The only time I had seen the teenage girl use her gift was to play with the raindrops on the window glass, causing them to flow in aimless patterns, until her interest waned and the streams she made sluiced away with all the rest. Sometimes, as my mother worked, the magistrate's wife would squander her expensive rouge and powders on me, idly coloring in my face and curling my hair with iron crimpers heated over a candle, but most of the time she sat at the window and did nothing at all.

But the magistrate's wife was not important. She, too, was just accessory to the tragedy.

The important thing, the truly important thing, had been

the magistrate, hadn't it? A good two decades older than his wife, striking in his crimson Tribunal coat, his polished boots, his mink-fur cap. He had ruffled a hand through my hair when he came across me in his wife's sitting room and called me "little blackbird," as though we were already familiar. The first time he requested my mother's assistance in mending a tear in his uniform coat, she sat at the dining room table, silent and impassive, while he stood over her and watched her work.

"You have a pretty girl," he told her, glancing over at me. His smile was warm, but something about it frightened me, and I shuffled behind her chair back. While his wife reminded me of a pet rabbit, with his sharply cropped brown hair, jet eyes, and severe features, he brought to mind a raptor. "She must get it from you. Your husband is not so pretty."

My mother offered a polite smile. "My husband is kind."

"Kindness can only bring so much satisfaction." He eased against the table, studying her with that same half smile. "It doesn't put food on the table."

The next time he called upon her, it was to mend a rip in the upholstered sofa, down below, so she had to kneel. And the time after that, she came to fit him for a new pair of uniform trousers.

On that third visit, she gripped my hand so tightly as we left that her fingers raised pink marks on my skin. When I looked up at her to tell her she was hurting me, the setting sun gleamed across her gritted teeth and the moisture brimming in her eyes. And something about that—knowing she was trying not to cry—terrified me. It seemed to go against some natural law, as if our places in the world had been reversed. And in that moment, I wanted desperately to comfort her.

"I won't go back, Tomochka," she whispered as we walked

home, still holding my hand rigidly. "I can't, no matter the cost. Oh, that girl. That poor girl."

Then had come the cave-in. Fifteen men buried alive, twenty others killed immediately, and my father one of the few brought out whole, which made him inherently dangerous. He was burnt on the pyre with all the rest, although I imagined not before the Troika priestesses had taken the proper precautions.

I had cried. I was sure that I had cried. But I had seen so little of him over the years—he spent over two-thirds of my life buried deep in the mines—that in my memory, he was a ghost carved in the glow of our hearth. A man who sat and ate by the fire. Or a motionless shape under the quilt when my mother and I rose early on winter mornings to heat the water.

Sometime after the funeral, the magistrate had shown up at our home to offer his condolences. My mother accepted them tranquilly, politely, and as she tried to shut the door, he wedged his polished cavalry boot in to block it. I saw it all from behind her, having spent the days since my father's death clinging to her skirt as though the hem had sewn itself to my fingertips.

"I heard something interesting about you today, Raisa," he said, smiling pleasantly.

"My daughter is hungry, and I need to cook dinner for her, sir." Her dark eyes were unwavering.

"They say that when your husband was placed upon the pyre, you tried to stop them." He took a step past the threshold, and the door slipped from her fingers and eased shut behind him. "The attendants had to hold you back."

"I was in shock." She kept her voice level, her expression as slack as the hands hanging limply at her sides. "In mourning."

"They say, you said that he must be buried whole. That he must be protected until his soul can pass. What did you mean by that?"

"Grief makes us mad."

"I see. Where did you say you were from again?"

"Vesnino."

"A strange accent for a city like that." His fingertips traced along her forehead, gently tucking an errant strand of soot-black hair behind her ear. She flinched at his touch. "You know, the heretics have a most unusual custom. They believe that if the dead are not interred whole, the soul will reach the afterlife as it is—fragmented, burnt, blinded. So, when one of theirs dies, they do not purify it through fire or division. They just sit there and wait for it to rot. You can't help but wonder if most of the monsters come from their own stock."

My mother didn't answer, and when he took a step deeper into the room, she remained where she was, only shifting to brush her hand over my back. "I can assure you, Oleg Sergeyevich, what you heard of, it was nothing more than a brief madness. A hysteria, if you will, as we women are prone to."

"Certainly. And please, there's no need for such formalities. Call me Olezhka." Still smiling, he turned to me. "Hello, little blackbird. I have something for you. A gift from my wife. The last time you visited, she caught you admiring it."

He squatted down and took a small rock-crystal dog from his pocket. It had been part of a carved stone menagerie displayed in a little gilded cage atop the fireplace mantel. I took it from his hand, and as I began to pull away, his fingers locked around my wrist.

"Say thank you," he reminded with a solemn nod.

"Thank you," I mumbled. The moment he let go, I retreated behind my mother.

The magistrate straightened to his full height. "Your daughter is lovely, but you are even lovelier."

"Your wife is very pretty too, sir."

"My wife is a vapid fool. Perhaps you should send your daughter to bed."

"She's been having nightmares since her father's death. We sleep together now."

"That's a shame. The nightmares, that is." He rubbed the faint shadow of stubble darkening his chin. "I should be going then, to leave you to your dinner. But before I forget, the pants you altered are unraveling at the inseam. For what I paid you, it is unacceptable. You will need to correct them."

"I can pick them up, sir, or you can have one of your attendants drop them off if you please."

He didn't answer, just smiled at her, and after a moment she drew in a shallow breath and nodded.

"When would be a good time for me to come by?"

"Tomorrow evening at seven o'clock." Turning away, he opened the front door. "And don't bring your daughter this time."

That was the beginning of the end. I knew it in my heart. Because the moment the door had shut behind him, she had bolted it. We'd eaten leftover gruel for supper that night as she sat at the kitchen table in just her bloomers and shift, immersed in the act of embroidering her mourning dress. Black thread upon black wool, a candle held to the fabric to track her progress. And when she'd gone to visit him the next evening, she had been wearing my rushnyk.

30

I was torn from sleep by a shrill, undulating sob. Moisture ran down my face, gathering on my eyelashes and in the trough of my lips. My parched tongue found the droplets. Clean. Rainwater or tears.

Slowly, I cracked open my eyes. Overhead, layers of fog sifted through the branches. I caught the faintest whiff of wood smoke when the breeze changed directions, but its source was far from here.

The sobbing continued for a few moments longer, garbled and distorted. The cry of a newborn. I was too exhausted to feel more than a stirring of trepidation, much less summon the energy to sit up and wipe at the tears rising in my eyes.

Close to my ear, I heard the metallic click of a rifle bolt sliding into place. "Just the drekavcy," Vanya murmured, not to me, maybe only to himself. "Do you think they feed?"

I watched the mist snake and coil through the pine canopy. Even after the drekavac's cries died into eerie silence, the weight of them seemed to linger around me as though suspended in the fog.

The drekavcy were harbingers of death, my mother had told me on our doomed journey, and she had been right. I wondered if she knew it then, if she could hear it in the spirits' screams—that they were singing a dirge for her.

After all this time, my memories were coming home to me, but over the years, they'd lost their substance and feeling. I had been so young then. I hadn't even realized what was happening right before me.

Looking back, I felt divided—both the girl who had stood there watching, and another girl, a stranger one born to the wilderness. I wished I could leave those memories with the first girl, the child, Tomochka. For how much I'd thought I wanted to find myself, I wished I'd never gone looking at all.

Carefully, I eased to a sitting position. I rested in a natural windbreak alongside a dry riverbed, an overhang formed by the eroded bank and a net of gnarled roots belonging to the pine tree looming overhead.

"I'm glad you're awake," Mikhail said quietly from beside me, Stanislav's rifle angled across his crossed legs.

"What happened?" I looked around, struggling to shake away my daze. "Where are we?"

"Mikhail and I dragged you as far as we could," Vanya said, sitting at my other side. "It's all right. You're safe now."

"The train?"

Vanya shook his head. "I doubt it's even there still, and if it is, we can't go back. The screaming stopped about thirty minutes ago, but…" He trailed off.

Slowly, I sank against the dirt wall. I just wanted to go

home, but I knew in my heart that without Galina, that place would never be my home again.

A couple of raindrops splashed on my head. I looked up at the rumbling clouds, wiping my watery eyes with the back of my hand. A miserable laugh pressed against the back of my throat. As if this day couldn't get any worse.

"Toma?" Mikhail asked, and I slowly shifted my gaze to his calm, composed features. Even now, he kept up his barricades. Cold. Hardened.

"This close," I said, showing him the distance between my thumb and index finger. "I was this close to touching her, to saving her. And now I'll never see her again."

Mikhail sighed, running a hand through his hair. I could tell he was struggling to find the right consolatory words, and that only made me angrier. He was the one who had gotten me involved in all this. It was his fault Galina was gone. He could at least look at me.

"You can't give up," he said at last.

I shook my head. "Don't you get it? It's over. She's gone. We've lost."

My mother had known when to give up. She had relinquished her rushnyk to me before stepping between the trees, because she knew that sometimes we could not win. Sometimes, there were no happy endings.

"That doesn't sound like the Toma I know," Vanya said, although with none of his usual lightheartedness.

"Now's not the time for jokes," I snapped.

"The Toma I know wouldn't give up like this." His green eyes met mine. "She would keep fighting."

A strangled laugh escaped my throat. "How? The train is gone."

"We go to Eyry," Mikhail said, rising to his feet. He drew the rifle sling over his shoulder and offered me a hand. "It can't be far now, so we continue on foot. We walk all night if we have to. And once we get there, we find Koschei and end this once and for all."

At the boys' behest, I rested for twenty minutes until the rain lightened to a miserable drizzle. By the time I convinced them that I was well enough to start walking, I had begun to feel a little more in control. They were right. It wasn't over. This wasn't like back then with my mother. There was still time to save Galina.

Rolling my lower lip between my teeth, I followed behind the others. I didn't want to think about all the things Koschei might do to her. I tried to focus on the forest ahead. One step after another. Dead leaves. A slug. A cloud of gnats.

As we walked, I thought I heard soft laughter. I looked around and spotted a mavka studying us through the trees. She was a different creature than the one who had stalked us when we had first left Vanya's village. This mavka had straight blond hair instead of wild black curls, and a smatter of freckles stood out against her pale skin. A cloud of blue swallowtail butterflies followed her, flitting in and out of the gaps between her exposed ribs, where cocoons hung like crooked teeth.

She tried to catch our attention by beckoning, then by crooning wordlessly in a crackly voice like the rustling of dead leaves. Vanya hurried on ahead, keeping his eyes directed at the ground at his feet, and she followed close beside him, teasing him. Just as I picked up a rock to scare her off, she disappeared into the trees, giggling all the while.

"I think she likes you, Ivan," Mikhail said.

"Would you kindly shut up, Your Highness?"

"Must be all that rusalka blood you have in you."

Vanya was so busy glowering at Mikhail that he didn't notice the puddle ahead until he stepped in it, burying his boot up to the ankle.

"No!" he groaned, tearing his boot free. He sighed at the thick, dripping mud and scraped his shoe on the ground. "You know, my father used to say that if you leave yarn or linen out for the mavki, they'll do something for you in return, like watch over your grazing livestock. It's also why your clothes sometimes disappear when you hang them out to dry. He told me the mavki steal them."

"Can you stop talking about your father?" Mikhail growled.

Vanya looked almost as stunned by Mikhail's outburst as I was. "What's wrong about me talking about him?"

"I'm sick of hearing about it. You just never shut your mouth. Don't you realize that you're the only one here who gives a damn about what your father said?"

"I care," I said.

Vanya cocked his head, challenging Mikhail with a sarcastic smile. "All right, Tsarushka, let's hear about your father then. Enlighten us."

"No." Mikhail glared at him. "I'm not going to talk about him just so you can twist around everything I say and mock me."

As they bickered, I searched the forest once more, but there was no sign of the mavka. I sighed, shoving my hands into my coat pockets. The dead could only return once. For saving Galina, this would be my only chance.

"Someone slept poorly this morning," Vanya said, and walked on ahead, leaving Mikhail and me alone in awkward silence.

"Mikhail, what's wrong?" I asked softly, once Vanya had put some distance between us.

"Nothing, I just…I'm sick of hearing him talk about it." Mikhail's voice caught on the last word. He cleared his throat and continued. "Why does he feel the need to tell us about what his father was like?"

There was something almost defensive about the way Mikhail said it, as if he had taken personal offense to Vanya's stories. It nagged at the back of my mind as we continued walking.

Mikhail took a deep breath. "You need to understand. My father. My father…"

The muscles tensed in his throat as he struggled with what he wanted to say, as if the words actually had physical weight.

"My father *hated* me," Mikhail forced out, a pained grimace contorting his features. "Ever since I could remember, he never told me that he loved me. Never hugged me, never comforted me. Growing up, it felt like he was constantly testing me, but I wouldn't realize they were tests until I saw his disapproval. I couldn't even befriend other boys without him remarking on their class, or their uncouthness, or…or the way I acted around them. If I so much as greeted a stable boy or a servant, he'd call me a disgrace, a dishonor to the crown. And nothing I did was ever enough."

The moment the words left his mouth, the rigid muscles in his neck and shoulders relaxed, and his hard jawline softened. He exhaled slowly, as if a great burden had been lifted from his back.

I imagined Mikhail as a child, trying to impress his father with a show of his powers or a snippet of new information learned from his tutors. And then what? No reaction, not even a hint of a smile? Or just indifferent silence?

It was all beginning to make sense now. Over the years, Mikhail had built a shell for himself, a barrier to distance himself so that he would never suffer from rejection or want of affection. Always on the inside, and always an outsider.

"Mikhail, I'm so sorry," I said, pierced by sadness.

"I've never told that to anyone," he said at last, a vague smile tugging at the corners of his lips. "I don't know why."

This journey was changing all of us. It was only when Mikhail turned ahead again, his back straight and head held high, that I realized I didn't just want to save Galina anymore—I wanted to watch Mikhail regain his throne and transform the empire into what it was meant to be all along.

No. I didn't want to watch. I wanted to be a part of it.

We took shelter in a shallow cave as the sun began to set. The storm had relented after a few hours, dark clouds unfurling to reveal a full moon rising.

I prodded a stick into the depths of the fire we had built at the cave's entrance, where the smoke could escape and trees provided a natural windbreak. The burning logs crackled, spewing a mist of red and gold sparks into the night sky. I snapped the branch in two and fed it to the flames, rubbing my hands to warm them.

Joining Mikhail on the ground, I pressed my hand against my lower stomach, wincing as a painful cramp stitched my side. Just hunger or gas. If I remained on schedule, it would be another week or so until my bleeding started again. I hoped to be on my way home with Galina by then, or at least somewhere with a supply of clean rags.

A breeze rattled the pine boughs and churned sparks from the fire.

"If it gets any colder, it might not be the monsters that kill us," Vanya mused, wrapping his arms around himself as he shivered. "It'll be this damn cold."

"Don't be so negative," I said.

He grinned. "That's asking too much of me."

A thin smile touched my lips. I unpinned the amber brooch that fastened my rushnyk around my shoulders and unfolded it. At its full length, the cloth was just barely wide enough to cover all three of us if we sat shoulder to shoulder, hip to hip.

"It's not much of a blanket, but it'll keep out the wind," I said when Mikhail gave it a questioning look as I extended one end in his direction.

"Thank you." He drew the embroidered fabric over himself. "At least I won't die from the cold."

I settled back, trying to drift off. After lying awake for almost thirty minutes, my skin crawling with anxious tension, I fell into a restless sleep.

In my dream, I was back in Vanya's apartment during that hazy time of day when you couldn't tell if it was dusk or dawn. Vanya sat in the chair by the unlit fireplace, dressed in the clothes he had been wearing on the day we met. He wouldn't acknowledge me. His green eyes were focused on a stain on the wall.

We didn't speak. As a shadow edged across the room, his shirt's gold embroidery tarnished until it was as dark as ink.

"I'm so tired," Vanya mumbled, but I didn't think he was talking to me. In the distance, a bell began to toll, and the shadow swelled until it touched him. "I just want to sleep."

Suddenly, I jolted awake, startled by loud voices. For a moment, I thought that the yelling was a part of my dream. A harsh light shone in my eyes, blinding me.

"Show us your hands!" a man shouted. "Your hands! Put up your hands!"

Shapes emerged from the forest's edge—men carrying long-arms, their faces garish in the red glow of our fire's embers.

Mikhail shifted out from under my rushnyk, began to rise, and then abruptly sat down again. He lifted his arms in the air, his gray eyes flickering from man to man. "We don't want any trouble."

"Is that so?" One soldier laughed sardonically, eying Mikhail's sage-green greatcoat. "You don't want any trouble. Some way to greet your comrades, isn't it?"

Vanya groaned, still in the clutches of sleep. Squinting into the harsh lantern light, he wiped his mouth with the back of his hand. "Whuuuh?"

"I said show me your hands!"

I followed Mikhail's example, and Vanya, evidently awake enough now to recognize basic commands, raised his hands as well.

A mustached man in a peaked hat strode forward, close

enough that I could smell the musk of tobacco smoke and sweat clinging to his body. He picked up the rifle Mikhail had leaned against the cavern wall, turning it over in his hands as though to admire its craftsmanship.

"I suppose your uniforms weren't the only thing you stole from us, hmm?" Underneath the glossy leather brim of his cap, the soldier's dark-amber eyes regarded us—flat, intelligent eyes with heavy lids, the eyes of a bloodhound.

My stomach dropped at the sight of heavy-jowled features— he had been on the train, and Zemfirka had greeted him as Lieutenant Dronov with a nervous titter and unease in her eyes. In private, she had told me that out of all the soldiers who had served in the Serebrograd brigade with her and Dima, Lieutenant Dronov had been the most unpredictable—and the most cruel.

"Listen, we can explain—" Vanya began, and was about to say more when Dronov slammed the stock of his rifle into his stomach. Collapsing forward, Vanya hacked for breath.

"Vanya!" I scrambled forward, only to stop dead as one of the lieutenant's underlings leveled his bayonet at me.

I sank back onto my knees and discreetly gathered my rushnyk against myself, protecting my vital organs. I wished Vanya and Mikhail hadn't shifted out from under the tapestry. If it could protect me from a bogatyr's magic, then maybe it would shield us from bullets as well.

"Give me one reason why we shouldn't kill you where you sit," Dronov said, pacing before us. His gaze lingered on Mikhail before shifting to me. He narrowed his eyes. "You, girl. You were on the train."

"No, I…" I gulped. "You're mistaken."

"Is that so?"

"I wasn't. I don't even know what train you're talking about."

With a sneer, he glanced at his companions. "Notice anything strange here, boys?"

The other men just looked tired and irritated, although a few had a hungry glint in their eyes that I didn't care for at all.

"She sounds different from the others, Lieutenant Dronov," a blond-haired man said.

In the corner of my eye, I watched Vanya wheeze and grip the dirt in fistfuls. Grass grew from between his fingers in long, glossy fronds.

Using his rifle's barrel, Lieutenant Dronov pointed at us each in turn.

Vanya. "The Edge. Strannik filth."

Mikhail. "Somewhere to the north of here. The capital is my guess."

Me. "And you sound like a damned Grozniy to me."

"She doesn't sound like a Grozniy," Vanya broke in, his voice ragged. "She just—"

"They're spies working for the Otzvuk. They were probably the ones who warned the bogatyri that the Premier was on the train."

"Damn it, we're not spies," Mikhail snapped. "Have you even heard a Grozniy speak before?"

"Lucky for you three, we won't kill you like the other Otzvuk stragglers we've come across tonight." A dull smile touched Dronov's thin, bloodless lips. "We'll let Koschei decide your fates."

31

The first ruby gash of dawn light burned on the horizon, backlighting the mountains that curled in a jagged backbone along the valley's crest. Coils of fog sifted at our feet. Each time I inhaled, the damp vapors settled heavily in my lungs.

The Fraktsiya soldiers marched us down the road. Vanya was deep in conversation with two of his captors, making self-deprecating jokes and laughing uneasily while Mikhail ruminated in dark silence.

Lieutenant Dronov passed a flask around, and after the men had taken their fill, it made its way back to us. Vanya took a shuddering sip, sloshing half a mouthful on his shirt collar.

"Now this—this is a really funny one." His voice clicked in his throat. "Do you know that the Goddess actually has four faces, not three?"

"Where's the fourth one?" drawled the dark-haired soldier with watery blue eyes and a knotted scar splitting his face from brow to chin cleft.

"She keeps it shoved up her ass." Vanya chuckled, but it was strained. The moment the men's laughter died down, his gaze strayed away, and face went slack. He stared into the forest, but all I could see was the many-eyed trunks of the birch trees, their branches tangled overhead like a net of dismembered limbs.

"What is it?" Mikhail asked.

"Nothing." He took another, deeper glug of the drink. "Just remembering, I forgot to feed my cat."

In the distance, a drekavac screamed, and the soldiers huddled closer to each other, their fingers edging toward their rifles' triggers.

When the flask reached me, it was nearly empty. To smooth my raw nerves, I drained the rest. The liquid burned my throat on the way down, sharper than vodka, with an unpleasant aftertaste. Even so, it did the trick in relaxing me and quieting the torrent of thoughts rushing through my head.

The first chance I got, I tied my rushnyk around my waist, looping one end over my shoulder to secure it in place. I didn't remove the amber brooch from my pocket, afraid that our captors would take it from me.

"That's a pretty rushnyk," the soldier nearest to me said. He had the thin, tight face of a weasel and a pair of small, gleaming eyes to match, but his smile was pleasant enough.

"Thank you," I said.

"I've never seen one quite like it."

"It was my mother's," I mumbled, trying not to recoil when he grasped my shoulder, running his fingers over the raised red embroidery.

"Beautiful. Incredible craftsmanship. The patterns are exquisite." He stared at me as he said it. My skin crawled, maybe from the drink, maybe from the way his eyes glinted in the lantern light, flat and lifeless.

His smile didn't seem friendly anymore. His teeth were small like his eyes, and there seemed to be too many for his mouth, too closely spaced.

My stomach lurched in repulsion as I recognized the desire in his eyes. Yanking away from him, I drew the rushnyk tighter around my shoulders. I tugged on the knot to secure it, afraid that a sudden harsh wind might blow the cloth away. I needed its protection now more than ever.

When we neared a crumbling stone bridge stretched across the river, one of the men retrieved an iron talisman from his coat pocket and rubbed it restlessly. Held it to his lips. Whispered to it.

On our side of the bridge, a lantern post had been driven into the soil. Yet, as we neared, I noticed another object resting in the lantern's shadow.

My mouth went dry. I turned away, horrified, then helplessly looked back again.

A hand was nailed to the post, desiccated and skeletal. The skin was so thin that it was see-through and pearly; scaly webbing gathered between the fingers like tattered lace. Dried liquid streaked the wood and stained the ground black.

"Rusalka territory," a soldier in front of me said, spitting into the gurgling water. A white arm skimmed across the river's surface, gleaming as wetly as an eel's skin.

I paused to get a better look, but all I could perceive of the creatures below was luscious, dark hair and sleek, shifting limbs. The dimness, drifting algae, and lily pads obscured their true nature.

"Keep going," the man behind me said, pushing me forward. His hand dug cruelly into my shoulder. The tension was so thick in the air, it could have been torn with a bayonet. A pungent smell descended over us, not just pregnant with the rusalki's fermented fish odor, but also the men's fear, sweat, and dirt.

The sight of those strange, pale figures wafting through the black depths didn't frighten me, not after I had seen rusalki swimming beneath the ice so many winters in a row and they had never tried to harm me. I sensed that, as a fellow woman, the river spirits would treat me far kinder than the soldiers in my company. Even if a vodyanoy might be lurking in those depths, I would have tested my luck by jumping from the bridge, if in doing so, I wouldn't be abandoning Vanya and Mikhail to certain death.

Ahead, a dripping figure climbed over the stone wall and dropped in our path, landing on all fours. Fish-belly-white skin and hair the color of red algae. The rusalka's eyes gleamed with a pale silver fluorescence. She had no pupils, only a basin of eerie light against the jaundiced whites. Her face was ethereally beautiful, but her teeth were as slim as curved needles and just as sharp, dozens jutting from her black gums.

Amazed, I froze where I stood. I couldn't move my feet— it was as though they had taken root.

She was horrifying. She was glorious.

"Kill it!" Lieutenant Dronov screamed, reeling back. "Damn it, kill it!"

A rifle blast exploded in my ears, and the creature collapsed onto her side, revealing a stomach slit through with pulsing gills. She rose again on spidery limbs. Glistening blue blood poured from her midsection.

Mikhail backed away from the rusalka and nearly struck me. His breath hissed through his clenched teeth.

"There are more," another man cried, looking down into the water. "They're coming up here!"

Vanya leaned over the stone wall, staring at the river below. He didn't seem conscious of the other men's terror. His face shone with awe, his eyes wide and lips parted. What he saw in the water, I didn't know. Maybe only someone who loved women would know.

"Do something," Lieutenant Dronov ordered shrilly. "Give them a distraction."

The soldiers' eyes roved wildly around us. The weasel-faced man took a step toward me then hesitated. Dronov lunged at Vanya, who had begun to back away from the barrier, and drove him against it instead.

"Let go of me." Vanya bucked in the man's grip. Where his boot heels touched, moss and grass spread across the stones. "Damn you, get your rotten hands off me."

"No!" I cried.

Vanya twisted around in Dronov's hold, grappling with him. The lieutenant slammed his knee between Vanya's legs. With a hoarse moan, Vanya collapsed against him.

"No," Mikhail shouted. "Stop!"

"Don't," I screamed as Dronov lifted Vanya. "He doesn't know how to swim!"

Whatever Dronov had done, it had practically incapacitated Vanya. His face was dead white, and low choking sounds left his mouth like he was going to vomit. His hands loosely grasped at the soldier's greatcoat, struggling to gain purchase, and then his hips scraped against the stones. Then Dronov gave one hard push, and he was gone.

If Vanya cried out as he fell, the noise was drowned beneath a splash and the thrashing of many limbs.

"You Fraktsiya bastards, what have you done?" Mikhail yelled, struggling in the grasps of two other soldiers.

"No!" I shrieked, rushing toward the stone wall. Leaning over the edge, I frantically searched the inky river below.

Rusalki swarmed in a killing frenzy, an entangled mass of limbs, gnashing teeth, and flared gills.

Hands seized me and yanked me back. I kicked at the weasel-faced soldier, trying to break free. I wanted to choke Dronov. Wanted to kill him. "Why did you do that? Let me go."

I twisted in my captor's grip and slammed my fist into his face. His nose broke with a gristly crack both sickening and satisfying.

He wheeled back, clutching a hand to his face as he spat broken swears at me. Dropping his hand, he lunged at me. I dodged him, and as he struck the wall, I gave him a violent shove. The force of the blow sent him over the edge, screaming into the void below.

Lieutenant Dronov swung his rifle in my direction. Without hesitation. I vaulted over the wall, surrendering myself to the darkness and the fall.

32

A rusalka broke my fall. My hand landed on her cheek, a hair's width from her gnashing teeth. Rolling off her, I went under. Orbs of light drifted through the water. Eyes, I realized. Their eyes.

Webbed fingers trailed across my arms, tugged at my wrist, my flowing rushnyk. A billowing drift of hair brushed against my lips.

A current dragged me along, pulling me farther away from the bridge. My boots weighed me down like anchors. I fought against the flow and surfaced for air. The rusalki ignored me as I swam toward them and instead swarmed around better prey. Reaching the knot of writhing bodies, I shoved them aside.

Needle teeth grazed my wrist. Inky plumes spread through the water; I tasted it in my mouth, harsh and coppery. Blood. Not my own. No. Please. Not Vanya.

An arm. A shoulder. Sodden clothes. I pulled the body free

from the mass of rusalki, and all the air rushed from my lungs as a mauled face framed by short blond hair confronted me.

Blond hair. I let go of the body. Blond hair and a weathered face. Not Vanya. The weasel-faced soldier.

I surfaced, gasping for breath. My wet clothes and boots conspired to drag me down again. Blinking water out of my eyes, I searched the banks for Vanya, praying that he had managed to swim ashore while the rusalki swarmed the fallen Fraktsiya soldier.

I allowed the current to carry me farther away, kicking to the side as I neared the riverbank. Ahead, where boulders lined the bank, I spotted a disheveled form hanging from a rock. I could have mistaken it for discarded clothes caught by the current, if not for the hand that emerged to grasp weakly at clefts in the stone.

"Vanya. Vanya." Croaking his name, I clambered onto the rocky shore. My entire body trembled from the cold, teeth chattering so violently I could barely speak.

He dragged himself up, coughing and spitting out water. His waist emerged from the river, a pair of spidery hands curled over his hips.

"Get away from him," I screamed, staggering to my feet. The ground seemed to tilt beneath me, rolling like the river. I stumbled forward, half-delirious with terror, certain that by the time I reached him, the rusalka would have already dragged him back under.

Except then his thighs slid onto the algae-coated stone, and the webbed fingers slipped down to his knees. My breath caught in my throat. The rusalka was *helping* him.

As I reached Vanya, he curled atop the boulder, coughing.

The rusalka let go of him and retreated beneath the surface before I could get a good look at her.

"Are you okay?" I asked, falling to my knees beside Vanya.

"Toma," he mumbled, sitting up laboriously. Water trickled down his chin, his body trembling in the cold. He had lost his stolen cap in the river, and his hair hung in dripping coils over his face. "You jumped in to save me…"

Lantern light shone through the trees. Branches crunched and twigs snapped under heavy feet. Vanya's features tightened.

"You need to run," Vanya whispered, his voice cracking. "I'll take care of Mikhail."

I shook my head vehemently. "No, I'm not leaving you."

I wouldn't even consider it, not after everything we had been through. This wasn't where our journey would end. Whatever happened next, we would face it together.

"Please, Toma, now isn't the time to argue. Please run." He clenched his jaw, his gaze welling with fear. He put a hand on my forearm. "These men—"

Before he could finish, three Fraktsiya soldiers emerged from the tree line and rushed toward us. As the lantern light raced down their bayonet blades, I felt a sinking dismay. If I had run, I probably wouldn't even have made it to the cover of the forest, but at least I would've had a chance.

"Get up," one of the soldiers said, and brutally wrenched me to my feet, his fingers digging into my shoulder like a set of iron jaws.

Slowly, Vanya rose as well. He took my hand only long enough to give it a reassuring squeeze.

The soldiers herded us away from the river. My boots squelched as I walked, my toes numb from the cold.

Back on the road, the remaining soldiers were gathered in a circle a safe distance from the bridge. As we approached, the soldiers turned in our direction, their circle widening enough that I could see Mikhail curled on the cobblestones, grasping his shoulder. His head was thrown back, his face contorted in terrible pain.

Blood already darkened the sleeve of his coat, a black stain against the lighter fabric.

No. I froze, shocked. No. I had healed him.

"This one's useless," Lieutenant Dronov said, and stepped forward, drawing his gun from its holster. He pointed it at Mikhail's head. "We can leave him for the rusalki."

"Stop!" I wrenched against my captor's hands. "He's—"

"The Tsar," Vanya said suddenly.

Mikhail's eyes flashed open, the air hissing from between his clenched teeth.

Dronov narrowed his eyes, turning to us. "What did you just say?"

"He's the Tsar," Vanya repeated, the waver of uncertainty in his voice smoothing over. He stepped forward, or at least tried to, only to be yanked back again. "If you kill him, Koschei will hang you. He'll execute your entire unit."

Slowly, Dronov lowered his pistol and returned it to its holster. His jaw worked silently as he peered down at Mikhail. "Show me your face, boy."

Laboriously, Mikhail sat up, his entire body racked by his panting breaths. Sweat shone on his brow, and his skin grew

paler by the moment. He flinched as Dronov seized his chin
and twisted his face this way and that.

"Lantern," Dronov barked.

One of the soldiers stepped forward and raised the lantern
to Mikhail's face.

"By the Three," Dronov muttered, his mouth sagging
open. "There is some resemblance… But why were you on
the train?"

"To kill Koschei and reunite with the Otzvuk," I said,
thinking quickly.

"I didn't ask you, girl," Dronov growled, before turning
his attention back to Mikhail. "If you truly are the Tsar, then
who are these two?"

"Duchess Aloisia." Mikhail sagged in Dronov's hold, his
head falling. Blood oozed from his mouth, and the dark stain
on the shoulder of his uniform jacket inched slowly toward
his elbow. "Fourteenth in line to Groznaya's throne… Sent as
a diplomat before the insurrection… She was captured with
me and agreed to help in exchange for a marriage pact…"

Dronov's amber eyes scanned over me, taking in the sight
of my medic's uniform, my dripping hair. I looked down at
my feet to escape his burning gaze, shivering as a cold wind
swept across the road.

"What about you, Strannik?" Lieutenant Dronov asked, his
voice thick with condescension as he turned to Vanya. "I don't
suppose you are royalty, too? Not with that accent of yours."

Vanya cleared his throat. His thick accent, his provincial
charm, the way he spoke so casually, so carefree even in the
presence of our enemies—all these things worked against him

now. At least my shyness could be mistaken for noble modesty, but there was no hiding who he truly was.

"No, sir," Vanya said quietly, running a hand through his wet hair. "They paid me to smuggle them aboard the train. It was all my idea. If you—if you hurt Duchess Aloisia, Groznaya won't stand for it. If you so much as touch her, they'll do everything in their power to wipe out the Fraktsiya in retaliation. She'll be far more valuable to you alive, as a bargaining piece."

The lieutenant's gaze returned to me. For a second time, I looked away, half-afraid he would see the deception in my eyes.

"I see," Dronov said at last. "In that case..."

Down the road, hooves clomped against cobblestones. Lieutenant Dronov swiveled around and drew his pistol from its holster, while the remaining soldiers readied their rifles.

Beside me, Vanya sighed deeply, his shoulders sagging. He caught my gaze and offered a weak smile, as if trying to convince me everything would be okay. But it wouldn't be, would it?

The hoofbeats grew louder, accompanied by the rumbling of wagon wheels. A light flickered past the trees, where the road curved.

The blood pounded in my ears. I gnawed on my lower lip, racking my brain for an escape plan. Even if the soldiers took us to a nearby encampment, it would soon become clear to them that I wasn't Duchess Aloisia. Vanya and I would be killed, and Mikhail would be returned to Koschei's custody. I couldn't just stand here and let that happen. What should I do? Damn it, what should I do?

A wagon appeared from around the bend. It was overladen with crates and barrels, the two horses straining on their leads. Just a farmer or a traveler. Not someone who could help us.

"Stop," Dronov called, stepping into the middle of the road.

The wagon trundled to a stop. Another cart traveled behind it, drawn by four horses. My heartbeat quickened as I spotted the second cart's cargo—a massive gun mounted on wheels, with a short barrel as thick around as my thigh. The weapon vaguely reminded me of the lead toy cannon Galina had found one summer in the river muck, one of her most precious belongings. Except this was no toy, and the two Fraktsiya soldiers who sat behind the gun looked well prepared to use it.

Dronov stepped forward to the man in the first wagon. Spoke. Gestured back at us.

My heart sank.

As the two men talked, Dronov turned and pointed at Vanya. I heard the word *rusalki* and then I heard *koldun*.

Vanya caught my gaze. Held in my own, his hand trembled like a captured bird.

Dronov returned to us, carrying a bundle of rope and a machete. He dropped one end of the rope on the ground, where it curled like a noose, and cut sections from the other end. He handed a length of rope to the dark-haired soldier with the knotted scar bisecting his face from brow to chin. "Tie her hands, Ilyich."

I tucked my hands against my chest and stared at the bayonet blades aimed at me. If I refused, the men would shoot me. If I tried to run, the men would shoot me. I could try grabbing Ilyich's rifle, but then there would still be half a dozen other soldiers to deal with, not to mention the gun crew, and one or the other would, inevitably, shoot me.

Reluctantly, I stretched out my arms. I tensed as the rope tightened around my wrists, my breath hissing from my lungs. It seemed insane to just stand and obey. Why wasn't I fighting? Why did it feel like my legs were frozen?

"The duchess and Tsar are going to go for a little wagon ride," Dronov said, once another soldier had bound Mikhail's wrists. "You two help them to the wagon. If one of them tries to run, aim for the legs."

"What about Vanya?" My voice echoed in my ears, small and tinny. It sounded as though it belonged to a stranger, perhaps the Tomochka who'd run from her mother's screams, the one who had been weak. "He has—he has to come, too."

"There's no need for that," Lieutenant Dronov said.

Vanya's gaze clouded over. He hadn't moved from beside me. His hands hung limply at his side, his expression empty.

"No," Mikhail panted as a soldier dragged him to his feet. His legs buckled, and he would have fallen if not for the hands supporting him. "No."

"We'll tie him to a tree a little ways into the forest." There was nothing behind Dronov's smile. "If he tries hard enough, within thirty minutes or so, he should be able to escape."

"We're not going without Vanya." I took a step toward Vanya and the two soldiers flanking him, but Ilyich seized me by the shoulders and yanked me back. Growling, I struggled to break free. "Let go of me. He's coming with us. Let go!"

Vanya's mouth wrenched into a smile, but his eyes were haunted. There was something ancient in his gaze, like he had watched this situation play out a thousand times before. "I'll be fine. Don't worry about me. I'll be fine."

"Vanya." Mikhail's breath hitched in pain. "They—"

"It was an honor, Tsar." He turned, regarding me with polite indifference. "Duchess. Goodbye."

Ilyich dragged me toward the wagon and hauled me into its bed. I landed hard on my side, twisted around, and struggled to sit up. Mikhail joined me moments later, grunting as he struck the grain sacks piled on the floor. The soldier hopped into the wagon and sat on a crate, holding his rifle in both hands. Lieutenant Dronov handed off the machete and the rest of the rope to one of the three men staying behind, then joined us in the wagon.

"Don't even think about jumping out," Dronov said, once the wagon began moving. He eased onto another crate, angled his rifle across his knees, and lightly nudged Mikhail's side with the toe of his boot. "You royalty have fragile bones. I'd hate for you to break a leg."

I wormed into a sitting position and leaned to the side, trying to see past the cart behind us. I could just barely make out Vanya and the three remaining soldiers standing at the tree line.

Vanya lifted his hand. It almost looked as though he was crying.

A queasy feeling settled in my stomach as the wagon rumbled farther down the road. His last words replayed in my head. Goodbye, goodbye. There had been something so final about that statement. Something permanent.

No. This couldn't be farewell. It was too soon for that. We'd see each other again, wouldn't we? We had to.

Back the way we came, the trees shuddered, their trembling barely visible against the indigo sky. But there was no wind. I watched in horror as the trunks swayed, accompanied by the groan of splintering wood.

"No, what are you doing to him?" I yelled, struggling to my feet. I tried to jump from the wagon, but Ilyich seized me before I could take a step. "Stop it. Stop!"

The trees' shuddering intensified as Ilyich tackled me to the floor. I bruised my knees on the boards, his body pressing down on me, smothering me. Writhing beneath him, I fought to haul myself up. I kicked back blindly, hoping to land a blow or throw him off me, but only ended up striking crates and bags.

"Stop struggling," he growled and shifted his grip to my neck.

"Vanya!" I shouted, lifting my head.

The trees had begun to still. It was too late. I could feel it in my chest, an oppressive weight pressing down on my heart.

Gone. He was gone.

"You bastards. You murderers, you—" Before I could finish, Ilyich folded his arm around my throat, hooking his elbow under my jaw. As I strained against his hold, woolly darkness enveloped my brain, and my eyelids grew heavy. I struggled to keep them open. It was a losing battle. The night sky descended rapidly, falling, plummeting, and then there was nothing but the dark.

33

I awoke on a hard, jostling surface, bruised and sore. My entire body ached, but the worst of the pain was in my neck and back, where it felt as though my spine had been stomped cruelly underfoot.

I looked around, my head swimming with nausea as I took in the sight of hemp sacks weeping buckwheat, stacked crates, worm-gnawed wagon boards.

Wadded fabric pressed down on my tongue. My gorge rose at the scent and taste of mildew. I bit into the rag, the muscles in my jaw and neck working desperately to expel the fabric. Useless. A rope had been tied across my cheeks, holding the gag in place.

More rope tightened around my ankles. Contorting my body, I twisted around to find Ilyich tying my feet together. Instead of acknowledging me, he rose to his feet and returned to his perch on a nearby crate.

Once Ilyich was seated, he took out his pocket watch to

check the time, as if nothing significant had happened. His dark hair hung in oily strings over his brow. In the lantern light, the wiry scar that bisected his face appeared to writhe, as though it weren't a scar at all but a tapeworm beneath his skin.

The sob that welled in my throat was smothered by the gag. I wanted to die so I'd never have to think of Vanya again. Maybe I could have helped save him had I done something differently. I should have fought back more. I should have screamed louder, trying to convince the soldiers that Vanya was a good person. All he wanted was to help people, but justice and human goodness meant nothing in this world.

Neither Ilyich nor Lieutenant Dronov would care how warm Vanya had been even to strangers, or that he always knew what to say, or that his voice changed when he spoke Strannitsky, deepening into a low, rumbling purr. To his killers, he hadn't been an actual person, just an enemy.

I'm sorry, Vanya. Tears poured down my cheeks. *Forgive me. I never asked you about your father, or what it was like growing up.*

All of a sudden, I felt an aching desire to know these things. Vanya had probably been the only one alive in his immediate family, and now that line was gone forever.

Tell me about all the people you loved, Vanya. Had you ever gone this far in your life? If you could travel anywhere in the world, where would you go?

I bit back my sobs, taking deep, rapid breaths through my nose as I fought the urge to scream curses through my gag.

None of those questions mattered anymore. They would never be answered.

I would make them all pay. For as long as I lived, I would never forgive the Fraktsiya for everything they had done. For tearing Galina from me. For killing Vanya, destroying all that he was and could be.

Beside me, Mikhail lay motionless on the grain sacks, deathly pale against the burlap. His entire shirtsleeve was soaked in blood, and the cloth they had tightly bound around his shoulder grew redder by the minute. Each time the wagon lurched, he groaned, his breath cutting off in a hoarse gasp. He opened his eyes and looked at me, his gaze drowning in pain and misery.

"Toma, I saw him. His head. His face." Tears flooded his eyes. "I…I'm so sorry."

My teeth gnashed into the wadded fabric.

"I'm so sorry," he repeated, more forcefully this time.

I placed my bound hands on Mikhail's arm and shook my head firmly. I wished I could tell him it wasn't his fault. He wasn't to blame for what had happened.

"I liked him," Mikhail whispered, his voice torn with wrenching grief. "I *liked* him."

Turning away from me, he curled into a fetal position. Subdued sobs racked his body.

All this time, Mikhail had tried so hard to hide his emotions and maintain a strong façade. His mask had cracked when Aleksey had died, and again in Kraylesa. Now, it had finally broken.

I felt as if a part of myself had shattered, too. Had Vanya been terrified or had it been quick and painless?

"He could be so aggravating." Mikhail's choked voice became quick and fervent, as if by talking about Vanya, he could bring him back. "But he spoke—he spoke to me like an equal. And it was genuine, instead of just empty praise. He wasn't just trying to impress me or get something in return. Nobody ever spoke to me that way before, and I kept telling myself I hated it, but I liked it. Oh, Toma. I really admired him for it."

Shut up, just shut up, I thought, the words straining in the back of my throat. *Stop talking about him that way.*

I couldn't stand to hear Mikhail talk about Vanya in the past tense. It made it all the more real. Vanya was already gone, and there was no going back. No matter how much Mikhail spoke about him or how many tears I shed, there was no way to rewind the clock.

I twisted away from Mikhail, my sobs cracking into anguished wheezing. Suddenly, the wagon lurched to a halt, and a fiery radiance spilled into the bed of the wagon. Low voices and laughter echoed in my ears.

"Wait here with them," Dronov said, rose to his feet, and climbed down from the wagon. "I'll find a medic."

"Understood, sir," Ilyich said, his gaze flickering toward me. He had wide-set, watery blue eyes framed by paunchy lids, like the eyes of a catfish. His sagging mouth and thin, wilted mustache only added to the impression.

I despised him.

Minutes later, rapid footsteps crunched through the leaves beyond the wagon.

"Where is he?" a familiar voice said.

I cracked open my eyes as Zemfirka climbed into the wagon. She froze as still as a deer in lantern light, her jet eyes widening behind her gunmetal-rimmed glasses.

"Is something wrong?" Dronov snapped as she rested her canvas medic's satchel on the floor.

"No, sir." Carefully, she knelt down beside me and turned

Mikhail onto his back. His head lolled senselessly to the side, eyes closed and lips crusted with blood. Averting her eyes from my pleading gaze, she pressed her fingers beneath his jawline, waiting a moment before turning to Dronov. "It's too risky to move him in his condition without first stabilizing the bleeding. I'll need boiled water and clean rags."

"Do you hear her?" Dronov turned to Ilyich. "What are you waiting for? Go get them."

"Understood, sir." Ilyich clambered down from the wagon and offered the lieutenant a hasty salute before hurrying off.

"I'll also need a bottle of iodine and two rolls of gauze," Zemfirka said. "They're still in the tent."

"Do I look like a handmaid to you?" Dronov snarled.

"With all due respect, we don't have time for this, sir." Behind her round glasses, her eyes blinked, cool and unperturbed. "I need to immediately begin stabilizing the bleeding."

"Fine, just don't untie either of them. Don't even talk to them." Raking a hand through his coarse brown hair, he swiveled around and strode off in the direction he had come.

As soon as Dronov was out of sight, Zemfirka opened her medic's bag and rooted through it. Her gaze flicked to me twice, but she didn't speak to me or try lowering my gag before devoting her full attention to Mikhail's wound. She began by cutting away the sleeve of his jacket and unraveling the bandages I had wrapped around his arm and chest.

My breath caught in my throat. Beneath the gauze, blood coursed from the gunshot wound ravaging his shoulder. My careful embroidery hung in tatters, reduced to a snarl of loose thread.

Zemfirka's fingertips traced over the torn embroidery. "Is this your work, Toma?"

I nodded rapidly, my tongue straining against the gag. *I can help*, I tried to say, but all that came out was a low, plaintive groan.

"I recognize it from your rushnyk." She reached over and slipped the rope down to my chin.

I spat out the gag and drew in urgent gasps that felt dangerously close to becoming hacking sobs, my eyes still watering uncontrollably. "Zemfirka, you need to untie me now. Let me fix the embroidery."

"You know I can't do that. It would be treason." Shifting her gaze back to Mikhail, she carefully tweezed the dirt and gravel from his wound, wiping up the blood that welled free with each shallow breath. "I don't know what you are, but tell me what I should do. Quickly."

"Please. I'm the only one who can save him."

She looked at me hesitantly and reached for my wrist.

"What are you doing?" Lieutenant Dronov demanded, leaning over the wagon's door. "I told you not to take her gag off."

"I'm sorry, sir." Zemfirka cast her eyes downward, adjusting her glasses on her nose's narrow bridge. "I just wanted to know if she was the one to originally tend to the deserter's wound."

"Don't concern yourself with that. Just stabilize him for transport." Dronov turned to me. "I'll deal with this one."

As he lowered the door to the wagon, cold steel nipped against my palm. My fingertips tested its shape—a thin pick that terminated in a teardrop-shaped blade.

A scalpel.

34

Resting against my palms, the scalpel felt as precious as an icon, imbued with a far greater power than the tempered steel it was composed of. I curled my fingers around the tool, maneuvering it so that the handle lay flat against my inner wrist and the blade pointed upward.

Thank you, I mouthed to Zemfirka, but she had already turned away.

As Lieutenant Dronov tried to force the rag back into my mouth, I bit at his fingers, trying to draw blood. He slapped me hard enough that my head cracked sideways and sparks flew across my vision. The metallic tang of my own blood welled in my mouth, sharp and bizarrely thrilling, spurring my heartbeat into a violent pounding. My limbs trembled with nervous energy, and I strained against my bonds like a dog on a taut leash, my nerves screaming at me to fight him, hurt him, even if it meant using my own nails and teeth.

"Hardly behavior suiting a duchess," Dronov hissed, righting the rope that held the wadded cloth in place. He wrenched me from the wagon so violently that I nearly landed on the ground, his fingers digging into my armpits with such force, I thought he'd dislocate my shoulders from their sockets. My bound ankles struggled to gain purchase on the loose soil, and when that failed, I let my limbs go limp and imagined myself as a boulder or a rooted tree, something solid and unmoving.

Swearing, he dropped me. A hard, bruised ache climbed my tailbone as I landed on the ground, and I coiled over myself to protect my head and face from the blows I feared would come next. But instead, he just dragged me up again, and this time slung me over his shoulder as though I were nothing more than a dressed deer, something gutted and senseless, whose only worth was to die.

As he dragged me through the camp, my vision swayed in nauseating circles, giving me a whirling view of several burning fires, stacked trunks and barrels, and a scatter of tents. I writhed in his grasp, but he continued forward undauntedly.

Every time I spotted a crate, I leaned forward, searching for air holes. Galina's name gnashed in the back of my throat.

Dawn blazed across the horizon like a wall of fire, painting the skyline in shades of gold and indigo. Within an hour, the sun would rise, except I might not live long enough to see it.

We entered a tent occupied by a few rickety bookshelves, a table covered in maps, and an unused cot. Men surrounded the table, their conversation stilling as Dronov carried me into the room and dropped me unceremoniously onto the dirt.

Struggling to my knees, I tightened my grip around the scalpel's handle, terrified that the men would spot the glint of metal through my locked fingers. A hot line of blood unraveled down my wrist where the blade had cut me.

The tall blond man at the rear of the tent turned around. Even in the lantern light, the golden striations in Koschei's eyes appeared to radiate a low, pulsating glow.

Couldn't these men see what he was? Or did they just not care?

"Ah, so we meet again," Koschei murmured, stepping around the table. His long fingers traced over the map absently, toppling Otzvuk and Fraktsiya flag markers alike. "My men tell me that you are Duchess Aloisia, but there is no Duchess Aloisia of Groznaya. So, you must be Toma."

I blinked rapidly to clear the stinging sweat from my eyes. How could he know that? I was certain I had never given him my name.

"I spoke with your sister," Koschei said, resting against the edge of the table. Framed by his ashen lashes, his hooded leonine eyes regarded me aloofly. "Rest easily knowing that her first death was not in vain. By her very nature, she is invaluable to this empire's future prosperity."

Beside me, Lieutenant Dronov shifted uneasily. "Sir..."

"Leave us." He gestured to the other soldiers in the tent. "You as well. I'll call you when I'm ready. In the meanwhile, prepare the Tsar for transport as soon as his wounds are stabilized. Within the hour, we depart for Eyry Castle."

Once they had slipped out, he crossed the room and tugged the gag free. I expected his fingers to feel cold and slimy, like how I imagined a drekavac or vodyanoy might feel. Instead, they were shockingly warm to the touch—even more so than the humans he surrounded himself with.

I strained against the ropes, panting. "Where's Galina? What do you intend to do with her?"

"Merely unlock the source behind her resurrection and that of all beasts."

"But why?"

"Would you like to know the one greatest commodity produced by war?" He squatted down so that we were at eye level. "Death. In the war with Grozniya, I was afforded my first look at true carnage in the trenches. Soldier boys blown apart by artillery, and others drowning on dry land in the fog the Grozniy troops had distilled from vodyanoy gallbladders. We didn't always have time to tend to the dead, so we would leave our lost comrades behind in the trenches or burn them in mass graves, and come nightfall, we would pray that if they returned, they would seek out those who had harmed them. But that wasn't always the case. Sometimes, they came back for us as well."

"I...I don't understand."

"Your sister is remarkable in that she is self-aware. Imagine if someone could communicate with upyri. If someone could control them and all the revenants." Koschei's silken baritone echoed in the chamber of my skull, low and irresistibly compelling. It stifled even the hatred I felt at the sight of him, until a part of me wanted desperately, inexplicably to nod along to his every word. "No one would dare raise their hand against an empire with that power at its helm. It would spell the end to all wars."

It was even worse than I had thought. He didn't just want the key to immortality—he wanted absolute power to go along with it.

"You're mad," I whispered, and he smiled.

"I am a visionary. The upyr will become a martyr to this

cause. I will find the secret behind her sentience, and once I do, I will learn how to harness and control it."

"She's just a child!"

"What is the life of one child compared to the rape and butchering of millions? That is what war becomes." His gold-striated eyes regarded me. "Despite what you may believe, I want only the best for this country. After all, as a soldier, I devoted my life to it."

"You think you're fooling anyone?" A hoarse, jagged laugh pushed from my lungs. I leaned forward, forcing myself to confront his unforgiving gaze. "I saw what you did to those Otzvuk soldiers. The only thing you care about is power and control."

Ignoring my accusations, he rose to his full height. "While I appreciate your spirit, you are unfortunately of little use to me. You have potential, but that makes you a threat."

As he stepped past me, I writhed against the ropes. "Wait, come back here! Don't you dare hurt her, Koschei."

"Lieutenant, why don't you reacquaint her with her friend?" he said, parting the tent's fold. "The rest of you, get ready to move out once the Tsar is stabilized."

"Get back here!" I screamed as Dronov stepped back into the tent.

"Don't forget to dispose of the parts properly and do it far from here," Koschei added indifferently, as an afterthought. "Kill any animal that gets within ten paces of her. A koldunia's blood will only spoil the earth."

Then he was gone, and I was alone with the lieutenant.

Dronov stopped in front of me, eclipsed by the lantern light. When he bent down to tie a spare rope around the cord connecting my wrists, his eyes gleamed like those of an animal.

I could sense it in the way his tongue anxiously flicked over his lips and his nostrils flared in urgent breaths—he felt the same wild tension that made me want to bite and thrash and spill his blood. Anything to survive.

Once the makeshift lead was secured, he cut the cords around my ankles. I resisted the impulse to run, knowing I'd never make it out of the tent with my wrists bound. Every second counted, but so did every action I took. I needed to prepare myself.

"Don't bother screaming," he said, giving his rope a cruel tug that wrenched me to my feet. Another hard yank sent me stumbling after him as he exited the tent. "It's not going to save you. You brought this upon yourself."

Gritting my teeth, I winced with every step. My ankles were sore and swollen, and my toes tingled as though they were still immersed in icy water.

Once his back was turned, I fumbled with the scalpel. I angled the blade inward, slid it between the entwined rope, and began sawing back and forth. Bits of hemp scratched my palms, the ropes digging into my skin as I strained to cut myself free.

Lieutenant Dronov dragged me past the tents. At the edge of the encampment, he retrieved an axe from a nearby chopping stump.

My blood pounded in my ears, and my vision blurred around the corners. I imagined the axe swinging down, the sound it would make, the resounding thud of impact. I imagined my mother striding between the snow-laden trees.

Was this how she had felt just before it happened? Was it how Vanya felt? I thought of how he had stood at the forest's edge, smiling even as he struggled to hold back tears. Tears of my own flooded my eyes. Why hadn't I been able to protect him?

I took a steady breath, exhaling slowly as Dronov led me into the forest. *Take deep breaths and keep going. Get ready. Make him pay.*

We walked until the camp noises faded into silence. The sky grew steadily lighter as the sun rose past the mountains, but in the depths of the forest, there were still many shadows. A dim orchid haze settled over the trees.

Clumps of fiber fell between my hands. The sickening fear that rolled around in the pit of my stomach was dwarfed by a sudden sense of anticipation. Any moment now, I would do what I needed to do and fight.

"We're almost there," Dronov said.

The scalpel grazed my inner wrist as the rope around my arms gave way. I felt no pain at all, simply a dampness slipping down my skin as I jerked my hands free. Lieutenant Dronov spun around with a low growl of surprise, likely having felt the rope go slack. I lunged at him.

My scalpel found Dronov's shoulder with a soft *squelch*. He didn't collapse like I had hoped but screamed in pain and turned so suddenly that the scalpel's handle was torn from my hand. The blade remained embedded in him for a moment after I released it, before falling to the ground.

Bellowing in rage, Dronov swung the axe at me. I ducked down as it cleaved through the air above my head. Before he could try for another strike, I reeled back, nearly slipping in the slick leaves and moss. I swiveled around and rushed into the forest.

Branches shuddered and snapped behind me. Dead leaves were pulverized beneath pounding feet. I didn't dare look back.

"Stop!" Dronov screamed. "Stop, or once I find you, I'll make sure you suffer! I'll make it slow!"

In the brightening daylight, the firs and spruces appeared as sharp as blades, each bough bristling with a thousand needles. After a few minutes of running, I could no longer hear his shouts, but I kept going. My throat felt nearly as raw as my abraded wrists. Parched and breathless, I ran, panting like an animal. I felt like I was trapped in a nightmare—everything was hazy but the path ahead, my thoughts blurring until all I could focus on was the need to *go*.

Downhill, the ground was loosened by rainfall, deadly treacherous. I had to force myself to slow down, unable to escape from the conviction that if I returned to the Vesna River, I'd find Vanya, alive and whole.

Scrambling through a thorny bramble, my feet touched empty air. I plummeted down the steep ridge of a gully, grasping onto stones and branches in a futile attempt to control my descent. At the bottom, I rolled to a stop. The pain from my bruised ribs pushed the breath from my lungs in one sudden gasp.

Overhead, the dawn sky glowered down as though inflamed. Dazed, I watched as several blue swallowtail butterflies drifted from the foliage and danced around me.

My body ached, even in muscles I hadn't realized existed. Still too weak to rise, I looked up at the slope I had tumbled down. No sign of Dronov, but I wouldn't feel safe until I had put more distance between us. I needed to keep going.

As I hoisted myself onto my hands and knees, the underbrush rustled at the other end of the gully. Through the gaps between the shrubbery, I caught a glimpse of sage-green fabric. Fraktsiya green.

35

The leaves parted to reveal a person in fragments. Bare limbs, the sun-bleached swell of an exposed spine, pin-straight blond hair that glowed like fire in the dim light.

The mavka regarded me with her chin cocked, maple-brown eyes blinking unperturbed. A Fraktsiya cap perched rakishly on her head, the leather visor tilted sideways. More spoils overflowed from her cradled arms—an Otzvuk coat adorned with purple piping and blood-drenched epaulets, half a brown gabardine pant leg severed at the knee, a single boot.

It was the same mavka who had teased Vanya after we'd fled from the train. All this time she had been following us, or at least lingering nearby. Maybe she'd sensed the pall of death that hung over Vanya and had been drawn to it like a moth to a flame.

From deeper into the gully came the leaden thud of an axe striking wood.

We stared at each other in perfect stillness.

"I know you're here," Lieutenant Dronov called, his voice raspy from thirst or exhilaration. "I hear you moving, girl."

"Help me," I whispered to the mavka, but she had already turned away in disinterest. Swallowtail butterflies darted from her rib cage as she slipped the partial pant leg on one arm, tugging it upward before abandoning the effort. She handled the garments the way I might have handled a radio—shaking the boot this way and that until blood and dirt poured from its inner sole and plucking at the coat's gilded buttons, ignorant to their function.

As her boot slipped to the ground, Dronov laughed. He sounded even closer than before, the noise of his approach echoing off the gully's high walls. Twigs snapped beneath his heavy tread. Closer, closer. I edged for the cover of the bushes cradling the edge of the gully and pressed my body down to conceal myself, knowing that if I ran now, he'd be relentless in his pursuit.

Undisturbed by his approach, the mavka slipped on the Otzvuk uniform jacket. She traced her fingertips along the ornamental cords draped from shoulder to chest.

"Please, he'll kill me," I begged, and this time her gaze returned to me. A strange light entered her eyes, and her brow furrowed. For the first time since she'd emerged from the underbrush, I sensed she was truly seeing me.

At the other end of the gully, Dronov stepped from between the trees. His eyes landed on the mavka, and he reacted in an instant, lunging toward her with a wild cry. "Otzvuk pig!"

She turned to face him, and the rage in his eyes snuffed out in an instant, his thin lips drawing back in shock or horror. The axe swerved off-course; she caught the weapon by the handle on its way down and held it steady.

Swearing and panting, Dronov tried yanking the axe free of her grip. When that failed, he stumbled back and reached for the service pistol on his belt.

I watched, transfixed, as the mavka hooked her hand under his armpit as if she meant to wrench his arm free from its socket. Instead, her fingers riffled along his side. A spasm racked Dronov's body, the tremor so violent that it sent the pistol slipping from his fingers. He collapsed to the ground, twisting and turning as she crouched over him and brought her other hand up along his side.

Then he began to laugh—deep, guffawing bursts that shook his entire frame.

Vanya's words echoed in my head: *The forest spirits only tickle men. A pleasant death, if you ask me.*

Dronov writhed on the ground, his body trembling in the force of his hysterical laughter. By the second, his face grew redder, flushed with blood until it was nearly purple. His gaze landed on me, and he reached out a hand, still guffawing uncontrollably.

"Girl—" another burst of laughter twisted his spine "—kill it."

Slowly, I rose to my feet and approached him.

Tears glistened down his cheeks, tinted pink in the glow of the rising sun. A film of blood spread across his left eye, and ruby pinpricks dotted his cheeks and nose. He was laughing with such force, the vessels beneath his skin had burst.

"Please, it's a monster," Dronov gasped, his face contorting in agony even as a rictus of a grin stretched across his lips.

"No," I said, and retrieved his pistol from the ground. "You are."

As I turned to leave, he screamed after me, punctuating each laugh with vile curses. I found stable footing in the roots and crevices lining the gully's wall and began to climb. By the time I reached the top, I could no longer tell whether he was laughing or sobbing.

"Shoot me," he croaked as I paused at the brink. "I'm begging you. Just shoot me."

I glanced back. "Tickling is a pleasant death, if you ask me."

36

Long after Dronov's laughter faded behind me, I found myself freezing at every rustle, gripping the pistol so tightly that my knuckles blanched white. The cackling of crows and grackles scraped at my nerves, spurring me into a panic that verged on delirium. I blundered through the woods, searching for a path, I thought, or Vanya, or my mother—we were far from the Edge, but maybe I'd find her after all these years, with ivy reaching through her rib cage and her jawbone bulging with a crust of dead moss and monkshood.

With time, I reached the road and followed the wagon tracks—not toward the camp, but in the direction of the bridge, until the sun exposed a sprinkling of dried blood left in the dirt.

I entered the woods with my pistol bared in front of me, my teeth clenched to stifle my ragged breathing. My legs trembled uncontrollably beneath me. Two hundred paces from the road, I came to a devastated stand of pines whose malformed trunks curled over me like a cage. Roots emerged from the soil in a tangled net.

Standing on the soil, still loose and mucky from a recent disturbance, I stared at the congealed gore marbling the mud. Who knew whether it had spilled from a human or even an animal? The wilderness was alive with all manner of beasts.

In my own mouth, I tasted blood. I snared my inner cheek between my incisors and bit down until the taste became real. Unpeeling my gaze from the ground with some difficulty, I looked across the glade, drawn by another smear of red.

A body lay sprawled against one of the trees.

No, not him. It couldn't be him. As I stumbled toward the corpse, a low groan squirmed up my throat. No sooner had I taken five steps than I froze.

The man's head lolled crookedly against the tree trunk, bark and pine needles growing into his cheek, his eye socket. His brown hair obscured the worst of the damage Vanya's power had wrought to his face but failed to hide the devastation below. Branches emerged like grasping fingers from his chest.

I searched the glade. Another Fraktsiya soldier lay entangled in roots, his glazed eyes rolled up as if to track the blister of a sun that rose in the maroon sky.

The brutality of their deaths took my breath away. It spoke to Vanya's desperation in these moments, and his terror.

So where was he? And hadn't there been a third soldier?

My gaze returned to the puddle of blood. Streaks led across the glade, where the dark gash of the river glimmered through the trees. Bearing Dronov's pistol in front of me, I followed the trail of blood. As the river's low murmur filled my ears, I envisioned Vanya injured and terrified but alive, dragging himself toward the water. The rusalki would protect him, I knew they would, just as the upyri had protected me all these years. The monsters in this world were more than what they seemed.

More blood glistened on the pebbles lining the shore. I stopped at the river's edge, searching the green water for any sign of him. For the first time since I had started running, I heard the birds singing.

A boot bristled from the mud nearby. Maybe Vanya's, but more likely just twin to the one the mavka had stolen. I scooped it up to get a better look. It was far heavier than it should've been, like it was filled with stones.

I peered inside.

An uncontrollable scream swelled from my throat, and before I knew it, I had thrown the boot down. My fingers tangled in my hair, clawed at my cheeks. Tears welled from my eyes in an instant. I twisted my body away and collapsed to my knees, seized by grief so overwhelming, I thought it would tear me in two.

I felt strangled by the inevitability of Vanya's death. If I hadn't left with Mikhail, none of this would have happened. And then Vanya would have died during the riot in his village. Or afterwards, accused of being a koldun and butchered by his own neighbors.

Was it a curse or was it fate? Had the Goddess or the Three Sisters—*let's face it, Tomochka, they're one and the same, aren't they? All Tsarinas of Death*—had they sanctioned this?

A large body sloshed through the river, tearing me from my thoughts. I watched, stupefied, as a shape emerged from beneath the waves. Milk-white skin. Loose, sleek curls of burgundy hair.

Before the being's chest surfaced, my heart tremored with a brief hope that Vanya had heard my weeping and returned to me. But he did not have hair that fell halfway down his back or heavy, pendulous breasts.

The rusalka waded toward me, her eyes like banked embers. She held a dripping wool mound in her arms, the green cloth streaked with blood and algae. With infinite care, she laid it down on the shore beside where the boot had landed.

Another rusalka broke the surface, smaller than the other. She must have died so young. She brought a limp arm, detached from its partner and stippled with fish bites. It joined the rest of the pile.

My throat closed around the sob that rushed from my lungs, reducing the sound to a thin, watery moan. The Fraktsiya hadn't just dumped Vanya's body into the river. They had mutilated him so that he could never return, for even the rusalki were reborn whole.

An arm here. A leg there. Just a calf missing its ankle. Some dark, dripping handful crested with suckling leeches. A procession of rusalki came and went, each laying an offering onto the mound of flesh and stained wool.

Tears pouring down my face, I crawled over to the pile and laid a trembling hand upon Vanya's limp fingers. The edges of his nail beds were a deep, bruised indigo, and two of his fingernails were broken. How could it be possible that just hours ago, this hand had touched me?

As a wretched sob escaped my lips, I could almost feel the lingering warmth he'd left across my skin—those fingers tracing the scars scouring my forearm, as though each mark were something precious. Proof that I had survived.

A final figure emerged from the Vesna River as the other rusalki disappeared beneath its restless waters. When she had helped Vanya ashore in the night, her face had been lost to the shadows, reduced to the wet gleam of eyes and teeth, and the scalpel-sharp curve of her cheekbones. In daylight, her chiseled features were strikingly familiar—they mirrored those of the head she cradled in her arms.

Instead of laying his head down with the rest of his remains, the rusalka stopped at the edge of the bank and held it out to me. I took it from her, his hair as slippery as oil against my palms.

She didn't speak, but when she looked at me, I *felt* her grief inside of me. The moment her hands were empty, they gravitated to her stomach. Her gills swelled in long, heaving pulses as she stroked the space above her belly button, where I imagined she once must have felt an infant kick.

"I'm sorry," I wept, holding his head against my chest. "I'm so sorry. I couldn't stop them."

She reached out and laid a hand upon my hip. No. Upon the rushnyk fastened around my waist, tugging at the loose knot with her long, webbed fingers. The brooch popped off and landed on my knee. With my hands full, I couldn't keep her from untying the cloth. I didn't try to stop her. Maybe she would take the rushnyk back up the Vesna River, into the rain and silence of the wilderness, to Mama.

The rusalka slid her fingers over the embroidered patterns, snagging her hooked nails on the threads. Her lips parted, revealing a fringe of teeth as sharp and delicate as an ivory comb.

"Bring him back," she hissed in a voice like wind and the sluice of water. Her pupilless silver eyes pierced into me. Looking into them, I felt as though she could peer into everything I ever was and would be, my conscience split open like a mavka's back and exposed in all its vulnerability.

"I can't—" I began, but she had already let go of the rushnyk and retreated beneath the waves, leaving Vanya and me alone on the shore.

37

Resting Vanya's head in my lap, I forced myself to gaze at his face. His eyes were closed, a small mercy. If I looked at him from the neck upward, I could almost pretend that he was asleep. But dirt plugged his nostrils. There were dead leaves in his hair, and his mouth had been stuffed with moss and monkshood.

Sobbing even harder, I cleared out the moss and dried purple flowers and held his jaw shut until his lips remained closed. There would be no kisses or caresses for him anymore, only the cruel beaks and talons of ravens.

Cradling his head in my arms, I lifted my gaze to the sky, searching for a sign. An answer for why these terrible things happened over and over.

"Voserka," I shouted. "If you're there, show yourself!"

Just the soft lapping of the river and the breeze. From their roost in the guelder rose, the wrens continued to sing.

"Kosa, Voyna, Seredina." The names tore from my throat in a scream. "Someone. Anyone. I don't care. Are you there?"

If the Three Sisters were watching, it was with the same indifference as Voserka.

My shoulders slumped under the weight of Vanya's death.

"You are no mother." Closing my eyes, I pressed my forehead to the crown of Vanya's head. "You are no sisters."

Whether one or three, the only thing they propagated was suffering.

At first, all I felt was despair so deep it seemed on the verge of swallowing me whole in its depths. Then suddenly it was as though a candle flared to life in my head, and in an instant, I could sense it—a vast and uncontrollable force more palpable than that of any bogatyr or monster I had come across.

My eyes flew open.

The Unclean Force.

Raising my head, I searched the looming trees for its source. Where was it? *Who* was it?

"Please, I'll do anything if you bring him back to me." My voice broke, and the final words left my lips in a thin croak. "Just bring him back. Please."

Silence, and the river ahead, and the ruby droplet of a sun that hung suspended on the water.

My breath caught in my lungs. The presence I sensed wasn't coming from around me—it rose from within. I felt it resonate in my blood, and the pounding beat of my heart, and the trembling of my limbs as I held Vanya's head against myself.

A wild laugh escaped my lungs. How could we be so blind? We had been such fools. The Unclean Force had been within us—*all of us*—this whole time. It always had been.

All we had to do was reach out and grasp it.

My breath quickened into urgent panting as I gathered my

rushnyk in my arms and used my amber brooch's sharp edge to free a loose thread. Half in delirium, I tore at the cloth, ripping the embroidery free of it with my fingers and teeth, and unwinding the red floss into an overflowing mound.

My birth mother had not been a koldunia. She had simply wanted to mourn my father in the only way she knew how, and to an outsider with vulgar intentions, that had been enough to condemn her. If she had sensed this power within her at the end, she had turned away from it rather than sully herself.

I would not turn away. I knew what I had to do.

Once I had gathered a substantial amount of thread, I broke the pin off of the brooch and wrapped the strand around its end, forming a rudimentary needle. I began with his neck, embroidering a garland of diamonds and interlocking arrows around his torn throat. The thread kept slipping from the needle, forcing me to retie it. His skin was already so cold.

"Not you." A sob choked me as I wiped the blood from his neck with the corner of my rushnyk. "I won't let them take you."

Bit by bit, stitch by stitch, I made Vanya whole again. I freed his foot from his shoe. I tugged the leeches off him, their greedy, suckling mouths leaving circular wounds. The needle pricked my fingers, our blood merging. The thread darkened, first to burgundy then to a slick ink-black.

I adorned Vanya's hips in the twisting, intricate symbols that ran up my mother's rushnyk—for love, for protection. Time seemed to slow. Spirals, interlocking lines, stars with forked tips. My eyes ached from crying, and tender blisters rose on my index finger and thumb. I fell into a gray haze as I worked on his chest, shivering from the cold. The needle felt as unwieldy as a dagger. Then it slipped from my fingers and fell to the ground.

"No, no, no." Moaning, I grasped amid the leaves, frantically searching for the needle and its trailing thread. When I found it after several minutes of searching, I sobbed in relief, gripping the sliver of metal so tightly that it dug a divot into my skin.

By the time I tied off the final stitch, my fingertips were blued from the cold and trembling uncontrollably. The sun had begun its slow descent toward the tree line. Hours must have passed since I had first started, but it felt even longer, like a nightmare I couldn't awake from.

I held Vanya's body against myself, stroking his burgundy hair, which now more than ever resembled dried blood. Blood like the scabs that crusted my fingers. Blood like the cracked, trickling flows that stained his limbs.

"Come back," I whispered, pressing my lips against his cold shoulder. "Please, come back to me. I love you. I need you."

He had endured so much. He didn't deserve to die. Not like this. Not out here in the mud and the wilderness, where his body would decay and be eaten by animals, and nobody but the rusalki would come to mourn him.

Let his flesh rot if it meant he would become an upyr. Let his teeth grow into fangs. Let the embroidered crevices fissure and scale—even becoming a vodyanoy would be better than dead and cold and never coming back.

"Damn you, come back to me," I yelled as he slipped from my numb arms. His eyes were closed, his lashes dusted with dirt, lips parted but not in exhalation. His neck fell lifelessly to the side as he collapsed against the ground.

Stricken with shock, I rose to my feet and stared down at

him, waiting. Waiting. At last, I picked up my ruined rush-nyk and laid it over his body, tenting his face. Even if I'd had a shovel, the ground was too loose to bury him. At the next heavy rain, he might rise to the surface.

Looking at those obscene sutures that the rushnyk failed to conceal, the enormity of what I had done finally dawned on me. How disrespectful and hopeless. How profane. How could I have thought that I'd be able to bring him back to life? That I actually had the power to make a difference?

I couldn't save anyone. Not Vanya, nor Mikhail, nor Galina.

I was no koldunia. I was simply powerless.

Why had I ever thought I could change that?

I turned and retreated up the slope in a daze. Now that all hope was gone, the wrenching grief that filled its place was so immense, I could barely breathe. It felt like something had been torn from me, ripped free, and left in ruins like Vanya's body. The Fraktsiya soldiers had taken more than his life, more than his ability to make change and the beautiful impact he had on the world. They had also stolen the sole tie I had to my heritage and the newfound family Vanya and Mikhail had given me.

Cloth rustled. Leaves crackled. I froze, terrified to look behind me. If I turned around and Vanya was where I had left him, it would destroy me. He wasn't going to return. I knew it in my heart. When I looked back, he would still be lifeless and unmoving.

Better if I kept going. Just put down one foot after another and continue walking. At least then I would never have to know if he was dead or alive.

"Toma," a voice said quietly.

38

My heart broke as I turned around, confronting a pair of green eyes glowing almost as intensely as the reflection of the sun on the river. A sob of relief welled up in my throat as I rushed to his side.

"Toma," Vanya repeated, his voice trembling. He drew his arms around his naked chest, shuddering fingers tracing the sutures lining his stomach, his wrists, his forearms. "Something happened to me. Something. Something happened."

I fell to my knees in front of him, my eyes flooding with tears. I clasped his upper arm, touching warm skin that moments before had been as cold as the mud we sat in.

"You're safe now." My voice trembled violently. "Nobody's going to hurt you again."

As he looked down at his hands, a low moan tore from his throat. "What…"

"Don't be afraid. It's okay. You're okay." I took his hand, staring into his eyes as I did it. A part of me feared that if I looked down at his wounds, they would suddenly begin bleeding again. And he would be as dead as before.

"I remember. The darkness. I remember. It was black. It was so wet and dark and there was, there was nothing. Nothing at all. Nothing. There was nothing, and I was sinking, and then something was touching me." His voice grew hoarse with despair, each word as empty and hollow as the thudding of distant artillery blasts. He shielded his face with his hands, diluted blood oozing from the suture lines. Moments later, when he began sobbing uncontrollably, so did I, as if our hearts were conjoined by the same thread that garlanded his limbs.

Grief, relief, rage, love. As he buried his face against my shoulder, the storm of feelings roaring through me lost their distinction and became raw noise and moisture. Weeping, I clung to him, as though if I let go, I'd drift away.

This was what we needed—to be here, to be held.

Our sobs slowly faded into quiet tears and then into hitched, rough breaths and soothing silence. Vanya settled onto his knees, wiping his wet eyes with the backs of his hands. Tears trickled down his cheeks, vaguely pink in the glow of the rising sun.

I climbed to my feet and picked up his greatcoat. Although the rusalki had retrieved scraps of his trousers, shirt, and undergarments, the Fraktsiya coat he'd stolen from the train was the only article of clothing to survive mostly intact. The surviving soldier must have wrapped his desecrated body in it before tossing him into the river.

As I lifted the coat, meaning to draw it over his shoulders, he took it from my hands.

"I can do it on my own," Vanya muttered, sliding his arms into the sleeves. He struggled to wedge the buttons into their holes, but after several tries succeeded. The coat hung to his calves, sparing me the sight of his disfigured body.

I picked up my rushnyk and wrapped it around my neck. It was too torn to serve as a shawl or sash, but it sufficed as a scarf. It took me a bit of looking, but I found my dropped pistol as well, and stuck it into my dress pocket.

I helped Vanya to his feet and walked beside him, my arm around his back. Bushes rustled. Maybe an animal. Maybe a mavka or vodyanoy. But the monsters of the forest didn't frighten me the way humans did.

Vanya shivered against me, teeth chattering. Each breath he took was choked and abrupt, like he was trying to relearn how to breathe.

We made it to the glade, where flies had begun to gather on the two soldiers' corpses. I avoided looking too closely at them as I searched their bodies for anything that might aid us. One of the soldiers had a bag of supplies, which I slung over my shoulder after sticking Dronov's pistol into an outer pocket. I turned away as Vanya took the man's boots and clothing.

The boots proved to be a greater challenge than the buttons had. His blued fingertips fumbled with the laces, and after several tries, he swore and pressed his hands over his face, tears welling anew in his eyes.

"Don't worry," I said softly, kneeling down to tie his boots for him. "You're tired, that's all. You'll feel better after you've rested."

He said nothing until we left the clearing for untamed forest, only to ask, "Mikhail? Is he…?"

"He had a good medic to take care of him, so physically, he's probably fine. They were preparing to take him to Eyry Castle."

Returning to the camp would be pointless and deadly. Hours had passed since I had fled, and there was no doubt in my mind that Mikhail and Galina were long gone by now.

"These stitches." Vanya's voice was thick. "You were the one who did it, weren't you?"

My voice shriveled in my throat. I nodded once, twice, unable to speak.

His fingers edged to his throat, touched the embroidery there. "How long?"

"What?" I stammered.

"How long was I...was I gone for?"

From the haunted look in his eyes, it was clear he remembered some of his fight with the Fraktsiya soldiers, if not all of it.

I swallowed hard. His question carried such weight, it must have meant far more to him than he let on. It had taken me seven or eight hours to bring him back, I supposed, but how long was that really? Was that enough time for the first hint of decay to spread beneath the skin? For the blood that hadn't run into the river to go cold and congeal?

"Not long," I said at last.

He didn't answer.

"I saw your mother," I murmured. "When I went down to the river, she came to me."

Silence.

"She helped me save you. She wanted you to live. You were brought back for a reason." I felt in my heart that this was no coincidence. Everything in the world had meaning and significance.

Vanya's body tensed, his shoulders curling up like I had struck him. He drew in a deep breath, his hesitation heavy with unspoken meaning.

"You were brought back for a reason," I repeated, my voice firm with conviction. "And these stitches, they're proof that you survived."

"Thank you, Toma," Vanya whispered, looking over at me. His lips rose in a wrenching smile, and although no more tears welled from his eyes, I sensed that he was crying on the inside for everything he had lost and for a life that would never be the same.

39

Rain clouds rolled in from the east, transmuting the sunlight from gold to lead. Watching the storm approach, I shivered with a sudden foreboding. Some of the worst moments of my life had been preluded by storms, and now more than ever the weather felt like an omen of destruction.

As we walked, Vanya remained uncharacteristically quiet. He didn't want to talk about what had happened to him. He didn't want to talk at all. Several times I tried to start a conversation, only for it to fizzle out after the first few minutes. I didn't want to push him, and I didn't mind not talking—after seven years in the wilderness, I'd learned that silence in many ways was more natural than sound. Especially among those who came back.

Except, as the minutes passed, the silence began to disturb me in a way it never had before, allowing dark thoughts to ferment in my mind. So many hours had passed since I had escaped the Fraktsiya encampment, I knew that Galina and

Mikhail must already be at Eyry Castle. Still, I sensed in my heart that there was time to save them. We had come so far now, it was too late to stop, too late to wonder. If Vanya's death had taught me anything, it was that I must never give up on the people I loved.

Exhaustion weighed on my shoulders, growing heavier with each step. It had been over a day since I had last eaten, and my mouth was so dry. I wanted to go down to the river and drink from the flow, but I sensed I'd never be able to sip it now without tasting Vanya's blood. The river's purity was sullied in my mind forever.

We reached a break in the woods and found ourselves at the edge of a stony ridge. In the distance, clouds fought to engulf a castle built at the summit of a tall, pine-encumbered peak.

"Eyry Castle," I whispered, before movement below drew my gaze downward.

A convoy of horses, wagons, and marching soldiers trundled down the road that crossed through the valley. The procession was followed by six armored machines.

"Tanks," Vanya said. "They use a Yezmirskiy motor, but they're imperial in design."

Standing in the shadow of the pines, we watched the group pass. The horsemen's purple flags, adorned with the crossed sword and wheat sheaf, marked them as Otzvuk.

"What are the tsarists doing here?" I asked.

"I don't want to know," Vanya said, and gently tugged on my wrist, drawing me toward the cover of the forest.

I looked back just as roiling storm clouds engulfed the setting sun. The road darkened like an incision cut into the rocky skin of the earth, and the soldiers were reduced to droplets of blood or ink.

After Kupalo, the sight of the Otzvuk's indigo banners should have made me sick with anger, but that was before Lieutenant Dronov and the river. I didn't know what we were fighting for anymore, or for whom. The only important thing now was saving Galina and Mikhail.

Some distance in, we came across the ruins of an izba. It had been many years since anyone had lived there. In the owner's absence, nature had had her way with the home, ensnaring its hewn-log walls in ivy and planting moss and saplings across the dirt floor. The oven was just a pile of bricks and plaster.

Vanya and I walked to the well by the overgrown swine pen. I pushed off the lid, the boards splintering into pieces the moment they struck the ground.

A bucket trailing a chain lay beside the well, an enameled ladle not far away. Vanya lowered the pail into the hole until we heard a splash, and then he hoisted it up again.

He held the ladle out to me, and I drank from its cup. The water ran down my throat, so cold, pure, and delicious. I offered it to him next, but he shook his head.

"I'm not thirsty."

"You have to drink."

Hesitantly, he took a few sips. I sensed from how he grimaced that it hurt to swallow, or the water tasted horrendous to him. Even though he remained close enough for me to touch, I felt the distance between us growing wider.

"Look, blackberries," Vanya said, pointing to the bramble crawling over the fence. "Why don't you sit down and rest while I pick some?"

"We don't have time for that," I said, although hunger gnawed away at my guts.

"Toma, you look like you're going to collapse." He tucked an errant curl behind my ear, his fingers lingering on my cheek. "Twenty minutes, that's all I ask."

"But Mikhail and Galina—"

"You won't be able to help them if you're too weak to stand."

"All right." Sighing in defeat, I placed my hand over his, drew his knuckles to my lips, kissed them. His skin was soft and warm. I tried not to think about how, just hours ago, I had picked this hand from the dirt. How still it was. How cold.

There must also be parts of him that hadn't been there before. There was river water flowing through his veins and rusalka hair entangled in his guts. He had once said that he felt drawn to the Vesna River—and now she was inside of him forever.

As if sensing my thoughts, Vanya pulled his hand away and tucked it against his stomach, hiding the embroidery with the folds of his greatcoat. His smile was strained, like it might crack at any moment. Something told me that he needed this even more than me.

"Just rest," he said quietly, and turned away.

While Vanya picked berries, I sat down in the grass and leaned against the well, the stones blissfully cool against my back. The moment I relaxed my tensed muscles, I became aware of a dozen aches and pains. My feet throbbed so badly that I didn't have to take off my boots to know that blisters covered my tortured soles.

Vanya gathered the berries in the hem of his coat and returned to me with several handfuls. When he tried to sit, one leg nearly collapsed beneath him. I reached for him with a low cry, but he shook his head and said, "I'm fine. I'm *fine*."

The stitches necklacing his throat were gummed with blood and worse, and I was afraid to look at them for too long, as if to acknowledge them might cause them to bleed anew. Whatever thread of magic I had used to bind his soul to this world, it was fragile, and I didn't know how long it would last.

Even the undead could die again, and it scared me to wonder if in bringing him back to this world, I might have deprived him of eternity in the world to come. But perhaps his killers had already done that when they had discarded his body in the water, and that whatever feral power flourished within those patches of wilderness—the forest, the swamplands, the potter's field—it had gone into him and cut him off from the divine forever.

But in the end, maybe the Unclean Force and the divine were two sides of the same coin. Maybe it was by the divine's will that the dead were brought back in order to finish what they had been unable to complete, or so that they may have a second chance at the life they had lost.

I mulled over these things as I ate. The blackberry juice coated my tongue, sour and muddled. I forced myself to eat another fistful and then drink the water, metallic from its long rest in the well.

I gathered the surviving berries in the cup of my palm. When I held out my hand, he looked at me with a blank expression.

"You need to eat," I said. "Just one or two, or at least drink a little more."

He licked his lips. His mouth was dry—I could tell by the

way he swallowed painfully. "Thank you, but I'm not hungry. Don't worry. I'll eat, just not now."

"Vanya," I said, and his gaze slowly lifted.

His chest rose and fell, so that meant he was still breathing, and though his hands were bruised, it was not from the blood settling in his limbs. He was still alive, or the closest thing to it.

"Eat," I repeated, and when he refused to take the berries, I shocked myself by pushing my hand against his mouth. He turned his head to the side, but I refused to budge, smashing the berries against his lips until he shoved me away. Black pulp dropped to the ground as we stared at each other. His eyes were flared wide, and his lips pulled back to show his teeth.

"I said I'm not hungry," he snapped, rising to his feet. He wiped his face with the back of his hand, leaving a long streak of juice smeared across his cheek like a bloodstain.

"Why won't you just try one?" My voice rose uncontrollably.

"Because it disgusts me!" he snarled, his green eyes flashing. "And I'm not hungry, and if I eat them, they'll just rot inside of me."

A twinge of horror pierced me to the core. I had spent my entire life surrounded by monsters. I wondered if I'd just inadvertently created one.

"I understand," I whispered, and his shoulders slowly loosened. "Okay? I understand."

As we continued walking, I kept at a distance at first, but slowly edged closer until I was up against his side, and my hand found his. His skin was warm against my palm, and when I traced my thumb along his inner wrist, I caught the steady beat of his pulse. Then I found the stitches by accident, and even as I began pulling my hand back, he turned away from me and drew his arms around himself. He tucked his hands under his armpits, his gaze on the ground. His lips were pressed together so tightly, they trembled.

"I guess there is one bright side," he said as we kept going.

I looked over at him.

"Well, now we know for sure that you're a koldunia." His laughter came out forced, but in his voice, I caught a trace of the Vanya I knew.

I rolled my eyes. "Best be nice to me from now on, or I might put a curse on you."

We smiled at each other for a moment, because we needed this. We needed to know that we were both okay. A few steps later, he placed his hand briefly upon my shoulder, far enough away from my hand that I wouldn't be tempted to touch him, and a step behind so that I wouldn't see the relics of his death.

Hearing the drone of an engine, I looked up. Three dirigibles passed overhead in an arrow-shaped formation. The emblems painted on their rudders glowered down at me like a pair of eyes—green circles bisected by the Fraktsiya's broken chain.

"We can't be far now," Vanya said. "They're going in for a landing at the city's airbase."

I watched as the airships diminished into shapeless blots, thinking of how I used to watch the passing dirigibles with anticipation back in the wilds. Back then, I hadn't associated the vessels with the fact that they were weapons of war. I'd simply felt such awe at being so close to other living people, when in reality I hadn't been close at all.

A chill crept down my spine at the thought of fifty more years of hunting deer, hewing wood, hunger, fear of bears and wolves, endless winters trapped inside, and oh the *silence*. Now that I actually knew how much humans spoke to each other, I couldn't stand the idea of the heavy silence that would confront me when Galina and I returned home. As much as I loved my parents, I didn't think I was ready anymore to spend the rest of my life in the wilderness.

Long after we continued on our way, the thought weighed heavily on my mind. To even think about the future felt like tempting fate, but I couldn't stop returning to it. If this ordeal had taught me anything, it was that even a single person could have a profound impact on those around her. I didn't need to have powers or wear a crown to make a difference in the world, and the most vicious of monsters were built from the same flesh and blood as everyone else.

As the sun began to set, we reached the top of a grassy knoll crested by overgrown tombstones. The fortress was close enough now that, though it still towered in the distance, I could make out its individual domes and towers and see the winding steps cut into the cliff's sheer face.

You'd better be waiting, Koschei, I thought, gritting my teeth. *You said I had potential. You called me a threat. I'll show you just how much of one I am now.*

40

Pine needles and pinecone husks crunched beneath our feet as we followed a steep path formed by the daily migration of mavki or wildlife. Nestled on the peak above, the castle emerged from the evening fog before being swallowed up once more.

"There has to be a way to get up there," Vanya said, staring up at the castle, which rested upon high limestone walls built flush with the cliffside. "A mountain route."

I turned, sensing movement in the corner of my eye. A mavka emerged from the bramble like a feral goddess. Twigs and leaves bristled from her copper hair, her luminous hazel eyes studying us with solemn curiosity. There was something in the way she looked at us, and how she crossed her hands over her bare body as if in shyness or modesty, that made me wonder if her transformation had occurred more recently than the two forest spirits I had encountered before her.

"Hey, can you help us?" I called, against my better judgment.

Vanya looked around in confusion, noticed who I was talking to, and hid his eyes as if afraid the mavka might enchant him. "Toma, what are you doing? Why are you talking to her?"

"We're looking for a way inside the castle," I told the mavka, taking a step closer. "Do you know of a way we can get up there?"

The mavka looked from me to Vanya and then back again. She smiled slyly, as if she knew a secret, and dipped her chin in a slight nod.

"Can you show us, please?" I asked.

She didn't respond.

Remembering what Vanya had once said about mavki coveting human clothing, I took off my medic's capelet and held it out to her. She edged forward and took it in both hands, marveling at the wool and brass buttons.

Cradling the garment against herself, she stepped onto the natural path Vanya and I had followed from the roadside. Even when she walked on thorns and stones, her movements were as smooth and agile as those of a stalking lynx.

"I can't believe it," Vanya murmured, slowly lowering his hands. "You just let her steal your clothes."

"Come on," I said, hurrying after her.

Vanya sighed and followed beside me. "If she tickles me to my second death, I'm blaming you."

"You wouldn't be the only one."

Our conversation faded into tense silence as we pursued the copper-haired mavka through the woods. Moths flitted from the crevice in her back, battering harmlessly against my hands and face.

We wove in and out through the trees. Leaves crunched beneath our boots. She teased me and Vanya every time we lost ground, stopping only long enough for us to catch up, her lips curled in a playful smile.

We reached a creek engorged with rainwater and followed it along. The mavka strode through the shallows, her legs immersed up to her knees. It almost seemed as though she had no feet at all. Bile flooded my mouth as I recoiled at the memory of how Vanya had looked. How his *legs* had looked.

"Are you all right?" Vanya whispered as I closed my eyes, struggling with the urge to vomit.

"I'm fine," I choked, forcing myself to open my eyes and look down at his legs.

I told myself the worst was over. I'd never have to see him that way again. Like mine, his scars would never be beautiful, but they would be proof that he had survived.

As I walked, I fumbled through the bag I had taken off the dead soldier's body. I came across a tobacco tin, dried bundles of monkshood and moss wrapped in wax paper, a small bottle of gun oil, and, aha, matches.

When I lifted my head, the mavka was gone. Confused, I looked around before spotting her waiting for us near a narrow cleft in the hillside. From a distance, it looked like a rock formation or a vein of darker stone, but as we neared, the streak acquired a depth that betrayed it as something more than simple shadow—a cave blocked by an iron grate.

"Thank you," I said, approaching the mavka. "Is there anything else I can do to repay you?"

She stared at me and Vanya in silence, her hazel eyes darkening to black as the sun sank below the trees. A ghost of sadness drifted over her features.

Who were you once? I wanted to ask her. *You must have had a name. Had a family. What happened to you?*

Young women who died in the woods became mavki. I wondered, had she died naturally or was she murdered? Had it been quick and painless, or had it been terrifying?

Without a word, the mavka turned away and retreated into the underbrush, leaving me and Vanya alone at the cave's entrance. I tugged on the door of the grate, but it was locked tight, no way inside.

"Let me try," Vanya said, and he bent down to bury his hands in the earth. I retreated to a safe distance as roots punched through the soil and ensnarled the grate. The ground split with an earthen rumble, followed by the groan of twisting metal as the roots pried apart the bars. Within moments, the grate gave way, exposing the darkness of the tunnel beyond.

"Can I have some of your coat's lining to make a torch?" I asked Vanya as we stopped in the shadow of the rock overhang.

"Fine, let's destroy my only set of clothes," he grumbled, unbuttoning his coat. My skin crawled at the rasp of tearing cloth. Moments later, he rebuttoned his coat and handed me a strip of cotton.

I found a thick branch in the drift of debris that last season's flooding had deposited at the cave's entrance and wrapped the cloth around the top of it. After saturating the cloth in gun oil, I lit it with a match.

As we entered, it was like being consumed—a clammy darkness with many teeth. Deeper, deeper, we went into the hill, passing several pools of unknown depth. Overhead, limestone stalactites hung from the ceiling, the outcroppings rimed with bands of crystal that glistened like saliva in our torchlight.

I walked close enough to Vanya that I could make out the stitches on his neck. In all the children's stories, the bogatyr and the tsarevna had a rushnyk tied around their clasped hands during their wedding ceremony, binding them for life. Vanya and I were bound now, too, with the thread of a rushnyk, with my own blood and labor.

Soon enough, in a cavern so low we had to duck our heads, we came across the first sign of human disturbance—a heap of rotting buckets discarded near a hole eroded in the ground. A pulley system was bolted to the ceiling, and the remnants of a rope dangled into the darkness below. I looked into the hole. Although it was too dark to see to the bottom, I heard the splash of water.

We kept going. Past the natural well, the tunnel widened into a cavern divided into sections by brick walls. Trestles suggested that the room had once been used for storage, but all that remained were broken barrels and rusted bands.

At the end of the storage cavern, we reached a winding staircase cut into the limestone. There was no banister, not even a rope or chain to grasp onto. I had to take the stairs slowly, one at a time, testing my footing with every step.

A door confronted us at the top of the stairs. I tested the knob, but it refused to budge.

"Let me see if I can get this open," Vanya said.

As he lifted his hands, I grabbed his wrist.

He looked back at me, furrowing his brows. "What?"

"I…" I moistened my lips, afraid to admit just how terrified

I was that something might happen to him. If Koschei captured us, he wouldn't kill Vanya, not after seeing my embroidery. I had brought Vanya back to life, but what if in doing so, I had only guaranteed him a future of pain and terror?

As if sensing my fear, Vanya placed his hand over mine. He lifted my hand to his lips and kissed my knuckles, his breath warming my cold fingers.

"Everything's going to be all right," he murmured, his voice low and reverberating in the staircase's narrow confines. "I'll never let them hurt you."

It's you *I'm worried about*, I wanted to tell him, but to say so aloud felt like tempting fate.

He placed his hands upon the door, and straightaway the wood began to fissure and distort. I held my breath as the groaning of wood and twisting metal filled the air, my heart knocking against my ribs as I waited for shouts of alarm to rise from the other side of the door. Hinges snapped as twigs grew from the wood, bursting into bud and leaf, and the entire door collapsed into a pile of boards that looked halfway to becoming branches. There was no one on the other side.

Vanya stepped quickly through the doorway and peered around. He waved me into the windowless room.

Crates and barrels were stacked against the walls, while shelves contained bottles and clay crocks. Wood shavings crunched beneath our feet as we crossed the room.

"Looks like medical or chemistry supplies," Vanya said, glancing into one of the open crates. "I don't think there's anything in here that can help us. Except..."

Trailing off, he retrieved a small oil lamp from within one

of the crates. "I suppose this will be a little less primitive than carrying a torch around?"

Along with several more oil lamps, the crate contained extra wicks, glass shades, and oil. While Vanya filled and lit the oil lamp, I returned to the staircase and pitched the torch into the darkness. There was nothing that could catch fire down below, and if the flame wasn't smothered in the initial descent, surely it would be extinguished once it struck the cavern's damp limestone floor.

The door across the room led to a brick corridor. In spite of the modernity of the unlit electrical lights lining the passage, the flickering glow of our oil lamp made me feel as though I had been transported back to the wilderness, following Galina through the ice-choked ruins.

No windows. We must still be below the earth.

Vanya walked on ahead, eclipsing the oil lamp's glow. Trailing behind him, I was once more seized by a gut-wrenching foreboding that something would happen to him here.

"Vanya," I whispered, and he looked back at me.

"What is it?"

"Just… Just be careful, okay?"

He smiled a little. "Don't worry. I'll be fine."

As he turned ahead again, I bit my inner cheek to keep from telling him what I truly wanted to say: *I can't bear the thought of losing you again. I love you. Please, don't go. Stay here. Let me protect you.*

The corridor opened into a large room. Cages were stacked along the walls; most were empty, but some contained sickly-looking dogs and cats, and one held something even stranger. Surrounded by harsh electrical lights positioned on all sides of his cage, a drekavac knocked his swollen head against the bars, his shadow shriveled to an inkblot.

Deeper into the room, a water tank was nestled between two bookshelves. An indignant rusalka glowered at us through the algae-streaked pane; there wasn't enough room for her to swim, so she treaded water.

Vanya walked over to her.

"We can't just leave her like this," Vanya murmured, pressing his hand against the glass.

"If we break her out, will she be able to walk on dry land?" I asked.

He sighed, his hand falling. "No. I don't think so."

"We need to keep going," I said, pressing my hand over his. "We can come for her later, after we find my sister and Mikhail. Maybe we can find a way to carry her down to the caverns."

"You're right," he said, and continued across the room.

I looked at the rusalka, staring into her unblinking silver eyes. I wanted to believe that if we freed her, she wouldn't turn on us. My encounters with Vanya's mother and the mavki had only reinforced my certainty that the monsters of this world weren't all that they appeared to be.

We stepped through the next door into a room set up like an office, containing a table draped in a white cloth, a desk, and counters covered in glass bottles and vials. A brown-haired man dressed in a medic's gray coat stood with his back to us, scrubbing his hands at the porcelain washstand.

As we neared, he turned. He had the tight, triangular face of a mink and concave cheeks that bristled with stubble. His gaze swept to the pistol in my hand, before straying to Vanya.

"You fools do realize that the sign is up on the door for a reason?" he said levelly, narrowing his eyes. "I need absolute solitude in my work."

He spoke to us so boldly, it took me aback. Then I realized I was still wearing the Fraktsiya medic's uniform, while Vanya was dressed in a soldier's garb. For all the man knew, we were comrades to him.

"Your work is the last thing you should be worrying about," I snarled, leveling the pistol I had taken from Dronov. "Where's my sister?"

"What?" he asked, befuddled.

"She's an upyr. I know she was brought here. Tell me where she is!"

The doctor's eyes widened. "Ah...ah... It can't be..."

Suddenly, he made a dash for a door at the other end of the room. Vanya took off after him and tackled him to the floor. When the man tried to rise, Vanya linked his arms around the man's throat.

The man strained under Vanya's body, frantically thumping his palms against the ground. He grasped hold of the sheet covering the table and pulled on it, trying to haul himself up. The cloth puddled around him as his thin face reddened then began turning purple, and his eyes bulged from his skull. He tried to scream, but he could only manage a thin, guttering moan. After fifteen seconds, his wheeling limbs stilled, and he lay motionlessly beneath Vanya.

Vanya unfolded his arms from around the doctor's neck and pressed a finger under his jaw. Hesitated.

"He's just unconscious," Vanya said, but I barely heard him. All my attention was directed at the table now. With the sheet pooled on the floor, the table's surface was exposed to the harsh glow of the electrical light overhead. A pile of rags had been heaped in the center.

A groan escaped my throat as I registered what I was seeing. The pistol fell from my hand and clattered to the floor.

Galina lay motionless on the wicker-paneled table, drowning in her dress's fraying lace and linen. Surrounding her were the tools of crude butchery: bone saws, scalpels, picks, and needles.

Her head hung askew on her neck, partially attached with coarse sutures.

I froze, petrified by shock and horror. It couldn't be. Not this. Not after everything that had happened. All that we had endured and faced on our journey here—this wasn't how it was supposed to end.

"Galina," I whispered, and walked forward on feet that suddenly felt as insubstantial as smoke. "No. Oh, please, no."

She didn't respond. She was just a corpse now. The corpse of a child left for so long, she had started to mummify.

Whatever power had held her here was gone. Gone. She was gone.

"Toma," Vanya said softly, and when he tried to take my wrist, I jerked away, his touch excruciating. If he hugged me, I'd burn to ashes.

"I need to bring her back," I said frantically, searching the countertop for needles. It took me a moment to realize we had interrupted the scientist's suturing, and that a needle still hung from the thread trailing down her neck.

"Toma, I don't think—"

"Shut up!" I snapped. If he told me she wasn't coming back,

his words would curse her. I needed absolute silence to make this work. "Shut up, and just let me save her!"

Vanya backed away as I snatched up the needle. Cloth rustled behind me, and the doctor groaned, but I didn't look back to see what Vanya was doing. Didn't care. I had to focus.

I immersed myself in my embroidery. The stitches came out crooked and ugly. My vision blurred from panic and exhaustion and my hands trembled violently. I bit my lip to keep from sobbing as I slid the needle in and out, tugging the thread tighter than I would have dared if Galina had still been moving. I tried to find it in me to pray for a miraculous recovery, but prayers had never done anything for me. Even now, I didn't know who to turn to for help.

The blisters that had formed during those nightmarish hours along the riverside now burst from the pressure of gripping the needle. Tacky with my own blood, my fingertips burned as if I'd grabbed fistfuls of stinging nettles.

As I worked, I sensed in my heart that it was too late. No amount of pain or tears would make a difference. I had been able to bring Vanya back because he had died only once, but how could I restore Galina to health when she had already perished and become something else?

Vanya joined me at the table. He gently rested his hand upon my forearm. "Toma…"

"I can't do it," I sobbed, dropping the needle. I slammed my fist into the table, scraping open my knuckles on the brass rivets lining its edge. "It's not working. She's—she's not going to come back."

"No," Vanya said, circling around to the other side of the

table. His features hardened with resolve. "No. We're going to bring her back together."

I blotted at my eyes with the back of my hand, my mouth trembling so violently, I could hardly speak. "What do you mean?"

"The first time I used my power wasn't on a plant—it was on a dead mouse our cat had brought back. I wasn't able to heal it, not exactly, but the fur began to fill in."

I remembered Detskaya and the way the chair's leather upholstery had grown patches of fur atop it. How it had swelled shallowly as though in exhalation.

"Plants were always easier. They didn't feel as...intimate." He shifted his gaze away. "I think I'm ready to try now, but I can't do it when she's like this. Not without your help. Keep sewing."

Vanya's unshakable confidence gave me renewed hope. I picked up the needle again and turned my attention back to the task at hand. The trembling in my fingers died down by the time I snipped the sutures' dangling end and drew a new thread through the eye of the needle. I tried to pretend her skin was the aged linen that its pigment resembled, but I couldn't separate myself from my love for her. Every time I made another stitch, I was forced to acknowledge that this was what Galina had become, that I might not be able to bring her back, but that I *must* fight for her until the end.

Years ago, my sister, Galina, had saved me. I couldn't give up on her now, not when I had come so far to find her. Whatever it would take, we'd return home together.

While I worked, Vanya brushed his hand through her thinning hair, gathering it behind her head. The moment I tied off the final stitch, he placed one hand gently over her face and the other upon her wasted chest.

At Inga's factory in Detskaya, his power had been fuelled by rage and grief. But now, he seemed in absolute control of himself, his features as solemn and measured as those of a corpse guarder.

The table groaned, splinters raining to the floor as willow twigs burst from the wicker panels. Blood oozed from the bracelets of embroidery around Vanya's wrists and landed on Galina's neck.

A barbed-wire knot of fear twisted in my gut at the sight of his blood. "Vanya—"

"It's okay." His voice was strained, each breath shallow and abrupt. "Just don't talk."

Slowly, the sutured incision on Galina's neck began to close. He slid his hand through her hair, smearing his blood over her forehead. Her wrinkles and folds receded into smooth pink skin. My stitches unraveled and fell apart, uncoiling down her neck to reveal a circlet of silvery scar tissue.

Awe and shock filled me. It was working. I bit my inner cheeks to keep from crying out in joy, afraid that any noise would puncture this moment like a dream.

Galina's cheeks filled out and regained the soft flush of life, her lashes growing in dark and thick. Her chest swelled as she inhaled, the first breath I had ever seen her take. I felt witness to an extraordinary birth.

As Galina opened her eyes, Vanya shut his. He staggered against the counter, breathing even more heavily than before, then slipped to his knees.

In an instant, my excitement was replaced by stomach-churning terror.

"Vanya!" I rushed around the table, my heart slamming into my breastbone. At any moment, I expected him to topple over, dead as before, as if in saving Galina, he had exchanged his rebirth for her own.

"I'm fine," he croaked, pressing his hand against his throat. Thin rivulets of blood oozed between his fingers.

"No, you're not!" I tried to touch his throat to stop the bleeding, but he pushed my hand away and shook his head.

"I said I'm fine, just—just check on her."

"Toma?" a tiny, clear voice said from behind me.

I turned around.

Galina sat up, holding the white sheet against her chest. She rubbed her eyes with one hand. Eyes. Actual eyes—a dark and gorgeous brown.

As I hurried to her side, she reached out to touch me. I grabbed her hand and held it against my chest, marveling at her skin and body heat. She was so heavy, so warm. I stroked her thick, silky hair, for once not afraid that clumps would fall out under my fingers.

"Galechka, look at you," I whispered, my voice choked with tears. "You're beautiful."

She laughed, a soft, sleepy sound like the cooing of mourning doves. She leaned against me and propped her index finger against her lips, sucking the first knuckle lightly. In the past, I had always admonished her whenever I caught her doing it, afraid she'd tear her skin. Now, she could do it for as long as she wanted, and oh, she was alive. She was alive again, and safe.

"What happened?" she asked drowsily. "Why do you look so different? Are we back home?"

"It doesn't matter. You're safe now." I pressed my lips against her forehead. She smelled so strange, not like dust or rotten wood, but clean skin, fresh linen, and a faint chemical odor.

"Is she okay?" Vanya mumbled from where he sat.

"She's fine." I laughed, wiping tears from my eyes.

"Good." Vanya said. When I turned, he smiled in weak relief. "I'm really glad."

Slowly, Galina lowered her hand from her mouth and looked at it in wonder. "Toma, I have… My hand…"

Trailing off, she drew up the frayed hem of her dress, revealing unblemished chubby knees and tiny toes. So small. It shocked me what it looked like for her to be six again, instead of an eternity old. When she wiggled her toes, I couldn't help but laugh, buoyant with relief.

"Are these mine?" she asked, her smooth brow wrinkling in confusion.

"All yours, Galechka. Let's get you down from there." Wrapping my arms around her, I lowered her to the ground. The weight of her body surprised me so much, I nearly dropped her. I held her carefully as her bare feet touched the ground, afraid that she might slip and fall. Once I was sure she had the strength to stand, I released her.

"Where are we?" Galina asked, looking around. Her eyes landed on Vanya, and she edged behind me shyly, grasping at my skirt.

"Galina, this is my friend, Vanya." I placed a reassuring hand on her shoulder. "He helped me save you."

She took a tentative step forward, cocking her head as she looked him up and down. She gasped in amazement. "Ooh, Toma, you gave him your pretty embroidery."

"At least someone likes it," Vanya said, with a faint laugh. He lifted his head, his green eyes clouded with exhaustion. "Toma, I'm so thirsty. I think I saw a carafe on one of the shelves…"

Turning, I spotted a glass carafe on the counter by the water basin. As I crossed the room, the doctor glared at me from where he lay squirming on the floor. Vanya had used medical gauze to bind his limbs and gag him.

A ring of keys rested nearby on the counter. I slipped it into my pocket then turned my attention to the carafe. I sniffed the water and sampled it before bringing a cup back to Vanya.

"Thank you," Vanya mumbled as I handed him the tumbler. Once he had taken a few shuddery sips, spilling water on himself in the process, he leaned against the counter.

Droplets of blood clung to the skin below his sutures. Just the sight of them nauseated me with fear.

"Let me bandage you," I said, searching the counter for another roll of gauze. Bundles of bandages were lined up in the glass-doored cabinets, and I retrieved one from the stack.

"Just need to rest," Vanya said, his eyes fluttering shut as I tore the bandages with my teeth. "Just ten minutes…"

"Not here." Considering Koschei's obsession with those who came back, it was too much of a risk to let Vanya recuperate in the lab. After dressing his neck and wrists, I hooked my arms under his armpits and helped him to his feet. "Galechka, follow me."

Slowly, I guided him across the room, supporting his back.

His feet dragged, as if we were walking through quicksand. Galina hurried alongside us.

It took us nearly two minutes to reach the storage room. Once we were safely inside, he sank into a sitting position and leaned against one of the crates. Almost immediately, his breathing grew slow and heavy. When I said his name, he didn't answer.

I gnawed my lip nervously, resting my hand upon his breastbone. His heartbeat was slow but even. There were so many uncertainties, so many things that could go wrong. I wanted desperately to stay with him until he awoke, but how could I? Time was running out, and I had to make a choice.

"I'll be back," I whispered, brushing the hair away from his face.

He didn't respond. His thick lashes trembled as his eyes flicked beneath their lids.

"Galechka, I need you to watch him for me," I said, turning to her. "If you hear someone coming, wake him up. And if you can't wake him up, run. That door leads into caverns down below. Go through them and get to the woods. There are mavki there. They will be able to protect you."

Her eyes widened. "Wait, you're leaving? Where are you going?"

"I need to find another friend of ours." I took her hand and gave it a firm squeeze, something I wouldn't have dared to do just a few days before. "Stay strong until I get back."

"Please, don't go, Toma," Galina whimpered, wrapping her arms around me. "Let's just go home. Please, I want to go home."

It was too late for that. I had already seen and experienced too much of the world to justify leaving now. Galina's safety was paramount, but Mikhail was still out there, and if I abandoned him, how many others would perish as a result? How many other families would this war tear apart?

"Shh, shh, it's all right." I slipped out of her grasp. "I won't be gone long. Just do everything Vanya says and stay out of sight."

"But—"

"I love you." I took a deep breath, leaned down, and kissed the top of her head. As she sniffled, I untied the bead bracelet from around my wrist and showed it to her.

Her eyes widened. "Is that mine?"

"Yes, Galina, it's all yours." I tied it around her wrist, knotting it off in a bow. "Once we return home, we'll find the rest of the beads, all right? We'll spend all day hunting. But you need to stay hidden now. I'll be back."

As I left the storage room, I resolved not to look back. No matter what happened next, there could be no hesitation, no doubt. I retrieved my pistol from the floor and carried it at my side, resting my finger on the trigger guard.

I must fight.

Crossing the laboratory, I thought of the men who had collapsed under Koschei's onslaught, reduced to shriveled husks and bare bone. If he could slaughter thirty bogatyri effortlessly, I would stand no chance without some protection of my own.

I had no time to embroider my own limbs with my mother's protective symbols, nor the stomach for it, but maybe there was an alternative. I paused at the counter, ignoring the doctor who writhed on the floor, muffled protests rising from his gagged mouth as he glowered at me. Stacks of journals lined the shelf above the rolls of medical gauze, along with spare ink pots and writing supplies.

I retrieved a fountain pen and tested it on my palm. Black ink drizzled down my wrist. Rolling up my sleeve, I tried to recall the symbols that had adorned my mother's rushnyk in perfect detail. She had taught me well, first by copying them out in charcoal and then by devoting them to embroidery. I should have known that they had always been more than what they seemed.

Line by line, I drew the runes across my own arm, pressing down the pen nib as hard as I could dare, trying to raise welts or even blood, because maybe blood and pain were a part of it.

I marked my other arm similarly, then copied the final rows of embroidery down each knee. As I rose to my feet and continued on my way, I hovered my fingertips over the glistening lines crawling over my wrist. I could only pray that the symbols were just as powerful in ink as they were in cotton and madder.

The door at the other end of the laboratory opened into the vestibule of a winding staircase. I ascended the steps slowly, squinting in the gloom. Around the turn, a light burned, but the stairs were still immersed in shadows. I held on to the banister with one hand, and with the other, brandished my pistol in front of me.

Reaching the landing, I found myself in a white hallway with gilded columns and ornate stuccowork. As I rushed down the corridor, my boot heels echoed on the mosaic floor, matching the roar of blood pounding in my ears.

Although the lamps in the passageway were no brighter

than those in the laboratory below, I felt like a moth backlit by candlelight. My ruined rushnyk and inked armor wouldn't protect me here, not against ordinary humans.

Frantic footsteps. Loud, demanding voices.

Ducking against one of the pillars, I squatted down to make a smaller target of myself. I couldn't look away from the mud my shoes had smeared across the tiles, my heartbeat slamming into my ribs like the whacks of an axe. Would they notice my footprints?

"It's even worse than we thought, sir," a woman said. "The garrison at the old courthouse wired us thirty minutes ago, saying they were under attack, and all our attempts at reaching them have been unsuccessful. And now we've lost all contact with Eyry's south airbase."

"No doubt we have an informant in our midst," Koschei said, his voice icy smooth. "I do hope your unit will do everything in its power to find where our lines of communication were intercepted."

"Y-yes, sir. Our reinforcements will arrive here any minute, but should we initiate the emergency protocol? There are caverns that empty out into the valley below. If you leave now…"

"I'm not leaving," Koschei said dully. "Now is our chance to deal a fatal blow to the tsarists."

As the footsteps neared, I became hyperaware of my breathing, loud and ragged. The pair passed the pillar I hid behind, their shadows skittering across the floor. Even if I wanted to shoot them, I'd have to emerge from behind cover to do so. And they would be armed, too. That much I was sure of.

The footsteps receded.

Slowly, I released my breath and looked out from behind

cover. I glanced up and down the corridor before edging out into the open. Against my better judgment, I headed in the direction that Koschei had gone only moments before.

I couldn't run around the castle searching for Mikhail. My best option would be to follow Koschei and see where he went.

I hurried silently down the hall and peeked around the corner, where the corridor opened into a large atrium with a domed stained-glass ceiling. The walls were adorned with exquisite gilt filigree reminiscent of flames and ivy, while marble columns reached to the wraparound balcony of the floor above.

Koschei climbed the staircase to the second floor, still in conversation with the female soldier. I shuddered involuntarily at the sight of him, my breath catching in my throat. Maybe it was because I had spent so many years with my family in the wilderness, but I could *sense* it. There was a distortion in the air around him, as though he were too heavy for gravity to sustain. Only, instead of keeling under its force, it was gravity that yielded to him.

To others, his raw, overbearing energy must have been captivating, but even at a distance, it sickened me and made my skin crawl. This was the man who was to blame for everything. This was the witch.

We both were.

Koschei stopped at the landing and said something else to the woman, who nodded and retreated back down the stairs.

My throat narrowed to a pinhole. I pressed my back against the wall and held my breath, praying the soldier wouldn't re-enter this hall. Her footsteps neared, passed, receded. A door creaked open and then closed.

After counting to ten, I looked back into the atrium. From where I stood, it seemed deserted. If there were other soldiers guarding the castle, they must be dispersed around the entrance and grounds. Koschei was nowhere in sight.

I slipped off my boots and rested them against the wall. The chill of the stone floor leached through my holey socks. My medic's uniform, ragged and covered in dirt and brambles, would make it impossible for me to blend in with the Fraktsiya soldiers. There was no hiding that I was an outsider.

I raced across the atrium and hurried up the stairs. The woven runner muffled my footsteps, while the stairs, carved from the same limestone as the hill the castle stood on, were silent beneath my weight. I ascended in a crouch, hoping that, with its thick urn-shaped spindles, the banister would hide me from any soldier who happened to pass below.

Once I reached the top of the staircase, I darted for cover behind a tall urn. Breathing heavily, I peered into the hall beyond.

No sign of Koschei. Had he gone into one of the rooms?

I glanced behind me, making sure that no one was coming up the stairs, before edging into the passage. The drapes were drawn over windows. Electrical lights glowed in filigree cradles, casting shadows that resembled writhing serpents across the floor.

Every few steps, I looked behind me, expecting at any moment to find myself surrounded by soldiers. The corridor was empty. So far so good.

At the first door I came across, I squatted down and pressed my eye against the keyhole, queasily aware that if the door were to suddenly open, I'd be knocked flat on my back. Blackness confronted me.

I rose to my feet and went to the next door, listening keenly for any sign of life beyond the solid oak panel. No movement, no voices. Just silence and an unlit room.

Koschei must have come down this passage, so where was he?

A blade of light gleamed through the bottom of the next door. I looked through the keyhole and gasped.

The room on the other side was as decadent as the rest of the castle's furnishings, with hand-carved furniture and decorative stuccowork. But the floor was covered with a blood-splotched sheet instead of a luxurious rug, and heavy chains stretched across the bed.

A figure lay motionless atop the mattress. All I could see of him was a shackled arm, bloody clothes, and a dark tangle of hair.

Mikhail.

I took out the pair of keys I had found in the laboratory and inserted the larger one into the lock. The lock clicked, and when I turned the knob, the door swung outward with ease.

"Mikhail," I said softly, entering the room.

No response.

I eased the door shut behind me, slipped the keys into my pocket, and went to his side.

He lay in a deep slumber. An assortment of bottles and medical supplies rested atop the small bedside table. His wrists were shackled to the bed frame's carved posts, the chains long enough that he could move and sit up, but not reach for anything beyond the bed's confines.

"Mikhail," I repeated, tapping his cheeks with my fingertips. His skin was cool and clammy. If not for the slow, even breaths that lifted his chest, I would have thought he was dead.

What should I do?

It briefly crossed my mind that I could wrap him in the sheet and drag him through the castle the same way I had transported him through the woods. No good. I wouldn't be able to take him down the stairs. Even if I could somehow maintain my grip on him during our descent, his head would strike the stone with every step.

I needed to go back and get Vanya. The two of us would be strong enough to carry Mikhail to safety.

"Toma?" Mikhail whispered, cracking open his eyes.

"You're awake!" I said, barely able to contain the relief in my voice.

"Where am I?" His voice was slurred.

I set my pistol on the bedside table and took his hand in both of mine, the chains clinking together as I squeezed his fingers. "You're in Eyry Castle. Hold on, I'm going to remove these shackles. We need to get you out of here."

I fitted the second key in the shackle around his right wrist and twisted it. There was some resistance, and then the tumblers aligned with a soft click, and the cuff opened. As I crossed around to the other side of the bed to free his left wrist, Mikhail's eyes widened in horror.

Movement flickered in the corner of my vision. As I began to turn around, something struck me from the side, slamming against my temple so hard that sparks swarmed in my eyes. I dropped the key ring and fell to the ground, dazed by the embers dancing across my vision. The taste of blood bloomed in my mouth. By the time I realized I had bitten my tongue during the fall, Koschei's hands were already around my throat.

Looming over me like a bad moon, his face blurred so that I could only see a pale smear. When I blinked, his features resolved into high cheekbones and a finely chiseled nose. His leonine eyes bored into mine, searing in the low lamplight.

As his hands squeezed tight, I struggled beneath him, gasping for breath. One knee pinning my leg, the other jabbing into my side like an anvil, his full weight was boring down on me. I tried to wrench his hands free, but he was too strong. He took a hand from my throat only so that he could place it on my forehead, his fingers digging into my temples.

"I see you've found yourself." His voice was low and dark like the rumble of distant thunder. "The spark I sensed in you has become a flame. I should have snuffed it out when I had the chance, but instead, I think I'll take it for myself."

His grip on my forehead tightened, the pressure in my skull becoming excruciating. He was too strong. In a panic, working against the natural impulse to try prying the fingers of his left hand from my throat, I reached up and seized his right hand with both of mine, dragged it down. His sweaty skin brushed against my lips. I sank my teeth into the base of his thumb. Hot blood flooded my mouth.

Koschei jerked his hand away, his eyes flaring in confusion and outrage. Clearly, the Strannitsky runes worked as well against a koldun's magic as a bogatyr's.

"What are—" Before he could finish, a deafening explosion racked the building. The chandelier swung overhead in slow pendulum motions, crystal prisms tinkling against each other. As he looked up, his grip loosened around my throat just enough that I was able to wrench free and scramble out from beneath him.

I staggered to my feet, wheezing through my bruised throat. It felt as if he had crushed my windpipe. The floor shuddered in the concussion's aftermath, and the window-panes rattled like chattering teeth.

"It can't be," Koschei murmured. For a moment, a ghost of wonder flitted across his features, and then his eyes returned to me and his expression chilled. "You brought the Otzvuk here."

As he took a step forward, rot spread across the white tarp. The linen unspooled into frayed strands, and even the luxurious rug beneath it began to decay. I felt his power ripple across the soles of my feet like icy water, tingling between my toes and spilling as high as my ankles, before receding.

His eyes narrowed. "What are you?"

I didn't answer. My gaze flicked to the bedside table where I placed my gun. It seemed like a world away.

"I suppose it doesn't matter. Bogatyr or koldunia, you'll bleed just the same." His hand curled around the handle of the sword at his hip. As he drew the blade from its niello sheath, I made a dash for the gun.

Koschei lunged at me, and I leapt out of the way. All my years in the wilderness hadn't taught me how to fight humans, but they had taught me how to be agile and swift. I dodged his shashka's curved blade, ducking and darting out of the way of every blow.

This pulsing redness immersing the corners of my vision,

this trembling in my limbs, the taste of copper in my mouth and the sudden flood of saliva—was this terror?

Koschei seized a fistful of my dress and threw me off balance. I knocked into the bedside table, tipped it over, fell. Medicine bottles and instruments clattered to the floor. My pistol skidded out of sight.

"Leave her alone!" Mikhail shouted, straining against his chain. "Don't hurt her!"

I landed on all fours, broken glass cutting into my palms. My hands slipped over the floorboards, greased up with salve and oily tinctures.

A boot slammed into my side before I could rise to my feet, leaving me gasping for breath, tears blurring my vision. I fell onto my side, my ribs screeching in pain.

Shattered bottles and rolls of gauze littered the floor. A gleam of steel caught my eye, but then Koschei kicked me again, and I landed hard on my back. Glass crunched beneath me as I hoisted myself up, my body a knot of agony.

The tip of Koschei's shashka rested a mere finger's width from my face. I held my breath, afraid that if I inhaled, he would take that movement as an invitation to shove the sword through my throat.

"Don't, Koschei, don't do it." Mikhail leaned forward as far as his shackled wrist would allow, the chain strained taut. "She isn't a part of this!"

"Why are you doing this?" My voice came out thin and scratchy. "I don't understand. Don't you realize how many innocent people are dying because of you?"

If not for the war, so many lives would be spared.

"They are martyrs whose legacies will live on through the

revolution." As distant gunfire and shouts echoed through the walls, Koschei's gaze bored into me. "Do *you* realize how many people have died under the bogatyri's oppression? How many homes have been burned, how many families torn apart? Even now, the Otzvuk are scorching the earth they're driven from. They believe it's their divine destiny to rule over us lesser men, but would you like to know something? Their powers are no different than those of kolduny. The only difference is that the bogatyri gain their powers through blood, through privilege, while we gain ours through suffering and need."

Another explosion racked the building, this time powerful enough to stagger Koschei. His sword swung to the side, narrowly missing me as I splayed my fingers across the floor to keep from falling. My thumb found cold metal. Wincing as the point nipped me, I looked down. A pair of medical shears.

As Koschei regained his balance, I lunged forward. He swung his sword. I ducked, the blade cutting the air above my skull. I slammed into him. Underneath his military uniform, he was all hard muscle and bone, sharp angles that made for a painful collision.

As we reeled back, my shears found his chest. The blade sank up to the hilt in him when I slipped on the spilled salve and fell. His shashka clattered to the floor and I landed on top of him, still clutching the shears' handle.

Dust rained from the ceiling as a third explosion racked the castle. I couldn't tell whether the building itself had been hit or if the Otzvuk artillery units were firing at the outposts I had spotted near the mountain's base, but the explosions were close—their glow flared through the window, bathing the room in palpitations of crimson light.

As I rolled off him and lumbered to my feet, Koschei lay where I felled him, groaning in pain. Blood oozed between his fingers and ran down his side, black in the fading firelight.

Rushing over to the other end of the bed, I snatched the key from the mattress and unlocked Mikhail's last shackle. He sagged heavily against me. His legs nearly gave way as I helped him toward the door.

"Kill him, Toma," Mikhail mumbled. "Stake him to the earth and dismember him, so he stays that way."

The scissors skittered across the floor, coming to a rest at our feet. The blade was stained with gore. I looked over my shoulder as Koschei lumbered onto his hands and knees, his fingers already closing around his sword's hilt. Thin strings of blood oozed to the floor, the flow stemming by the second.

Slowly, Koschei raised his head, his lion-bright eyes burning into me. And he smiled.

41

A cacophony of gunfire and mortar blasts filled my ears as Mikhail and I escaped down the hall. I hurried alongside him, encircling my arm around his back to provide needed support. Whatever drug he had been given to stanch his pain had also left him stumbling and lethargic, as if he existed in a realm separate from the deafening concussions of artillery shells and the screams of dying men.

Somewhere deeper in the castle, a wall or ceiling crashed down with an ear-shattering roar. Surely, the Otzvuk intended to bring the fortress to the ground.

We reached the stairs and took them painstakingly slow. I wished I was strong enough to carry Mikhail. Every second we delayed meant another second closer to Koschei catching up to us or the castle's destruction. If the Otzvuk swarmed this place, they wouldn't waste time trying to differentiate civilians from soldiers. Nor would they recognize Mikhail, in his current state, for the tsar he had once been.

"Just leave me," Mikhail mumbled, his gray eyes as bleak and desolate as urns of ashes.

"I'm not leaving you! You never abandon the people you care about."

As we reached the bottom step, a door banged open high above.

"Tsar, are you really going to try this again?" Koschei's voice was hoarse with pain, and even so, it resounded through me with all the power of an artillery blast. "You've left a trail for me to follow."

I swore, looking down. Blood dripped down Mikhail's side from his soiled bandages, leaving a smatter in our wake.

"I thought that simply taking your powers would be enough to neuter you, but perhaps I was mistaken." Though his footsteps rang high above, his voice seemed to come from somewhere intimately close, as though he murmured it a mere hair's breadth away from my ear. "Instead of a bargaining chip, you have become a thorn in my side."

At the bottom of the stairs, I ducked through the second door I came across, entering a round ballroom whose center was encircled by marble statues on malachite pedestals—larger-than-life depictions of the Three Sisters and the Empire's founding bogatyri. Shafts of moonlight illuminated their faultless white faces, blind eyes boring down at me as I passed, as though to condemn us.

Mikhail and I split ways, each going down another side of the circle. At the other end of the room, we found ourselves at a solid wall. No way out. Cursing myself for not cutting off Koschei's head while I had the chance, or at least taking his sword, I scanned the room for another weapon.

My gaze landed on the statue of Voyna. She held a gold balance scale aloft in one hand, and a sovnya in the other. The polearm's curved blade gleamed lethally in the lingering glow of another artillery blast.

I clambered onto the statue's plinth and pried the sovnya from her hand. She relinquished the polearm with ease—it was a genuine weapon, the edge sharp to the touch. As I jumped down from the pedestal, the door crashed open behind us. I sank to a crouch, my back against the cold malachite.

"On the train, Toma, I told you that with every death comes an echo," Koschei said, stepping deeper into the room. His call rippled across the hall's grand expanse and rising columns, until his voice seemed to come at me from all sides. As for his footsteps, I could barely hear them over my pounding heartbeat and the blood rushing through my ears. "I wonder what sort of echo your death will produce, girl."

By the second, the room seemed to darken. Flakes of marble sifted down from the statue, dusting my hair and shoulders. I lifted my head, biting my tongue to keep from crying out. Cracks spiderwebbed across the statue's face.

Horror filled me as I looked down. On my own arms, the inked symbols were flaking away by the second. I didn't have much time left. No wonder the past warriors had carved the symbols on their weapons and armor—engraved in metal, they would have likely withstood far more abuse than simple ink.

Step by step, the room grew even darker still. The drapes frayed into piles of rotting silk, dappled with mold. Even the gilt carvings in the high ceiling flaked away until the exposed wood began to rot as well.

Edging around the side of the statue, I caught a glimpse of Koschei drawing deeper into the room. He traced his fingertips across the statue of Tsarina Yelena, the first empress of Kosa, and she crumbled beneath his skin.

"Bogatyr or koldun," he said. "There isn't much difference, you know. And how is being spoiled any worse than being blessed? It is how you use your gifts that counts. For years now, the bogatyri have gorged themselves on the blood and sweat of the common man like ticks. Like parasites. And now they have the hubris and arrogance to deride my gift as evil when they themselves have committed sins innumerable. You have seen that, haven't you?"

I swallowed hard, tightening my hold around my knife. His words worked their way inside me, burrowing deep like a blood worm, and all I could think about was my mother holding me close, pressing me against her body as a man set afire strode through the forest, hunting us.

Tomochka, whatever you do, don't make a sound.

So, I had hid under the thornbush, biting my own arm to keep from crying out. And when she had started screaming, I had run and not looked back.

This time, I would not run. This time, I must fight.

"Would you like to know how I became what I am today?" Koschei asked, eroding a second statue's face and arm in an instant with a touch as light as any lover's. Chunks of marble rolled across the floor.

I didn't answer. I didn't want to hear it. If my own power had emerged after seven years of struggle in the wilderness and after losing both my mother and Vanya, I hated to think what he had gone through to be granted his.

"It was in the trenches of Teykhst, within the Edge. The Grozniy troops had pushed us back as far as Shteynov to the south and Kupalo to the west. Death did not divide us in those days—it surrounded us on all sides. Teykhst was...different. We had managed to keep the Grozniy troops at bay by the time the 7th Bogatyr Regiment arrived; they were not involved in the actual fighting at that point. Too valuable. Not like us common men within the 12th Infantry Regiment. We bled in the trenches. We suffered. We died. We came back." His rolling timbre filled my ears, as low and somniferous as a chant. "So, we saw bogatyri fighting for the first time, and when there was a lull in the battle, we saw the way in which the 7th Bogatyr Regiment prevented the resurrection of us lesser beings. By burning the wounded and the dead alike, including our own. That would have been enough. That would have been enough, but then we were given an order. Go into Teykhst and raze it to the ground. Burn all cropland, kill all cattle. If anyone resists, they are traitors and they must be slaughtered."

Closer, closer. He paused at another statue—a tsar whose gilded crown and scepter disintegrated into rust and gold leaf beneath his spoiling touch. The malachite pedestal split in two as the statue came crashing to the floor in pieces, and the air between us was filled with a smothering cloud of marble dust. He was just a shadow now in the moonlit haze.

"The Grozniy encroachment appeared inevitable at that point. Even with the deployment of bogatyr regiments, it seemed only a matter of time before the Grozniy troops marched deeper into the Edge. So, by order of the crown, we would leave nothing behind that they could use. I was young and spirited, and it was in that moment, I made a decision. It was in that moment, I killed, and I found what I am today."

A shiver racked my body, and a slow, nauseating horror dawned on me. It was him. He was the one who had come from the wilds, the one who had made my home what it was today—a steppe of bones and decay. He was the one Galina had seen during her last moments.

He was the monster.

Koschei prowled even closer still, and more stone chips nipped into my scalp. Cracks spread through Voyna's face and shoulders; her head split apart and her chest caved in. As chunks of marble rained down on my shoulders like a barrage of beating fists, I darted out from behind the statue and rushed at Koschei.

"This is for Galina!" I snarled, driving the sovnya toward his stomach.

My sleeves were the first to fail, disintegrating to loose threads even as the inked runes upon my arms persisted. Gold dust flaked from the honed edge of the sovnya's blade.

He sidestepped my thrust of the weapon. As I swung the sovnya in a sweeping curve, he raised his own shashka and met me head-on.

Sparks rained to the floor as my polearm and his sword clashed against each other. In the hazy moonlight, his eyes radiated an eerie inhuman radiance.

"There you are," he purred, boring down on me. I darted out of the way as his blade came crashing down. He was stronger, but I was faster, and the sovnya had three times the range of his saber. And I would prove to him what I had learned during those years in the wilderness. I would show him what it meant to survive out there.

"Ah, I see how you have persisted for so long," he said, striding forward. "The Strannik you were with, the one my men killed—did he teach you those?"

The marks were almost gone now, and I could feel the weight of Koschei's power crashing down on me, as though by the second I was sinking deeper and deeper into some deep-sea void.

In the corner of my eye, I caught a flash of movement flicker behind the statue to my right. Keeping my gaze trained on Koschei, I stepped backwards, luring him closer still.

"My mother," I said.

He was about to say more, only to have his words cut out by the slick squelch of tearing flesh. He looked down, watching in stunned silence as the gilt sickle held by the statue of Kosa emerged from his chest.

With a wild cry, Mikhail thrust the crescent-moon blade even deeper. Trails of blood welled from Koschei's mouth as he reached down, grasping the sickle and reducing it to rust beneath his fingers. As the last smears of ink flaked from my arms, I spun the sovnya in a smooth arc overhead and brought it down upon him.

Koschei's head struck the floor, but his body remained upright. He took one step forward, then another, before the shashka fell from his slackening fingers and his body came crashing to the polished marble.

Lowering the polearm, I stepped forward uncertainly. As I looked down at his head, he looked up at me—his pupils dilating, the lids still blinking ever so slowly.

His lips trembled as though he meant to speak, but I had cleaved his vocal cords in two. Blood bubbled from one corner of his mouth, spilling down his chin in a froth of red saliva. And his lips continued to move in excruciating slowness, forming the shapes of words.

In time, you will understand... His irises' golden filaments glowed like fire—even now, as the shadow of death crept across his features, I felt pierced by those eyes, as if he could peer straight into the depths of me... *Who the true monsters are.*

Koschei's lips stilled, and his blood inched in a slowly widening circle across the tile floor. As the unnatural radiance of his irises diminished, the golden striations faded into an ordinary hazel. And I knew then that he would not be coming back.

42

Deeper in, part of the fortress collapsed with a deafening boom. Dust sifted from the ceiling, and the chandelier crashed to the floor with enough force to fling its crystal prisms across the room.

As we hurried into the corridor and headed toward the cellar stairs, two Fraktsiya soldiers turned the corner and froze at the sight of us. I barely had enough time to drag Mikhail into the cover of an alcove before they opened fire. Gilded splinters spewed across my shoulders as bullets pulverized the decorative woodwork above our heads. I landed on my rear, gasping for breath.

Koschei's shashka clattered to the floor beside me, slipping from my trembling fingers. I snatched it up again. The sword would do little good against rapid artillery, but it came as a small comfort to be armed again. I'd hooked the scabbard onto my medic's belt, and it slapped against my thigh with each step.

A deafening crash shook the walls, and a cloud of plaster dust rolled in from the corridor. In the explosion's aftermath, the gunfire died into an eerie quiet, punctuated only by distant shouts and the crackling of fire.

"Come on!" I hauled Mikhail to his feet and hurried back into the hall. The ceiling had collapsed farther down the corridor, littering the floor in rubble and blocking off the soldiers' route.

Gagging on the dust filling the air, I rubbed my stinging eyes with the back of my hand and looked around in bewilderment. Where was the door to the basement? Could it have gotten buried in the debris?

Through the screen of white powder, I spotted a wooden door partially hidden behind fallen lumber. Sheathing the shashka, I ran over and yanked at one of the beams, struggling to move it. So heavy. It wouldn't budge.

Mikhail joined me, grabbed the other end, and tugged.

"Can't you use your powers?" I asked frantically.

He shook his head, his features strained. "If I could, don't you think I would've done so by now?"

Chunks of plaster cascaded down the pile of rubble and snapped beneath our feet as we dragged the support beam free. I threw open the door, wincing as one of the hinges snapped.

We didn't have much time left. Any minute, this building would fall apart over us.

Dust rained down on our heads as we followed the staircase down into the earth. Vanya emerged from the laboratory just as we reached the bottom.

"No. No." Mikhail veered away, horror in his eyes. He

tripped over the stair's first step but caught onto the wall before he could fall. His entire body trembled with his frantic breaths. "You're dead. I know it. You're *dead*."

"Is that any way to greet your friend?" Vanya smiled wryly before turning to me. "Galina's in the caverns. We need to hurry. This castle's going to collapse any moment."

"Toma, that's not him," Mikhail stammered, grabbing my arm as I stepped forward. "It's not Ivan. It—it's some sort of monster."

"That's cruel, Tsarushka," Vanya said, and although there was still a ghost of humor in his voice, his eyes revealed how truly hurt he was. "First you call me a koldun, now you call me a monster? Wouldn't you say that's a bit excessive?"

"I saw you," Mikhail stammered. "I saw your head. That soldier brought out your head."

I realized that when I had passed out, Mikhail must have still been conscious. He must have witnessed the horrific aftermath I could only imagine—a soldier emerging from the woods, gripping a bloody machete in one hand and a handful of burgundy hair in the other.

Vanya's smile faded, and he raised a hand to his bandaged throat. "Oh. That's...I wish you hadn't mentioned that."

I decided that I should intervene before the ceiling crashed down on our heads. "Mikhail, it's really him. I brought him back with the same embroidery that I used to stitch up your wound."

Mikhail didn't answer. His lower lip quivered as he stared at Vanya, and then he stepped tentatively toward him. He reached out and gently touched Vanya's cheek as if to make sure he was truly there. Then, upon touching warm skin, Mikhail leaned forward and embraced him.

Vanya gave a brief squeeze in return, before they parted. He glanced up as another explosion shook the castle, the blast followed by rapid gunfire.

"I hate to cut our reunion short, but I'd rather not get killed a second time," Vanya said, and hurried into the next room. We passed through the laboratory, where I snatched up the lit oil lamp.

The brown-haired scientist thrashed on the floor, muffled shouts straining through the medical gauze Vanya had shoved in his mouth. His eyes flared in terror, pleading silently with me as I passed, but I barely even looked at him. If the collapsing fortress didn't kill him, the Otzvuk would. Seven years in the wilderness had hardened me and opened my eyes to one truth—kindness would save no one, least of all myself.

Down, down, down into the cold limestone vaults. By the time we entered the cavern filled with the remnants of barrels and shelves, the world above had gone silent. No time to rest. Who knew if these tunnels might survive the castle's destruction?

"Galina!" I coughed, my throat still hoarse and scratchy from inhaling plaster dust, not to mention the throttling Koschei had given me. "Galina, where are you?"

She crawled out from behind the crossed trestles, carrying an oil lamp in one tiny hand. Tears glistened on her cheeks as she set down the lamp and threw herself at me, sobbing my name.

"Shh, shh, it's okay," I murmured, running my free hand through her hair. "You're safe. I'm here now."

"Galina?" Mikhail said in quiet awe.

"Up we go," Vanya said, and scooped her into his arms. "Sorry, Tsar, but you're going to have to save your questions for later. I'm not waiting around to see if this hill can withstand whatever artillery the Otzvuk's been lobbing our way."

We descended deeper into the caverns. At times, Vanya was forced to set Galina down and bow over to avoid scraping his head on the ceiling. The oil lamps provided insufficient light, and halfway down, Mikhail's elbow jostled me and I accidentally dropped mine. In the darkness, the tunnels felt even longer and more convoluted than they had been before, as if they might stretch on forever.

Finally, I spotted a patch of light.

"That's it," I said. "We're almost there."

I stepped between the rows of stalactites and emerged into the night. The tension drained from my limbs as I took in grateful breaths of fresh air.

Finally. We were free.

Suddenly, an intense glow emerged from the trees. Men surrounded us in an instant, yelling for us not to move.

I pushed Galina behind me, shielding her with my body. "Wait, don't hurt us! We have a child!"

As she clutched at my skirt, I blinked rapidly, struggling to adjust to the sudden glare after so long spent in the dark. The fiery glow was moving...and growing.

Slowly, it dawned on me the glow wasn't from a lantern, but a man. A mustached man cloaked in an inferno and still standing, peering down at us with a haughty scowl as flames cocooned his limbs.

At his side stood a uniformed woman whose skin gleamed like polished iron, her blue eyes cold and merciless. On the breasts of their coats, embroidered in black, were the crossed sword and wheat sheaf of the Otzvuk.

"Identify yourselves," the burning man shouted. He had an accent like Mikhail's, refined and resonating. Another deposed nobleman.

Mikhail pushed past me and stopped before the line of soldiers. He leveled his chin and confronted the burning man head-on. "My name is Mikhail Vladimirovich of House Morev, and under the authority of the Kosa throne, I am commanding you and your soldiers to lower your arms."

The bogatyr strode toward us and stopped close enough that the heat radiating from his body made my face prickle tightly. The flames receded, but grew brighter, lighter, until they were almost as incandescently blue as his searing eyes.

Mikhail stood tall, his back held straight and rigid, shoulders squared even as his knees swayed beneath him. Then, slowly, a smile spread across his lips. "Colonel Fyodorov, it's been a while. If you're here, then this must be the 5th Artillery Division."

Slowly, the bogatyr's suspicious scowl loosened into a gape of amazement. The flames surrounding his arms died down, and wisps of smoke wafted from his fingertips and clothes.

"I can't believe it," the man murmured. "By the Three, it's really you…"

Almost immediately, the bogatyr sank to one knee. The soldiers in his company looked at each other in befuddlement, be-fore lowering their rifles and following their leader's example.

"Forgive me for my transgression, Your Highness," the bogatyr said, bowing his head. "My soldiers and I are yours to command."

43

In the streets of Eyry, war was being waged, but in the city's Tribunal courthouse, all was calm. By the time we arrived there, the doors and windows of the three-story building were already fortified, and sandbags were piled up along the entrance and walls. If there were any Fraktsiya casualties, their bodies had been disposed of inconspicuously.

Colonel Fyodorov hosted us in the judge's office, a cave-like space with rugs adorning the walls and dark, carved furniture. He was accompanied by Staff Captain Lokteva, the blonde bogatyr who could harden her skin like steel armor. Rather than take a seat, she coolly observed us from where she leaned against the wall.

I sat in one of the chairs with Koschei's shashka angled across my knees. Galina curled up on the rug by my feet, a cushion from one of the chairs wedged under her head. She'd been so tired, she had fallen asleep on the way here. Vanya had to carry her in.

Exhaustion weighed down on me, reducing my limbs to numb weights. It was a struggle to remain awake, and even the distant sounds of fighting failed to rouse me from my daze.

Mikhail appeared equally subdued. He gazed down at his palms as the colonel spoke, and though he didn't say so aloud, I had a feeling he was thinking about his powers. About how they still hadn't come back. About how killing Koschei hadn't ended the war, just changed its tide.

Over glasses of rich red wine, Colonel Fyodorov detailed the Otzvuk's next course of action. "Once we seize Eyry, we will reclaim the rest of the motherland and drive those revolutionary pigs out to the Edge. After that, it won't be long until we rein the rest of your territories back in, Your Highness. With Koschei dead, I suspect that the Fraktsiya will cease to exist within the next year, if not the next six months."

"And what of the civilian casualties in the Edge?" Vanya asked the moment the bogatyr paused to refill his wineglass.

The colonel's gaze shifted to him, and his expression hardened. "Excuse me? Did you just interrupt—"

Mikhail raised two fingers, and the colonel's mouth snapped shut. Leaning forward in his seat, he gazed unflinchingly at the bogatyr. "Is it true that your men have been targeting civilians?"

"That..." The colonel cleared his throat and took a hasty sip of wine. "I don't know where you heard that from, Tsar, but let me assure you—every drop of blood we spill is for the glory of the motherland. Sometimes, innocent people get in the way. The Fraktsiya uses them as shields."

"I want full reports of any skirmishes that have resulted in significant civilian casualties, regardless of which side is to blame."

Colonel Fyodorov choked on his wine. "With all due respect, Your Highness, there are hundreds."

"We also want reports on how many people have been accused of being kolduny," I added, getting ahead of myself, and the colonel nearly sprayed his mouthful of wine in my face. He stared at me, beads of red wine gathering in his mustache, looking so confused I almost felt bad for him.

Mikhail nodded. "She's right. Compile an audit of the Tribunal's investigations and executions in the months since the uprising, along with any and all acts of citizens taking judgment into their own hands."

"Colonel, I'll reach out to our troops and auxiliaries and have them compile a list of incidents," Staff Captain Lokteva said crisply, and turned to Mikhail. Even with her powers stifled, her skin still seemed to gleam in the dim lighting, her nails darkly metallic as she traced her fingertips over the edge of the desk. "Would Your Highness also like the reports documenting atrocities committed by the Fraktsiya?"

"Yes, I would." Now that he was back in his own element, Mikhail's entire demeanor had changed. He no longer approached conversations as if expecting confrontation, instead responding calmly and decisively to every remark and question.

"Is there anything else you would like us to prepare?" the colonel asked.

"Yes, one more thing, actually," Mikhail said, and the colonel stiffened as though preparing for a blow. He turned to me with a smile. "Arrange for travel to the Edge. I believe my friend Toma and her sister are looking to return home."

44

Outside the dirigible's window, a steppe of fluffy white clouds stretched to the horizon. I pressed my fingertips against the glass, peering between the gaps in the cloud cover in hope of recognizing the layout of the land below.

Galina stretched out on the bench's wooden slats and fell asleep with her head in my lap. I ran my fingers through her thick chestnut hair, stroking it out of her eyes, which flicked beneath their closed lids. If she suffered from unpleasant dreams, she did so silently, her features as calm and peaceful as the sky surrounding us. This high above the clouds, it was difficult to believe that the empire was still engulfed in a civil war.

So far, the way back had been nearly as stressful as the journey to Eyry, not because Galina was gone, but because I was terrified of losing her once again. The Otzvuk leadership managed to arrange transport for us with an envoy sent by the neutral nation of Yezmirny, in order to provide much-needed food and medical supplies for expats and citizens of Yezmir-skiy descent. The envoy had fortunately received travel per-mits from both Otzvuk and Fraktsiya officials, who were in no rush to make enemies with the technologically advanced nation beyond the Black Steppe.

However, despite these precautions, up until this point the journey itself had been nerve-racking. Rather than traveling by the old logging routes, we had taken off from Eyry's airbase in a dirigible bearing the crimson wolf emblem of Yezmirny, a sleek vessel of cupro-aluminum and tan canvas. Loaded with supplies, it had made a slow track across the mountains, stopping at airbases in cities and towns with sizable Yezmir-skiy populations to distribute aid and rendezvous with com-munity leaders.

Despite Galina's begging, each time we had landed, I re-fused to let her leave the ship, wary of the soldiers milling about and the pall of smoke that lingered on the horizon. Even Vanya seemed frightened, and in confidence, he told me that he was afraid to even inquire about his village, wor-ried of what he might find. He had left the airship only long enough to send telegrams to Inga and Annushka, assuring them of our survival.

"The captain says we should land within the half hour," Vanya said, sinking into the seat across from me. He hadn't told me if he planned to return to Kupalo, even though Mikhail had provided him with an imperial pardon, travel permits to cross through Otzvuk-ruled territories, and sev-eral hastily drafted and unprecedented documents identify-ing him as a bogatyr of common blood.

Throughout our flight, Vanya had kept the papers in

their sealed envelope, dropped carelessly atop our room's storage shelf. Whenever the three of us moved around the small windowless cabin, shifting past each other to reach the double-bunked cots, Vanya and I avoided even looking at the envelope, or the nearly identical one that Mikhail had given me. The knowledge of what would come once the airship landed hung over us like a falling object, something heavy and plummeting at incredible speed.

Galina shifted, mumbling in her sleep. I smiled as she sucked on her knuckle. When I looked up, I found Vanya watching me with stormy eyes.

"What will you do if we aren't able to heal them?" he asked, and now more than ever, I sensed it—that weight boring down with great velocity.

"I'll stay," I said.

"And if we do?"

"I'll stay, too. Vanya, they're my family." The words spilled from my mouth helplessly. I didn't feel in control of them— it was the debt I owed Mama and Papa for saving me. I was the only thing keeping my family together, even now, and if I left, they would fall apart without me. It was inevitable.

"So, you'll spend the rest of your life in isolation?"

I found myself at a loss for words.

Vanya sighed, running a hand through his hair. His gaze shifted out the window. "Maybe I should stay, too."

"I can't expect that of you." Just the words made my heart ache. He didn't belong in the wilderness. It was not his world. But I was beginning to sense that it wasn't mine either; for seven years, I had only been a visitor there.

"It would be fitting, wouldn't it?" A wry smile touched his

lips, and his fingers strayed to the bandages around his wrist. "The wilderness is for kolduny and monsters."

"You're not a monster, Vanya."

"Aren't we all?"

As he glanced out the window, I stared down at his hands. The broken nails hadn't grown in yet, and his cuticles were marred by purplish bruises. His skin was so fair that I could see the bluish branching of veins beneath—the only proof that his blood still flowed.

But that did not make him human.

It had been many days since he last ate, and at night he strayed restlessly through the airship's dark bowels. He could only choke down a few mouthfuls of water at a time, and if he tried to drink more than that, he gagged and coughed until it welled from his mouth, pink with diluted blood.

It frightened me. He was not an upyr, but not alive either.

Deathless or not, Vanya's ability to feel hadn't been taken away. I could tell that he was worried for the people in his town, but if he had confided in Mikhail about his concerns before we set out on the journey home, he had done so in private. He had made it clear to both of us that he didn't want the Otzvuk to know he was Strannik. I couldn't say that I blamed him and felt uncomfortable divulging my own heritage as well.

Whenever Vanya was in the presence of Otzvuk officers, he became standoffish, anger and loathing buried in his gaze. In confidence, he told me that he couldn't forgive the Otzvuk for what they had done in his town.

"I hate them for it," he said, when we had been given a moment alone after our meeting with Colonel Fyodorov. "I *despise* them. But the way I see it, there are only two options. I can learn to tolerate them the way Inga did, or I can leave and do what? Run to Yezmirny or Groznaya? No. This is my country. This is the country my father died for. I'm not just going to stand by and let it burn. Here, I can make a difference. I think we can actually change things, Toma. Mikhail is different. If he regains his throne, he won't be like his father."

I was slowly realizing that he saw siding with Mikhail as something different than siding with the tsarists—the two were irrevocably linked, but not the same in Vanya's eyes. Ever since we'd ended up in Otzvuk custody, I had thought long and hard about Vanya's decision to help Mikhail. It wasn't out of greed or hunger for power, but a profound desire to change the empire from within, through diplomacy and policy instead of violent upheaval. Despite Vanya's cynicism, I sensed that he truly did wish to believe in human kindness and empathy.

His ability to move beyond his own outrage and indignation only made me admire him even more. I wanted to emulate him, to adopt his confidence and unwavering self-conviction. I wanted to become part of the change.

I was stirred from my thoughts as a four-bell chime rang through the dirigible. Moisture beaded on the glass as the vessel began to sink.

Galina yawned as I shifted out from under her. She sat up, rubbing her eyes, and looked at me blearily. "Are we there?"

"We're descending," Vanya said.

The dirigible shuddered as we passed through the cloud cover, buffeted like a ship on a stormy sea. Outside the window, mist coiled and wisped against the windows. Then we were in the clear, and a vast expanse stretched below—

primordial pine forests flanked by the jagged snow-tipped spine of the mountains.

I pressed my palms against the glass, mesmerized. Those gouges in the earth ahead could only be the Teykhst trenches, and beyond the mountains, I discerned Kupalo's domed steeples, ruined fortress, and mill.

As we sank lower still, more details filled in. After ten minutes or so, Flight Lieutenant Doğan appeared at the other end of the observation deck.

"The captain requests your presence," he said, ushering us up a flight of stairs to the cockpit at the front of the vessel— a semicircular room of exposed cupro-aluminum girders and glass windows, whose walls were fitted with porcelain dials and small fluid-filled tubes used to measure altitude and air pressure.

Captain Şahin stood examining the instruments as we entered. Her chin shifted subtly in our direction, her raven hair moving to reveal the khaki gabardine strap crossed over her left eye. Though the fabric hid the devastation of her socket, it couldn't so easily hide the scar that coiled down her face, raising her mouth in a perpetual half smile.

"Toma, would you please point out the direction of your home for me? We have reached the proper coordinates."

As I did, she made several adjustments to the dials on the wall. Taking her place at the wheel, she guided the dirigible into a smooth descent along the flat span of earth between our izba and the river. When we were close enough to the ground that I was a little afraid the observation desk's floor would make contact with it, she braked the dirigible until it

idled at a near standstill and signaled for the mooring team
to rappel down.

At the different cities, it had taken her crew only minutes to
tether the vessel to the mooring poles constructed at airfields
and on state-owned land. As we waited, Şahin explained to
me that in Yezmirny the technology was already being developed to create crafts that were capable of landing without
the need for mooring.

I nodded along, only half listening. If I squinted, I could
just make out our izba. It looked so small, as if it were on the
verge of collapsing.

At last, the ship was stabilized, and the gangway lowered
from its tip. I stepped down onto the rocky field. So bright.
Shielding my eyes with my hand, I waited for my vision to
adjust to the sun's glare.

"Look how colorful it is, Toma!" Galina exclaimed, jumping down from the gangway. Her new leather shoes made
puffs of dirt. "Look how green the grass is. And the trees!"

Vanya remained at the other end of the gangway platform,
within the shadow of the dirigible's canvas-lined frame.

"Aren't you coming?" I asked.

"Go have your reunion. I'll catch up in a few minutes."

I nodded and turned back ahead. It had been less than a
month since I had first set out on my journey, but it felt like
a lifetime had passed since I last opened the izba's creaking
door. As I crossed the uneven ground, I had to keep from
trembling, half in excitement and half in dread.

I could envision it clearly in my head. The hearth would
be filled with cold ashes, mold would blanket the bowl of
fresh mushrooms, and on the floor, I'd find a scatter of bones

and rotting fabric, with a pair of hand-carved wooden masks bristling from it all.

I was torn from my thoughts as Galina suddenly broke free of my hand and rushed on ahead.

"Galina, wait!" I shouted, running after her. "If you fall, I won't be able to sew it up this time."

Laughing, she reached the izba and cast open the door. It banged shut behind her, and for a moment, all I could do was freeze at the wooden pane, waiting for a scream of horror and anguish.

Galina's silvery laughter echoed from within. My parents' voices were so soft, the door stifled them to crackly whispers.

"Toma, what are you waiting for?" Galina hollered. "Come inside."

I drew in a shuddery breath and opened the door, stepping into the cool, familiar dim. The hearth was unlit, as I had envisioned, and everything else remained as I had left it—the walls covered in quietly ticking timepieces, and the bundles of dried herbs nailed to the crossbeams, and my parents in their shrouds of fur and decaying fabric.

I came forward on watery legs, reaching out for them as if I were just a child again, tears flooding my eyes uncontrollably. There was so much I wanted to tell them but that I could spend an eternity trying to put into words, so all I could choke out was, "I brought her back. It's just like I said. I told you I would."

45

By the time I had finished telling my parents about Galina's resurrection, my sister had fallen asleep on my straw-stuffed mattress and Vanya was waiting for me outside with a crate of medicine and essentials from the dirigible's hold.

Wrapped in canvas and twine, Koschei's sword rested atop the box. Not a souvenir, but a reminder of what I'd done. Of the blood I spilled. Of what it meant to survive in the outer world.

Vanya carried the items inside, and the moment he caught sight of Mama and Papa lingering by the masonry oven, the crate nearly slipped from his arms. For the first time, I saw my parents through his eyes—spindly constructs of rotten fabric, bone, and buckskin, with the hearth-light pooling on their carved birchwood masks and relinquishing the rest to shadows.

"Don't be afraid," I murmured, placing my hand on his arm. He drew in a deep breath, steadied his features.

"You must be Toma's mama and papa," Vanya said, his voice wavering ever so slightly. He rested the crate on the bench that ran the length of the wall and brushed off his hands on the seat of his pants. As he stepped forward to greet them, the apprehension drained from his gaze, and he smiled warmly. "Ivan Zoravich, but I've never been one for formalities, so Vanya will do."

Mama and Papa dipped their chins in mute greeting. From their silence, I realized they were afflicted by the same nervousness that sent my stomach fluttering.

"Mama, let's try you first." As I turned to her, I couldn't keep from grinning.

She came forward tentatively, laying her outstretched hand in mine. As I began to untie the suede cords crisscrossed over her layers of wraps, she hesitated and slipped her fingers away.

"What is it?" I asked, baffled.

"No." Her voice left her like the rustle of the breeze through tall grass.

"No?" I repeated, certain I had misheard.

She turned to Papa, and though their carved faces remained unmoving, I felt a tension crawl over me.

I stepped forward. "Mama."

"Toma, we have lived for so long." She drew her arm against herself. The folds of fabric slipped away to expose what I had never seen before—the pale swell of her knuckles, held together by copper splints of Papa's careful creation. There was no skin left at all in places. "We are so tired."

"But Vanya and I can heal you." My voice warbled. I swallowed hard, feeling dangerously close to tears. "We can bring you back."

"You will bring us back to sickness. To pain. To thirst and hunger."

"Allow us this," Papa said quietly. "Our remaining time here, and then a deep and well-earned rest."

I choked for a response. "How can you—"

The airship's whistle pierced the izba's confines, cutting off my cry in my throat.

Vanya glanced toward the door. He furrowed his brow as the dirigible blared twice more. "Toma, they're not going to wait forever. Do you want me to ask them for more time?"

"No. Go." The words pushed from between my gritted teeth one at a time. It felt like spitting out nails.

"Toma." His hand closed around my shoulder. I couldn't even look at him. How could I?

"You have a war to win, Vanya." I had known in my heart all along that we weren't destined to be together. That was why he had left the residency permit and pardon unopened in the envelope Mikhail had given him. He had never intended to linger. "Please. Just go."

"Won't you just look at me and talk—"

"I said, go!" I wrenched away from him, swiveling around to confront him. He stared at me in shock, but then his face smoothed over. He too knew how to make farewells less painful—he had done it once before.

"I understand," he murmured, taking my hand only long enough to kiss my fingers, those fingers that had brought him back. "I'll return when this is over. Mikhail, too. This is not farewell."

As soon as the door swished shut behind Vanya, a deep,

numbing exhaustion fell over me. I sank onto the bench, cradling my forehead in my hand.

Wasn't this what I had wanted all along? To come home?

Images passed through my mind. The corpses of suspected kolduny hanging from an oak tree. A crimson pool forming under Koschei's headless body. Dronov writhing in the leaves, laughing uncontrollably until bloody tears rippled down his cheeks.

Vanya and I had blood on our hands. Blood that had already been spilled, and blood yet to come. How could I stay, knowing that I would be responsible for whatever happened next?

My birth mother had hidden that she was Strannik out of fear and necessity, and all these years, I had hidden in the wilderness, afraid to become a part of civilization. I was tired of hiding. I wanted to see a world untouched by the violence and hatred that had made me.

And a part of me—a part that I tried to bury deep inside myself so I could focus on Galina—desperately wanted to stay with Vanya. I cared about him deeply, and he offered the key to discovering my past and understanding my heritage. He could teach me Strannitsky, and perhaps together we could learn more about the special symbols adorning my mother's embroidery.

But how could I ever leave?

"Toma?" Galina said, and I slowly lifted my head to find her standing next to me. The dirigible's horn must have stirred her from her nap.

"What is it, Galechka?" My voice came out thick. I swallowed hard to clear it.

"I want to hunt for the rest of the beads."

"Oh, okay," I mumbled, trying to summon the energy to stand. "In a minute."

Moisture trickled down my cheek. I looked at the ceiling, but there was no leak, and then a wretched sob escaped from deep inside me, somewhere so far within I hadn't realized it existed until now, not really.

"Why are you crying?" Galina asked, her own lower lip trembling.

"I'm not crying." I wiped the tears away and then the thin line of mucus that escaped one nostril. "I just...I miss Vanya."

He said he'd come back, but that could be months or years from now, and in the time between, he'd lose his brightness in my memory, and I'd forget his jokes and the rolling timbre of his voice, and one day he might step through the door with his cat-green eyes, his clever smile, and burgundy hair, and I wouldn't even recognize him.

"You need to go to him," Mama murmured, coming up to us as silently as a shadow. She eased onto the bench beside me, her fingers tracing small circles in my back.

"I can't. I need to keep the two of you together. To keep our family together."

"You must live, Toma." Her mask shifted to Galina. "The both of you must."

The dirigible blared for a third time. If I just sat here a little while longer, I could go outside and it would be as though nothing had changed at all, as though we'd never left the izba in the first place.

"There will come a day when you will die, my child." Papa's sibilant murmur passed over me like the wind through willows. He sank to a crouch before me, his mask's beatific face raised skyward. As he wiped away my tears with his tattered wrappings, the hearth-light danced over his barren sockets and baroque-pearl teeth. There was nothing left beneath. "And when you do die, I pray that your bones will sleep undisturbed and hallowed. But if something draws you back to this world and you find yourself wandering as we once wandered, know that we will be waiting to brush the grave soil from your face and clear the moss from your mouth. Know that we will bring you home. And wherever you go from here, always remember—all that you love will return to you."

As Mama and Papa led me to the door, a three-bell chime echoed through the izba, the sign of the dirgible's approaching departure. The moment I opened the door, it was as though something seized hold of me, a force as irresistible as gravity that urged me across the threshold, beyond the shadow of the eaves.

I broke into a run, feet pounding across the gravel and dirt. The wind whipped at my face and threw my hair in a black banner behind me, its chill exhilarating me. I expected to spot the dirigible rising past the decaying forms of the nearby izbas, but as I neared, the airship remained earthbound.

"Vanya, we're coming," I shouted, and shocked myself by laughing. This feeling that spurred my heart into a frantic beat, the warmth flooding my face, the grin that tugged at my lips—this was joy. This was what it meant to return home.

★ ★ ★ ★ ★

AUTHOR'S NOTE

I began working on *Bone Weaver* during a period of self-discovery, after I had hit a dead end in researching my father's side of the family and decided to look into where my mother's family had come from. Ultimately, my new search just took me down a rabbit hole even more convoluted than the former, and I realized that when my mom said most of her ancestors had come from "Russia," she really meant imperial Russia. More specifically, parts of modern-day Ukraine, Lithuania, and western Russia.

After hitting enough walls thanks to butchered transliterations, lack of records, and disappearing towns, I lost interest in the genealogy research, and instead became fixated on the absences—the circumstances that led to my mom's ancestors immigrating to America during the 1900–1910s, the persecution and war that they fled, what life was like in imperial Russia, the political and social strife of that period, and the construction of identity and nationality. One thing led to another, and along with reading about imperial Russian and Eastern European history from the 1700–1900s, I also became deeply interested in Slavic (and to a lesser degree, Baltic) folklore, monsters, and superstitions.

Although by the end of my research, I had enough material to begin a novel set in imperial Russia, I didn't quite feel emotionally ready to write a historical fantasy. That would come with my next manuscript, *The City Beautiful*. So, *Bone Weaver* began as a way to experiment and tentatively toe around the brutality of the real-life persecution and violence explored in *The City Beautiful*. It felt safer that way, less personal.

While this is a secondary world fantasy, many of the world-building aspects of this story were inspired by my research into Eastern European folklore and history. All of the monsters come from Slavic (but not solely Russian or Eastern Slavic) folklore, along with concepts like the Unclean Force and spoiling. *Bone Weaver*'s lexicon and location names are, for the most part, drawn from Russian; however, there are other lingual inspirations as well. Strannitsky, for instance, has a vaguely Germanic base with roots in several languages, Yezmirny is an echo to Ottoman Turkey, and some of the town names like Teykhst and Shteynov are also intentional chimeras.

At its core, this is a story about feeling like an outsider. It is a story about identity, and what it means to be deprived of parts of your identity, and what it takes to reclaim autonomy.

GLOSSARY

bannik: A bathhouse spirit said to be capable of foreseeing the future. The very brave—or very foolish—can request the bannik to tell their fortune by standing with their back to the steam bath's open door. A light stroke of its fingertips brings good tidings, while a clawing foretells something far worse. *plural* **banniki.**

banya: A steam bath. In rural villages, these often consist of simple steam rooms constructed on private land. In larger towns and cities, they can also be found at communal bathhouses.

The Black Steppe: A vast and uninhabited grassland separating Kosa from Yezmirny, sharing its northern borders with the Kosa mainland and the southwestern tip of the Granary. Its geography is largely flat and treeless, although staired plateaus and basalt columns can be found along its southern and eastern rims, dotted with the collapsed ruins of ancient Strannik settlements. Entire swathes of the steppe are buried beneath molten ebony sand and chunks of porous stone, the relics of a catastrophic event known as the Great Burning (Str: *tzer Grohdler Korbrendt*). Once the Stranniki's ancestral homeland, it is now considered to be cursed land spoiled by the Unclean Force.

blight ward: The designated term for former battlefields that are still seeded with unexploded ordnance or toxic chemicals. Blight wards are common across the Edge and along Groznaya's borders. These areas are dangerous, both due to the man-made contamination of the land, and the presence of the Unclean Force caused by the widespread death and suffering. Strange malformations of natural fauna and flora have been reported in blight wards dating to the Fifth Groznaya-Kosa War. Some speculate the mutations are caused by the leftover canisters of toxic gas Grozniy forces derived from vodyanoy gallbladders.

bogatyr: An individual endowed with magical powers. Troika belief states that a bogatyr's power comes from the three goddesses of creation—with Tsarina Yelena's reforms several hundred years ago, this doctrine has been codified into imperial law.
plural **bogatyri.**

drekavac: A harbinger of doom created when an infant dies before its time. It is said that when a drekavac crosses through a person's shadow, woe is certain to follow.
plural **drekavcy.**

dreynikit: (noun/adjective, *Strannitsky*) feminine and gender-neutral term for a worshipper of the Three Sisters. Dreynik is the masculine equivalent.

plural **dreynikiten/dreyniker.**

The Edge: Kosa's northwestern territory, stretching from the Ice Plains in the north to the Granary in the south. It shares a border with Groznaya, and as a result has been host to the worst of the frontline fighting between Kosa and the neighboring empire.

Fraktsiya: Collective name for the revolutionary factions controlled by Koschei, consisting mainly of civilian workers, conscripted peasants, and imperial soldiers loyal to the Fraktsiya cause. What they lack in magic, they make up for in unit cohesion and resentment at centuries of the bogatyri's oppression.

The Granary: The Kosa Empire's southwestern territory and agricultural hub. With its fertile soil and favorable climate, it provides much of the empire's wheat, kasha, sunflower oil, and cotton.

grevka: The currency of the Kosa Empire. Grevka is used both as a singular unit and a collective plural (e.g., one grevka, twenty grevka).

Groznaya: The Kosa Empire's northwestern neighbor, sharing borders with the Edge and the unsettled Ice Plains. No conflicts have occurred between Groznaya and Kosa since the devastating war ten years ago. While Groznaya has not yet interfered in the power struggle between the Fraktsiya and the Otzvuk, there has been an increased military presence along the Groznaya-Kosa border in recent weeks.

Holy Tribunal: The ecclesiastical body responsible for overseeing the trials and executions of suspected kolduny and heretics, under the authority of the Ministry of Heritage. Installed by Tsarina Inessa a hundred years ago to replace the previous vigilante system, the Tribunal's stated goal is to preserve the cultural and religious integrity of the Kosa Empire.

The Ice Plains: The region to Groznaya and Kosa's far north, a frigid and inhospitable expanse of tundra and glacial seas. Small whaling communities and mining camps can be found near the Groznaya and Kosa borders. Expansionist efforts from both empires have failed in the past, and those who venture into the region's depths seldom return. It is rumored that the tsarina of witches rules the Ice Plains from her moving castle, and puzzling tracks found in the snow only seem to reinforce that theory.

koldun: A male witch. Koldunia is the female equivalent. Unlike the bogatyri, it is believed that kolduny derive their powers from the Unclean Force, and lurk in all strata of society. *plural* **kolduny.**

Kosa: The goddess of harvest, homeland, and fertility, she is one of the Three Sisters of creation and the Kosa Empire's namesake. Her sigils are the reaping hook and wheat sheaf.

Koskiy: The official language spoken in Kosa and its territories. As per imperial law, it is the mandatory language used in state schools, military institutions, and government transactions and proceedings.

mavka: A female forest spirit. In addition to stealing garments left out to dry, mavki are notorious for tickling men to death—usually to grotesque effect.
plural **mavki.**

Otzvuk: The coalition of factions loyal to the tsarist regime and determined to restore Tsar Mikhail to power. Composed of the deposed nobility, the remnants of the military police and the imperial army, and the civilians they've conscripted to their cause. Although not all members of the Otzvuk are bogatyri, bogatyri play a central leadership role in its armies.

prahvekht: (affirmative, *Strannitsky*) True, absolutely.

rusalka: A female river spirit. Although they are seldom found in lakes and ponds, it isn't uncommon to come across them in saltwater bays and estuaries.
plural **rusalki.**

rushnyk: An embroidered tapestry, commonly used to adorn the Troika home and altar, as well as in marriage and burial rites.
plural **rushnyky.**

schväst: (noun, *Strannitsky*) Tail.
plural **schvästen.**

Seredina: The goddess of fate, technology, and weaving, and one of the Three Sisters of creation. Her sigils are the distaff and spindle.

sovnya: A polearm with a long, curved blade. One of the sigils of the goddess Voyna.

spoil: To be cursed or corrupted by the Unclean Force.

Strannik: One of Kosa's largest minority groups. Within the imperial mainland and its territories, the Strannik population ranges from 0.2% (the Kosa interior) to 7.0% (the Edge). Prior to the rise of bogatyri, the Stranniki were known as Strazhniki, or guards, due to the pacts of fealty they pledged to the now-eradicated noble houses in exchange for rights to settle. Despite being forbidden from carrying firearms and bladed weapons, the Stranniki's legacy as combat servants has continued under the Morev Dynasty in the form of forcible conscriptions to Kosa's frontline infantry—often starting in their early teens, of boys and girls alike.
  plural **(Kos) Stranniki, (Str) Stranniker/Strannikiten.**

Sudrekht: (noun, *Strannitsky*) Colloquial term for the Holy Tribunal.

Svet: Kosa's political ally to the west. What the kingdom of Svet lacks in military might, it makes up for in a powerful economy and friendly diplomatic relations with foreign powers. In the months preceding Tsar Mikhail's dethronement, discussions were underway of a marriage between the Tsar and Princess Agathe.

Troika: Ecclesiastical term for the Three Sisters, the goddesses of creation. Also refers to the worshippers of the Three and the faith in general (e.g., a Troika temple, Troika worshippers).

tsurästvo: (noun, *Strannitsky*) A riot or attack.
  plural **tsurästvim.**

tza slovanakh: (exclamatory phrase, *Strannitsky*) The stench.

Unclean Force: A dark energy capable of spoiling crops and bringing death and sickness. Said to be the force that powers witches' magic, as well as that which resurrects the dead as monsters.

upyr: A wandering revenant that preys upon the dead and living alike, often spotted scavenging through potter's fields and waste pits. Typically, an upyr's flesh mummifies with age. However, specimens have also been found with wet rot or the pickling characteristic of bog burials.
  plural **upyri.**

vasyem: (noun, *Strannitsky*) Water.

vodyanoy: A male water spirit. Can typically be found in marshes and swampland. Characterized by their two sets of teeth and froglike eyes.
  plural **vodyanye.**

Voserka: The three-faced goddess worshipped by the Stranniki, often depicted with a blacksmith's hammer. It is said that she smithed the first humans at the hearth of creation, and that the Unclean Force rose from the cinders left over. Some believe the Three Sisters and the goddess Voserka to be manifestations of the same divine being, though heresy accusations have been raised over less.

Voyna: The goddess of war and retribution, and one of the Three Sisters of creation. Considered the patron of bogatyri, it isn't unusual for soldiers to wear travel icons of her into battle. Her sigils are the sovnya and balance scales.

Yezmirny: A large and powerful kingdom separated from the Kosa Empire by the Black Steppe, it is at the vanguard of the continent's technological revolution. It is an open secret that the import of Yezmirskiy tanks and dirigibles was as much responsible for Kosa's victory over Groznaya as the belated deployment of the empire's bogatyr regiments. So far, Yezmirny has remained a neutral observer in Kosa's civil war, intervening only to assist in humanitarian efforts and arrange evacuations of Yezmirskiy diplomats.

ACKNOWLEDGMENTS

Without the help and support of the people below, this novel wouldn't have been possible.

First of all, I would like to thank my literary agent, Thao Le, whose strong advocacy for my work allowed this book to reach the wonderful people at Inkyard Press.

I would also like to thank my editor, Stephanie Cohen, who deeply understood the story I was trying to tell here and helped me find and draw out its soul. Stephanie's invaluable insight allowed me to build the Kosa Empire into a fully formed world and bring my characters to life on the page.

I would also like to thank everyone at Inkyard Press for their hard work and dedication in getting this book out into the world. In particular, I would like to thank Brittany Mitchell, Justine Sha, and Bess Braswell.

In addition, I would like to thank my critique partners, Laura Samotin, Laura Creedle, Brenda Marie Smith, Sonya Doernberg, Alexandra Gill, Kathryn Donovan, and Cassandra Farrin, whose notes and critiques were vital in shaping this book to be the best work possible.

As this book is inspired by specific cultures, time periods, and locations, during the drafting process, it was important for me to do as much as I could to ensure that I was properly honoring these influences. Special thanks goes out to Tamara Atoian, who provided Russian sensitivity reads both during the early drafting process and the final proofreading, Sonya Doernberg and Alexandra Gill, who further helped with Russian lexicology and cultural details, and Cyrus McGoldrick and Burcu Kocakurt, who provided Turkish sensitivity reads.